Praise for
Troubled Daughters, Twisted Wives

"This fascinating collection of stories represents a long-overdue tribute to mystery writers who laid the foundation for those of us working in the field today. The remarkable range and complexity of these tales is a humbling reminder of the importance of the trailblazers whose work established psychological suspense as the backbone of crime writing both then and now."

> —Sue Grafton, *New York Times* bestselling author of *V Is for Vengeance*

"Sarah Weinman knows everything about crime fiction, and in her amazing anthology, she introduces an array of brilliant female writers who know more than they should about the dark side of the human psyche. Each story features a woman who's 'good and mad' in her own shocking way, and *Troubled Daughters, Twisted Wives* is an important and riveting read."

> —Lisa Scottoline, *New York Times* bestselling author of *Don't Go*

"Troubled, twisted, and terrific. Where have these women been? Sarah Weinman's *Troubled Daughters, Twisted Wives* serves up stellar short stories, forgotten gems by some of the finest authors of their era."
> —Hallie Ephron, author of the bestselling *There Was an Old Woman*

"A short unabashed fan letter for a first-rate job. My compliments to Ms. Weinman. It was like opening gifts, one story to the next, from a very young Patricia Highsmith to Shirley Jackson in her prime. A rare and worthy collection of suspense pioneers."

> —Carol O'Connell, *New York Times* bestselling author of *It Happens in the Dark* and *Crime School*

"At last, the anthology we have been waiting for: a veritable gold-mine of spellbinding, psychologically rich tales. Masterfully curated by crime fiction expert Sarah Weinman, *Troubled Daughters, Twisted Wives* not only brings much-deserved attention to fourteen unjustly neglected, pioneering writers—it also changes the way we think about the history, and the future, of the suspense genre."

—Megan Abbott, Edgar Award–winning author of *Dare Me*

"*Troubled Daughters, Twisted Wives* proves that women were writing smart, dark, twisty tales long before anyone thought to label their work a subgenre, and often by subverting gendered cultural expectations. Sarah Weinman serves as an expert curator to this wonderful collection, providing a coherent narrative tying these trailblazing stories to one another and to a new wave of female-led psychological suspense. This is a must-read for crime fiction fans."

—Alafair Burke, author of *If You Were Here*

"These thoughtfully selected and very readable crime stories give us an unusually revealing and subtle portrait of the curtailed real lives of women in the mid-twentieth century and the fantasies that would free them." —Sheila Kohler, author of *Becoming Jane Eyre*

"Sarah Weinman has dug up hidden treasure. Not only are these stories compelling gems in their own right—their exploration of the darker side of the relationships that link women to their lovers, husbands, fathers, and mothers also provides a thought-provoking perspective on contemporary crime writing. Strong women characters and strong women writers did not appear out of nowhere—this is the background, these are the pioneers."

—Lene Kaaberbøl, *New York Times* bestselling coauthor of *The Boy in the Suitcase* and *Death of a Nightingale*

"A captivating selection of finely tuned suspense stories from masters of their craft: brilliant depictions of seemingly ordinary women, some with far from ordinary motivations, and others compelled by extraordinary circumstances. It was a delight to experience stories from old favorites Charlotte Armstrong, Shirley Jackson, Margaret Millar, and Patricia Highsmith—with a sparkling entry from Dorothy B. Hughes—and to discover a cluster of immensely talented writers I'd never read. Insightful introductions by Sarah Weinman for each story sharpened the pleasure of delving into these gems from past decades."   —Sara J. Henry, award-winning author of
Learning to Swim and *A Cold and Lonely Place*

"We tend to view the past through a rosy lens, imagining it as a simpler, gentler time. *Troubled Daughters, Twisted Wives* buries that fantasy by exploring the dark drama festering beneath the façade of domestic bliss. The stories by these pioneering female crime writers range from the quietly menacing to the out-and-out devastating. Editor Sarah Weinman has assembled an extraordinary collection that shows just how great a debt modern crime writers owe to the past, and proves that, once again, the female is the deadlier of the species."   —Hilary Davidson, author of *Evil in All Its Disguises*

"In this book, Weinman has expertly curated near-forgotten works by some of the most gifted women crime writers of all time. These chilling, provocative stories prove just how harrowing domestic suspense can be and together provide an eye-opening perspective on the evolution of the psychological thriller. *Troubled Daughters, Twisted Wives* delivers page after page of pure, dark pleasure."
—Koethi Zan, author of *The Never List*

"A revealing glimpse into the dark hearts and secret lives of mid-century women."   —Christa Faust, author of *Choke Hold*

PENGUIN BOOKS

TROUBLED DAUGHTERS, TWISTED WIVES

SARAH WEINMAN is the news editor for Publishers Marketplace, the book industry service that produces the widely read daily newsletter *Publishers Lunch*. Weinman also writes the monthly "Crimewave" mystery and suspense column for the *National Post*, and has contributed to publications including the *Wall Street Journal*, *Los Angeles Times*, the *Washington Post*, the *New York Observer*, *Slate*, and the *New Yorker*'s Web site. Her short fiction has appeared in *Ellery Queen's Mystery Magazine*, *Alfred Hitchcock Mystery Magazine*, and the anthologies *Long Island Noir*, *Dublin Noir*, and *Baltimore Noir*. Weinman lives in Brooklyn, and can be reached on the Web at www.sarahweinman.com and on Twitter (@sarahw).

TROUBLED DAUGHTERS, TWISTED WIVES

STORIES FROM THE TRAILBLAZERS
OF DOMESTIC SUSPENSE

Edited by

SARAH WEINMAN

A PENGUIN BOOK

PENGUIN BOOKS
Published by the Penguin Group
Penguin Group (USA), 375 Hudson Street,
New York, New York 10014, USA

USA | Canada | UK | Ireland | Australia | New Zealand | India | South Africa | China

Penguin Books Ltd, Registered Offices: 80 Strand, London WC2R 0RL, England
For more information about the Penguin Group visit penguin.com

First published in Penguin Books 2013

The author has made diligent efforts to contact all rights holders for the stories included
in this anthology and gratefully acknowledges their cooperation in allowing their stories
to be reprinted. In some cases locating the rights holders was difficult and one case
impossible. Rather than exclude any story, they are all presented here with thanks to those
rights holders who gave permission and to those who could not be found.

LIBRARY OF CONGRESS CATALOGING-IN-PUBLICATION DATA
Troubled daughters, twisted wives : stories from the trailblazers of domestic suspense /
edited by Sarah Weinman.
pages cm
ISBN 978-0-14-312254-8
1. American fiction—Women authors.   2. Suspense fiction, American.
3. Domestic fiction, American.   I. Weinman, Sarah, editor of compilation.
PS647.W6T67 2013
813'.01089287—dc23   2013011939

Printed in the United States of America
1   3   5   7   9   10   8   6   4   2

Set in Adobe Caslon Pro
Designed by Elke Sigal

To my mother, Judith,
and my father, Jack (1936–2012)

CONTENTS

ACKNOWLEDGMENTS

A PASSION project like this cannot possibly happen without the help, hard work, and input of a great many people.

First and foremost, the rights holders, permissions managers, and other literary representatives who granted kind permission to republish these stories as they were originally meant to be read: Jack Callahan; Christopher Harrington; Evan Harrington; Barry Malzberg; Roger Schwed; Shira Hoffman at MacIntosh and Otis; Craig Tenney at Harold Ober; Charles Schlessiger and Lina Granada at Brandt & Hochman; Linda Allen of the Linda Allen Literary Agency; Vianny Cruz at ICM; Dara Hyde at Grove/Atlantic; Lynda Gregory of the Blanche Gregory Literary Agency; and Claire Morris and Ruth Murray at Gregory & Company.

Thanks to those who were instrumental in tracking down physical copies of the stories and with additional research: Jackie Sherbow and Janet Hutchings at *Ellery Queen's Mystery Magazine*; Noreen Tomassi and Brenda Wegener at the Center for Fiction; Steve Viola, Maggie Griffin, Kizmin Reeves, and Maggie Topkis at Partners & Crime (sadly missed, more than I can possibly express); Bud Webster; Anne Besig Forwand; the New

York Public Library; Greg Shepard; Jessica Ferri; Rick Cypert; Tom Nolan; Charles Ardai; Jason Pinter; Christa Faust; Tina Wexler; Oline Cogdill.

Friends, colleagues, and family helped in ways big and small, and this list is by no means comprehensive: Megan Abbott; Jami Attenberg; Dov Berger; Michael Cader; Hilary Davidson; Roe D'Angelo; Robin Dellabough; Juliet Grames; Sara J. Henry; Jennifer Jordan; Stuart Krichevsky; Aline Linden; Michael Macrone; Mark Medley; Bryon Quertermous; Jonathan Santlofer; Jacob Silverman; Michele Slung; Jack Weinman, z"l; Jaime Weinman; Judith Weinman; Joe Wallace; Sharon Avrutick Wallace; Dave White; Emily Williams; Jennifer Young. Special thanks to Michelle Wildgen, who commissioned the essay at *Tin House* that started me on the road leading to this anthology, and beyond.

At Penguin, Stephen Morrison, for listening to my excitable rant at lunch one day, suggesting there might be an anthology in it, and turning the idea into reality; Becca Hunt, for invaluable help and support at early critical junctures; Elda Rotor, for key advice and understanding; Henry Freedland, for his patient phone manner; Sam Moore, for able permissions work; Lynn Buckley, for the amazing cover; Lavina Lee, for the most thoughtful copyedits I've ever received; and Tara Singh, who got what I was trying to do with absolute clarity, vision, and action. I'm lucky to be part of this publishing village.

To my agent, Shana Cohen, for being the best advocate, sounding board, neurosis-deflector, and, above all, friend I could ever have.

And to Ed Champion, for everything.

INTRODUCTION

AS WE speak, the current crop of crime writers who excite and inspire me the most are women. These authors are very much rooted in the present, exposing our most potent fears and showing the most insidious effects of human behavior in ways that are fresh, smart, and forward-looking, but—consciously or otherwise—draw on the rich tradition crime writing has to offer. Their books color outside the lines, blur between categories, and give readers a glimpse of the darkest impulses that pervade every part of contemporary society. Especially those impulses that begin in the home.

With each passing year I've grown more picky and discerning about my crime fiction reading. The books I'm drawn to are most often written by women, about women. Their authors speak to me as a reader, as a feminist, and as one who cares about the greater good.

Consider Gillian Flynn's *Gone Girl*, 2012's most popular and critically acclaimed suspense novel, with more than two million copies sold as of this writing. It's a masterful look at a marriage that seems like pure bliss to outsiders, but to the husband and wife in question, bears greater resemblance to the 1989 movie *The War of the Roses*, the ultimate poisonous battle of the sexes.

Flynn is just one of the many standouts at the vanguard of psychological suspense that addresses matters of great relevance to women. Edgar Award–winning author Megan Abbott moves smoothly from feminine-subversive midcentury noir in novels like *Die a Little* or *Bury Me Deep* to taut, almost hallucinatory examinations of teenage girls making sense of their hearts, bodies, and minds, as in *The End of Everything* or *Dare Me*. In her most recent suspense novel *And When She Was Good*, Laura Lippman illuminates the world of the suburban madam with expert empathy, as she did with a kidnap victim's battle of wits with her former tormentor in *I'd Know You Anywhere*. And Attica Locke, in *The Cutting Season*, restarts a disquieting but necessary conversation on America's slavery past through the lens of a plantation-turned-tourist attraction overseen by a single mother.

The burgeoning renaissance has an international flavor, too, with successful authors like Tana French of Dublin, Sophie Hannah of London, Louise Penny of Canada, and the duo of Lene Kaaberbøl and Agnete Friis of Denmark. They may nominally be writing police procedurals, but what they really do, book after book, is take a scalpel to contemporary society and slice away until its dark essence reveals itself: the ways in which women continue to be victimized, their misfortunes downplayed by men (and women) who don't believe them, and how they eventually overcome.

In marveling at these women, I began to wonder about who came before them. They certainly could not have existed without the efforts of the generation immediately preceding them, who collectively furthered the cause of women in the genre and coalesced into the group Sisters in Crime, founded in 1986. At that point four women—Liza Cody, Sue Grafton, Marcia Muller, and Sara Paretsky—were making critical and commercial inroads into the identifiably male private detective story, transmuting the darkness, nobility, humor, and detection savvy of the form from the vantage point of their investigating heroines Anna Lee, Kinsey Millhone, Sharon McCone, and V. I. Warshawski.

Over the next two and a half decades, where there was a market, women were there to fill it, master it, and put their distinct stamp on it. The police procedural, long a male-dominated category, gave birth to the splinter group of the forensic thriller, pioneered by Thomas Harris but made mainstream by Patricia Cornwell and, later, Kathy Reichs, Val McDermid, and Karin Slaughter. And when a crime story demanded a vivid sense of place in settings stretching from upstate New York to Appalachia to the West and the South, women like Julia Spencer-Fleming, Margaret Maron, Vicki Lane, and Margaret Coel rose up to meet those goals and gain devoted readerships for their region-flavored fare.

When I reached back further in time I discovered, much to my surprise, an entire generation of female crime writers who have faded from view. Their work spanned a period of three decades, from the early 1940s through the mid-1970s. At the time, their work, about the concerns of women, didn't easily fit within the genre's two marquee categories, which had come of age during the Great Depression and flourished thereafter: the male-dominated hard-boiled story made famous by the likes of Raymond Chandler, James M. Cain, and Dashiell Hammett; and the tonally lighter and less violent cozy, which grew out of the success of Agatha Christie, Dorothy L. Sayers, Margery Allingham, and Ngaio Marsh, known colloquially as the "Queens of Crime."

The crime genre, concerned as it is with the righting of wrongs and playing by rules, is less comfortable with blurred boundaries. It's especially uneasy about stories that feature ordinary people, particularly women, trying to make sense of a disordered world with small stakes, where the most important worry is whether a person takes good care of her children, stands up to a recalcitrant spouse, or contends with how best to fit—or subvert—social mores. The bombast of global catastrophe, the knight-errant detective's overweening nobility, or the gaping maw of total self-annihilation has no place in these stories. A subtle approach to the human condition with a more domestically oriented view attracts far less notice than books with grand ambitions writ large, but they are no less deserving of appreciation and understanding.

With cultural conversations increasingly focused on women's issues, from the "war on women" waged during the 2012 American election cycle, hand-wringing over whether women can "have it all," and books saluting or decrying the end of men, this misplaced generation of female crime writers deserves, more than ever, to take their place at the literary table. Understanding the time and place in which these women created some of the best and most influential works of crime fiction ever written will allow their branch of the genre's family tree—what we think of as domestic suspense—to be properly recognized.

War is the ultimate chaotic event; World War II in particular. While the men fought their enemies overseas, the women had no choice but to transcend their day-to-day lives as homemakers and caregivers and try something else. They worked in munitions factories, nursed wounded soldiers back to health, and wrote and spoke about what they saw and heard.

Seismic changes were also taking place in genre fiction, and help to explain the rise of the domestic suspense story during and after the World War II. Before the war, most working writers made their money producing stories by the word for the pulps or the slicks. The pulps, named for the cheap paper quality, included magazines like *Black Mask*, *Dime Detective*, and *Argosy*. And with very rare exceptions, they almost always published men. The slicks (for higher quality paper) paid writers better, with outlets like *Collier's*, *The Saturday Evening Post*, and *The American* publishing more mainstream stories for a middlebrow audience. Women fared better in these markets, but the stories published there were less overtly psychological or suspenseful in nature.

That left a void, filled when the most popular mystery writing team of the day—cousins Manfred Lee and Frederic Dannay, aka Ellery Queen—launched their eponymous magazine in 1941. In its early years, *Ellery Queen's Mystery Magazine* published works designated as detective stories, featuring the greats like Dashiell Hammett, James M. Cain, Raymond Chandler, Margery Allingham, Dorothy L. Sayers, and Agatha Christie during their peak. But they also made room for crime stories, those that didn't rely on the detective as a plot device, and this is where a number of women found a viable market to explore more domestic-minded subjects. *EQMM* published tales of wives struggling with poisonous marriages, daughters seeking to escape parental high expectations, elderly women neglected and at the behest of others, and teachers, nurses, and social workers who felt shackled by their work.

When World War II ended and the men came home, the social order of the day was restored, with men returning to their absent lives and jobs as family providers. Or at least that's what was supposed to happen. Once disrupted, like Humpty Dumpty's fragments, it's impossible to put a social order back together again. The 1950s certainly tried, wanting desperately to stick with the prewar status quo in which men provided and women stayed at home. That decade gloried in conspicuous consumption, emphasizing the value of owning cars, kitchen appliances, and large suburban houses. But a growing number of women found themselves questioning their lives, which centered around their husbands, children, and home. Many found comfort in what they could buy, watch on television, or read in magazines. Others found a welcome outlet in the written word, channeling their frustrations of unattainable domestic perfection into suspense stories read by an audience of other women who understood these anxieties all too well.

The mystery magazine business was not immune to disruption, either. The pulps started dying off, but *EQMM* flourished, as did new magazines like *Manhunt*, *Alfred Hitchcock's Mystery Magazine*, and *The Saint Mystery Magazine*. What these women wrote broadened the general short story market, paving the way for writers to start their careers in front of a small but influential and devoted readership, and were particularly good at widening the range of mystery short stories published—especially those by women. Their work, in short form or in novels, could be tough or tender, reflecting contemporary anxiety or finding a way to subvert it. And they were justly rewarded by their peers.

With the genre's escalating postwar popularity—the "Christie for Christmas" marketing slogan for the annual Hercule

Poirot or Miss Marple bestseller by Agatha Christie came about in the mid-1940s—some critics felt the need to knock down crime fiction. Edmund Wilson's 1944 *New Yorker* essay "Who Cares Who Killed Roger Ackroyd," which took Sayers, Christie, Chandler, and others to task for not measuring up to appropriate literary greatness, remains the most infamous of the genre-snob bunch, and the standard from which most recent literary put-downs deviate from. But essays by Wilson and his ilk had a more positive by-product: the formation of the Mystery Writers of America in 1945. Its slogan: "crime does not pay enough." Its mission: to better the status, career prospects, and payments for mystery writers. Its crown jewel: the annual Edgar Awards banquet, honoring the best in mystery year after year.

The Edgars proved to be very kind toward works of domestic suspense fiction, and many of the selections in this anthology won or were nominated for the Edgar, or their authors won or were nominated for novels or other stories. The very first winner of the Best Novel Award, in 1952, was female, Australian writer Charlotte Jay. *Beat Not the Bones* concerned itself with a young woman determined to uncover the truth about her anthropologist husband's death, which was ruled to be suicide but was, she believed, murder. The novel earned praise for its superior suspense and depiction of its exotic New Guinea setting.

Critics like the writer and editor Anthony Boucher, who wrote the "Criminals at Large" column between 1951 and his death in 1968, were also impressed by domestic suspense tales. Boucher never hesitated to put novels by the likes of Margaret Millar, Charlotte Armstrong, Dorothy Salisbury Davis, Dorothy B. Hughes, and Celia Fremlin—all included in this anthology—on his best-of-the-year lists, praising their skillful plots, exemplary characterization, and incisive portraits of human behavior. But critical acclaim alone doesn't sustain writing careers. These women had a steady readership willing to part with their money whenever a new title arrived. Their stories chiefly concerned women, but their audience encompassed both genders. They were published almost exclusively in hardcover format—their work deemed to be more sophisticated than the paperback houses that replaced the pulp magazines en masse and quickly propagated, with great success, in the 1950s and 1960s.

Then the social order changed once more, inch by incremental inch, in the mid-1960s. Women dissatisfied and frustrated by the expectations of domesticity found kinship in the identification of a feminine mystique, which in turn opened the door to a movement looking for equal rights. Those who helped forge that movement took extreme tacks at first, risking accusations of being fringe, crazy, or worse. But without them, more moderate concerns like making room for working women, earning comparable pay to men, and dialing down the sexism could never have been addressed.

As the feminist movement grew in prominence, and female writers made bold strides into what was formerly thought of as "male" territory, a funny thing happened in the crime genre: readers turned away from the domestic suspense story, and the pioneering writers seemed to fall off the map. Their work struggled to remain in print, their champions fewer than the men of the paperback pulps. Domestic suspense writers did not have their versions of Barry Gifford, whose Black Lizard paperback reprint project throughout the 1980s helped restore the reputations of a great many male writers from that era, or Geoffrey O'Brien, who helped define their importance in the first place in *Hardboiled America* (1981) while playing down, or in many instances leaving out entirely, their female counterparts.

Writers like Jim Thompson, David Goodis, and Charles Willeford may have been published initially with the lackadaisical indifference given to lesser peers, but their reputations have since been restored and polished to high gloss, with Thompson and Goodis novels now part of the Library of America (overseen by O'Brien). Writers like Fremlin, Hughes, and Millar, heralded while they lived, did not have the same institutional backing as their male peers. Worse off were those women writers who wrote domestic suspense short fiction exclusively.

Once a pendulum swings one way, it's only natural it begins to swing back in the other direction. And now the balance that's worked against the proper recognition of domestic suspense can be recalibrated.

Who, then, are these women, the fourteen authors represented in this collection? Most of them were mothers and wives, writing fiction in brief moments of respite from raising children and keeping the house in order. Some never married at all or married late in life, spending their wartime youth (First or Second, depending on the woman) working in army factories, passing out rudimentary birth control, or helping out with the Nazi resistance. A fair number went to college; a couple earned graduate degrees. Some traveled the world, alone or with their husbands. Some stuck close to their hometowns or original states of birth, telling stories that reflect their deep regional roots. Others settled in California, siphoning off money from the Hollywood spigot. All of them understood uniquely, absolutely, and bravely what it was like to be a woman, to be trapped in situations, and to summon up the fortitude to overcome them, expressed in novels and stories.

The collection includes a number of women who published short stories only, or predominantly, during their careers. This meant they didn't attract as wide a reputation or critical acclaim as those who spent the bulk of their careers on novels. Rediscovering writers like Joyce Harrington, Barbara Callahan, and Miriam Allen deFord—all of whom excelled at the mystery short story—has been a welcome delight, one I'm glad to share with readers here.

I've included Patricia Highsmith's first published short story, "The Heroine," as an intriguing "path not taken" choice. The story fits the domestic suspense bill by featuring a young nanny who must reckon with her increasingly morbid fascinations. But Highsmith, though her body of work is clearly oriented around human psychology, found her footing writing about the male sociopath. By her own estimation, she didn't relate as well to women as leading characters, with the exception of *The Price of Salt* (1952), the excellent lesbian novel she published under a pseudonym, and *Edith's Diary* (1977), a more jarringly uneven epistolary suspense novel.

As with any anthology, there are notable omissions, the three key ones being Joyce Carol Oates, Ruth Rendell, and Mary Higgins Clark. Oates certainly concerned herself with the terror of the domestic, but her crime-writing self did not emerge in full until the early 1980s, with the books she wrote as Rosamond Smith (after that, it was as if Oates opened a vein and crime stories came rushing out). Rendell began her career in the early 1960s, but did not commit herself fully to psychological suspense territory until she published with a pseudonym of her own, Barbara Vine, with 1987's *A Dark-Adapted Eye*. Higgins Clark, too, frequently published suspense stories in the 1960s, and was both a peer and influence upon several writers included here, such as Dorothy Salisbury Davis and Joyce Harrington. But her career in domestic suspense only began in earnest with the 1975 publication of *Where Are the Children?*, and Higgins Clark spent the bulk of her time thereafter on novels.

The fourteen stories that made the cut come from voices so bursting with life that domestic matters were a subversive way of showcasing large ambitions. These tales may concern themselves with the everyday, the mundane, those pesky "women's issues" that are really human issues. But they deal with matters of great import to females of all ages, which is why I've presented these stories in a loose chronological order by the age of the protagonists, starting with adolescents to single young adults to married women with young children to the elderly.

These stories may be subtle, even quiet, but don't let that fool you. The women who ruled over the domestic suspense genre during the mid-twentieth century turn our most deep-seated worries into narrative gold, delving into the dark side of human behavior that threatens to come out with the dinner dishes, the laundry, or taking care of a child. Their stories of domestic suspense frighten precisely because in depicting ordinary, everyday life—especially in the context of larger anxieties about rapid societal change—the nerves they hit are really fault lines that, despite tremendous progress, show no signs of going away anytime soon.

TROUBLED DAUGHTERS, TWISTED WIVES

PATRICIA HIGHSMITH

1921–1995

PATRICIA HIGHSMITH may well be the most famous and unusual choice for this anthology. Highsmith largely wrote about, and was more comfortable with, men. When she wrote about domestic situations in her novels and stories, they were largely to do with male perception, misunderstanding, and delusion. One of her story collections was even titled *Little Tales of Misogyny*. The two key exceptions are *The Price of Salt* (1952), the lesbian novel she published under the pseudonym Claire Morgan, and *Edith's Diary* (1977), an epistolary account of a woman's slow descent into madness, taking a male loved one with her.

As I state in the introduction, I regard Highsmith's first published short story, "The Heroine," as a "path not taken" tale. The story, which Highsmith wrote as a student at Barnard College, concerns itself with a young woman, Lucille, hired as a nanny for the well-to-do Christiansen family's two children, nine-year-old Nicky and five-year-old Heloise. Every gesture, from pouring coffee to tidying rooms to making beds, appears innocent on the surface but masks layers of increasing dread.

"The Heroine," first published in *Harper's Bazaar* in 1945 and awarded an O. Henry Prize, holds up masterfully on its own while also demonstrating why Highsmith was so good so early in her career.

Highsmith's twenty-two novels and eight short story collections include some of the greatest psychological suspense novels ever written, including her debut, *Strangers on a Train* (1950), *The Talented Mr. Ripley* (1955), and four follow-up books, *The Blunderer* (1954), *Those Who Walk Away* (1967), and *The Tremor of Forgery* (1969). Her depictions of disordered, sociopathic minds resonated with disturbing force largely because her narrators descended into aberrant, even murderous behavior with ample justification—even if they were ultimately fooling themselves first. Her characters were outsiders, like Highsmith, who was born in Fort Worth, grew up and spent early adulthood in New York, and then decamped for Europe, which showered critical acclaim on her during her lifetime. She wouldn't get proper American due until after her death, from aplastic anemia, in 1995.

THE HEROINE

THE GIRL was so sure she would get the job, she had unabashedly come out to Westchester with her suitcase. She sat in a comfortable chair in the living room of the Christiansens' house, looking in her navy blue coat and beret even younger than 21, and replied earnestly to their question.

"Have you worked as a governess before?" Mr. Christiansen asked. He sat beside his wife on the sofa, his elbows on the knees of his gray flannel slacks and his hands clasped. "Any references, I mean?"

"I was a maid at Mrs. Dwight Howell's home in New York for the last seven months." Lucille looked at him with suddenly wide gray eyes. "I could get a reference from there if you like . . . But when I saw your advertisement this morning I didn't want to wait. I've always wanted a place where there were children."

Mrs. Christiansen smiled, but mainly to herself, at the girl's enthusiasm. She took a silver box from the coffee table before her, stood up, and offered it to the girl. "Will you have one?"

"No, thank you. I don't smoke."

"Well," she said, lighting her own cigarette, "we might call them, of course, but my husband and I set more store by appearances than references . . . What do you say, Ronald? You told me you wanted someone who really liked children."

And fifteen minutes later Lucille Smith was standing in her room in the servants' quarters back of the house, buttoning the belt of a new white uniform. She touched her mouth lightly with lipstick.

"You're starting all over again, Lucille," she told herself in the mirror. "You're going to have a happy, useful life from now on, and forget everything that was before."

But there went her eyes too wide again, as though to deny her words. Her eyes looked much like her mother's when they opened like that, and her mother was part of what she must forget. She must overcome that habit of stretching her eyes. It made her look surprised and uncertain, too, which was not at all the way to look around children. Her hand trembled as she set the lipstick down. She recomposed her face in the mirror, smoothed the starched front of her uniform.

There were only a few things like the eyes to remember, a few silly habits, really, like burning little bits of paper in ashtrays, forgetting time sometimes—little things that many people did, but that she must remember not to do. With practice the remembering would come automatically. Because she was just like other people (had the psychiatrist not told her so?), and other people never thought of them at all.

She crossed the room, sank onto the window seat under the blue curtains, and looked out on the garden and lawn that lay between the servants' house and the big house. The yard was longer than it was wide, with a round fountain in the center and two flagstone walks lying like a crooked cross in the grass. There were benches here and there, against a tree, under an arbor, that seemed to be made of white lace. A beautiful yard!

And the house was the house of her dreams! A white, two-story house with dark-red shutters, with oaken doors and brass knockers and latches that opened with a press of the thumb . . . and broad lawns and poplar trees so dense and high one could not see through, so that one did not have to admit or believe that there was another house somewhere beyond . . . The rain-streaked Howell house in New York, granite pillared and heavily ornamented, had looked, Lucille thought, like a stale wedding cake in a row of other stale wedding cakes.

She rose suddenly from her seat. The Christiansen house was blooming, friendly, and alive! There were children in it. Thank God for the children! But she had not even met them yet.

She hurried downstairs, crossed the yard on the path that ran from the door, lingered a few seconds to watch the plump faun blowing water from his reeds into the rock pond . . . What was it the Christiansens had agreed to pay her? She did not remember and she did not care. She would have worked for nothing just to live in such a place.

Mrs. Christiansen took her upstairs to the nursery. She opened the door of a room whose walls were decorated with bright peasant designs, dancing couples and dancing animals, and twisting trees in blossom. There were twin beds of buff-colored oak, and the floor was yellow linoleum, spotlessly clean.

The two children lay on the floor in one corner, amid scattered crayons and picture books.

"Children, this is your new nurse," their mother said. "Her name is Lucille."

The little boy stood up and said, "How do you do," as he solemnly held out a crayon-stained hand.

Lucille took it, and with a slow nod of her head repeated his greeting.

"And Heloise," Mrs. Christiansen said, leading the second child, who was smaller, toward Lucille.

Heloise stared up at the figure in white and said, "How do you do."

"Nicky is nine and Heloise six," Mrs. Christiansen told her.

"Yes," Lucille said. She noticed that both children had a touch of red in their blond hair, like their father. Both wore blue overalls without shirts, and their backs and shoulders were sunbrown beneath the straps.

Lucille could not take her eyes from them. They were the perfect children of her perfect house. They looked up at her frankly, with no mistrust, no hostility. Only love, and some childlike curiosity.

". . . and most people do prefer living where there's more country," Mrs. Christiansen was saying.

"Oh, yes . . . yes, ma'am. It's ever so much nicer here than in the city."

Mrs. Christiansen was smoothing the little girl's hair with a tenderness that fascinated Lucille. "It's just about time for their lunch," she said. "You'll have your meals up here, Lucille. And would you like tea or coffee or milk?"

"I'd like coffee, please."

"All right, Lisabeth will be up with the lunch in a few minutes." She paused at the door. "You aren't nervous about anything, are you, Lucille?" she asked in a low voice.

"Oh, no, ma'am."

"Well, you mustn't be." She seemed about to say something else, but she only smiled and went out.

Lucille stared after her, wondering what that something else might have been.

"You're a lot prettier than Catherine," Nicky told her.

She turned around. "Who's Catherine?" Lucille seated herself on a hassock, and as she gave all her attention to the two children who still gazed at her, she felt her shoulders relax their tension.

"Catherine was our nurse before. She went back to Scotland because of the war. I'm glad you're here. We didn't like Catherine."

Heloise stood with her hands behind her back, swaying from side to side as she regarded Lucille. "No," she said, "we didn't like Catherine."

Nicky stared at his sister. "You shouldn't say that. That's what I said!"

Lucille laughed and hugged her knees. Then Nicky and Heloise laughed too.

A colored maid entered with a steaming tray and set it on the table in the center of the room. She was slender and of indefinite age. "I'm Lisabeth Jenkins, miss," she said shyly as she laid some paper napkins at three places.

"My name's Lucille Smith," the girl said.

"Well, I'll leave you to do the rest, miss. If you need anything else, just holler." She went out, her hips small and hard-looking under the blue uniform.

The three sat down to the table, and Lucille lifted the cover from the large dish, exposing three parsley-garnished omelets, bright yellow in the bar of sunlight that crossed the table. But first there was tomato soup for her to ladle out, and triangles of buttered toast to pass. Her coffee was in a silver pot, and the children had two large glasses of milk.

The table was low for Lucille, but she did not mind. It was

so wonderful merely to be sitting here with these children, with the sun warm and cheerful on the yellow linoleum floor, on the table, on Heloise's ruddy face opposite her. How pleasant not to be in the Howell house! She had always been clumsy there. But here it would not matter if she dropped a pewter cover or let a gravy spoon fall in someone's lap. The children would only laugh.

Lucille sipped her coffee.

"Aren't you going to eat?" Heloise asked, her mouth already full.

The cup slipped in Lucille's fingers and she spilled half her coffee on the cloth. No, it was not cloth, thank goodness, but oilcloth. She could get it up with a paper towel, and Lisabeth would never know.

"Piggy!" laughed Heloise.

"Heloise!" Nicky admonished, and went to fetch some paper towels from the bathroom.

They mopped up together.

"Dad always gives us a little of his coffee," Nicky remarked as he took his place again.

Lucille had been wondering whether the children would mention the accident to their mother. She sensed that Nicky was offering her a bribe. "Does he?" she asked.

"He pours a little in our milk," Nicky went on, "just so we can see the color."

"Like this?" And Lucille poured a bit from the graceful silver spout into each glass.

The children gasped with pleasure. "Yes!"

"Mother doesn't like us to have coffee," Nicky explained, "but when she's not looking, Dad lets us have a little like you did. Dad says his day wouldn't bc any good without his coffee, and I'm the same way. Gosh, Catherine wouldn't give us any coffee like that, would she, Heloise?"

"Not her!" Heloise took a long delicious draught from her glass which she held with both hands.

Lucille felt a glow rise from deep inside her until it settled in her face and burned there. The children liked her, there was no doubt of that.

She remembered now how often she had gone to the public parks in the city, during the three years she had worked as maid in various houses (to be a maid was all she was fit for, she used to think), merely to sit on a bench and watch the children play. But the children there had usually been dirty or foul-mouthed, and she herself had always been an outsider. Once she had seen a mother slap her own child across the face. She remembered how she had fled in pain and horror.

"Why do you have such big eyes?" Heloise demanded.

Lucille started. "My mother had big eyes too," she said deliberately, like a confession.

"Oh," Heloise replied, satisfied.

Lucille cut slowly into the omelet she did not want. Her mother had been dead three weeks now. Only three weeks and it seemed much, much longer. That was because she was forgetting, she thought, forgetting all the hopeless hope of the last three years, that her mother might recover in the sanatorium. But recover to what? The illness was something separate, something which had killed her.

It had been senseless to hope for a complete sanity which she knew her mother had never had. Even the doctors had told her that. And they had told her other things, too, about herself.

Good, encouraging things they were, that she was as normal as her father had been.

Looking at Heloise's friendly little face across from her, Lucille felt the comforting glow return. Yes, in this perfect house, closed from all the world, she could forget and start anew.

"Are we ready for some dessert?" she asked.

Nicky pointed to her plate. "You're not finished eating."

"I wasn't very hungry." Lucille divided her dessert between them.

"We could go out to the sandbox now," Nicky suggested. "We always go just in the mornings, but I want you to see our castle."

The sandbox was in back of the house in a corner made by a projecting ell. Lucille seated herself on the wooden rim of the box while the children began piling and patting like gnomes.

"I must be the captured princess!" Heloise shouted.

"Yes, and I'll rescue her, Lucille. You'll see!"

The castle of moist sand rose rapidly. There were turrets with tin flags sticking from their tops, a moat, and a drawbridge made of the lid of a cigar box covered with sand. Lucille watched, fascinated. She remembered vividly the story of Brian de Bois-Guilbert and Rebecca. She had read *Ivanhoe* through at one long sitting, oblivious of time and place just as she was now.

When the castle was finished, Nicky put half a dozen marbles inside it just behind the drawbridge. "These are good soldiers imprisoned," he told her. He held another cigar box lid in front of them until he had packed up a barrier of sand. Then he lifted the lid and the sand door stood like a porte-cochere.

Meanwhile Heloise gathered ammunition of small pebbles from the ground next to the house. "We break the door down and the good soldiers come down the hill across the bridge. Then I'm saved!"

"Don't tell her! She'll see!"

Seriously Nicky thumped the pebbles from the rim of the sandbox opposite the castle door, while Heloise behind the castle thrust a hand forth to repair the destruction as much as she could between shots, for besides being the captured princess she was the defending army.

Suddenly Nicky stopped and looked at Lucille. "Dad knows how to shoot with a stick. He puts the rock on one end and hits the other. That's a balliska."

"Ballista," Lucille said.

"Golly, how did *you* know?"

"I read it in a book—about castles."

"Golly!" Nicky went back to his thumping, embarrassed that he had pronounced the word wrong. "We got to get the good soldiers out fast. They're captured, see? Then when they're released that means we can all fight together and *take the castle!*"

"And save the princess!" Heloise put in.

As she watched, Lucille found herself wishing for some real catastrophe, something dangerous and terrible to befall Heloise, so that she might throw herself between her and the attacker, and prove her great courage and devotion. She would be seriously wounded herself, perhaps with a bullet or a knife, but she would beat off the assailant. Then the Christiansens would love her and keep her with them always. If some madman were to come upon them suddenly now, someone with a slack mouth and bloodshot eyes, she would not be afraid for an instant.

She watched the sand wall crumble and the first good soldier marble struggled free and came wobbling down the hill. Nicky and Heloise whooped with joy. The wall gave way completely, and two, three, four soldiers followed the first, their stripes turning gaily over the sand.

Lucille leaned forward. Now she understood! She was like the good soldiers imprisoned in the castle. The castle was the Howell house in the city, and Nicky and Heloise had set her free. She was free to do good deeds. And now if only something would happen . . .

"O-o-ow!"

It was Heloise. Nicky had mashed one of her fingers against the edge of the box as they struggled to get the same marble.

Lucille seized the child's hand, her heart thumping at the sight of the blood that rose from many little points in the scraped flesh. "Heloise, does it hurt very much?"

"Oh, she wasn't supposed to touch the marbles in the first place!" Disgruntled, Nicky sat in the sand.

Lucille held her handkerchief over the finger and half carried her into the house, frantic lest Lisabeth or Mrs. Christiansen see them. She took Heloise into the bathroom that adjoined the nursery, and in the medicine cabinet found mercurochrome and gauze.

Gently she washed the finger. It was only a small scrape, and Heloise stopped her tears when she saw how slight it was.

"See, it's just a little scratch!" Lucille said, but that was only to calm the child. To her it was not a little scratch. It was a terrible thing to happen the first afternoon she was in charge, a catastrophe she had failed to prevent. She wished over and over that the hurt might be in her own hand, twice as severe.

Heloise smiled as she let the bandage be tied. "Don't punish Nicky," she said. "He didn't mean to do it. He just plays rough."

But Lucille had no idea of punishing Nicky. She wanted only to punish herself, to seize a stick and thrust it into her own palm.

"Why do you make your teeth like that?"

"I—I thought it might be hurting you."

"It doesn't hurt any more." And Heloise went skipping out of the bathroom. She leaped onto her bed and lay on the tan cover that fitted the corners and came all the way to the floor. Her bandaged finger showed startlingly white against the brown of her arm.

"We have to take our afternoon nap now," she told Lucille, and closed her eyes. "Goodbye."

"Goodbye," Lucille answered, and tried to smile.

She went down to get Nicky and when they came up the steps Mrs. Christiansen was at the nursery door.

Lucille blanched. "I don't think it's bad, ma'am. It—it's a scratch from the sandbox."

"Heloise's finger? Oh, no, don't worry, my dear. They're always getting little scratches. It does them good. Makes them more careful."

Mrs. Christiansen went in and sat on the edge of Nicky's bed. "Nicky, dear, you must learn to be more gentle. Just see how you frightened Lucille!" She laughed and ruffled his hair.

Lucille watched from the doorway. Again she felt herself an outsider, but this time because of her incompetence. Yet how different this was from the scenes she had witnessed in the parks!

Mrs. Christiansen patted Lucille's shoulder as she went out. "They'll forget all about it by nightfall."

"Nightfall," Lucille whispered as she went back into the nursery. "What a beautiful word!"

While the children slept, Lucille looked through an illustrated book of *Pinocchio*. She was avid for stories, any kind of stories, but most of all adventure stories and fairy tales. And at her elbow on the children's shelf there were scores of them. It would take her months to read them all. It did not matter that they were for children. In fact, she found that kind more to her liking, because such stories were illustrated with pictures of animals dressed up, and tables and houses and all sorts of things come to life.

Now she turned the pages of *Pinocchio* with a sense of contentment and happiness so strong that it intruded on the story she was reading. The doctor at the sanatorium had encouraged her reading, she remembered, and had told her to go to movies too. "Be with normal people and forget all about your mother's difficulties. . . ." (Difficulties, he had called it then, but all other times he had said "strain." Strain it was, like a thread, running through the generations. She had thought, through her.)

Lucille could still see the psychiatrist's face, his head turned a little to one side, his glasses in his hand as he spoke, just as she had thought a psychiatrist should look. "Just because your mother had a strain, there's no reason why you should not be as normal as your father was. I have every reason to believe you are. You are an intelligent girl, Lucille. Get yourself a job out of the city—relax, enjoy life. I want you to forget even the house your family lived in. After a year in the country—"

That, too, was three weeks ago, just after her mother had died in the ward. And what the doctor said was true. In this house where there were peace and love, beauty and children, she could feel the moils of the city sloughing off her like a snake's outworn skin. Already, in this one half day! In a week she would forget forever her mother's face.

With a little gasp of joy that was almost ecstasy she turned to the bookshelf and chose at random six tall, slender, brightly colored books. One she laid open, face down, in her lap. Another she opened and leaned against her breast. Still holding the rest in one hand, she pressed her face into *Pinocchio*'s pages, her eyes half closed.

Slowly she rocked back and forth in the chair, conscious of nothing but her own happiness and gratitude. The chimes downstairs struck three times, but she did not hear them.

"What are you doing?" Nicky asked, his voice politely curious.

Lucille brought the book down from her face. When the meaning of his question struck her, she flushed and smiled like a happy but guilty child. "Reading!" she laughed.

Nicky laughed too. "You read awful close."

"Ya-yuss," said Heloise, who had also sat up.

Nicky came over and examined the books in her lap. "We get up at three o'clock. Would you read to us now? Catherine always read to us till dinner."

"Shall I read to you out of *Pinocchio*?" Lucille suggested, happy that she might possibly share with them the happiness she had gained from the first pages of its story. She sat down on the floor so they could see the pictures as she read.

Nicky and Heloise pushed their eager faces over the pictures, and sometimes Lucille could hardly see to read. She did not realize that she read with a tense interest that communicated itself to the two children, and that this was why they enjoyed it so much. For two hours she read, and the time slipped by almost like so many minutes.

Just after five Lisabeth brought in the tray with their dinner, and when the meal was over Nicky and Heloise demanded more reading until bedtime at seven. Lucille gladly began another book, but when Lisabeth returned to remove the tray, she told Lucille that it was time for the children's bath, and that Mrs. Christiansen would be up to say good night in a little while.

Mrs. Christiansen was up at seven, but the two children by that time were in their robes, freshly bathed, and deep in another story with Lucille on the floor.

"You know," Nicky said to his mother, "we've read all these books before with Catherine, but when Lucille reads them they seem like *new* books!"

Lucille flushed with pleasure. When the children were in bed, she went downstairs with Mrs. Christiansen.

"Is everything fine, Lucille? I thought there might be something you'd like to ask me about the running of things."

"No, ma'am, except . . . might I come up once in the night to see how the children are doing?"

"Oh, I wouldn't want you to break your sleep, Lucille. That's very thoughtful, but it's really unnecessary."

Lucille was silent.

"And I'm afraid the evenings are going to seem long to you. If you'd ever like to go to a picture in town, Alfred, that's the chauffeur, will be glad to take you in the car."

"Thank you, ma'am."

"Then good night, Lucille."

"Good night, ma'am."

Lucille went out the back way, across the garden where the fountain was still playing. And when she put her hand on the knob of her door, she wished that it was the nursery door, that it was eight o'clock in the morning and time to begin another day.

Still she was tired, pleasantly tired. How very pleasant it was, she thought, as she turned out the light, to feel properly tired in the evening (although it was only nine o'clock) instead of bursting with energy, instead of being unable to sleep for thinking of her mother or worrying about herself.

She remembered one day not so long ago when for fifteen minutes she had been unable to think of her name. She had run in panic to the doctor.

That was past! She might even ask Alfred to buy her a pack of cigarettes in town—a luxury she had denied herself for months.

She took a last look at the house from her window. The chintz curtains in the nursery billowed out now and then and were swept back again. The wind spoke in the nodding tops of the poplars like the high-pitched, ever-rippling voices of children.

The second day was like the first, except that there was no mishap, no scraped hand—and the third and the fourth. Regular and identical like the row of Nicky's lead soldiers on the playtable in the nursery. The only thing that changed was Lucille's love for the family and the children—a blind and passionate devotion which seemed to redouble each morning.

She noticed and loved many things: the way Heloise drank her milk in little gulps at the back of her throat, how the blond down on their backs swirled up to meet the hair on the napes of their necks, and when she bathed them the painful vulnerability of their bodies.

Saturday evening she found an envelope addressed to herself in the mailbox at the door of the servants' house. Inside was a blank sheet of paper and inside that a new $20 bill.

Lucille held it by its crisp edges. Its value meant nothing to her. To use it she would have to go to stores where other people were. What use had she for money if she were never to leave the Christiansen home? It would simply pile up, $20 each week. In a year's time she would have $1040, and in two years $2080. Eventually she might have as much as the Christiansens and that would not be right.

Would they think it very strange if she asked to work for nothing? Or for $10 perhaps?

She had to speak to Mrs. Christiansen, and she went to her the next morning. It was an inopportune time. Mrs. Christiansen was making up a menu for a dinner.

"It's about my salary, ma'am," Lucille began.

"Yes?" Mrs. Christiansen said in her pleasant voice.

Lucille watched the yellow pencil in her hand moving swiftly over the paper. "It's too much for me, ma'am."

The pencil stopped. Mrs. Christiansen's lips parted slightly in surprise. "You *are* such a funny girl, Lucille!"

"How do you mean—funny?" Lucille asked curiously.

"Well, first you want to be practically day and night with the children. You never even want your afternoon off. You're always talking about doing something 'important' for us, though what that could be I can't imagine. And now your salary's too much! We've never had a girl like you, Lucille. I can assure you, you're different!"

She laughed, and the laugh was full of ease and relaxation that contrasted with the tension of the girl who stood before her.

Lucille was rapt in the conversation. "How do you mean different, ma'am?"

"Why, I've just told you, my dear. And I refuse to lower your salary because that would be sheer exploitation. In fact, if you ever change your mind and want a raise—"

"Oh, no, ma'am . . . but I just wish there was something more I could do for you—and for the children."

"Lucille! You're working for us, aren't you? Taking care of our children. What could be more important than that?"

"But I mean something bigger—I mean more—"

"Nonsense, Lucille," Mrs. Christiansen interrupted. "Just because the people you were with before were not so—friendly as we are doesn't mean you have to work your fingers to the bone for us."

She waited for the girl to make some move to go, but still she stood by the desk, her face puzzled. "Mr. Christiansen and I are very well pleased with you, Lucille."

"Thank you, ma'am."

She went back to the nursery where the children were playing. She had not made Mrs. Christiansen understand. If she could just go back and explain what she felt, tell about her mother and her fear of herself for so many months, how she had never dared take a drink or even a cigarette . . . and how just being with the family in this beautiful house had made her well again . . . telling her all that might relieve her.

She turned toward the door, but the thought of disturbing her or boring her with her story, a servant girl's story, made her stop. So during the rest of the day she carried her unexpressed gratitude like a great weight in her breast.

That night she sat in her room with the light on until after twelve o'clock. She had her cigarettes now, and she allowed herself three in the evening, but even those three were sufficient to set her blood tingling, to relax her mind, to make her dream heroic dreams. And when the three cigarettes were smoked, and she would have liked another, she rose, very light in the head, and put the cigarette pack in her top drawer to close away temptation.

Just as she slid the drawer she noticed on her handkerchief

box the $20 bill the Christiansens had given her. She took it now, and sat down again in her chair.

From the packet of matches she took one, struck it, and leaned it, burning end down, against the side of her ashtray. Slowly she struck matches one after another and laid them strategically to make a tiny, flickering, well controlled fire. When the matches were gone, she tore the pasteboard cover into little bits and dropped them in slowly. Finally she took the $20 bill and with some effort tore bits from it of the same size. These, too, she meted to the fire.

Mrs. Christiansen did not understand, but if she saw *this*, she might. Still *this* was not enough. Mere faithful service was not enough either. Anyone would give that, for money. She was different. Had not Mrs. Christiansen herself told her that?

Then she remembered what else she had said: "Mr. Christiansen and I are very well pleased with you, Lucille."

The memory of these words brought her up from her chair with an enchanted smile on her lips. She felt wonderfully strong and secure in her own strength of mind and her position in the household. *Mr. Christiansen and I are very well pleased with you, Lucille.* There was really only one thing lacking in her happiness. She had to prove herself in crisis.

If only a plague like those she had read of in the Bible . . . "And it came to pass that there was a great plague over all the land." That was how the Bible would say it. She imagined waters lapping higher against the big house, until they swept almost into the nursery. She would rescue the children and swim with them to safety, wherever that might be.

She moved restlessly about the room.

Or if there came an earthquake . . . She would rush in among falling walls and drag the children out. Perhaps she would go back for some trifle, like Nicky's lead soldiers or Heloise's paint set, and be crushed to death. Then the Christiansens would know her devotion.

Or if there might be a fire. Anyone might have a fire. Fires were common things and needed no wrathful visitations from the upper world. There might be a terrible fire just with the gasoline in the garage and a match.

She went downstairs, through the inside door that opened to the garage. The tank was three feet high and entirely full, so that unless she had been inspired with the necessity and importance of her deed, she would not have been able to lift the thing over the threshold of the garage and of the servants' house too.

She rolled the tank across the yard in the same manner as she had seen men roll beer barrels and ashcans. It made no noise on the grass and only a brief bump and rumble over one of the flagstone paths, lost in the night.

No lights shone at any of the windows, but if they had, Lucille would not have been deterred. She would not have been deterred had Mr. Christiansen himself been standing there by the fountain, for probably she would not have seen him. And if she had, was she not about to do a noble thing?

She unscrewed the cap and poured some gasoline on a corner of the house, rolled the tank farther, poured more against the white shingles, and so on until she reached the far corner. Then she struck her match and walked back the way she had come, touching off the wet places. Without a backward glance she went to stand at the door of the servants' house and watch.

The flames were first pale and eager, then they became yellow with touches of red. As Lucille watched, all the tension that was left in her, in body or mind, flowed evenly upward and was lifted from her forever, leaving her muscles and brain free for the voluntary tension of an athlete before a starting gun. She would let the flames leap tall, even to the nursery window, before she rushed in, so that the danger might be at its highest.

A smile like that of a saint settled on her mouth, and anyone seeing her there in the doorway, her face glowing in the lambent light, would certainly have thought her a beautiful young woman.

She had lit the fire at five places, and these now crept up the house like the fingers of a hand, warm and flickering, gentle and caressing. Lucille smiled and held herself in check. Then suddenly the gasoline tank, having grown too warm, exploded with a sound like a cannon shot and lighted the entire scene for an instant.

As though this had been the signal for which she waited, Lucille went confidently forward.

NEDRA TYRE

1912–1990

NEDRA TYRE, a native of Offerman, Georgia, was the author of six crime novels published in a twenty-year period, including *Mouse in Eternity* (1952), *Hall of Death* (1960), and *Twice So Fair* (1971), as well as more than forty short stories, largely published by *Ellery Queen's Mystery Magazine*. Tyre was educated at Emory University in Atlanta and the Richmond School of Social Work in Virginia, and her experience as a social worker, librarian, and teacher particularly informed her fiction, which was deeply psychological and empathetic in nature. Tyre also wrote primarily about the American South, especially Georgia and Virginia, doing so years before the Southern regional mystery took off as a subgenre.

After 1971, though, Tyre stopped publishing novels and her short story output slowed down. Part of this was due to her taking on a staff job for an agency that gave financial assistance to poor children in third-world countries. A larger reason was ill health, including total deafness that struck her in the late 1970s. Tyre was also known to be a woman of great convictions and quirks: According to the Web site *Recovering Nedra*, devoted to returning Tyre to literary prominence, her friends recalled her "storing books in her oven, only eating lunch at restaurants that provided cloth napkins, traveling the world as a single woman, corresponding with all she met, and developing fondness for teddy bears."

"A Nice Place to Stay," first published in *Ellery Queen's Mystery Magazine* in 1970, is among Tyre's best and most anthologized works, and thus an excellent reintroduction to this unjustly neglected writer. Here Tyre is unflinching about the wretched state of poverty her protagonist grows up in, longing as the girl does for a real home and people who will love her. Naturally, the title takes on multiple meanings, with the last one the most horrifying, if inevitable.

A NICE PLACE TO STAY

ALL MY life I've wanted a nice place to stay. I don't mean anything grand, just a small room with the walls freshly painted and a few neat pieces of furniture and a window to catch the sun so that two or three pot plants could grow. That's what I've always dreamed of. I didn't yearn for love or money or nice clothes, though I was a pretty enough girl and pretty clothes would have made me prettier—not that I mean to brag.

Things fell on my shoulders when I was fifteen. That was when Mama took sick, and keeping house and looking after Papa and my two older brothers—and of course nursing Mama—became my responsibility. Not long after that Papa lost the farm and we moved to town. I don't like to think of the house we lived in near the C & R railroad tracks, though I guess we were lucky to have a roof over our heads—it was the worst days of the Depression and a lot of people didn't even have a roof, even one that leaked, plink, plonk; in a heavy rain there weren't enough pots and pans and vegetable bowls to set around to catch all the water.

Mama was the sick one but it was Papa who died first—living in town didn't suit him. By then my brothers had married and Mama and I moved into two back rooms that looked onto

an alley and everybody's garbage cans and dump heaps. My
brothers pitched in and gave me enough every month for Mama's and my barest expenses even though their wives grumbled
and complained.

I tried to make Mama comfortable. I catered to her every
whim and fancy. I loved her. All the same I had another reason
to keep her alive as long as possible. While she breathed I knew
I had a place to stay. I was terrified of what would happen to me
when Mama died. I had no high school diploma and no experience at outside work and I knew my sisters-in-law wouldn't take
me in or let my brothers support me once Mama was gone.

Then Mama drew her last breath with a smile of thanks on
her face for what I had done.

Sure enough, Norine and Thelma, my brothers' wives, put
their feet down. I was on my own from then on. So that scared
feeling of wondering where I could lay my head took over in my
mind and never left me.

I had some respite when Mr. Williams, a widower twenty-
four years older than me, asked me to marry him. I took my
vows seriously. I meant to cherish him and I did. But that house
we lived in! Those walls couldn't have been dirtier if they'd been
smeared with soot and the plumbing was stubborn as a mule.
My left foot stayed sore from having to kick the pipe underneath
the kitchen sink to get the water to run through.

Then Mr. Williams got sick and had to give up his shoe repair shop that he ran all by himself. He had a small savings account and a few of those twenty-five-dollar government bonds
and drew some disability insurance until the policy ran out in
something like six months.

I did everything I could to make him comfortable and keep

him cheerful. Though I did all the laundry I gave him clean sheets and clean pajamas every third day and I think it was by my will power alone that I made a begonia bloom in that dark back room Mr. Williams stayed in. I even pestered his two daughters and told them they ought to send their father some get-well cards and they did once or twice. Every now and then when there were a few pennies extra I'd buy cards and scrawl signatures nobody could have read and mailed them to Mr. Williams to make him think some of his former customers were remembering him and wishing him well.

Of course when Mr. Williams died his daughters were johnny-on-the-spot to see that they got their share of the little bit that tumbledown house brought. I didn't begrudge them— I'm not one to argue with human nature.

I hate to think about all those hardships I had after Mr. Williams died. The worst of it was finding somewhere to sleep; it all boiled down to having a place to stay. Because somehow you can manage not to starve. There are garbage cans to dip into—you'd be surprised how wasteful some people are and how much good food they throw away. Or if it was right after the garbage trucks had made their collections and the cans were empty I'd go into a supermarket and pick, say, at the cherries pretending I was selecting some to buy. I didn't slip their best ones into my mouth. I'd take either those so ripe that they should have been thrown away or those that weren't ripe enough and shouldn't have been put out for people to buy. I might snitch a withered cabbage leaf or a few pieces of watercress or a few of those small round tomatoes about the size of hickory nuts—I never can remember their right name. I wouldn't make a pig of myself, just eat enough to ease my hunger. So I managed. As I say, you don't have to starve.

28 · NEDRA TYRE

The only work I could get hardly ever paid me anything beyond room and board. I wasn't a practical nurse, though I knew how to take care of sick folks, and the people hiring me would say that since I didn't have the training and qualifications I couldn't expect much. All they really wanted was for someone to spend the night with Aunt Myrtle or Cousin Kate or Mama or Daddy; no actual duties were demanded of me, they said, and they really didn't think my help was worth anything except meals and a place to sleep. The arrangements were pretty makeshift. Half the time I wouldn't have a place to keep my things, not that I had any clothes to speak of, and sometimes I'd sleep on a cot in the hall outside the patient's room or on some sort of contrived bed in the patient's room.

I cherished every one of those sick people, just as I had cherished Mama and Mr. Williams. I didn't want them to die. I did everything I knew to let them know I was interested in their welfare—first for their sakes, and then for mine, so I wouldn't have to go out and find another place to stay.

Well, now, I've made out my case for the defense, a term I never thought I'd have to use personally, so now I'll make out the case for the prosecution.

I stole.

I don't like to say it, but I was a thief.

I'm not light-fingered. I didn't want a thing that belonged to anybody else. But there came a time when I felt forced to steal. I had to have some things. My shoes fell apart. I needed some stockings and underclothes. And when I'd ask a son or a daughter or a cousin or a niece for a little money for those necessities they acted as if I was trying to blackmail them. They reminded me that I wasn't qualified as a practical nurse, that I might even get into trouble with the authorities if they found I was palming myself off as a practical nurse—which I wasn't and they knew it. Anyway, they said that their terms were only bed and board.

So I began to take things—small things that had been pushed into the backs of drawers or stored high on shelves in boxes—things that hadn't been used or worn for years and probably would never be used again. I made my biggest haul at Mrs. Bick's where there was an attic full of trunks stuffed with clothes and doodads from the twenties all the way back to the nineties—uniforms, ostrich fans, Spanish shawls, beaded bags. I sneaked out a few of these at a time and every so often sold them to a place called Way Out, Hippie Clothiers.

I tried to work out the exact amount I got for selling something. Not, I know, that you can make up for theft. But, say, I got a dollar for a feather boa belonging to Mrs. Bick: well, then I'd come back and work at a job that the cleaning woman kept putting off, like waxing the hall upstairs or polishing the andirons or getting the linen closet in order.

All the same I *was* stealing—not everywhere I stayed, not even in most places, but when I had to I stole. I admit it.

But I didn't steal that silver box.

I was as innocent as a baby where that box was concerned. So when that policeman came toward me grabbing at the box I stepped aside, and maybe I even gave him the push that sent him to his death. He had no business acting like that when that box was mine, whatever Mrs. Crowe's niece argued.

Fifty thousand nieces couldn't have made it not mine.

Anyway, the policeman was dead and though I hadn't wanted him dead I certainly hadn't wished him well. And then I got to thinking: well, I didn't steal Mrs. Crowe's box but I had stolen other things and it was the mills of God grinding exceeding fine, as I once heard a preacher say, and I was being made to pay for the transgressions that had caught up with me.

Surely I can make a little more sense out of what happened than that, though I never was exactly clear in my own mind about everything that happened.

Mrs. Crowe was the most appreciative person I ever worked for. She was bedridden and could barely move. I don't think the registered nurse on daytime duty considered it part of her job to massage Mrs. Crowe. So at night I would massage her, and that pleased and soothed her. She thanked me for every small thing I did—when I fluffed her pillow, when I'd put a few drops of perfume on her earlobes, when I'd straighten the wrinkled bedcovers.

I had a little joke. I'd pretend I could tell fortunes and I'd take Mrs. Crowe's hand and tell her she was going to have a wonderful day but she must beware of a handsome blond stranger—or some such foolishness that would make her laugh. She didn't sleep well and it seemed to give her pleasure to talk to me most of the night about her childhood or her dead husband.

She kept getting weaker and weaker and two nights before she died she said she wished she could do something for me but that when she became an invalid she had signed over everything to her niece. Anyway, Mrs. Crowe hoped I'd take her silver box. I thanked her. It pleased me that she liked me well enough to give me the box. I didn't have any real use for it. It would have made a nice trinket box, but I didn't have any trinkets. The box seemed to be Mrs. Crowe's fondest possession. She kept it on the table beside her and her eyes lighted up every time she looked at it. She might have been a little girl first seeing a brand-new baby doll early on a Christmas morning.

So when Mrs. Crowe died and the niece on whom I set eyes for the first time dismissed me, I gathered up what little I had and took the box and left. I didn't go to Mrs. Crowe's funeral. The paper said it was private and I wasn't invited. Anyway, I wouldn't have had anything suitable to wear.

I still had a few dollars left over from those things I'd sold to the hippie place called Way Out, so I paid a week's rent for a room that was the worst I'd ever stayed in.

It was freezing cold and no heat came up to the third floor where I was. In that room with falling plaster and buckling floorboards and darting roaches, I sat wearing every stitch I owned, with a sleazy blanket and a faded quilt draped around me waiting for the heat to rise, when in swept Mrs. Crowe's niece in a fur coat and a fur hat and shiny leather boots up to her knees. Her face was beet red from anger when she started telling me that she had traced me through a private detective and I was to give her back the heirloom I had stolen.

Her statement made me forget the precious little bit I knew of the English language. I couldn't say a word, and she kept on screaming that if I returned the box immediately no criminal charge would be made against me. Then I got back my voice and I said that box was mine and that Mrs. Crowe had wanted me to have it, and she asked if I had any proof or if there were any witnesses to the gift, and I told her that when I was given a present I said thank you, that I didn't ask for proof and witnesses, and that nothing could make me part with Mrs. Crowe's box.

The niece stood there breathing hard, in and out, almost counting her breaths like somebody doing an exercise to get control of herself.

"You'll see," she yelled, and then she left.

The room was colder than ever and my teeth chattered.

Not long afterward I heard heavy steps clumping up the stairway. I realized that the niece had carried out her threat and that the police were after me.

I was panic-stricken. I chased around the room like a rat with a cat after it: Then I thought that if the police searched my room and couldn't find the box it might give me time to decide what to do. I grabbed the box out of the top dresser drawer and scurried down the back hall. I snatched the back door open. I think what I intended to do was run down the back steps and hide the box somewhere, underneath a bush or maybe in a garbage can.

Those back steps were steep and rose almost straight up for three stories and they were flimsy and covered with ice.

I started down. My right foot slipped. The handrail saved me. I clung to it with one hand and to the silver box with the other hand and picked and chose my way across the patches of ice.

When I was midway I heard my name shrieked. I looked around to see a big man leaping down the steps after me. I never saw such anger on a person's face. Then he was directly behind me and reached out to snatch the box.

I swerved to escape his grasp and he cursed me. Maybe I pushed him. I'm not sure—not really.

Anyway, he slipped and fell down and down and down, and then after all that falling he was absolutely still. The bottom step was beneath his head like a pillow and the rest of his body was spreadeagled on the brick walk.

Almost like a pet that wants to follow its master, the silver box jumped from my hand and bounced down the steps to land beside the man's left ear.

My brain was numb. I felt paralyzed. Then I screamed.

Tenants from that house and the houses next door and across the alley pushed windows open and flung doors open to see what the commotion was about, and then some of them began to run toward the back yard. The policeman who was the dead man's partner—I guess you'd call him that—ordered them to keep away.

After a while more police came and they took the dead man's body and drove me to the station where I was locked up.

From the very beginning I didn't take to that young lawyer they assigned to me. There wasn't anything exactly that I could put my finger on. I just felt uneasy with him. His last name was Stanton. He had a first name of course, but he didn't tell me what it was; he said he wanted me to call him Bat like all his friends did.

He was always smiling and reassuring me when there wasn't anything to smile or be reassured about, and he ought to have known it all along instead of filling me with false hope.

All I could think was that I was thankful Mama and Papa and Mr. Williams were dead and that my shame wouldn't bring shame on them.

"It's going to be all right," the lawyer kept saying right up to the end, and then he claimed to be indignant when I was found guilty of resisting arrest and of manslaughter and theft or robbery—there was the biggest hullabaloo as to whether I was guilty of theft or robbery. Not that I was guilty of either, at least in this particular instance, but no one would believe me.

You would have thought it was the lawyer being sentenced instead of me, the way he carried on. He called it a terrible mis-carriage of justice and said we might as well be back in the eigh-teenth century when they hanged children.

Well, that was an exaggeration, if ever there was one; nobody was being hanged and nobody was a child. That policeman had died and I had had a part in it. Maybe I had pushed him. I couldn't be sure. In my heart I really hadn't meant him any harm. I was just scared. But he was dead all the same. And as far as stealing went, I hadn't stolen the box but I had stolen other things more than once.

And then it happened. It was a miracle. All my life I'd dreamed of a nice room of my own, a comfortable place to stay. And that's exactly what I got.

The room was on the small side but it had everything I needed in it, even a wash basin with hot and cold running water, and the walls were freshly painted, and they let me choose whether I wanted a wing chair with a chintz slipcover or a modern Danish armchair. I even got to decide what color bedspread I preferred. The window looked out on a beautiful lawn edged with shrubbery, and the matron said I'd be allowed to go to the greenhouse and select some pot plants to keep in my room. The next day I picked out a white gloxinia and some russet chrysanthemums.

I didn't mind the bars at the windows at all. Why, this day and age some of the finest mansions have barred windows to keep burglars out.

The meals—I simply couldn't believe there was such delicious food in the world. The woman who supervised their preparation had embezzled the funds of one of the largest catering companies in the state after working herself up from assistant cook to treasurer.

The other inmates were very friendly and most of them had led the most interesting lives. Some of the ladies occasionally used words that you usually see written only on fences or printed on sidewalks before the cement dries, but when they were scolded they apologized. Every now and then somebody would get angry with someone and there would be a little scratching or hair pulling, but it never got too bad. There was a choir—I can't sing but I love music—and they gave a concert every Tuesday morning at chapel, and Thursday night was movie night. There wasn't any admission charge. All you did was go in and sit down anywhere you pleased.

We all had a special job and I was assigned to the infirmary. The doctor and nurse both complimented me. The doctor said that I should have gone into professional nursing, that I gave confidence to the patients and helped them get well. I don't know about that but I've had years of practice with sick people and I like to help anybody who feels bad.

I was so happy that sometimes I couldn't sleep at night. I'd get up and click on the light and look at the furniture and the walls. It was hard to believe I had such a pleasant place to stay. I'd remember supper that night, how I'd gone back to the steam table for a second helping of asparagus with lemon and herb sauce, and I compared my plenty with those terrible times when I had slunk into supermarkets and nibbled overripe fruit and raw vegetables to ease my hunger.

Then one day here came that lawyer, not even at regular visiting hours, bouncing around congratulating me that my appeal had been upheld, or whatever the term was, and that I was as free as a bird to leave right that minute.

He told the matron she could send my belongings later and he dragged me out front where TV cameras and newspaper reporters were waiting.

As soon as the cameras began whirring and the photographers began to aim, the lawyer kissed me on the cheek and pinned a flower on me. He made a speech saying that a terrible miscarriage of justice had been rectified. He had located people who testified that Mrs. Crowe had given me the box—she had told the gardener and the cleaning woman. They hadn't wanted to testify because they didn't want to get mixed up with the police, but the lawyer had persuaded them in the cause of justice and humanity to come forward and make statements.

The lawyer had also looked into the personnel record of the dead policeman and had learned that he had been judged emotionally unfit for his job, and the psychiatrist had warned the Chief of Police that something awful might happen either to the man himself or to a suspect unless he was relieved of his duties.

All the time the lawyer was talking into the microphones he had latched onto me like I was a three-year-old that might run away, and I just stood and stared. Then when he had finished his speech about me the reporters told him that like his grandfather and his uncle he was sure to end up as governor but at a much earlier age.

At that the lawyer gave a big grin in front of the camera and waved good-bye and pushed me into his car.

I was terrified. The nice place I'd found to stay in wasn't mine any longer. My old nightmare was back—wondering how I could manage to eat and how much stealing I'd have to do to live from one day to the next.

The cameras and reporters had followed us.

A photographer asked me to turn down the car window beside me, and I overheard two men way in the back of the crowd talking. My ears are sharp. Papa always said I could hear thunder three states away. Above the congratulations and bubbly talk around me I heard one of those men in back say, "This is a bit too much, don't you think? Our Bat is showing himself the champion of the Senior Citizen now. He's already copped the teenyboppers and the under thirties using methods that ought to have disbarred him. He should have made the gardener and cleaning woman testify at the beginning, and from the first he should have checked into the policeman's history. There ought never to have been a case at all, much less a conviction. But Bat wouldn't have got any publicity that way. He had to do it in his own devious, spectacular fashion." The other man just kept nodding and saying after every sentence, "You're damned right."

Then we drove off and I didn't dare look behind me because I was so heartbroken over what I was leaving.

The lawyer took me to his office. He said he hoped I wouldn't mind a little excitement for the next few days. He had mapped out some public appearances for me. The next morning I was to be on an early television show. There was nothing to be worried about. He would be right beside me to help me just as he had helped me throughout my trouble. All that I had to say on the TV program was that I owed my freedom to him.

I guess I looked startled or bewildered because he hurried on to say that I hadn't been able to pay him a fee but that now I was able to pay him back—not in money but in letting the public know about how he was the champion of the underdog.

I said I had been told that the court furnished lawyers free of charge to people who couldn't pay, and he said that was right, but his point was that I could repay him now by telling people all that he had done for me. Then he said the main thing was to talk over our next appearance on TV. He wanted to coach me in what I was going to say, but first he would go into his partner's office and tell him to take all the incoming calls and handle the rest of his appointments.

When the door closed after him I thought that he was right. I did owe my freedom to him. He was to blame for it. The smart alec. The upstart. Who asked him to butt in and snatch me out of my pretty room and the work I loved and all that delicious food?

It was the first time in my life I knew what it meant to despise someone.

I hated him.

Before, when I was convicted of manslaughter, there was a lot of talk about malice aforethought and premeditated crime.

There wouldn't be any argument this time.

I hadn't wanted any harm to come to that policeman. But I did mean harm to come to this lawyer.

I grabbed up a letter opener from his desk and ran my finger along the blade and felt how sharp it was. I waited behind the door and when he walked through I gathered all my strength and stabbed him. Again and again and again.

Now I'm back where I want to be—in a nice place to stay.

SHIRLEY JACKSON

1916–1965

SHIRLEY JACKSON was born in San Francisco in 1916 and spent much of her life in the college town of Bennington, Vermont, with her husband, the literary critic Stanley Edgar Hyman, and their children. She first received wide critical acclaim for her short story "The Lottery," published in *The New Yorker* in 1948 and anthologized countless times since. Her novels include *The Road Through the Wall* (1948), *Hangsaman* (1951), *The Bird's Nest* (1954), *The Sundial* (1958), *The Haunting of Hill House* (1959), and *We Have Always Lived in the Castle* (1962), and while they are most often characterized by the mixing of realistic settings with elements of horror and the occult, they are just as informed by the mundane terror of domesticity and raising children, which she treated with humor in her two books of nonfiction, *Life Among the Savages* and *Raising Demons*. Jackson also wrote four books for children, with the last, *Famous Sally*, published posthumously in 1966.

Jackson was a prolific short story writer as well, her many tales delving in themes common to her novels but with a sharper bite. A prime example of Jackson at her peak is "Louisa, Please Come Home," first published in *Ladies' Home Journal* in 1960. Here Jackson twists the missing girl trope by having the girl herself as narrator, describing how she'd run away from home several years earlier though her parents were convinced she'd been abducted. And after years of impostors coming forward to claim the reward, finally, Louisa is ready to return home. Except, as Jackson shows with uncanny insight, myths often have a more powerful hold than the truth, and what you see is not necessarily what you believe.

LOUISA, PLEASE COME HOME

"LOUISA," MY mother's voice came over the radio; it frightened me badly for a minute. "Louisa," she said, "please come home. It's been three long long years since we saw you last; Louisa, I promise you that everything will be all right. We all miss you so. We want you back again. Louisa, please come home."

Once a year. On the anniversary of the day I ran away. Each time I heard it I was frightened again, because between one year and the next I would forget what my mother's voice sounded like, so soft and yet strange with that pleading note. I listened every year. I read the stories in the newspapers—"Louisa Tether vanished one year ago"—or two years ago, or three; I used to wait for the twentieth of June as though it were my birthday. I kept all the clippings at first, but secretly; with my picture on all the front pages I would have looked kind of strange if anyone had seen me cutting it out. Chandler, where I was hiding, was close enough to my old home so that the papers made a big fuss about all of it, but of course the reason I picked Chandler in the first place was because it was a big enough city for me to hide in.

I didn't just up and leave on the spur of the moment, you know. I always knew that I was going to run away sooner or later, and I had made plans ahead of time, for whenever I decided to go. Everything had to go right the first time, because they don't usually give you a second chance on that kind of thing and anyway if it had gone wrong I would have looked like an awful fool, and my sister Carol was never one for letting people forget it when they made fools of themselves. I admit I planned it for the day before Carol's wedding on purpose, and for a long time afterward I used to try and imagine Carol's face when she finally realized that my running away was going to leave her one bridesmaid short. The papers said that the wedding went ahead as scheduled, though, and Carol told one newspaper reporter that her sister Louisa would have wanted it that way; "She would never have meant to spoil my wedding," Carol said, knowing perfectly well that that would be exactly what I'd meant. I'm pretty sure that the first thing Carol did when they knew I was missing was go and count the wedding presents to see what I'd taken with me.

Anyway, Carol's wedding may have been fouled up, but *my* plans went fine—better, as a matter of fact, than I had ever expected. Everyone was hurrying around the house putting up flowers and asking each other if the wedding gown had been delivered, and opening up cases of champagne and wondering what they were going to do if it rained and they couldn't use the garden, and I just closed the front door behind me and started off. There was only one bad minute when Paul saw me; Paul has always lived next door and Carol hates him worse than she does me. My mother always used to say that every time I did something to make the family ashamed of me Paul was sure to be in it somewhere. For a long time they thought he had something to do with my running away, even though he told over and over again how hard I tried to duck away from him that afternoon when he met me going down the driveway. The papers kept calling him "a close friend of the family," which must have overjoyed my mother, and saying that he was being questioned about possible clues to my whereabouts. Of course he never even knew that I was running away; I told him just what I told my mother before I left—that I was going to get away from all the confusion and excitement for a while; I was going downtown and would probably have a sandwich somewhere for supper and go to a movie. He bothered me for a minute there, because of course he wanted to come too. I hadn't meant to take the bus right there on the corner but with Paul tagging after me and wanting me to wait while he got the car so we could drive out and have dinner at the Inn, I had to get away fast on the first thing that came along, so I just ran for the bus and left Paul standing there; that was the only part of my plan I had to change.

I took the bus all the way downtown, although my first plan had been to walk. It turned out much better, actually, since it didn't matter at all if anyone saw me on the bus going downtown in my own home town, and I managed to get an earlier train out. I bought a round-trip ticket; that was important, because it would make them think I was coming back; that was always the way they thought about things. If you did something you had to have a reason for it, because my mother and my father and Carol never did anything unless *they* had a reason for it, so if I bought a round-trip ticket the only possible reason would be that I was coming back. Besides, if they thought I was coming back they would not be frightened so quickly and I might have more time to hide before they came looking for me. As it happened, Carol found out I was gone that same night when she couldn't sleep and came into my room for some aspirin, so all the time I had less of a head start than I thought.

I knew that they would find out about my buying the ticket; I was not silly enough to suppose that I could steal off and not leave any traces. All my plans were based on the fact that the people who get caught are the ones who attract attention by doing something strange or noticeable, and what I intended all along was to fade into some background where they would never see me. I knew they would find out about the round-trip ticket, because it was an odd thing to do in a town where you've lived all your life, but it was the last unusual thing I did. I thought when I bought it that knowing about that round-trip ticket would be some consolation to my mother and father. They would know that no matter how long I stayed away at least I always had a ticket home. I did keep the return-trip ticket quite a while, as a matter of fact. I used to carry it in my wallet as a kind of lucky charm.

I followed everything in the papers. Mrs. Peacock and I used to read them at the breakfast table over our second cup of coffee before I went off to work.

"What do you think about this girl disappeared over in Rockville?" Mrs. Peacock would say to me, and I'd shake my head sorrowfully and say that a girl must be really crazy to leave a handsome, luxurious home like that, or that I had kind of a notion that maybe she didn't leave at all—maybe the family had her locked up somewhere because she was a homicidal maniac. Mrs. Peacock always loved anything about homicidal maniacs.

Once I picked up the paper and looked hard at the picture. "Do you think she looks something like me?" I asked Mrs. Peacock, and Mrs. Peacock leaned back and looked at me and then at the picture and then at me again and finally she shook her head and said, "No. If you wore your hair longer, and curlier, and your face was maybe a little fuller, there might be a little resemblance, but then if you looked like a homicidal maniac I wouldn't ever of let you in my house."

"I think she kind of looks like me," I said.

"You get along to work and stop being vain," Mrs. Peacock told me.

Of course when I got on the train with my round-trip ticket I had no idea how soon they'd be following me, and I suppose it was just as well, because it might have made me nervous and I might have done something wrong and spoiled everything. I knew that as soon as they gave up the notion that I was coming back to Rockville with my round-trip ticket they would think of Crain, which is the largest city that train went to, so I only stayed in Crain part of one day. I went to a big department store where they were having a store-wide sale; I figured that would land me in a crowd of shoppers and I was right; for a while there was a good chance that I'd never get any farther away from home than the ground floor of that department store in Crain. I had to fight my way through the crowd until I found the counter where they were having a sale of raincoats, and then I had to push and elbow down the counter and finally grab the raincoat I wanted right out of the hands of some old monster who couldn't have used it anyway because she was much too fat. You would have thought she had already paid for it, the way she howled. I was smart enough to have the exact change, all six dollars and eighty-nine cents, right in my hand, and I gave it to the salesgirl, grabbed the raincoat and the bag she wanted to put it in, and fought my way out again before I got crushed to death.

That raincoat was worth every cent of the six dollars and eighty-nine cents; I wore it right through until winter that year and not even a button ever came off it. I finally lost it the next spring when I left it somewhere and never got it back. It was tan, and the minute I put it on in the ladies' room of the store I began thinking of it as my "old" raincoat; that was good. I had never before owned a raincoat like that and my mother would have fainted dead away. One thing I did that I thought was kind of clever. I had left home wearing a light short coat; almost a jacket, and when I put on the raincoat of course I took off my light coat. Then all I had to do was empty the pockets of the light coat into the raincoat and carry the light coat casually over to a counter where they were having a sale of jackets and drop it on the counter as though I'd taken it off a little way to look at it and had decided against it. As far as I ever knew no one paid the slightest attention to me, and before I left the counter I saw a woman pick up my jacket and look it over; I could have told her she was getting a bargain for three ninety-eight.

It made me feel good to know that I had gotten rid of the light coat. My mother picked it out for me and even though I liked it and it was expensive it was also recognizable and I had to change it somehow. I was sure that if I put it in a bag and dropped it into a river or into a garbage truck or something like that sooner or later it would be found and even if no one saw me doing it, it would almost certainly be found, and then they would know I had changed my clothes in Crain.

That light coat never turned up. The last they ever found of me was someone in Rockville who caught a glimpse of me in the train station in Crain, and she recognized me by the light coat. They never found out where I went after that; it was partly luck and partly my clever planning. Two or three days later the papers were still reporting that I was in Crain; people thought they saw me on the streets and one girl who went into a store to buy a dress was picked up by the police and held until she could get someone to identify her. They were really looking, but they were looking for Louisa Tether, and I had stopped being Louisa Tether the minute I got rid of that light coat my mother bought me.

One thing I was relying on: there must be thousands of girls in the country on any given day who are nineteen years old, fair-haired, five feet four inches tall, and weighing one hundred and twenty-six pounds. And if there are thousands of girls like that, there must be, among those thousands, a good number who are wearing shapeless tan raincoats; I started counting tan raincoats in Crain after I left the department store and I passed four in one block, so I felt well hidden. After that I made myself even more invisible by doing just what I told my mother I was going to—I stopped in and had a sandwich in a little coffee shop, and then I went to a movie. I wasn't in any hurry at all, and rather than try to find a place to sleep that night I thought I would sleep on the train.

It's funny how no one pays any attention to you at all. There were hundreds of people who saw me that day, and even a sailor who tried to pick me up in the movie, and yet no one really *saw* me. If I had tried to check into a hotel the desk clerk might have noticed me, or if I had tried to get dinner in some fancy restaurant in that cheap raincoat I would have been conspicuous, but I was doing what any other girl looking like me and dressed like me might be doing that day. The only person who might be apt to remember me would be the man selling tickets in the railroad station, because girls looking like me in old raincoats didn't buy train tickets, usually, at eleven at night, but I had thought of that, too, of course; I bought a ticket to Amityville, sixty miles away, and what made Amityville a perfectly reasonable disguise is that at Amityville there is a college, not a little fancy place like the one I had left so recently with nobody's blessing, but a big sprawling friendly affair, where my raincoat would look perfectly at home. I told myself I was a student coming back to the college after a week end at home. We got to Amityville after midnight, but it still didn't look odd when I left the train and went into the station, because while I was in the station, having a cup of coffee and killing time, seven other girls—I counted—wearing raincoats like mine came in or went out, not seeming to think it the least bit odd to be getting on or off trains at that hour of the night. Some of them had suitcases, and I wished that I had had some way of getting a suitcase in Crain, but it would have made me noticeable in the movie, and college girls going home for week ends often don't bother; they have pajamas and an extra pair of stockings at home, and they drop a toothbrush into one of the pockets of those invaluable raincoats. So I didn't worry about the suitcase then, although I knew I would need one soon. While I was having my coffee I made my own mind change from the idea that I was a college girl coming back after a week end at home to the idea that I was a college girl who was on her way home for a few days; all the time I tried to think as much as possible like what I was pretending to be, and after all, I *had* been a college girl for a while. I was thinking that even now the letter was in the mail, traveling as fast as the U.S. Government could make it go, right to my father to tell him why I wasn't a college student any more; I suppose that was what finally decided me to run away, the thought of what my father would think and say and do when he got that letter from the college.

That was in the paper, too. They decided that the college business was the reason for my running away, but if that had been all, I don't think I would have left. No, I had been wanting to leave for so long, ever since I can remember, making plans till I was sure they were foolproof, and that's the way they turned out to be.

Sitting there in the station at Amityville, I tried to think myself into a good reason why I was leaving college to go home on a Monday night late, when I would hardly be going home for the week end. As I say, I always tried to think as hard as I could the way that suited whatever I wanted to be, and I liked to have a good reason for what I was doing. Nobody ever asked me, but it was good to know that I could answer them if they did. I finally decided that my sister was getting married the next day and I was going home at the beginning of the week to be one of her bridesmaids. I thought that was funny. I didn't want to be going home for any sad or frightening reason, like my mother being sick, or my father being hurt in a car accident, because I would have to look sad, and that might attract attention. So I was going home for my sister's wedding. I wandered around the station as though I had nothing to do, and just happened to pass the door when another girl was going out; she had on a raincoat just like mine and anyone who happened to notice would have thought that it was me who went out. Before I bought my ticket I went into the ladies' room and got another twenty dollars out of my shoe. I had nearly three hundred dollars left of the money I had taken from my father's desk and I had most of it in my shoes because I honestly couldn't think of another safe place to carry it. All I kept in my pocketbook was just enough for whatever I had to spend next. It's uncomfortable walking around all day on a wad of bills in your shoe, but they were good solid shoes, the kind of comfortable old shoes you wear whenever you don't really care how you look, and I had put new shoelaces in them before I left home so I could tie them good and tight. You can see, I planned pretty carefully, and no little detail got left out. If they had let me plan my sister's wedding there would have been a lot less of that running around and screaming and hysterics.

I bought a ticket to Chandler, which is the biggest city in this part of the state, and the place I'd been heading for all along. It was a good place to hide because people from Rockville tended to bypass it unless they had some special reason for going there—if they couldn't find the doctors or orthodontists or psychoanalysts or dress material they wanted in Rockville or Crain, they went directly to one of the really big cities, like the state capital; Chandler was big enough to hide in, but not big enough to look like a metropolis to people from Rockville. The ticket seller in the Amityville station must have seen a good many college girls buying tickets for Chandler at all hours of the day or night because he took my money and shoved the ticket at me without even looking up.

Funny. They must have come looking for me in Chandler at some time or other, because it's not likely they would have neglected any possible place I might be, but maybe Rockville people never seriously believed that anyone would go to Chandler from choice, because I never felt for a minute that anyone was looking for me there. My picture was in the Chandler papers, of course, but as far as I ever knew no one ever looked at me twice, and I got up every morning and went to work and went shopping in the stores and went to movies with Mrs. Peacock and went out to the beach all that summer without ever being afraid of being recognized. I behaved just like everyone else, and dressed just like everyone else, and even *thought* just like everyone else, and the only person I ever saw from Rockville in three years was a friend of my mother's, and I knew *she* only came to Chandler to get her poodle bred at the kennels there. She didn't look as if she was in a state to recognize anybody but another poodle-fancier, anyway, and all I had to do was step into a doorway as she went by, and she never looked at me.

Two other college girls got on the train to Chandler when I did; maybe both of them were going home for their sisters' weddings. Neither of them was wearing a tan raincoat, but one of them had on an old blue jacket that gave the same general effect. I fell asleep as soon as the train started, and once I woke up and for a minute I wondered where I was and then I realized that I was doing it, I was actually carrying out my careful plan and had gotten better than halfway with it, and I almost laughed, there in the train with everyone asleep around me. Then I went back to sleep and didn't wake up until we got into Chandler about seven in the morning.

So there I was. I had left home just after lunch the day before, and now at seven in the morning of my sister's wedding day I was so far away, in every sense, that I *knew* they would never find me. I had all day to get myself settled in Chandler, so I started off by having breakfast in a restaurant near the station, and then went off to find a place to live, and a job. The first thing I did was buy a suitcase, and it's funny how people don't really notice you if you're buying a suitcase near a railroad station. Suitcases look *natural* near railroad stations, and I picked out one of those stores that sell a little bit of everything, and bought a cheap suitcase and a pair of stockings and some handkerchiefs and a little traveling clock, and I put everything into the suitcase and carried that. Nothing is hard to do unless you get upset or excited about it.

Later on, when Mrs. Peacock and I used to read in the papers about my disappearing, I asked her once if she thought that Louisa Tether had gotten as far as Chandler and she didn't.

"They're saying now she was kidnapped," Mrs. Peacock told me, "and that's what *I* think happened. Kidnapped, and murdered, and they do *terrible* things to young girls they kidnap."

"But the papers say there wasn't any ransom note."

"That's what they *say*." Mrs. Peacock shook her head at me. "How do we know what the family is keeping secret? Or if she was kidnapped by a homicidal maniac, why should *he* send a ransom note? Young girls like you don't know a lot of the things that go on, *I* can tell you."

"I feel kind of sorry for the girl," I said.

"You can't ever tell," Mrs. Peacock said. "Maybe she went with him willingly."

I didn't know, that first morning in Chandler, that Mrs. Peacock was going to turn up that first day, the luckiest thing that ever happened to me. I decided while I was having breakfast that I was going to be a nineteen-year-old girl from upstate with a nice family and a good background who had been saving money to come to Chandler and take a secretarial course in the business school there. I was going to have to find some kind of a job to keep on earning money while I went to school; courses at the business school wouldn't start until fall, so I would have the summer to work and save money and decide if I really wanted to take secretarial training. If I decided not to stay in Chandler I could easily go somewhere else after the fuss about my running away had died down. The raincoat looked wrong for the kind of conscientious young girl I was going to be, so I took it off and carried it over my arm. I think I did a pretty good job on my clothes, altogether. Before I left home I decided that I would have to wear a suit, as quiet and unobtrusive as I could find, and I picked out a gray suit, with a white blouse, so with just one or two small changes like a different blouse or some kind of a pin on the lapel, I could look like whoever I decided to be. Now the suit looked absolutely right for a young girl planning to take a secretarial course, and I looked like a thousand other people when I walked down the street carrying my suitcase and my raincoat over my arm; people get off trains every minute looking just like that. I bought a morning paper and stopped in a drugstore for a cup of coffee and a look to see the rooms for rent. It was all so usual—suitcase, coat, rooms for rent—that when I asked the soda clerk how to get to Primrose Street he never even looked at me. He certainly didn't care whether I ever got to Primrose Street or not, but he told me very politely where it was and what bus to take. I didn't really need to take the bus for economy, but it would have looked funny for a girl who was saving money to arrive in a taxi.

"I'll never forget how you looked that first morning," Mrs. Peacock told me once, much later. "I knew right away you were the kind of girl I like to rent rooms to—quiet, and well-mannered. But you looked almighty scared of the big city."

"I wasn't scared," I said. "I was worried about finding a nice room. My mother told me so many things to be careful about I was afraid I'd never find anything to suit her."

"*Any*body's mother could come into my house at any time and know that her daughter was in good hands," Mrs. Peacock said, a little huffy.

But it was true. When I walked into Mrs. Peacock's rooming house on Primrose Street, and met Mrs. Peacock, I knew that I couldn't have done this part better if I'd been able to plan it. The house was old, and comfortable, and my room was nice, and Mrs. Peacock and I hit it off right away. She was very pleased with me when she heard that my mother had told me to be sure the room I found was clean and that the neighborhood was good, with no chance of rowdies following a girl if she came home after dark, and she was even more pleased when she heard that I wanted to save money and take a secretarial course so I could get a really good job and earn enough to be able to send a little home every week; Mrs. Peacock believed that children owed it to their parents to pay back some of what had been spent on them while they were growing up. By the time I had been in the house an hour Mrs. Peacock knew all about my imaginary family upstate: my mother, who was a widow, and my sister, who had just gotten married and still lived at my mother's home with her husband, and my young brother Paul, who worried my mother a good deal because he didn't seem to want to settle down. My name was Lois Taylor, I told her. By that time, I think I could have told her my real name and she would never have connected it with the girl in the paper, because by then she was feeling that she almost knew my family, and she wanted me to be sure and tell my mother when I wrote home that Mrs. Peacock would make herself personally responsible for me while

I was in the city and take as good care of me as my own mother would. On top of everything else, she told me that a stationery store in the neighborhood was looking for a girl assistant, and there I was. Before I had been away from home for twenty-four hours I was an entirely new person. I was a girl named Lois Taylor who lived on Primrose Street and worked down at the stationery store.

I read in the papers one day about how a famous fortune-teller wrote to my father offering to find me and said that astral signs had convinced him that I would be found near flowers. That gave me a jolt, because of Primrose Street, but my father and Mrs. Peacock and the rest of the world thought that it meant that my body was buried somewhere. They dug up a vacant lot near the railroad station where I was last seen, and Mrs. Peacock was very disappointed when nothing turned up. Mrs. Peacock and I could not decide whether I had run away with a gangster to be a gun moll, or whether my body had been cut up and sent somewhere in a trunk. After a while they stopped looking for me, except for an occasional false clue that would turn up in a small story on the back pages of the paper, and Mrs. Peacock and I got interested in the stories about a daring daylight bank robbery in Chicago. When the anniversary of my running away came around, and I realized that I had really been gone for a year, I treated myself to a new hat and dinner downtown, and came home just in time for the evening news broadcast and my mother's voice over the radio.

"Louisa," she was saying, "please come home."

"That poor poor woman," Mrs. Peacock said. "Imagine how she must feel. They say she's never given up hope of finding her little girl alive someday."

"Do you like my new hat?" I asked her.

I had given up all idea of the secretarial course because the stationery store had decided to expand and include a lending library and a gift shop, and I was now the manager of the gift shop and if things kept on well would someday be running the whole thing; Mrs. Peacock and I talked it over, just as if she had been my mother, and we decided that I would be foolish to leave a good job to start over somewhere else. The money that I had been saving was in the bank, and Mrs. Peacock and I thought that one of these days we might pool our savings and buy a little car, or go on a trip somewhere, or even a cruise.

What I am saying is that I was free, and getting along fine, with never a thought that I knew about ever going back. It was just plain rotten bad luck that I had to meet Paul. I had gotten so I hardly ever thought about any of them any more, and never wondered what they were doing unless I happened to see some item in the papers, but there must have been something in the back of my mind remembering them all the time because I never even stopped to think; I just stood there on the street with my mouth open, and said *"Paul!"* He turned around and then of course I realized what I had done, but it was too late. He stared at me for a minute, and then frowned, and then looked puzzled; I could see him first trying to remember, and then trying to believe what he remembered; at last he said, "Is it possible?"

He said I had to go back. He said if I didn't go back he would tell them where to come and get me. He also patted me on the head and told me that there was still a reward waiting there in the bank for anyone who turned up with conclusive news of me, and he said that after he had collected the reward I was perfectly welcome to run away again, as far and as often as I liked.

Maybe I did want to go home. Maybe all that time I had been secretly waiting for a chance to get back; maybe that's why I recognized Paul on the street, in a coincidence that wouldn't have happened once in a million years—he had never even *been* to Chandler before, and was only there for a few minutes between trains; he had stepped out of the station for a minute, and found me. If I had not been passing at that minute, if he had stayed in the station where he belonged, I would never have gone back. I told Mrs. Peacock I was going home to visit my family upstate. I thought that was funny.

Paul sent a telegram to my mother and father, saying that he had found me, and we took a plane back; Paul said he was still afraid that I'd try to get away again and the safest place for me was high up in the air where he knew I couldn't get off and run.

I began to get nervous, looking out the taxi window on the way from the Rockville airport; I would have sworn that for three years I hadn't given a thought to that town, to those streets and stores and houses I used to know so well, but here I found that I remembered it all, as though I hadn't ever seen Chandler and *its* houses and streets; it was almost as though I had never been away at all. When the taxi finally turned the corner into my own street, and I saw the big old white house again, I almost cried.

"Of course I wanted to come back," I said, and Paul laughed. I thought of the return-trip ticket I had kept as a lucky charm for so long, and how I had thrown it away one day when I was emptying my pocketbook; I wondered when I threw it away whether I would ever want to go back and regret throwing away my ticket. "Everything looks just the same," I said. "I caught the bus right there on the corner; I came down the driveway that day and met you."

"If I had managed to stop you that day," Paul said, "you would probably never have tried again."

Then the taxi stopped in front of the house and my knees were shaking when I got out. I grabbed Paul's arm and said, "Paul . . . wait a minute," and he gave me a look I used to know very well, a look that said "If you back out on me now I'll see that you never forget it," and put his arm around me because I was shivering and we went up the walk to the front door.

I wondered if they were watching us from the window. It was hard for me to imagine how my mother and father would behave in a situation like this, because they always made such a point of being quiet and dignified and proper; I thought that Mrs. Peacock would have been halfway down the walk to meet us, but here the front door ahead was still tight shut. I wondered if we would have to ring the doorbell; I had never had to ring this doorbell before. I was still wondering when Carol opened the door for us. "Carol!" I said. I was shocked because she looked so old, and then I thought that of course it had been three years since I had seen her and she probably thought that *I* looked older, too. "Carol," I said, "Oh, Carol!" I was honestly glad to see her.

She looked at me hard and then stepped back and my mother and father were standing there, waiting for me to come in. If I had not stopped to think I would have run to them, but I hesitated, not quite sure what to do, or whether they were angry with me, or hurt, or only just happy that I was back, and of course once I stopped to think about it all I could find to do was just stand there and say "Mother?" kind of uncertainly.

She came over to me and put her hands on my shoulders and looked into my face for a long time. There were tears running down her cheeks and I thought that before, when it didn't matter, I had been ready enough to cry, but now, when crying would make me look better, all I wanted to do was giggle. She looked old, and sad, and I felt simply foolish. Then she turned to Paul and said, "Oh, *Paul*—how can you do this to me again?"

Paul was frightened; I could see it. "Mrs. Tether—" he said.

"What is your name, dear?" my mother asked me.

"Louisa Tether," I said stupidly.

"No, dear," she said, very gently, "your *real* name?"

Now I could cry, but now I did not think it was going to help matters any. "Louisa Tether," I said. "That's my name."

"Why don't you people leave us alone?" Carol said; she was white, and shaking, and almost screaming because she was so angry. "We've spent years and years trying to find my lost sister and all people like you see in it is a chance to cheat us out of the reward—doesn't it mean *any*thing to you that *you* may think you have a chance for some easy money, but *we* just get hurt and heartbroken all over again? Why don't you leave us *alone*?"

"Carol," my father said, "you're frightening the poor child. Young lady," he said to me, "I honestly believe that you did not realize the cruelty of what you tried to do. You look like a nice girl; try to imagine your own mother—"

I tried to imagine my own mother; I looked straight at her.

"—if someone took advantage of her like this. I am sure you were not told that twice before, this young man—" I stopped looking at my mother and looked at Paul—"has brought us young girls who pretended to be our lost daughter; each time he protested that he had been genuinely deceived and had no thought of profit, and each time we hoped desperately that it would be the right girl. The first time we were taken in for several days. The girl *looked* like our Louisa, she *acted* like our Louisa, she knew all kinds of small family jokes and happenings it seemed impossible that anyone *but* Louisa could know, and yet she was an imposter. And the girl's mother—my wife—has suffered more each time her hopes have been raised." He put his arm around my mother—his wife—and with Carol they stood all together looking at me.

"Look," Paul said wildly, "give her a *chance*—she *knows* she's Louisa. At least give her a chance to *prove* it."

"How?" Carol asked. "I'm sure if I asked her something like—well—like what was the color of the dress she was supposed to wear at my wedding—"

"It was pink," I said. "I wanted blue but you said it had to be pink."

"I'm sure she'd know the answer," Carol went on as though I hadn't said anything. "The other girls you brought here, Paul—*they* both knew."

It wasn't going to be any good. I ought to have known it. Maybe they were so used to looking for me by now that they would rather keep on looking than have me home; maybe once my mother had looked in my face and seen there nothing of Louisa, but only the long careful concentration I had put into being Lois Taylor, there was never any chance of my looking like Louisa again.

I felt kind of sorry for Paul; he had never understood them as well as I did and he clearly felt there was still some chance of talking them into opening their arms and crying out "Louisa! Our long-lost daughter!" and then turning around and handing him the reward; after that, we could all live happily ever after. While Paul was still trying to argue with my father I walked over a little way and looked into the living room again; I figured I wasn't going to have much time to look around and I wanted one last glimpse to take away with me; sister Carol kept a good eye on me all the time, too. I wondered what the two girls before me had tried to steal, and I wanted to tell her that if *I* ever planned to steal anything from that house *I* was three years too late; I could have taken whatever I wanted when I left the first time. There was nothing there I could take now, any more than there had been before. I realized that all I wanted was to stay— I wanted to stay so much that I felt like hanging onto the stair rail and screaming, but even though a temper tantrum might bring them some fleeting recollection of their dear lost Louisa I hardly thought it would persuade them to invite me to stay. I could just picture myself being dragged kicking and screaming out of my own house.

"Such a lovely old house," I said politely to my sister Carol, who was hovering around me.

"Our family has lived here for generations," she said, just as politely.

"Such beautiful furniture," I said.

"My mother is fond of antiques."

"Fingerprints," Paul was shouting. We were going to get a lawyer, I gathered, or at least Paul thought we were going to get a lawyer and I wondered how he was going to feel when he found out that we weren't. I couldn't imagine any lawyer in the world who could get my mother and my father and my sister Carol to take me back when they had made up their minds that I was not Louisa; could the law make my mother look into my face and recognize me?

I thought that there ought to be some way I could make Paul

see that there was nothing we could do, and I came over and stood next to him. "Paul," I said, "can't you see that you're only making Mr. Tether angry?"

"Correct, young woman," my father said, and nodded at me to show that he thought I was being a sensible creature. "He's not doing himself any good by threatening me."

"Paul," I said, "these people don't want us here."

Paul started to say something and then for the first time in his life thought better of it and stamped off toward the door. When I turned to follow him—thinking that we'd never gotten past the front hall in my great homecoming—my father—excuse me, Mr. Tether—came up behind me and took my hand. "My daughter was younger than you are," he said to me very kindly, "but I'm sure you have a family somewhere who love you and want you to be happy. Go back to them, young lady. Let me advise you as though I were really your father—stay away from that fellow, he's wicked and he's worthless. Go back home where you belong."

"We know what it's like for a family to worry and wonder about a daughter," my mother said. "Go back to the people who love you."

That meant Mrs. Peacock, I guess.

"Just to make sure you get there," my father said, "let us help toward your fare." I tried to take my hand away, but he put a folded bill into it and I had to take it. "I hope someday," he said, "that someone will do as much for our Louisa."

"Good-by, my dear," my mother said, and she reached up and patted my cheek. "Very good luck to you."

"I hope your daughter comes back someday," I told them. "Good-by."

The bill was a twenty, and I gave it to Paul. It seemed little enough for all the trouble he had taken and, after all, I could go back to my job in the stationery store. My mother still talks to me on the radio, once a year, on the anniversary of the day I ran away.

"Louisa," she says, "please come home. We all want our dear girl back, and we need you and miss you so much. Your mother and father love you and will never forget you. Louisa, please come home."

BARBARA CALLAHAN

1935–2009

BARBARA CALLAHAN was born in Philadelphia and spent much of her life in the area, eventually settling down in Cherry Hill, New Jersey, with her husband and five children. She graduated from Chestnut Hill College, a coeducational Roman Catholic institution, in 1956 and taught English and French at the middle school and high school level for three years before turning her attention to raising her family as well as founding the Women's Cursillo of South Jersey, which organized spiritual retreats, later volunteering with the Kairos Prison Ministry. Between 1981 and her retirement in 1995, Callahan worked as a writer and editor for Datapro Research Corporation, a company devoted to the creation of computer manuals.

Callahan began to write in the early 1960s, when her children were young, and eventually published more than twenty short stories, many of them suspense-oriented, the last appearing shortly before her death in 2009. *Ellery Queen's Mystery Magazine* published her first mystery story, "The Sin Painter," in 1974, about a group of people enthralled by an artist with sinister motives, and followed up two years later, in its September 1976 issue, with "Lavender Lady," nominated for an Edgar Award for Best Short Story and republished here. The story centers around Miranda, a singer of growing fame who's constantly asked by her devoted fans to sing the title song, though she's grown sick of doing so and has disassociated herself from the song's true meaning.

As Miranda narrates, she finds her way back to the terrible childhood circumstances that informed the creation of the song even as she wants nothing more than to block out those memories and to cast them off as untruths. But with each quoted lyric, the reader learns how closely aligned art and truth really are, and how terrible the repercussions of that creative convergence can truly be.

LAVENDER LADY

IT WAS always the same request wherever I played. College audiences, park audiences, concert-hall audiences—they listened and waited. Would I play it in the beginning of a set? Would I wait till the end of a performance? When would I play *Lavender Lady?*

Once I tried to trick them into forgetting that song. I sang four new songs, good songs with intricate chords and compelling lyrics. They listened politely as if each work were merely the flip side of the song they really wanted to hear.

That night I left the stage without playing it. I went straight to my dressing room and put my guitar in the closet. I heard them chanting "*Lavender Lady, Lavender Lady.*" The chant began as a joyful summons which I hoped would drift into silence like a nursery rhyme a child tires of repeating. It didn't. The chant became an ugly command accompanied by stamping feet. I fled to safety.

Milo, my manager, found me in the closet with my guitar. His dark eyes, reproving and cold, told me I would be without him if I did not go back onstage. I couldn't bear the thought of facing the night alone.

I stood in the wings and listened to him lie. "Miranda will be right back. She broke a string. She loves to sing *Lavender Lady* as much as you love to hear it."

The chanters applauded wildly. Milo slipped offstage and grabbed my arm.

"They'll forgive you this time," he snapped. "Now go out there."

"And you, Milo, you'll forgive me?"

"Yes, yes, but only this time."

Now I must play *Lavender Lady* at the end of every concert. I used to cry when I sang it but now I am drained so by it that Milo has to come onstage and carry me off. I slump over my guitar in a faint. I've been told that audiences love my finale.

I don't know exactly what happens to me when I play that song, I can remember only the introduction to it. After that the song takes over and tells me what to do.

It tells me to stare at a blankness over the heads of the audiences. In a review of my concert in Philadelphia a critic wrote: "Miranda Smith focuses on a fragment of space that becomes quite real to her. Perhaps lavender-colored ectoplasm materializes somewhere below the first balcony. The golden-haired folksinger becomes a medium for the expression of love offered and then terror unleashed. She begins *Lavender Lady* with a radiant smile and ends it with a sadness so overwhelming that it annihilates her. The last note of the song is like the final beat of her heart. Her arms slide limply over her guitar, her golden hair tumbles over the cold surface of the instrument. She becomes still, terribly still. Then the dark-haired prince, her manager, Milo McGee, comes to carry his Sleeping Beauty away.

"Once more the *Lavender Lady* has triumphed by pushing the

frail musician into a trance from which, according to McGee, she awakens the following morning. Who is this Lavender Lady and why does she exert such power over the millionairess-singer? McGee has hinted that she is Miranda's mother, the lovely socialite who abandoned the child when she was eight years old."

Milo is such a liar. He knows she isn't Mother, yet he told a magazine writer that the last time I saw Mother she was wearing a lavender gown. She was wearing a brown fur coat.

The women hired by my father to care for me were old and irritable. I was horrible to all of them. When Father interviewed the young woman with the long blonde hair, I knew I would like her. As soon as we were introduced, she hugged me. The lavender scent she wore tickled my nose and made me sneeze. She told me she wouldn't use it any more, but I wanted her to. The lavender was a lovely clue to her presence. I could always find her.

> Lavender Lady, so young and so dear,
> Lavender Lady, I know when you're near.

She taught me my lessons at home. We worked hard. Afterward we went down to the pond or to the grape arbor. We played wonderful games until I became tired. Then she put me on her lap and sang to me. At dusk I took her hand. We ran all the way home because we were two princesses being pursued by the Fiend of the Fields who wanted to change us into mushrooms.

Sometimes we tired of the arbor and the pond. We went outside the estate, across the road, and down to the rock pile. The rock pile was the moon and we climbed all over it. It was fun being a Moon Maiden until we met the Moon Monster.

The Lavender Lady never called him the Moon Monster.

She called him Jim. She told me Jim was our secret friend whom we had met in a secret place. I was never to tell anyone about Jim who sat with his arm around her while I scrambled on the rocks. I never told anyone our secret.

Lavender Lady, the secrets we shared,
Lavender Lady, I never was scared.

Milo keeps secrets well, I think. His lies please him more than the truth. He knows about the Lavender Lady and the Moon Monster. He's the only one I ever talk to about them. He knows how I begged her to send Jim away. He spoiled our games so finally she did.

I told Milo about our journey too. The Lavender Lady asked my father if she could take me to visit her mother. Father wanted the chauffeur to drive us, but the Lavender Lady refused. Her mother would be embarrassed, she told Father, if such a magnificent car pulled up in front of her shabby house.

The Lavender Lady and I took a bus. It was the first time I had ever been on one. "You poor little rich girl," the Lavender Lady said as she helped me onto the bus. After a while I didn't care much for the gaseous odor. I put my head on her shoulder and breathed in her lovely lavender scent until I fell asleep.

She shook me gently at our stop. I looked up and down the street but I didn't see a shabby house. We walked around the block and waited for another bus. As we sat on the bench the Lavender Lady reached into her large handbag. "Surprise," she said, "we're going to surprise my mother. She thinks you are a little blonde-haired girl. We'll fool her. I'll put this on you."

I laughed and laughed when I looked into the mirror of her

compact. I had become a red-headed little girl with pigtails. And I laughed again when she put the red bandanna with black bangs on it over her head.

Lavender Lady, so pretty and wise,
Lavender Lady, you loved to surprise.

Milo is cruel sometimes. I wish I had never told him about the wig. When I wanted to avoid recognition on a flight to Los Angeles, he put a red wig with pigtails on me. After I threw it on the floor, Milo refused to fend off passengers who came to me for my autograph.

I took off the red wig when we left the bus. The walk was long and hot. The Lavender Lady wanted to run but I told her that the Fiend of the Fields didn't live around there.

Her mother's house was so ugly. The paint was peeling off and the porch was falling apart. We walked up two rickety steps when the door was opened by the Moon Monster.

"Where is her mother?" I asked him.

"She went away," Jim said.

"Like my mother did?" I asked.

"I guess so," he answered.

I hugged the Lavender Lady tightly. Poor beautiful thing. I knew exactly how sad she must have felt.

Lavender Lady, such sadness you've known,
Lavender Lady, you won't be alone.

Jim pulled me away from her and kissed her. I didn't like that so I kicked him. He raised his arm to hit me but the Lavender Lady blocked him. She took me into the kitchen and heated some soup. It was chicken noodle but it tasted odd. I fell asleep at the table.

When I woke up I was lying on a dirty cot in a bedroom. Jim was sitting on a chair next to me.

"Where did she go?" I cried.

"To make a phone call. Now go back to sleep."

I tried to get up but Jim pushed me down. The room was so smelly. When she returned she would wrap me in her lavender scent and everything would be all right again. When I heard her footsteps downstairs I ran to the door. Jim picked me up and dumped me on that terrible cot, then locked the bedroom door when he left. I pounded and pounded but she must not have heard.

The next morning she brought me oatmeal. Then she washed my tear-stained face. When she rocked me back and forth in her arms I began to feel better. "Take me away from here," I begged.

"He won't let me do that," she said. "We'll just have to do what he says until we get our chance to escape. This is like one of our games by the pond. We're two princesses but we'll get away."

The Lavender Lady took me outside the awful house. We walked to a field where Stars of Bethlehem curtsied in the wind. She sat down and I made a garland for her hair. After I tired of picking flowers I wondered why we didn't walk through the fields into the woods, away from the ugly house and away from him.

"Now," I told her, "let's go now. He'll never know."

She shook her head. "He's upstairs in the house. He is looking at us through binoculars. He'll overtake us."

"But his car is gone. He drove away."

"No, little rich girl, that's a trick. He drove it around the back of the house. He's still there."

When he came walking through the field, smashing the flowers under his feet, she smiled at him. She could pretend so well. She jumped up and hugged him. Together they opened a suitcase filled with money. She tossed some of it into the air.

"Green snow," she sang, "green snow, the loveliest snow."

Her garland fell off as she danced around with Jim. I picked it up and pulled it apart.

> *In fields full of flowers, we spent happy hours,*
> *Beneath trees dark and shady, dear Lavender Lady.*

Milo is talking now to someone outside my bedroom door. He's saying, "She didn't care a hoot for her, you know, but the crazy kid thought she did."

"Miranda's naive," a voice answers.

It's my secretary. Milo is talking to her about me. He must be telling her about my mother. Milo is lying again. I always knew mother never cared a hoot for me.

When I was back on that filthy cot I could hear the Moon Monster and the Lavender Lady talking, just as I can hear Milo and my secretary now. The Moon Monster was saying something about getting rid of me because I would recognize him later. I became frightened until I heard her say that she would take care of me. Everything would be all right. She would take care of me.

The next morning he sat sullenly at the table while she made breakfast for us.

"Why feed her? Hurry up, will you?"

She flashed him a stern look that silenced him. She winked at me. I winked back. I knew we would be leaving him that day.

We walked slowly to the field of Stars of Bethlehem. When

we were down the hill I grabbed her hand. I touched something in it that was cold and hard. It fell to the ground into the flowers. The sunlight hit it while it was falling and it glistened like silver.

"My watch," she cried, "I dropped my watch."

She began to push aside the flowers but I pulled at her.

"Father will get you another one, come on."

She continued clawing at the flowers. I wanted her to leave. A game would do it. She loved games. I spread my arms and fluttered them.

"I'm a butterfly, a yellow butterfly. I'm flying, I'm flying. You're the Lavender Locust and you must catch me."

I flew away. I turned back once and saw her starting to get up. I flew up and down hills. I came to a stream. It was a good place to wait for her. I took off my shoes to wade for a bit

"Butterfly, butterfly, where are you?" she called.

She was coming. I was so happy.

"You can't catch a butterfly," I shouted. It was nice that she was playing the game. When she came closer I saw that there was something shiny in her hand. She had found her watch. She stopped by a tree to catch her breath. Then she started to run toward me.

But I liked being a butterfly. I liked having her chase me. I didn't want the game to end. I giggled when I saw the stepping stones a few yards from me. I ran in the water to the first one and then to the second. I jumped across on all of them, skidding only once on the green slime that covered them. I sat down across the stream to wait for her.

Her golden hair flying, she skipped from the first to the second stone. And to the third. But on the fourth stone her foot slipped on the green slime. I screamed as she fell backward and hit the side of her face on the third stepping stone. When her head rolled over I saw the reddish-purple bruise on her fair skin. She tried to get up but she fell back again, back on that hard terrible rock. The stream water next to her turned red.

> Lavender Lady, clear water runs red,
> Lavender Lady, you cannot be dead.

I cannot sleep tonight as I usually do after a concert. My eyelids have become reddish-purple curtains. They are the same color as the bruise on the Lavender Lady's face. They are the same color as that ghastly shirt Milo is wearing tonight. I've asked him not to wear it, but he told me my secretary likes it.

They're still talking outside my door. Milo is not talking about my mother. He is talking about the Lavender Lady and he is telling my secretary a vicious lie about her. I can bear his other lies, but not this one. He is saying that the silver thing I saw in the Lavender Lady's hand was not a watch, but a knife. He's saying, "She had a silver pocketknife with her to kill a kid who was born with a silver spoon in her mouth."

I'll have to prove to Milo it was a watch. I'll take him to that stream. Perhaps the watch is still there, rusted and buried under the stepping stone. When I take him, I'll ask him to wear the reddish-purple shirt. It will go well with his face if he happens to slip.

Reddish-purple, reddish-purple. What was the word printed on that colored pencil I had when I was a child? Magenta, yes, that's it, magenta.

Such a lyrical word. It should be in a song. I need a new

song, a new song that will captivate me just as *Lavender Lady* did. I'm getting a melody in my head right now. It is so sad it makes me cry. This song will be better than *Lavender Lady*. It will be a better ending for my concerts. It will thrill my audiences. It will overwhelm me.

I've got the first two lines. They go like this:

> *Magenta man, once kind and strong,*
> *Magenta man, you've done me wrong.*

VERA CASPARY

1899–1987

In her 1979 autobiography *The Secrets of Grown-Ups*, **VERA CAS-PARY** declared, "This has been the century of the woman, and I know myself to have been a part of the revolution." Caspary had good reason to make this claim: much of her work, which included eighteen novels, ten screenplays and four stage plays, focused on a woman's right to lead her own life, no matter the costs or the motives of others, especially men. As a screenwriter, Caspary commanded as much as $150,000 for adaptations like *Letter to Three Wives*. Her sixteen-year marriage to film producer Isidore "Igee" Goldsmith was a transatlantic love affair interrupted by war, disrupted by the HUAC anti-Communist hearings, and marked by financial instability.

Caspary, born and raised in Chicago, is likely best known for her 1943 novel *Laura*, about a private detective's obsession with a portrait of the titular missing woman. The film adaptation was released the following year starring Gene Tierney as Laura and Clifton Webb as her sinister nemesis Waldo Lydecker. (A stage version premiered in 1946.) The book marked a turning point for

Caspary, who previously published more mainstream fiction; from then on she devoted her fiction to suspense tales like *Bedelia* (1945), *The Murder in the Stork Club* (1946), and *The Weeping and the Laughter* (1950), a national bestseller when published in 1950. After Goldsmith's death in 1964, Caspary kept publishing, though she never quite reached the heights of her pre- and post-war heyday.

Though she didn't write many short stories, the majority of those, too, dealt with the highs and lows of women reaching for independence. "Sugar and Spice," first published in 1943 by *The American* magazine, is an inverted detective story. Though it follows the trajectory of a police procedural, as the detective in question looks into the murder of a young actress, the story is told from the perspective of his wife, and delves into the relationship between the actress and her close friend and sometimes rival. Caspary evokes the theatrical milieu as one wise and well-versed in its ways, and applies great psychological depth to the thorny relationship between friends, which may be decidedly more sinister.

SUGAR AND SPICE

I HAVE never known a murderer, a murder victim, nor anyone involved in a murder case. I admit that I am a snob, but to my mind crime is sordid and inevitably associated with gangsters, frustrated choir singers in dusty suburban towns, and starving old ladies supposed to have hidden vast fortunes in the bedsprings. I once remarked to a friend that people of our sort were not in the homicide set, and three weeks later heard that her brother-in-law had been arrested as a suspect in the shooting of his rich uncle. It was proved, however, that this was a hunting accident and the brother-in-law exonerated. But it gave me quite a jolt.

Jolt number two came when Mike Jordan, sitting on my patio on a Sunday afternoon, told me a story which proved that well-bred, middle-class girls can commit murder as calmly as I knit a sock, and with fewer lumps in the finished product. Mike had arrived that morning for an eleven o'clock breakfast, and after the briefest greeting had sat silent until the bells of San Miguel started tolling twelve.

This was unusual. Mike was not the taciturn type. But he

was independent almost to a point of arrogance and disliked asking favors. This I learned was the cause of the brooding silence. There is no greater favor you can ask a California hostess than the use of her telephone for a New York call.

I sat without speaking until the bells were still. Mike pulled out a roll of bills that reminded me of the old movie gangsters.

"Let me pay you now, Lissa. I don't want to make this call from the Officers Club. It may take two or three hours to get through, and there are always too many fellows waiting to use the phones. Believe me, this is a case of life and death."

When he put the call through I disappeared. A few minutes later Mike found me on the patio with the watering can in my discreet hands. It was a brilliant day, the wind high, the air sweet with the scent of sage and mimosa. Bees floated above the geraniums, and the cactus was coated with a film of silver dust. Loathing sunshine, Mike pulled a canopied chair into the shade of the pepper tree. He had the light skin that burns easily and a thick crop of flaming hair.

"Would you like to know who killed Gilbert Jones?"

My watering can clattered on the flagged floor of the patio. According to the latest reports, Gilbert Jones's death was still baffling the New York police. It was one of those conspicuous murders that take up front-page space usually reserved for the biggest war news. Gilbert Jones had been a leading New York actor who had also played in a few pictures, and there were two women involved in the case, one beautiful, the other a millionaire. They were cousins, and had both been in love with Gilbert Jones.

"How do *you* know who killed him?"

We were alone that Sunday afternoon. My husband was on duty at the Post and an eighth of a mile separated us from the nearest neighbor. Although there was no one closer than the passengers in the pygmy cars on the highway below our hill, Mike spoke softly. This story was close to his heart. . . .

Mike Jordan's mother was the sort of woman who, when she learned she was to have a child, looked at beautiful pictures and listened to great music. As a result, Mike grew up to make family gatherings more than usually hideous by his renditions of *The Melody in F* and Rachmaninoff's *Prelude*. His first music teacher had been a German, the local professor; when he died Mike took lessons from Mrs. Coles, a faded blonde with brown eyes, crimped hair, and a pair of pearl-button earrings which Mike was certain she wore when she bathed and slept.

Everybody in town felt sorry for Mrs. Coles because her husband had deserted her, and admired her because she supported herself when she might easily have depended upon rich relations. To Mike her independence seemed a bit rueful. At every lesson the piano students were made aware that she had been bred for better things than the career of music teacher. She had a lovely daughter to whom her gallant laments must have been as much part of the daily routine as the students' finger exercises.

One day—Mike was about sixteen at the time—Mrs. Coles interrupted a Chopin *Nocturne* by announcing, "Phyllis is so fond of you, Michael. She looks up to you with the greatest respect."

Mike's fingers crashed down upon the keyboard as though he were working on Liszt's *Second Hungarian Rhapsody*. He had always admired the piano teacher's daughter. She was very fair, with great, glowing dark eyes.

"She has something to ask you," Mrs. Coles continued. "But she's shy and has asked me to approach you first. I reminded her of the *Courtship of Miles Standish* and said, 'Why don't you speak for yourself, Phyllis?' but she said the tables were turned because John Alden was a man. A clever child, don't you think? So I wonder, Michael"—Mrs. Coles hesitated, adjusting a pearl earring—"if you'd like to escort Phyllis to Nancy Miller's party. It's to be at the club, a bit ostentatious, in my opinion, for such young people, but Nancy's mother, although she is my own sister, likes show. Perhaps you will enjoy it."

The invitation flattered and puzzled him. Nancy Miller was almost a legend in the town, a girl who went to fashionable boarding schools and spent her summers in Europe or at seashore resorts. There was hardly a profitable industry in the town that did not belong in some fashion to her father. They had a big place—an estate, the town called it—a couple of miles out on the river.

Mike's mother suggested that he might have been invited because he had won an interstate essay contest and had his picture in a Chicago newspaper. Mike laughed scornfully. Phyllis Coles might have had as her escort the senior class president or the captain of the football team. The prize essay had provided him with a sporty new outfit, white ducks and a blue Norfolk jacket. He was reading Schnitzler at the time, fancied himself a man of the world, and wondered if he dared appear with a carnation in his buttonhole.

On the day of the party he got as far as the door of Nick

Scarpas's flower store on Main Street, but there his courage failed. He arrived at the Coles house just as if he had come for a music lesson and, as the door was always open, walked in. Through yellow silk portieres he heard shrillness and sobbing. What, he asked himself, would a man of the world do in the circumstances? He trifled with the idea of sneaking away, returning, and announcing himself with a dignified knock. Then an inspiration visited him. He struck a pose beside the piano and began playing with one hand carelessly. No man of the world could have done it better.

The yellow drapes parted, Mrs. Coles skipped into the room, adjusted an earring. "How prompt, Michael! Phyllis isn't quite ready. Will you wait?"

Presently Phyllis came out. Her nostrils and the edges of her eyes, Mike noticed, were faintly pink. As they walked to the club she seemed more remote than ever. The month was June, the twilight fragrant. In every yard roses and iris bloomed, and bushes were garlanded with bridal wreath. Phyllis seemed as frail as a flower in a cloudy blue dress embroidered all over with small pink nosegays.

They walked timidly up the path that led to the club's great door and entered slowly. As they crossed the lobby a swarthy crone seized Phyllis and shouted, "Isn't she lovely?" Mike saw a witch's face rouged to the eyes, which were as black and hard as the jet pendants that dangled from her ears. "Pity," she muttered, "pity the party isn't given for her."

Another woman, ruffled and jeweled, peered at Phyllis through a rimless pince-nez. "Sweet child, I'm so glad you've come. How well you look in that dress."

Phyllis turned away. Her enchanting pallor was lost in a

rose-pink blush. Mike rubbed his left shoe against his right leg, embarrassed because Phyllis had neglected to present him to the ladies, who he knew must be old Mrs. Hulbert and her daughter, Mrs. Ulysses S. Miller.

It was a grand party. Sophisticated, the local paper called it. The ballroom was decorated in silver and black velvet, its tall columns twined with silver-leaved garlands, the bandstand draped with velvet and dripping with tinsel. Mike was about to express awe when he became aware of scorn in the tilt of Phyllis's nose and the slight smile curving her lips.

"Come along, Mike; Nancy will want to meet you."

He had last seen Nancy Miller when she was a fat little girl riding in a wicker basket behind a fat pony. Now that she was fifteen years old, he had imagined that she would have come to look like an heiress. If she had been merely homely, he would have been less disappointed than in this commonplace girl, still fat, and as lumpy as back-yard soil.

"Is this the *famous* Mike Jordan?" She had one of those insincere, heavily inflected, finishing-school voices, hideously unbecoming to a fleshy girl with big bones. Her enthusiasm, her synthetic charm, her schooled graces contrasted painfully with her cousin's pretty reticence. "I've heard *so much* about *you*."

"I guess you mean a couple of other fellows," he replied wittily. "I'm just the Mike Jordan nobody knows."

She smiled coyly. "A famous man shouldn't be so modest."

As Mike danced with Phyllis he noticed that Nancy's dark eyes were following them. Phyllis noticed, too, and smiled. Later, of course, Mike had to dance with his hostess. She was too heavy for him, too self-assertive, the sort of girl who had to control her instinct to lead.

"I read your essay," she said. "I think it was wonderful. It reminded me of Thomas Paine or Patrick Henry."

He accepted the tribute grudgingly.

"I was curious to meet the man who wrote such inspired words," Nancy added. And Mike actually felt himself blush as she went on, "That's why I asked Phyllis to bring you tonight. And"—she looked into his face brazenly—"I'm not disappointed in the writer, either."

When the music stopped he tried to break away, but Nancy clung to him, accompanying him in his search for Phyllis.

They found her on the porch, surrounded by boys. "Isn't my cousin the most popular thing?" Nancy squealed. "Men are always wild about her." She broke through the circle of Phyllis's admirers, encircled her cousin's waist with a strong, swarthy arm. "You're absolutely bewitching in that dress."

Phyllis froze. Muttering a sullen thanks, she went off to dance with Johnnie Elder. Nancy giggled, and later, at supper, attempted again to flatter her cousin: "Isn't Phyllis just too sweet in blue? That dress looks as if it were designed for her."

A couple of Nancy's girl-friends giggled. The significance of the scene was lost upon Mike then, and it was not until years later, when Nancy, herself, explained its peculiar agony, that he understood that certain traits of character are called feminine because they are implanted early in girl-children.

"Well, Mike, how did you like the party?" Phyllis asked, as they walked home in the moonlight.

He dared not show how thin was his lacquer of sophistication, so he answered dryly, "It was all right."

"It was ghastly. All that silver and velvet; just showy ostentation."

Johnnie Elder honked past them, waving from his brother's roadster.

Phyllis watched the vanishing taillights. Abruptly gripping Mike's arm, she whispered, "She hates me, Mike, she hates me desperately; she wishes I was dead."

"Who?"

"Don't be stupid. Didn't you notice anything? She's hated me ever since we were little kids, because they could buy her everything except looks. Her hair's as straight as an Indian's. And Grandma always felt sorry for me because my mother was poor and had to support us, so she always made a fuss over me instead. Once my grandmother gave me a big doll"—Phyllis's hands measured the height of this wondrous memory—"it was bigger than any doll Nancy got that Christmas. And it was only that I was poor and didn't have so many toys that Grandma gave me this big doll. Nancy was so jealous that she grabbed the doll out of my arms and deliberately smashed it. There's still a chip in the fireplace where she broke it. The head was in pieces. She hates me."

She stood quite still. Moonlight, shining through the catalpa tree, fell upon her so that half of her face, lighted in silver, was clear-cut and exquisite, while the other half was scarred by a shadow as jagged and irregular as a birthmark. Mike took her arm and jerked her out of the shadows.

As they walked through the shabbier streets to her mother's house, Phyllis told him of her ambitions: "I'm going to be an actress. I mean to be very successful and rich, and then I'll laugh at everyone."

The gate creaked as they walked up the untidy path. Phyllis looked at the moon and laughed. . . .

The next season she joined the Dramatic Club. Mike Jordan thought her the best actress in the high school, and when, in his senior year, he became a member of the club's executive board, he promoted Phyllis at every opportunity, just as though he were a silly old manager in love with a pretty actress.

Every year the club gave a show. Mike was then trying to write like O'Neill, and he wanted them to do *The Straw*, with Phyllis as the tubercular heroine. But Nancy had come to the high school that year. Her mother was ill and she was spending the winter in town. She had the whole school imitating her, fawning upon her, copying her attitudes. No elderly opportunist is ever so slavish as a youngster who finds that he can skate on a private pond, play tennis on fine courts, and be treated to quantities of pop and ice cream.

Nancy's word was law, her whims undisputed fashion, and when she said *Romance* was her favorite play, more than half the club board was willing to vote her ticket. Mike was too much the politician to tell them he thought it a bad play, so he argued that they could never afford the elaborate costumes and sets. He was voted down.

At the next board meeting he heard the proposal that they give Nancy the part so that her father would pay for their props and scenery.

Phyllis was her mother's gallant child. She uttered not a word of self-pity. Mike took her to the show, and as he sat beside her, studying her fine profile, he admired the dignity with which she hid her disappointment. After the final curtain she asked him to go backstage with her. Nancy's dressing-room was filled with extravagant floral offerings, tributes from her father's business associates.

Phyllis broke through the crowd of chattering girl-friends, kissed Nancy's rouged cheek, and cried sincerely, "You were wonderful, darling, simply wonderful."

That swarthy old lady whom Mike had seen at the party rose from a small chair beside Nancy's dressing table. She was dressed in rich, musty black silk. "You could have done it better," she told Phyllis.

"But Nancy has real talent and temperament, Grandma."

"You have beauty."

This was in May. At the end of June, Mike finished high school. He spent the summer as a counselor in a boys' camp, and in September went to New Haven. Mike's father was the editor of a small newspaper, and it was enough of a struggle to send his son to Yale without providing money for holiday trips.

During the next two summers Mike worked in Connecticut, but he never lost touch with the home town. His father sent him the newspaper, and he was still sufficiently interested in his old friends to read the society columns. Nancy Miller, daughter of Mr. and Mrs. Ulysses S. Miller, "came out" and was thereafter entitled to silver tinsel and black velvet decorations at her parties. Shortly afterward, Mr. and Mrs. Ulysses S. Miller announced the engagement of their daughter to John Price Elder II.

The Roman numerals amused Mike. Johnnie Elder's father had come to the town as a laborer, had worked himself up to foreman and then to plant manager in one of the mills. During a strike he had done the dirty work for the owners, dealing with scabs and gunmen brought to town to break the strike. Mike's father had nicknamed him "Judas Elder" and made him the butt of scathing editorials which were never noticed by the people who elected J. P. Elder to the City Council. The son Johnnie was a big, thick-skinned fellow, ruddy and good-looking, fullback on his college football team, and a god to the town girls.

To Mike he seemed a natural mate for Nancy.

Mrs. Coles died that same October. She had lived only a few hours after an emergency operation. Phyllis was nineteen years old and quite alone in the world. Her aunt persuaded her to sell her mother's furniture and come to live at their house until she decided what she wanted to do with her life.

Mike sold a story to a small magazine that year, and he had enough money to travel home for Christmas. On his first afternoon in the town, he borrowed his father's old car and drove it through the massive gates of the Miller place. A Negro butler opened the door and led him to the library, where Phyllis greeted him.

The room was staid, and Phyllis's black dress and pale hair, worn in a knot, seemed part of the dignified atmosphere.

Phyllis gave Mike her cold hand. They talked for a while about his work and his ambitions, and then he asked about her plans.

"I'm taking a secretarial course."

"What! You said in your letter that you wanted to come to New York and study dramatic art. I've looked up some schools for you."

She dismissed the notion with a weary gesture. "Uncle Ulie's had enough of my mother's family."

"He's got plenty of money."

"I can't take any more." Her hands were like carved ivory

hands clasping the oaken apples carved into the arm of the chair.

The telephone rang. Phyllis answered it, and when she had learned who was calling, her voice betrayed her. What she said, however, was quite casual: "She's not here. . . . I think she went to have some fittings, lingerie and things. . . . I don't know when she'll be back. . . . Oh, do! . . . Yes, Yes!"

She hung up the receiver and, without a word of excuse, hurried out of the room.

When she returned, Mike saw that she had rouged her lips and combed her hair. The smell of burning coal and the flat odor of steam were drowned by her perfume. She kneeled on the cushioned window seat that overlooked the drive. Wheels sounded on the gravel. A car door slammed; the bell rang; the butler walked slowly down the hall. Phyllis's cheeks had become rosy and her eyes were dancing.

Johnnie Elder came in. "Hello —" He tossed the greeting at Phyllis smoothly. His big fist crushed Mike's hand. The enthusiasm of his greeting was all out of proportion to his regard for Mike. While they talked of colleges and football teams, Johnnie's eyes were fixed on Phyllis. Mike felt like a man who has wandered by mistake into a peep show. He muttered something about having to leave. Just as Johnnie was crushing his hand for a second time, the door opened, and there was Nancy.

"Sorry to be late, dear. I didn't know you were coming over." She offered Johnnie her cheek.

"It's good to see you again, Mike." Nancy's face was flushed and wet with snow, and snowflakes glistened in her dark hair. She had grown slimmer, but she was still a big girl. "You can't leave now, Mike. Stay and have a drink with us."

The butler wheeled in a cart filled with glasses and bottles. Johnnie made Martinis, and Mike proposed a toast to the engaged couple. Phyllis merely touched her lips to the glass.

"Will you do me a favor, Mike?" Nancy asked.

"Anything I can."

"You've always had a lot of influence with Phyllis. Make her come to my New Year's Eve party."

"But I don't think I'd want to," Phyllis said. "After all, it's not two months since my mother . . ."

"Don't be so old-fashioned. Mourning's an obsolete custom."

"I knew your mother well, Phyllis." This was Mike's contribution to the argument, and later, when he saw the results, he was sorry he hadn't kept his opinion to himself. "There was nothing she liked better than your having a good time. She wouldn't want you to sit and mope on New Year's Eve."

"Do you really think so?" Phyllis brightened.

Because Mike felt sorry for her he embroidered on the idea.

Presently Phyllis said, "If you really think Mother would want me to, Mike . . ."

"Attaboy, Mike!" Nancy clapped him on the shoulder. To Phyllis she said, "I'll call Fred tonight."

Phyllis frowned. "So that's why you were so anxious?"

"Who's Fred?" Mike asked.

"Nancy's cousin on the other side, Fred Miller. Maybe you don't remember him, Mike; he was out of school before we got in. He went with an older crowd."

"They're in insurance," Johnnie said.

"I wouldn't have used my influence quite so freely if I'd known I was fixing it up for another fellow," Mike said.

"Don't worry, Mike. You're invited to my party, too, and we'll all dance with you," Nancy promised.

Johnnie, Nancy, and Mike drank another round of cocktails. Phyllis sat on the window seat, self-contained and aloof from their banter and their plans. Johnnie and Nancy chattered about the wedding, the ushers, the honeymoon, the bicycling in Bermuda, and tackle for deep-sea fishing. They seemed less like lovers than a pair of kids planning a holiday. Later Mike's father told him that the elder Elder had lost almost everything during the depression, and that a union with the Ulysses Miller interests would probably save him from bankruptcy. . . .

Nancy's party was, as usual, lavish. She wore a dress of some stiff gold material which made her look rather like a statue of Civic Virtue. Phyllis had left off her mourning, but showed, by fastening those same pearl buttons in her ears, that her mother had not been forgotten.

Whenever he looked at her, Fred Miller panted. He was the most unprepossessing man Mike had ever seen in tails and white tie. Sandy hair parted in the center tended to elongate his narrow head. He had a heavy cold, and every five minutes, or so it seemed to Mike Jordan, he drew out a miraculously clean handkerchief (he must have had dozens of them in his pockets) and blew a trumpeting note. "Sorry," he'd say each time.

Johnnie Elder tried to make Phyllis drink champagne.

"You know I never drink."

"You will tonight."

"What makes you think so?"

"Don't be a fool." Nancy's voice was rough. Their persiflage, commonplace as it was, annoyed her. "After all this is New Year's

Eve and you've been feeling sort of low lately. Champagne's just what you need. Tell her, Mike; you've got a lot of influence."

"If she doesn't want to drink, you can't make her." This was Johnnie Elder, suddenly belligerent.

Nancy sniffed. "Who was just trying to make her drink, Mr. Elder?"

"I can manage my women without your help," Johnnie snapped.

Evidently he had been celebrating with a few early cocktails, otherwise he could not have been so careless. The lids dropped over Nancy's dark eyes and her mouth was a narrow line.

Phyllis asked for a taste of the champagne. "If my refusing to drink makes people quarrel, I'd better have one."

Johnnie watched her from under his long lashes.

She sipped it, cried, "Why, it's not bad at all," and drained her glass.

"Phyllis can take it," Johnnie boasted.

"She's remarkable," Nancy said coldly.

Mike took her arm. "Come on, Nancy, let's dance."

Nancy and Mike were better partners than they had been at the other party, for Nancy had learned to follow a man. But there was no life in her dancing. She tried not to stare too obviously through the arched doorway that led to the bar, but whenever they approached that end of the ballroom, her eyes were drawn to the table where Fred Miller and Johnnie were competing for Phyllis's attention.

When the dance was over, Mike said, "Let's go up to the balcony and have a cigarette."

By the time he finished the sentence Nancy was at the bar. Johnnie pulled out a chair for her, the waiter brought another bottle of champagne, and Phyllis said, "The orchestra's good, isn't it?"

"Have a drink and catch up with Phyllis," Johnnie said. "She's going to town tonight. Here's to a girl who can take her liquor."

"I'm glad Phyllis is having such a good time."

Phyllis smiled. Her decorum was like a thin curtain before a flame. When the music began again she was off like a streak of lightning with Johnnie. Nancy danced dutifully with Fred Miller.

At midnight bells rang, the dancers flung serpentines and filled the air with the multi-colored rain of confetti. They sang, drank toasts, kissed their friends. Mike felt the heat of Nancy's bruised mouth against his cheek and the sweet quivering of Phyllis's lips.

When she came to Johnnie Elder, Phyllis flung herself into his arms, buried her mouth in his lips, then cried, "Let's have a happy year. Please let it be a good one, Johnnie, please!"

Dance music started again. The party grew wilder. Only a conventional crowd can become so thoroughly abandoned.

Phyllis caught the fever. Unless he had seen her that night Mike would never have believed that a girl so decorous as she could so completely abandon herself to a mood and a man. She and Johnnie danced like a pair of Siamese twins, joined for life.

Evidently the electrician had taken one too many, for in the middle of a fox trot the lights went out. Nobody cared. Lights from the bar and balconies fell in stripes across sections of the writhing crowd. The music was hot, slow, and sensual, with a rolling savage beat. Mike had gone up to the balcony for a cigarette. There he found Nancy bent over the rail, squinting down into the darkness.

A roll of drums announced supper. Nancy ran down the stairs, holding her golden skirt high above her ankles. The brilliant lights of the dining-room, after the dusk of the ball-room, was like a cold shock. At flower-decked tables men and women in paper caps blew horns and whirled steel-tongued clappers. A man blew a whistle in Nancy's ear and another tickled her with a feather-tipped wand.

She neither heard nor saw these antic attempts to capture her attention. Friends invited her to eat at their tables. She was as deaf to kindness as to jests.

"Drunk," someone said, "drunk as a lady."

She was unhappily sober.

To Mike Jordan the party had become unendurable. He knew then that he hated the town and its smug best people. Since Fred Miller was there to look out for Nancy, he left. As he walked down the ash-strewn icy path, he saw the glint of a gold gown among the automobiles. There was Nancy, her shoulders bare, peeking into parked cars.

He hurried after her, begged her to go in, warned her of the danger of catching cold. He even offered her his coat, thinking, as he peeled it off, of Sir Walter Raleigh and Queen Elizabeth. All he got for his gallantry was a sullen glance.

The next day he felt it was his duty to telephone Nick Scarpas, and order flowers to be sent with a note of thanks to Miss Miller. At ten o'clock that night his father and mother took Mike to the railroad station. He was not displeased at leaving the town and did not think he would soon return.

The train whistled and rushed through darkness. The sleeping car was quiet, berths made up, passengers hidden behind swaying green curtains. The porter, groaning aloud, carried heavy bags toward the drawing-room at the end of the car. As Mike came from the men's room, drawing his flannel robe tight about him and clutching at his leather toilet case, he saw the conductor and the Pullman man tap at the drawing-room door. It opened, and for a moment, in the greenish sleeping-car light, he caught a glimpse of Nancy Miller's sullen face and her dark, fierce eyes. . . .

The telephone rang with that insistent clamor which announces a long-distance call. Mike went to answer it, and I sat on the retaining wall, watching a parade of army trucks on the highway. In a few minutes Mike came out again. The operator had reported an hour's delay in his New York call.

"Your story doesn't sound like a mystery," I said. "It sounds like something that might have happened in my own crowd at college. I can't believe that people of their sort, girls like Phyllis and Nancy, could commit murder."

"I daresay any crime story, if you told it biographically, would sound normal. Except in cases of insanity and early criminal tendencies."

"Did Phyllis marry Johnnie Elder?"

Mike Jordan settled himself in the canopied chair, polished his dark glasses, and went on in his own deliberate way with the story. . . .

It was impossible for Phyllis to go on living with her aunt and uncle. Even her grandmother's efforts could not win back their affection. The poor girl sat patiently on the window seat, waiting for Johnnie Elder's car to roll through the iron gates. But Johnnie was in no position to marry a penniless girl.

For Phyllis there was only one refuge. She had not been trained to earn a living. In spite of her own sorry experience, Cinderella's mother had gone to her death believing that marriage is a girl's only way of security. For a girl with Phyllis's beauty a good marriage seemed almost guaranteed. But Phyllis was not able to wait. She had to get out of that gloomy castle.

She and Fred Miller eloped.

Mike Jordan found the news distasteful. Fred was only eight years older than Phyllis, but he seemed of another generation and was as dull as an insurance policy. He worked in his father's office on Main Street.

Theirs was a Sunday-dinner household — grapefruit before the soup, two kinds of dessert, and everybody falling asleep afterward. They furnished Phyllis's house in solid walnut, hung drapes of satin damask at her windows, and covered her bed with filet lace.

Once a week, when Phyllis's grandmother was driven to their house by Ulysses S. Miller's chauffeur, they heard about Nancy, who had gone to live in France. Her grandmother's reports were catalogs of glamour, lush with descriptions of Paris openings, week-end parties at historic châteaux, holidays at Biarritz and Monte Carlo.

Black, jet eyes peered at Fred Miller from under a scowling forehead thick with rice powder. "That's the life Phyllis ought to be having. She's wasted in this town."

"I'm going to take her abroad some day," Fred promised. "Just as soon as we've put away a little money, we're going to take that trip."

Phyllis took no part in these conversations. While her grand-mother insulted her husband and poor Fred tried to defend himself, she was wrapped in a dream of glory wherein celebrated heads turned and noble hearts beat swiftly as Lady Phyllis, in a Paris creation which had been photographed for the fifty-cent fashion magazines, entered The Casino. . . .

Mike finished college and went to New York, where he worked as copywriter in an advertising agency until he was able to get a job at half the salary on a morning newspaper. Then he became assistant dramatic critic on the *Globe-Telegram*.

His boss had chronic indigestion and when he was laid up Mike covered the openings. On a first night while he was gossiping in the lobby during intermission, he was confronted by a stranger who called him by his first name.

"So you don't remember me, Mike?"

Mike was puzzled. He had met a great many people in New York, but he remembered names and faces, and it seemed unlikely that he should have forgotten this vivid, cadaverous girl.

"The last time you saw me I was hunting bones in a graveyard. You were gallant and offered me your coat." Even her voice had changed The finishing-school shrillness had been replaced by a pleasant huskiness.

A gong announced the rising of the curtain. The crowd pushed them back into the theater. "Come up for cocktails," she called across several heads and shoulders. "I'll leave my phone number at your office."

Her place was magnificent, two penthouses made into a single apartment with a four-way view of Manhattan. It was modern in the best sense, simple, and without excess decoration.

It was a warm evening. They sat on the terrace, Nancy perched on the ledge, her back against the iron rail. The scene had the quality of an Italian primitive, in which foreground figures are large and solid, and in the background every minute object sharply outlined. Nancy had become so thin that her bones showed. This was not unbecoming, for she was well constructed and her face cut into interesting planes. She wore blue trousers and a white blouse with the sleeves rolled up, and on her right hand an enormous star sapphire.

"How handsome you are," Mike said.

Nancy's smile was cynical. "Don't kid me."

"Who's kidding? You're a handsome wench."

She flipped her cigarette stub over the iron rail. "I don't kid myself, Mike. I've survived so far without being beautiful and I guess I can get along for the rest of my life." He was about to remonstrate, when she said, "Have you seen Phyllis lately?"

There was a sudden crash of thunder.

"She's all right," Mike said. "Happily married to your cousin."

"Grandma thinks she's wasting her life. Fred isn't half good enough for her, Grandma says. He's a stick, according to Grandma."

"I disapprove of your grandmother," Mike said.

"She's always been mad about Phyllis. When I was a little girl, a horrid, fat child with bushy eyebrows, I'd get dressed up in a starched dress and sash, and Grandma would look at me and say, 'You'll have to be good, Nancy; you'll never be beautiful.' Mamma bought me the most exquisite things, handmade, imported, designed by children's couturiers, but Grandma would never forgive me for having these things while Phyllis, who was so lovely, was poor. Even when we were tiny children she made Phyllis hate me."

"Phyllis hate you?" Mike remembered how Phyllis's face had been scarred by the catalpa tree's shadow.

"I don't blame her. It was Grandma's fault; she instigated it and kept it alive. Even today she's resentful because Phyl's beauty deserves the luxury and I, who am homely and unworthy, get it all. I do think Phyllis hates me so much that she's often wished me dead."

Nancy walked to the opposite end of the terrace and stared down at the toy boats and bridges on the East River.

Thunder rolled above their heads and a bright arrow of lightning pierced the sky.

"Don't you hate Phyllis?" Mike asked.

Nancy wheeled around. "Why should I? She's always seemed a poor pathetic little thing. If she didn't hate me so horribly, I'd be fond of her. But she's always been so resentful, I could feel her bitterness. She'd look at me with those big, soft eyes as if I were a monstrosity. Once at a party — it was my first big party and I had a beautiful silver dress, but whenever Phyllis looked at me, I felt like a big, ugly pig and my dress seemed hideous, and the evening was ruined."

"Do you remember what Phyllis wore that night?"

Nancy shook her head.

"It was blue, I think. Blue thin stuff with flowers on it."

Nancy stiffened. "Yes, of course I remember now. It was a dress of mine. Mother had given it to her."

"Phyllis cried before the party. I always wondered why."

Nancy came across the terrace slowly, looking down at her tanned feet in rope sandals. "I teased her about the dress. Most of the girls knew it had been mine. We giggled."

Drops of rain, as big as pennies, spattered the terrace. Mike and Nancy gathered up the cocktail things and went inside. Nancy threw herself upon the yellow couch.

"She paid me out with Johnnie Elder." Nancy rolled over, picked up her glass, drank, and rolled on her back again.

"Were you in love with him?"

"He was the handsomest boy in town, all the girls were mad about his eyelashes, and I felt that it didn't matter that I wasn't pretty if he loved me. When a man proposes, you think he's in love with you." Nancy shuddered. "Women often call their own feelings love, Mike, when it's just balm for sore pride. Or fear that they'll be left behind. Probably I ought to be grateful to Phyllis, because Johnnie and I'd never have gotten along. But it was hell while it lasted."

Mike lit the fire. The room was cozy. And that was the last time, for many months, that they spoke of Phyllis.

They became close friends. Mike went with the sleek Broadway and prosperous Greenwich Village crowds. These people, after her life in France, were the sort Nancy liked. She had no talent of her own, but an enormous appreciation and excellent taste. Along with the boarding-school inflection had gone her admiration for romance and rococo. She was a realist, a product of the period, yet sufficiently independent to disagree, when it pleased her, with popular taste.

Mike soon fell into the habit of bringing her his short stories, asking for criticism and, more often than not, accepting it. They quarreled a lot, but these clashes were tonic to their friendship.

They had other quarrels which were not so healthy. Nancy pretended to be tough, but she was actually as thin-skinned as an adolescent. The old wounds had never healed. The scar tissue was frail. Some careless word, forgotten as soon as Mike had spoken it, would cause her to turn upon him cruelly.

Often Mike vowed never to see her again. But as suddenly as she had begun to brood, she relaxed, was herself again, tough, critical, merry, and tireless when there was any chance for fun.

When Nancy was called away by her grandmother's last illness, Mike realized that he had begun to depend upon her companionship. He wrote long letters, confessed that he found New York dull without her, outlined the plots of his new stories.

The day her grandmother was buried, she called Mike and told him she'd arrive at Grand Central the next afternoon. She promised a surprise. Knowing Nancy, he thought she'd bought a Great Dane or dyed her hair. He bought himself a new suit, filled her apartment with flowers, and decided that he'd bury the hardboiled act and tell her sentimentally how much he had missed her.

The surprise was Phyllis. Arm in arm, the girls confronted Mike. "She thought I ought to warn you," Nancy told him, "but I wanted a glimpse of your face when you saw us together."

Both kissed him.

Phyllis said, "I'm so happy, Mike. It's like old times again, almost as if we were kids."

"It's new times," Nancy laughed. "Grandma always set us against each other, but, now she's gone, the spell's broken and we can be friends."

Mike felt that he did not understand women at all. He could not believe that their grandmother's death had turned the girls' lifelong loathing into love. "Whence springs this sudden affection for your dear cousin?" he asked Nancy when they arrived at the apartment and Phyllis had gone off to change her clothes.

"Oh, Mike! If you only realized how deadly life is in that town. Fred and Fred's family would drive me to arsenic if I had to dine with them more than once every five years, and poor Phyllis has to have dinner there every Sunday."

"Are you sure it wasn't because you want to show her how much better your life is than if you'd married Johnnie Elder?"

Nancy turned scarlet. Mike was immediately remorseful. During her absence he had resolved to guard his tongue and her sensitivity. Instead of sulking, Nancy slapped his face.

For the rest of mat season there was little emotion in their relationship. They fell back into an easygoing camaraderie, and gave themselves to the pleasure of entertaining Phyllis.

Mike used his newspaper connections so that she could meet people whose names she had read in magazines about New York life.

It was never difficult to find an extra man for Phyllis, and it was inevitable that she made conquests. But she never forgot that she was a married woman. That remote, untouchable quality, more than her beauty, was Phyllis's greatest charm. Men felt that she was a prize almost beyond reach, that her favors were few, but, if given, would lead to ecstasy beyond imagining.

To Mike Jordan the happiest nights were those when they dined at Nancy's, sipped liqueurs or brandy, and he read aloud from the works of Jordan. He was at the dreary stage then, writing morbid little pieces about unpleasant people involved in sordid conflicts. Nancy listened attentively, a pencil and notebook beside her.

Much of his later success, Mike admitted, he owed to her

frankness and clarity. Phyllis never uttered a word except praise. Mike was an author, his work sacred.

Phyllis had planned to stay in New York for two weeks. Her holiday stretched on and on, until Mike quit asking when she intended to go home. Fred Miller wrote and wired, and went so far in extravagance as to telephone twice a week. Phyllis had always a new excuse — the opening of a play, a fitting, a concert the like of which she would never have another chance to hear; and, finally, the Beaux Arts Ball.

Phyllis was going with Mike, and his friend, Horace Tate, was taking Nancy. They had planned to go as characters out of Greek mythology. When Mike and Horace rang the bell of Nancy's apartment that night, they were admitted by a masked Diana.

Mike looked Nancy over critically. "You're too skinny to be classical. Zeus would have exiled you."

Phyllis came in, unmasked, but dressed in a white tunic, bound in gold and with a bunch of golden grapes in her hair. Fred Miller followed, blowing his nose lustily.

He grasped Mike's hand. "Glad to see you again, Jordan. A lot of water's flowed under the bridge since the last time we met. Getting to be quite famous, aren't you?"

"Fred surprised us," Phyllis explained to him. "We were totally unprepared. I'm terribly sorry, Mike, that I can't go with you."

"Haven't time," said Fred. "One of my clients has moved up to Boston but I'm still handling his business. Want to show him that I appreciate his loyalty."

Mike did not particularly like Fred nor care to see more of him, but he could not believe that anyone who lived in a dull, small town could be so indifferent to New York. He tried to persuade Fred to postpone his Boston engagement and let Phyllis go to the ball.

"A businessman can't do just as he pleases. You artists and Bohemians don't seem to understand that we've got responsibilities. Sure, I could get a kick out of the city, too, but I've got to think of others, not just myself."

"Think of Phyllis," Nancy said sulkily. "She's been planning on this party for weeks."

Phyllis took Fred's arm. "I'm going with my husband. But it won't be for long. I'm coming back; I'm going to live in New York some day."

And she did. The following September Fred drove their sedan, filled with suitcases and hatboxes, to New York. Phyllis must have worked hard to uproot a man whose life was woven so deeply into the life of his home town. What emotion she must have spent, what tears, artifices, pleadings, and reproaches it must have cost her. Fred tried to make a brave show, as though the move had been forced upon him by the insurance company for which he worked. Since his father had represented the company for thirty-two years, they decently gave Fred a job in their New York office.

At Phyllis's cocktail parties Fred was always busy, filling glasses, passing hors d'oeuvres, fetching ice from the kitchen. Whenever he had a moment between duties, he would corner some unfortunate guest and try to prove that an insurance man was no less interesting than a second-string dramatic critic. His body seemed never to fit comfortably into Phyllis's Victorian chairs. For she, knowing she could never afford anything like

Nancy's penthouse, had done wonders with a three-room suite in a remodeled house. Fred suffered shame because she had bought furniture secondhand.

Mike had started to write his play, and since Phyllis knew the home-town background so well, he consulted her nearly every day. Out of her resentment of the townspeople who had pitied and patronized the music teacher's daughter grew Mike's most vivid characterizations. She had a gift for mimicry, and when she had the chance to strip others of their emotional veils she shed completely the pretty reticence with which she guarded her own secrets.

They saw less and less of Nancy. In the beginning she had been splendid, generous in helping Phyllis furnish her apartment, never appearing at their door without gifts and gadgets, and putting on an apron to help with the serving when Phyllis gave her first party. No one could name the day when they had ceased to interest her. Perhaps it was Fred's conversation. Mike was too self-absorbed to worry about anyone's moods but his own. He did not see Nancy nor bother to telephone her until the play was finished.

"I thought you were dead," she said, when he finally called.

"This is the resurrection. I've written a play." As she did not hail this with a bravo, Mike's heart sank. "I'd like to read it to you," he said timidly.

"Come up tonight," she said. "How about dinner?"

That was in the morning, and the rest of the day passed like a century in a mortuary. To pass the time he took a long walk, and since a blizzard was beginning to blow up, he arrived with a purple nose and frostbitten fingers.

At dinner they chatted like long-separated school chums who had been living in different hemispheres.

They had their coffee and Courvoisier in the living-room. Then Nancy stretched on the couch and said, "Let's hear the play."

She seemed to accept his genius indolently, but he was as pleased as though she had compared him to Shakespeare. Now the writing of his play seemed a man's job rather than a gesture of unholy impudence. While he read she lay quiet, her face expressionless, and only once, when he made a particularly neat point, caught his eye. Finally it was over. They heard the hiss of burning wood, the wind in the airshaft, the distant hum of the traffic.

After a time Nancy said, "It's good, Mike. Some of it is very good."

He skipped to the couch, leaned over to kiss her. "Do you really think so?"

She turned away, unwilling to accept the kiss until she had finished telling him what she thought of his work. He might not, after all had been said, still want to kiss her.

"Take a drink first." She gave him three fingers of brandy. "It's a good play, Mike, except for two things. Two very important things. One is the way you solve the problem for your characters. You make it too easy."

"But the tragedy demands —"

"Tragedy, my eye," she interrupted. "You've given it a happy ending. No one wanted that woman to go on living. You killed her because it was convenient. You were afraid to face the bigger problem of keeping her alive."

Mike's silence seemed significant. Actually he had nothing to say. Presently he became solemn and remarked, "It's a good point. I'll think about it. What else?"

"The girl."

"What's wrong with her?"

"I don't believe her. She's always right, always the victim. She hasn't enough guts and evil to make her human."

"Perhaps you don't understand that sort of woman. There are females without evil in their hearts."

"Down in their secret souls," Nancy retorted, "all women are vipresses."

"Apparently you judge every other woman by your own limitations."

"Thanks for telling me what you really think of me, Mike."

"Listen; I know this woman. A small-town woman, pretty and poor, surrounded by snobs."

"I know that woman, too. We come from the same town, Mike."

"You never knew the people. You were shut away, protected from the problems of the sordid citizens, the rich girl living in your castle behind the stone wall."

Nancy stared into the fire. "Perhaps I can't judge this play at all, Mike. Perhaps it's too personal. I'm all tied up in prejudices. You ought to get someone else to read it."

It was then that Mike made a grotesque mistake: "Phyllis has read it and she thinks it's absolutely true to life."

"She would."

"Don't be a vipress, Nancy."

She neither spoke nor stirred. In her greens and reds and golds, with the big hoops in her ears, she was like one of those haughty, rebellious duchesses that Goya loved to paint. Mike lost his temper, screamed, called her an egotist and a snob. Furious because his anger seemed trivial beside her aloofness, he gathered up his things, thrust the play back into his brief case, stamped out into the hall for his hat, coat, scarf, and rubbers. As he let himself out he looked back at her. She sat in the same position, hunched before the fire, staring as if in a trance into the flames.

Three days later she left for Florida. When the season was over, she drove to Mexico. Through Phyllis, who got the news from her aunt, he learned that Nancy had taken a year's lease on a house in Taxco.

She had been right about the play. Mike heard the same criticism from his wisest friends, and in April he began to rewrite it. While he was working he thought constantly of Nancy. He felt that some measure of gratitude was due her, but he could never humble himself before Nancy nor beg her forgiveness.

In June he sold the play, and spent the summer making further changes. It opened on the thirteenth of September and was immediately a hit.

Gilbert Jones headed the cast, and at the party after the opening Mike introduced him to Phyllis.

When Mike saw them together on the dance floor, he was reminded of that New Year's Eve when she had danced so recklessly with Johnnie Elder. Excitement colored her cheeks. Above the flimsy black stuff that veiled her shoulders she was like a painting on ivory. She wore black jet earrings, fine old ones set in gold, an inheritance from her grandmother.

She and Gilbert Jones danced together, drank together, laughed, teased, flirted, and forgot that there were other people at the party. Behind them, like a shadow, hovered Fred Miller. He had caught his annual cold earlier than usual, and he blew his nose constantly.

Every woman at the party envied Phyllis. Gilbert wore his good looks like an advertisement of superior masculinity.

He was not a fine actor. He was too handsome to play any

part as well as he played Gilbert Jones. In Mike's play he was cast admirably as a vain and selfish bachelor who had been for years the lover of the heroine's mother. Gil loathed the part and the play, but it was a distinguished production and he could not have afforded to turn it down. He fancied himself a romantic rogue and believed that he would come into his own if he ever found a lush, heroic, swashbuckling part. He had a theory which he argued tirelessly whenever he found a listener. This weary and cynical world, Gil said, longed for escape into romance; the great play of the century would be three acts of capes and boots, duels and balconies.

While Mike's play was in rehearsal, its press agent, needing copy, sent out a paragraph about Gilbert Jones's quest for the perfect romantic role. It was a typical press-agent blunder, for Mike's play, which he had been paid to exploit, was anything but romantic escapism. The paragraph, printed by dramatic editors too bored to be careful, bore fruit. Gil received a flood of manuscripts by writers who agreed that the theater would be saved by swashbuckling romance. Most of the plays were too amateurish to bear reading, but finally one came in that fitted all of Gil's requirements. It was about the Cavaliers who settled in Maryland. A schoolteacher in Moline, Illinois, had written it.

Not long after Mike's play had opened and royalties were pouring in, Gil asked Mike to read the swashbuckling script. Mike read it and laughed. He had better use for his money than investment in that rose-garlanded tripe.

One day Phyllis came to see Mike. She said that Mike was shortsighted and stubborn, and that in refusing to put money in Gil's play he was losing the chance of his life.

"It's kind of you to be so interested in my career," Mike

teased, "but I happen to be making as much money as I need, and I'm not interested in the financial end of show business."

"But you love the theater," she said with pretty reproach. "I've often heard you say it needs a shot in the arm. Here's your chance, Mike, not only to make a fortune for yourself, but to do something really important for the theater."

"Since when have you become a patroness of the drama, Mrs. Miller?"

Suddenly angry, she cried, "Why do you always call me Mrs. Miller? You know me well enough to use my first name."

"I know why you're out procuring for the drama, Phyllis."

"But it's a great play. People are so tired of realism. Life is hard enough nowadays, with war and taxes and all; nobody wants to be reminded of it in the theater. They want escape."

"I've heard that before," Mike said. "From the source."

She shrank into a corner of the chair. Her love for Gil had influenced her taste in clothes. She had begun to seek picturesque, old-fashioned effects, which on her were charming. She had on a black velvet suit with white ruffles at wrist and neck, and a little black tricorne tilted over one eye and tied on with a black veil. As she sat in the wing chair, touching her nostrils with a lace handkerchief, she was appealing and beautiful.

"Mike," she murmured, "don't laugh at me. You know what my life's been. Can I help it if I've fallen in love? He's everything I've dreamed about all my life."

Mike's heart was affected, but not his pocketbook. He tried to make Phyllis understand that there was no hope for Gil's cumbersome, dated play. She listened politely, but Mike's arguments failed to move her. At the end he felt that he had grown as tiresome to her as Fred Miller.

She had become a woman with a mission. All of her energy was devoted to a single end. Loving Gil, she sought a means of proving herself worthy. She tried, in every way she knew, to find a backer for Gil's show.

One morning her telephone rang, and there was Nancy, just arrived by plane from Mexico City. She had also called Mike, and suggested that they all meet for lunch. It was like Nancy to have forgotten that she had departed in anger.

Mike and Phyllis hurried to Nancy's apartment. It was crowded with open trunks and packing cases, woven baskets, painted furniture, wooden plates, painted trays, serapes, and such an assortment of tin and silverware that it looked as if she were planning to open a shop. She crushed them both in enthusiastic embraces, kissed Mike's mouth and Phyllis's cheek, gave them extravagant presents, declared that she had always prophesied Mike's success, and called to her maid for tequila so they might drink to his career.

She looked serene and healthy. The cadaverous hollows were gone, the angles softened by a few becoming pounds of flesh. . . .

That night Phyllis proved she was the better woman by showing that she possessed something even more dazzling than Nancy's jewels and furs. The love of Gilbert Jones, his splendid masculinity, gave Phyllis such glamour that Nancy's sables might have been muskrat. There was no doubt that Nancy was impressed. As was his habit, Gil flirted with a new woman. Phyllis watched as an author might watch actors rehearse the scenes he has written. Her temper was so good that she laughed at Fred Miller's poor attempts at humor.

It was Mike Jordan's party. He had given it to celebrate

Nancy's return. Mike had not asked Gil to join these home-town friends, but Phyllis had managed to bring him along without embarrassing either Gil or his host.

Nancy had just seen Mike's play. "It's great," she said. "It's honest and beautiful, and it's you, Mike; I can see you in every line."

"It's you, too, Nancy. Didn't you notice that I took all your advice?"

"Nancy helped you with the play?" asked Gil.

"She saved it from being a dreary and morbid little phony. And a flop."

"Nancy has a great sense of theater, real intuition," Phyllis added. "She might have been a great actress."

Nancy laughed. She knew it was cheap flattery but she enjoyed being the center of attention.

Fred Miller pulled out his watch. "I don't like to break up this party, but —"

"Must we?" Phyllis interrupted. "Nancy's just come home and we're having such a good time."

"I can't help it if I'm tired, dear. Your friends must understand that a businessman can't burn the midnight oil like Bohemians."

Phyllis glanced quickly at Gil. He turned to Fred Miller. "Why don't you go on and let me bring Phyllis home?"

"That's kind of you, Jones. Thanks so much. Good night, everyone."

Farewells were curt. No one bothered to watch Fred go. Gil leaned toward Nancy, whispering some compliment that made her laugh. Phyllis approved.

Presently Gil turned to Mike Jordan: "I know you don't like my new play, but, frankly, I'm quite mad about it, and so is

Phyllis. I'm sure that if Nancy's critical sense is as sound as you say, she might be able to suggest whatever changes our play needs."

"Now, Gil," Phyllis pouted, "we mustn't be selfish. Nancy's only just got home and she wouldn't have time to read it now."

"I wouldn't mind," Nancy said. "Bring the manuscript around, will you?"

Mike Jordan sulked. It was contrary of him to be annoyed with Nancy, when his bad temper should have been visited upon Phyllis and Gil. Mike was less distressed by their opportunism than by Nancy's failure to see through their clumsy ruses. He meant to chide her.

As they rode uptown in a taxi Nancy said, "Did you ever see such an attractive man as Gil Jones?"

"He's a heel."

Nancy laughed. "How you loathe handsome men, Mike."

Mike retreated sullenly to his corner of the cab, deciding that if Nancy was so dull as to let a good-looking ham pull the wool over her eyes, she deserved a lesson. Nancy, enjoying his jealousy, continued to tease him. He lost his temper and reminded her of her faults and the mistakes she had made with other men. The evening was a failure.

The next morning Mike's agent called and told him that his Hollywood deal had been settled. Mike could get the salary he asked if he would leave immediately for California. The studio wanted him to rewrite a play which had been rewritten only eight times.

Naturally, he spent a frantic day between his agent's office and the bank and department stores. He closed his apartment and refurnished his wardrobe as though California were a desert island. But he did not intend to desert Nancy. At half-past five he rang her doorbell. The apartment was still cluttered with the woven baskets, silverware, and serapes. The maid, who knew him well, told him to go straight to the living-room.

Gilbert and Phyllis were there. Gil was reading the play. They resented the interruption and were not at all cordial.

"I'm going to Hollywood tomorrow," Mike announced.

"How nice for you," Nancy said.

Mike felt that she was glad to have him out of the way. . . .

A few weeks later Gil handed in his resignation to the manager of Mike's play, and announced that he was appearing in *Jackstraw, A Romance of Cavalier Maryland*. A new producer had come to Broadway; her name was Nancy Miller.

Apparently the radiance of Gil's personality so dazzled her that she had lost all critical judgment. It was a very bad play, and the author, who had come from Moline for rehearsals, refused to rewrite a line. They got Alexandra Hartman for the feminine lead and, while she gave the play some distinction, she was a hellcat at rehearsals. Gil was so busy appeasing his leading lady, convincing Nancy that they needed more money, and wheedling the author to change a line, that he hadn't a moment for Phyllis.

She was not allowed in the theater during rehearsals. That was Miss Hartman's unbreakable rule. Although Phyllis had worked so hard to get the show produced, found a backer, and listened to all the early discussions, she was now an outsider, brushed aside with a mechanical smile and polite promise when she waited in the lobby for Gil. She consoled herself with the hope of his gratitude in the happy future, after the show was on and a hit. Some day, she fancied, Gil would take her in his arms and whisper gratefully, "How can I repay you, darling Phyllis, for all that I owe you?"

They were opening in Baltimore, the historical scene of the play's action. Phyllis bought herself a new outfit, and was about to reserve a seat on the train, when Fred Miller put his foot down. They had the worst fight of their marriage, and Fred finally said, "The trouble with you is that you think you're Nancy, who can spend a thousand dollars on every whim."

The rebuke defeated Phyllis. It was like an echo of her grandmother's lament. As long as she could remember, Phyllis had been reminded that she could not expect the privileges which Nancy took as her right. She had no money of her own. Fred supported her. When he said, "I won't have you spending money on trains and hotels to see a show you can see here in a couple of weeks," she had to submit.

After the Baltimore opening Fred read the reviews and said, "Aren't you glad you didn't spend the money? They say it's the worst show in twenty years."

Anyone but Nancy would have been discouraged by the reviews. Instead of closing, she put more money into the production, extended the road tour, made drastic revisions in the script, and recast several parts. The author, frightened by the critics, agreed to revisions, but was not able to rewrite, and a play doctor was hired. They took the show on a nine-week tour. Gil was too busy to write a post card to Phyllis.

Fred Miller died suddenly of pneumonia. Phyllis had warned him against going to the office with a severe cold but Fred always had colds, and if he'd quit work every time he sniffled he would never have held a job. He tried to nurse it at night with

hot whisky, aspirin, and all the home remedies which he thought
as effective as anything a doctor could prescribe. Phyllis was
sleeping on a cot in the living-room. One morning she went into
the bedroom and found him unconscious. He died at the hospital twenty hours later.

She was very brave, managed everything, took the body
home to his parents and the family plot. Half the town attended
the funeral, and they said that Phyllis, pale and touching in her
black garments, was the prettiest widow they had ever seen.
Fred had left her quite a lot of money. She had no idea that the
big insurance premiums which she had always resented would
bring her a small fortune.

Jackstraw had meanwhile come to New York. Poor Phyllis,
cheated of rehearsals and the out-of-town opening, missed the
first night, too. She was determined to see it on the night of her
return to New York. Mourning or no mourning, she had her
duty to her cousin Nancy and to her friend Gil. She still felt
close to the play and cherished the memory that she had been
Gil's first audience for it. This thought gave her strength and
hope, and as she sat beside the window of the dining car she
decided that she would not telephone Gil that day, but would see
the play alone and afterward surprise him in his dressing-room.

With her coffee the waiter brought the morning paper.
She turned at once to the dramatic section, thinking that she
might read Gil's name in some press agent's notice. And thus
she learned that *Jackstraw* had closed on the previous Saturday
night.

It was the final irony. After all she had given to it, she had
not seen a single performance of Gil's play.

Forlornly she followed a porter through the cold station, and rode to her apartment alone in a drafty cab. The day was miserable. Rain streaked the taxi windows so that she could not even enjoy Fifth Avenue's brilliance. As soon as she got into her apartment, while the shades were still drawn and the radiators cold, she telephoned Gil. A switchboard operator's nasal voice informed her that Mr. Jones had given up his apartment.

She called Nancy. Her cousin uttered condolences on the death of Phyllis's husband, and Phyllis consoled Nancy on the death of her play.

Phyllis said, "How's Gil taking it?"

"Bearing up bravely, looking for a new part."

"I must let him know I'm back."

There was a long silence. A happy thought entered Phyllis's mind. Should Gil want to put on another show, there need be no long, agonizing search for a backer. Fred was no longer alive to remind Phyllis that she could not expect the privileges that Nancy enjoyed; the money Fred had put into insurance would back Gil's new play. She was so eager to speak to Gil, to console him with her golden promise, that she paid little attention to Nancy's unnatural silence.

She did not like to confess to Nancy that she was ignorant of Gil's whereabouts, and she decided to call his agent instead. She was very fortunate, for Gil had just come into the office. He also expressed sympathy, but he could not say much else as his agent was with him. He promised to come and see her that afternoon.

She dressed carefully; used her best perfume. The failure of *Jackstraw* did not seem so dismal now. She was almost grateful for it, knowing that as a result of disappointment Gil would be in a soft, self-pitying mood. She sent out for a bottle of his favorite whisky, arranged it on a tray with seltzer and glasses. When there was nothing else to be done, she watched raindrops roll down the windowpane.

The doorbell rang. She sat quiet for a moment lest she betray too large a measure of eagerness, then drew a deep breath and ran to the door.

Gil was not alone. There was Nancy, too. No woman who was not a millionaire would have appeared in public in such an old, streaked raincoat. She had on galoshes and had a green scarf tied around her head.

Gil took both of Phyllis's hands, gazed deep into her eyes. "Well, dear," he said, in a thick voice. They held hands until Nancy spoke sharply. "I wish you'd help me with these boots, Gil."

He turned to help Nancy. "We were sorry to hear about Fred."

"Thank you," said Phyllis.

Nancy took her wet things into the bathroom. For a couple of minutes Phyllis and Gil were alone. Neither spoke. They were aware of rain dripping against the window and the sizzling of steam in the radiator.

When Nancy came back, she asked, "Have you told her, Gil?"

He shook his head.

"You might as well know, Phyllis. Gil and I are married."

Phyllis handed around drinks, then raised her own. "To your happiness," she said, and finished the highball before she put down the glass. She saw the look of triumph in Nancy's eyes.

Gil and Nancy soon left; but on Saturday of that week Nancy happened to be in the neighborhood of Phyllis's apartment and stopped in. Phyllis was not at home, and Nancy said that she

would wait. She read a magazine, washed her face, and used the
telephone, which was in Phyllis's room between the twin beds.
Before she went, she wrote a note begging Phyllis to dine with
them the following Tuesday. Phyllis found it on the bed table,
tore it into small pieces, and threw it into the wastebasket.

"No use being a hypocrite about it," Phyllis remarked several
weeks later when she told the story to Mike Jordan.

On the Tuesday of Nancy's dinner party Gil was called to
the telephone by Phyllis's maid, who told them that Mrs. Miller
had been taken to the hospital. When she came to work that
morning, the maid said, she had found Mrs. Miller unconscious
in her bed. The doctor thought at first that she had taken an
overdose of sleeping medicine, but an analysis showed that she
had been poisoned. It was a poison that worked slowly and the
dose had been insufficient.

Gil suffered extravagant remorse. It was only natural for him
to blame himself for the poor girl's attempt at suicide. As soon
as she was allowed visitors he visited her at the hospital. She was
sitting up in bed, looking very frail and gentle in a white mari-
bou jacket with enormous sleeves.

She held out both hands. He took them. They were cold and
so soft that there seemed no bones under the thin flesh. His eyes
filled as he bent over to kiss her.

She looked up at him with burning eyes and whispered,
"Someone tried to kill me, Gil."

His hands dropped. He moved away and stared as though he
were looking at a ghost. She shook her head and repeated the
astonishing statement. "You don't believe I'd have done such a
thing myself?" she asked. "You know me so well, Gil, you know
I'm not brave enough for that."

It was discovered later that five or six poisoned capsules had been placed in the box with her sleeping pills. . . .

The telephone rang again. New York Operator Forty assured Mr. Jordan that she was still working on his call. When he came back to the patio, he said, "I'm thirsty, Lissa; may I have a drink?"

We went into the kitchen, which was on the east side of the house, and about twelve degrees cooler than the patio. I got out some cheese and crackers, and we sat with our drinks in the breakfast nook.

"Had someone tried to murder Phyllis, or was that merely an excuse because she was ashamed to admit that she had tried suicide?" I asked.

"Wait," Mike said. He was a playwright, and as keenly as he felt this story, he was still too much of a technician to give away the climax before recounting the events that led to it.

He finished his drink and held out his empty glass to me. While I squeezed a lemon, he began the final chapter. . . .

A few months later Mike Jordan came to New York on a Hollywood writer's holiday. He had a suite in an expensive hotel and went to night clubs at which he would never before have dreamed of spending money. He saw both Phyllis and Nancy, and each told him in precise detail her separate story.

Phyllis was being frightfully gay at this time, spending Fred Miller's money wildly and surrounding herself with good-looking young men. She had become extremely chic. This Mike thought was an affectation. Like so many bored women, she was seeking compensation for the dullness of her nights by exhibiting herself in costumes whose extravagance advertised her loneliness.

Frequently at parties or the theater she met Gil and Nancy. They and all of their friends dutifully appeared at all the smart places and saw the same people over and over again. To show that she bore them no malice, she invited Mr. and Mrs. Jones to a couple of her big parties, and Nancy returned the hospitality by inviting Phyllis to dine . . . with seven other guests, four of them male and attractive.

For a few months Gil and Nancy considered themselves the happiest couple in town. Nancy thought her husband the handsomest man in the world and herself an extremely fortunate woman. Gil was good-natured and disinclined to quarrel, and as long as his wife admired him, he was indulgent of her moods. The one subject on which they could not agree was the story Phyllis had told him about the poisoned sleeping pills. Gil still believed that someone had tried to murder Phyllis, and Nancy held to her theory that this was an excuse to cover an unsuccessful attempt at suicide.

Although they solemnly promised not to speak of it, they were tempted constantly to find arguments to support their separate attitudes. He thought her unnecessarily vindictive about her cousin, while she considered him a credulous fool. For a while they managed to keep their opinions to themselves.

One night they met Phyllis at a dinner party. Afterward Gil and Phyllis were partners at bridge. They won quite a lot of money, and on the way home Gil boasted about his game and, to show sportsmanship, praised his partner. Nancy stiffened. Aware of her displeasure, he hastily changed the subject.

Although her marriage had increased Nancy's self-confidence, she was still thin-skinned.

"You needn't be afraid to talk about Phyllis," she said coldly. "I know what a superior creature she is."

Gil did not speak again until they were in their apartment. His nerves were on edge. "Look here," he said when they were in the hall, taking off their coats; "this has gone far enough. Every time I mention Phyllis you act as if I'd insulted you. We've got to have this out once and for all."

They quarreled bitterly, brought out buried grievances, and led each other to the subject of the poisoned pills. Later, when she was questioned about this quarrel, Nancy said that she could not remember precisely what each of them had said, but only that Gil's gibes had so wounded her that she ran the length of the apartment into her bedroom and locked the door. For a while, she said, he had stayed in the corridor, shouting abuse.

The next day she could not force herself to speak to him. He addressed her politely, just as though they had not quarreled, but she seemed not to hear. It was Nancy's habit, when she was hurt, to brood for days. She regretted her moodiness, but had never been able to cure it.

This, more than the quarrel, upset Gil, for the actor's pride was fed by the response of his audience. Nancy's passionate silence destroyed his self-confidence and led to the distrust of his charm. And when, lunching alone at a popular restaurant, he ran into Phyllis, in a turban made all of violets and a purple veil tied in a bow under her chin, he invited her to have a drink with him.

He told her, as she later reported to the police, of Nancy's sulks. The news did not surprise Phyllis. She was well acquainted with this habit of Nancy's; it had always made family history. She advised Gil to feed Nancy a bit of her own stew and to treat her with the same black indifference.

The idea delighted Gil. When he donned a mood he wore it like a wig and tights. In contrast with his brooding melancholy,

Nancy's sulks were a pale fog beside a storm cloud. She was utterly bewildered. All of her life, Nancy had been given her own way; when she sulked and refused to talk, her parents and the servants had waited tremulously for her mood to lighten. Now she had a taste of the bitter medicine.

Gil noted the effect of his performance and was as pleased as though he had heard a first-night audience shouting bravos. Perhaps he kept it up longer than necessary. Her nerves were frayed. Too proud to beg forgiveness, she waited shyly for him to offer the first word.

The triumphant actor sought a wider audience. One woman was not enough for him. Daily he made reports to Phyllis. One day, when they had been having tea together, he went off with her gloves in his pocket. They were fuchsia-colored and size five and three quarters. Nancy's maid, going through Gil's pockets before she sent his suit to the cleaner's, found the gloves and brought them to her mistress with an air of sly innocence.

Nancy turned as pale as if a wound had drained the blood from her. That very day she had bought Gil a reconciliation gift, a costly morocco traveling case with gold fittings. It was in her closet, shrouded in tissue paper, ready to be presented after the first embrace. . . .

It was about four in the afternoon when the maid brought her the gloves. Gil came home at seven o'clock. When Nancy heard the door open she rushed at him, pallid, red-eyed, and screaming like a fishwife.

This was no time for sullen dignity. Gil used words he'd picked up backstage, filth which belonged to the riffraff of the theater, and which had never before soiled the lips of that dignified actor.

The two maids retired to the kitchen. According to their report, the quarrel lasted almost two hours. It thoroughly exhausted Nancy. Sobbing, she threw herself across her bed. The cook came out of the kitchen to ask cautiously if Mr. Jones wished dinner, but Gil turned and stalked out to the hall, put on his coat, and left the apartment.

According to the story which Phyllis told the police the next day, she was reading in her living-room, when the doorbell rang so furiously that her young Negro maid, who was washing dishes in the tiny kitchen, came out and begged Phyllis not to obey that nervous summons. Quite calmly Phyllis opened the door, and admitted Gil.

He walked to the center of the living-room and said quietly, "I've been through hell."

"Sit down," she said gently.

Gil strode up and down like a caged beast. Phyllis, not wishing the maid to overhear, bade her leave the dishes and go home.

"I'd rather die," Gil said, "than have to look at my wife's face again."

"Why? What's happened, Gil?"

"She's an evil woman." Gil shuddered. "Although I'm not a particularly virtuous man, wickedness in a woman horrifies me."

"Gil dear, be reasonable. Nancy's your wife and a fine, generous girl. She was spoiled at home, but she's wonderfully goodhearted and she loves you desperately. Won't you try to forgive her?"

Gradually, with such argument, she managed to calm him. He asked for a drink, and she brought out the whisky and soda. She did not count the drinks he poured for himself, but thought he must have taken four or five. Toward the end of the evening he became quite garrulous, and told her why he had married

Nancy. During rehearsals and the out-of-town tryouts of the play, they had been thrown together constantly. Nancy had been such a good sport about the money she lost on the play that Gil had tried to make it up as much as possible in offering her his friendship. She had interpreted his kindness as love, and showed her passion for him with shocking frankness. The marriage had been impulsive.

He now realized how grave had been the mistake. As sternly as he tried he could not reject his need for Phyllis. Her image was engraved indelibly, he had said, upon his heart.

"I can't sleep, I can't think, I can't work," Gil said, rising and crossing the room to the wide Victorian armchair where Phyllis sat. "I can't live with that woman another day. I'm going to tell her so . . . tonight."

"No, Gil. Think it over. Your marriage was an impulse, and this may be another. You know your own nature; you're too flexible, you allow yourself to be carried away too easily. Tomorrow you may feel differently about her."

"No. I'll never love her. And I'm too upset to let this thing go on any longer. I'll tell her, darling, that I love you."

"No, Gil. That you must never tell her. If it were any other woman —" Phyllis shrugged off the rest of the thought. "But you must never tell Nancy that."

"I'm going home. Tomorrow I'll let you know what I've done." He kissed her on the forehead tenderly like a fond uncle.

Phyllis put the whisky into a walnut cabinet which had once been a Victorian commode. She carried the soda water to the refrigerator and the glass to the sink. The dinner dishes had not been dried and put away. Phyllis ran hot water over them, dried them and tidied the kitchen. This was a habit developed by early training. All the women in the family, even when they had servants, were fussy housekeepers.

She barely slept that night, and at dawn fell into a fitful slumber made hideous by nightmares. She spent most of the day waiting for Gil to telephone.

When, at last, the doorbell rang, she hurried to it eagerly and, even before she had it open, said, "Gil, dear!"

There stood two detectives who had come to inform her of Gil's death, and when she had sufficiently recovered from the shock, to ask a number of questions. . . .

Nancy told a quite different story.

After Gil had left her sobbing on the bed, Nancy said, she was exhausted. The quarrel had been preceded by two hours of emotion and several days of tension. She fell asleep. When she awoke the clock was striking eleven. The maids had gone home, and she was alone. She had slept heavily and felt curiously light and fresh.

She bathed, put on a becoming new negligee, and awaited Gil's homecoming eagerly, because she felt that the noisy quarrel had released hidden resentments and it would be possible for them to make peace. She had eaten no dinner and was very hungry. There was cold chicken and applesauce in the icebox, and she sliced a couple of tomatoes. She had just poured boiling water into the drip coffeepot when she heard Gil's key in the lock.

He looked cold. His cheeks were almost blue. He had walked, he told her, from Seventy-ninth Street to Sixty-fifth. His mentioning Seventy-ninth Street, Nancy thought, was his way of confessing that he had been with Phyllis. She did not remark upon it, but asked if he would like a drink.

"I've had enough. My head's clear now; I want it to stay that way."

Nancy felt sturdy, calm, and capable of facing any situation. Her tears had washed away grief and anger, and her nap had erased all bitterness.

Of one thing she was certain. She must know the truth, however painful.

"I've been a heel," Gil said.

Since he was so clearly remorseful Nancy did not wish to rebuke him. "I've been pretty difficult myself."

"The worst thing I've done is to have gone to Phyllis with my troubles. It was stupid and selfish of me and unfair to you."

He offered contrition humbly, and she could afford to be magnanimous. "I'm hurt that you went to her, but probably it was my own fault. I'm spoiled and egocentric and willful. A vipress, Mike Jordan used to call me. If I ever let go with one of those moods again, I wish you'd horsewhip me."

"It'd be healthier," Gil said.

"Might even cure me." Nancy felt better. She laughed aloud. "My whole trouble is that we never used horsewhips at home. Even our horses were given their heads."

Gil wrapped his arms about himself and shivered.

"You did get a chill," Nancy said. "If you won't have a drink, let me give you some coffee. Have you had dinner?"

She heated the coffee and made a nice little cold supper. They ate at their regular places at the dining-room table. As she poured his coffee Nancy said steadily, "There is one thing I must know, Gil. Are you in love with her?"

He set his cup down hard. Some of the coffee spilled into the saucer. "Whatever gave you that idea?"

"You were in love with her before you met me."

"Did she tell you so?"

Nancy hesitated. "What about the suicide? There was no other reason why she should have tried to kill herself."

"Someone tried to murder her."

Nancy did not wish to renew the argument. Instead she said, "It's the way she acts about you. There's a sort of possessive righteousness about her, as if you'd been hers and I snatched you away."

"Great God!" he shouted. "You women act as if a man were a thing to be handed around on a platter. Phyllis couldn't possess me any more than you do. I loved you and asked you to marry me. Isn't that enough?"

Nancy's eyes filled. She tried to hide her emotion by eating, but she could not. As she sipped coffee, she looked at him over the cup and asked, "Do you love me, Gil?"

"I wouldn't live in a house with a woman I didn't love. I should think my past history would make that apparent."

"But I've been so nasty. A vipress."

"A man's unfortunate to love a vipress, but what can he do about it?"

"Come here and kiss me."

After the kiss he went back to his place and ate heartily. They seemed a pleasantly domestic couple again. Tremulously she asked her final question: "Did you tell Phyllis that you love me?"

He nodded. "I told her that I'd made up my mind not to see any more of her."

When they had finished eating, Nancy put the remaining food back into the icebox and washed the few dishes. Although she had been brought up in a house tended by servants, her grandmother had instilled in her a horror of sloppiness. She'd have been ashamed if the servants found the kitchen dirty when they came in the morning.

Her apartment had been designed originally as two penthouses, so that her bedroom and bath were at the opposite end from Gil's. This arrangement had amused them in the early days of their marriage, and they had enjoyed the adventure of traveling the length of the apartment when they visited each other at night.

When Nancy finished in the kitchen she went into Gil's quarters. He shouted from the bathroom that she should go to bed, and that he would come in and say good night. She had only her nightgown under the negligee and it took her but a couple of seconds to prepare for bed. She fell asleep almost immediately. The short nap had restored but a portion of the energy she had exhausted during the quarrel.

Gil had the actor's habit of sleeping late. But when, at one o'clock the next afternoon, he had not yet rung for his breakfast, Nancy opened the door of his bedroom softly. She found his body on the floor close to the bed. He had apparently tried to summon help before he died. Blood and dried vomit stained his pajamas and the light tan carpet. His protruding eyes were like glazed porcelain balls.

Nancy was shaken but remarkably self-possessed. The maids were amazed by her ability to withstand shock. It was she who telephoned for the doctor who had an office on the first floor of the apartment house.

There was no doubt that Gil had been poisoned. The doctor asked Nancy what he had eaten the night before, and she told him about the coffee, showed him the remnants of chicken, the half-used loaf, and what remained of the applesauce in a white china bowl. And there were four tomatoes in the cooler instead of the half-dozen which the cook had put there the day before.

Nancy told the doctor and, later, the detectives that she had eaten the same food, drunk coffee brewed in the same pot. She remembered that when she had asked Gil if he wanted a drink, he had answered that he had had enough. According to his own story, he had spent part of the evening on Seventy-ninth Street, which led her to think that he had been with her cousin, Phyllis Miller.

Analysis showed that the poison which had killed Gilbert Jones (and Mike Jordan made a special point of withholding its name) worked slowly. If its presence is known in time and an antidote administered, the victim can be saved. But no one had heard Gil's cries. Nancy had slept soundly at her end of the apartment.

By the time Gil's body was examined he had been dead for a few hours, but medical authorities could not say whether he had died at five in the morning or at seven-thirty. And the time element was further complicated by the fact that the poison might have killed him in six hours or nine. He had been a healthy man with a rugged heart. Experts could not name precisely the hour at which he had been given the poison, whether at ten o'clock at night or at one the next morning. And time was the determining factor.

From nine o'clock the night before, or a few minutes after, until approximately ten-forty, he had been with Phyllis. In this detail the girls' stories agreed. If he had left Phyllis around ten-forty, it was reasonable to believe Nancy's statement that the clock had been striking eleven when he opened the front door. He had sat up with her talking and eating, until somewhere around twelve-thirty.

There was a possibility, of course, that he had stopped on his way home at a bar or restaurant. Detectives questioned bartenders and waiters in the Third and Lexington Avenue places between Sixty-fifth and Seventy-ninth Street, but none of them remembered having served him. And if he had been accidentally poisoned in any of these places, there would certainly have been other victims.

There was one other possibility, suicide. This was not likely. He was not of a morbid nature, and since he had been married to Nancy he had no financial problems. His play had failed, but if actors committed suicide after every flop, there'd be none left to keep the theater going. And the day before he had been interviewed about a good part by an important manager. There was no reason for Gilbert Jones to have been suicidally unhappy. Two women had loved him, but that was more or less what he expected. In his way he had probably cared for both, which is to say that he loved neither, since he had room in his heart only for love of himself.

It must have been one of the women. They had both played emotional scenes with him, had both given him drinks. Their stories were in direct conflict. Each said that he had promised her to give up the other, and had gone so far as to play a farewell scene with the unhappy one. Although neither of them accused the other, each implied that the other was guilty. No poison was discovered in either apartment. But when a murderer washes the dishes, she might easily get rid of deadlier evidence. If there had been poison left in either apartment, the guilty woman could easily get rid of it. Modern plumbing provides a quick and easy way to dispose of such evidence. . . .

While Mike was summing up the points on both sides and adding to my suspense, the telephone rang. We were silent for a moment. All the color had left Mike's face. Into the phone he said, "This is Jordan. . . . All right; I'll hold on."

Although I was crazy to hear the conversation, I had been brought up to believe that there is no sin more despicable than eavesdropping. Virtuously I walked on tiptoe toward the patio.

"You heard the rest, you might as well hear this," Mike said, and I flew into the living-room.

It was on the west side of the house, and although the curtains had been drawn, the sun filtered light through the patterned green cloth. I sat on the couch as I used to sit in the dentist's waiting-room, my hands at my sides pressed hard against the seat.

After a seemingly endless interval I heard Mike say, "Hello, dear." He was silent for a few minutes, and then he turned to me and said, "She's crying."

"Who?"

He spoke into the telephone: "I know you wouldn't do such a thing, my dear. I know who did it. . . . Yes! If you do as I say, she'll have to confess." After another interval he said to her, "Because I know. Of course it's hard for you, but not half so hard as being accused, yourself."

Apparently she asked Mike to come to New York, for he told her that he was not free to leave, since he was in the Army. "I can't get away, you know, unless they subpoena me, which isn't probable, since I was three thousand miles away when the murder was committed. But I do know positively." His voice became gentler: "You'll have to handle this yourself. Tell her that you must talk to her privately, and get her to come to your apartment. She'll come if you tell her you've talked to Mike Jordan. I'm sure that she knows I know. You must let her think you're alone; but have someone there. If you're constantly under surveillance by the Homicide Squad, so much the better. Have your lawyer there, too, but concealed."

Again there was argument. Mike almost lost his temper. "Of course it's a horrid thing to do, but, my dear girl, you are suspected of murder."

She must finally have agreed, because Mike turned to me and nodded. Then he spoke again into the telephone: "Tell her that you know about her *first* murder."

I gasped. Probably there was as much astonishment at the other end of the wire, for Mike hastened to reassure her by saying, "Yes, indeed. I do know it. Tell her you know what caused Fred Miller's death."

Silence must have followed this revelation. Mike turned to see the effect upon me.

"Then it was Phyllis?" I muttered.

Mike said it into the telephone, "It wasn't jealousy that caused her to poison Gil. She was jealous, no doubt, and afraid of losing him. This made her hysterical, and you know how completely she'd abandon herself once she unlocked that shell of restraint. She probably pleaded with Gil, told him that he dared not desert her after what she'd done for him. I can't tell you exactly what her words were, but I'm sure she disclosed theatrically that she'd been driven to murder for Gil's sake.

"Knowing Gil, I feel that he was shocked at the thought

before he quite believed her. Instead of exciting him and in-creasing his passion, it turned him against her. You knew Gil better than I. He was vain enough to enjoy the spectacle of the two of you weeping and fighting over him, but he didn't want corpses as tribute on the altar of love. I know Gil's faults, too. He was vain and opportunistic, but there wasn't a malicious bone in his body. Think of his naïveté over that suicide business. As soon as she had confessed, whether he fully believed it or not, he began to loathe her. This cooled her considerably, I'm sure. When the hysteria died, she saw that he was dangerous to her, and put poison in his highball.

"She had the poison, you know," Mike continued. "It was the same stuff she'd put into the sleeping pills. After she discovered that Gil had married you and she'd killed poor Fred in vain, she tried to kill herself. She probably thought she was sincere about it, but the sincerity wasn't deep enough to make her go through with it. If she had died, Nancy, you would have been punished and your marriage with Gil haunted by her ghost. And since she recovered, she found it less embarrassing to appear the victim of a murder attempt than a frustrated suicide.

"That looked bad for you, too, you know. She probably tried to make believe that you'd poisoned her sleeping pills. Yes, she inferred it when she told me the story. Naturally, I never be-lieved it, Nancy; I knew you too well, and I also knew how Fred Miller died."

I did not hear the rest of the conversation, for there came into my mind then the image of a psychology professor, a pomp-ous little man he was, who once said to our class that suicide and murder are not far removed from each other; both, he told us, were born of the desire for revenge upon an individual or upon society. Suddenly, as Mike finished the long-distance call, I saw the pattern of the story. There was only one point which I did not understand.

"How did *you* know, Mike, that Phyllis had killed Fred Miller? I thought you said he'd died of pneumonia."

We were on the patio when I asked that question. The pepper tree's shadow had shifted and Mike sat upright in a metal chair under the striped umbrella. Sunlight and the brilliant hues of the geraniums hinted mockingly at the pleasure of being alive. The blossoms of the mimosa were fat yellow balls.

"There's no doubt that Fred died of pneumonia. In a hospital with a physician in attendance."

"But you said that Phyllis killed him."

"It's easy, Lissa, when a person has a bad cold, to give him pneumonia, particularly if you're his loving wife." In the hot light Mike shivered. "Don't ask me how she did it. That, Lissa, is something I'll never tell anyone again."

"You told her how to do it, Mike? Why? Why did you tell her how to kill her husband?"

Mike rose and walked to the edge of the patio, stood at the wall looking down on the valley and the highway. His fists were clenched so tightly that the bones shone through the skin.

"I gave her the recipe for murder."

"How, Mike?"

Mike did not immediately answer. He stood beside the wall, looking down at the shadows on the hillside and the lively road. "Long ago, Lissa, when I was trying my hand at fiction, I wrote a story. It was a young man's story, bitter and sordid, all about an unhappy wife who brought about her husband's death by a series of acts which caused a bad cold to develop into pneumonia.

"Each of these acts was described in the most minute detail, Lissa.

"I read the story to Phyllis and Nancy. They were the only ones who ever heard it, for after Nancy'd got through telling me what she thought of my little masterpiece, I burned the manuscript. She was pretty tough with me that night, asked if I was crazy enough to suppose that anyone would ever publish a story that gave such precise instructions to potential murderers.

"After Nancy had attacked the story so violently, Phyllis could not very well praise it. She listened quietly and neither praised nor criticized the tale. But she must have remembered. I knew —" Mike turned abruptly and raised his voice at me as though I were guilty. "I knew as soon as I heard of Fred Miller's death. In a way I feel as if I had committed murder."

How blind men are. When he told me how heavily his conscience was burdened, I told Mike Jordan that this was not his first sin against the cousins. He took off his dark glasses and glared at me. "A sin of omission," I said. "Are you so stupid, Mike, that you've never realized how Nancy loved you?"

After a moment he said quietly, "That's very female of you, Lissa."

"Since she was fifteen and made such an odious exhibition of herself in the silver and black dress at her party. Every time she succeeded in getting close to you, Phyllis came along and dazzled you with her beauty and that mystery which was only a disguise for her coldness and jealousy. Her sole purpose in life was revenge against Nancy, and you were her victim as well as Gilbert and Fred."

"But Nancy fell in love with other men, with Gil and Johnnie Elder. She flirted quite a lot in Europe and almost got engaged while she was in Mexico."

"She tried to make herself fall in love with them, Mike. Partly because she was trying to get you out of her system, and partly because it was only natural for her to want to take something away from Phyllis. She had shared hope and failure with Gil, which softened her toward him. And, besides, he was not exactly repulsive to women."

Mike's hands fumbled in his pocket. He brought out the roll of bills again, hurried across the patio, and thrust them into my hands. When he spoke his voice was humble:

"Would you mind, Lissa, if I used your phone again? I'd like to call New York."

HELEN NIELSEN

1918–2002

HELEN NIELSEN was the author of more than a dozen novels published between the late 1940s and the mid-1970s, including *Dead on the Level* (aka *Gold Coast Nocturne*, 1951), *Detour* (1953), *Sing Me a Murder* (1961), and *The Brink of Murder* (1976), as well as a number of television scripts for shows like *Alfred Hitchcock Presents* and *Perry Mason*. Biographical details about Nielsen are scarce: she was born and raised in the Midwest and attended the Chicago Art Institute before working on aircraft designs as a draftsman during World War II. She later moved to Southern California, where her writing career flourished, before eventually settling in Arizona.

Aside from writing novels and TV scripts, Nielsen published dozens of short stories for *Manhunt*, *Alfred Hitchcock's Mystery Magazine*, and *Ellery Queen's Mystery Magazine*. Many of them featured a hard-boiled police detective, Mike Shelly, solving murderous crimes, but on occasion Nielsen would switch to tough-minded, cigarette-smoking female protagonists who try their best to get out from under the passions that ensnare them to unavailable men, but never manage to escape.

Loren, the narrator of "Don't Sit Under the Apple Tree," which was first published in *Manhunt* in 1959, is one such woman. Starting as a secretary to her married boss, then moving up the social ladder as his wife, she knows the precariousness of her place in life even as she would prefer to not think about it. But then mysterious hang-up calls in the middle of the night begin and force Loren to reexamine her life and whom she can really trust.

DON'T SIT UNDER THE APPLE TREE

IT WAS exactly ten minutes before three when Loren returned to her apartment. The foyer was empty—a glistening, white and black tile emptiness of Grecian simplicity which left no convenient nooks or alcoves where a late party-goer could linger with her escort in a prolonged embrace, or where the manager—in the unlikely event that he was concerned—could spy out the nocturnal habits of his tenants. Loren moved swiftly across the foyer, punctuating its silence with the sharp tattoo of her heels on the tile and the soft rustling of her black taffeta evening coat. Black for darkness; black for stealth. She stepped into the automatic elevator and pressed the button for the seventeenth floor. The door closed and the elevator began its silent climb. Only then did she breathe a bit easier, reassuring herself that she was almost safe.

There was an apex of terror, a crisis at which everything and every place became a pulsing threat. Loren wore her terror well.

A watcher—had there been an invisible watcher in the elevator—would not have been aware of it. He would have seen only a magnetically attractive woman—mature, poised, a faint dusting of pre-mature gray feathering her almost black hair. The trace of tension in her face and eyes would have been attributed to fatigue. The slight impatience which prompted her repeated glances at the floor indicator above the doors would have passed for a natural desire to get home and put an end to an over-long, wearisome day.

In a sense, the watcher would have been right.

The elevator doors opened at the seventeenth floor, and Loren stepped out into a carpeted corridor of emptiness. Pausing only to verify the emptiness, she hurried to the door of her apartment. The key was in her gloved hand before she reached it. She let herself in, closed the door behind her, and leaned against it until she could hear the latch click. For a moment her body sagged and clung to the door as if nailed there, and then she pulled herself upright.

Above the lamp on the hall table—the light turned softly, as she had left it—a sunburst clock splashed against the wall in glittering elegance. The time was eight minutes before three. There was work to be done. Loren switched off the lamp. The long room ahead became an arrangement of grays and off-blacks set against the slightly paler bank of fully draped windows at the end of it; but halfway between the hall and the windows, a narrow rectangle of light cut a pattern across the grays. The light came from the bedroom. Loren moved toward it, catching, as she did so, the sound of a carefully modulated feminine voice dictating letters.

To Axel Torberg and Sons,
Kungsgaten 47
Stockholm, Sweden.

Gentlemen.

In regard to your inquiry of February 11, last: I am sorry to inform you that full payment for your last shipment cannot be made until the damaged merchandise (see our correspondence of Jan. 5) has been replaced.

Having done satisfactory business with your firm for the past twenty years, we feel confident that you will maintain this good will by taking immediate action.

Very Truly Yours,
Loren Banion
Vice President
John O. Banion, Inc.

Loren entered the bedroom. The voice came again, now in a warmer and more informal tone.

Katy, get this off airmail the first thing in the morning. Poor old Axel's getting forgetful in his dotage and has to be prodded. Okay, Doll—?
Next letter:
To Signor Luigi Manfredi,
Via Proconsolo,
Florence . . . .

The room was heavily carpeted. Loren made no sound as she crossed quickly to the French windows, barely glancing at the dictograph which stood on the bedside work table. It was still partly open. The night wind worried the edges of the soft drapes which gave concealment as Loren, pulling them aside only a finger width, peered out at the scene below. The seventeenth floor was one floor higher than the recreation deck. The pool lights were out; but there was a moon, and young Cherry Morgan's shapely legs were clearly visible stretched out from the sheltering canvas sides of one of the swinging lounges. There were legs other than Cherry's—trousered legs; identity unknown. With her parents abroad, Cherry was playing the field.

> *. . . if you will wire this office on the date of shipment, we will have our representatives at the docks to make inspection on arrival. . . .*

The voice of Loren Banion continued to dictate behind her. Loren listened and slowly relaxed. She had, she now realized, been gripping at the draperies until her fingers were aching. She released the cloth and walked back to the bed—no longer swiftly, but with a great weariness as if she had come a very long distance, running all the way. She sank down slowly and sat on the edge of the bed. The dictograph was now a droning nuisance, but a necessary one. Cherry Morgan could hear it, and that was important.

". . . Honestly, Mrs. Banion, I don't know how you can work as late as you do! Sometimes I hear you up there dictating all night long."

"Not all night, Cherry. I never work past three. Doctor's orders."

"Doctor's orders? What a drag! I'm glad I don't have your doctor. If I'm going to work until three in the morning it's got to be at something more interesting than business correspondence!"

And the fact that Cherry Morgan frequently worked past three was the reason the dictograph continued to play.

... Very Truly Yours,

Oh, you know the rest, Katy. On second thought, give the sign off more flourish. Signor Manfredi probably sings Don Jose in his shower.

A small crystal clock stood beside the dictating machine. Loren glanced at it; it was six minutes before three. She had done well. A year of catching planes, meeting trains and keeping spot appointments, had paid off in timing. It was all over, and she was safe. The tension could ebb away now, and the heaviness lift; and yet, it was all she could do to raise up the small black evening bag she had been clutching in her left hand, open it, and withdraw the gun. She held the gun cupped in the palm of her right hand. She looked about the room for some place to hide it; then, unable to look at it any longer, jammed it back into the bag and tossed it on the table beside the clock. The time—five minutes before three. It was close enough. She got up and switched off the machine. Then she removed her gloves, shoes, coat, and went into the bathroom. She left the door open—the shower could be heard for some distance at this hour—and returned exactly five minutes later wearing a filmy gown and negligee. She got into bed and now switched off the light; but now her eyes were caught by a glittering object that would not let them go. It was such a frivolous telephone—French styling sprayed with gold. It was magnetic and compelling. It seemed almost a living thing; and a living thing could be denounced.

"Not tonight," Loren said. "You won't ring tonight."

It had all started with a telephone call—long distance, Cairo to New York City.

"Mr. Banion calling Miss Loren Donell . . . thank you. Here's your party, Mr. Banion."

And then John's voice, annihilating miles.

"Loren—? Hold on tight. I've got one question: will you marry me?"

It could have happened only that way. John wasted neither time nor words. She had clung to the telephone, suddenly feeling quite schoolgirlish and dizzy.

"But, John, what about Celeste?"

"What about her? She's flipped over a Spanish bullfighter, and he's expensive. We've finally struck a deal. She's in Paris now getting a divorce."

"I can't believe it!"

"Neither can I, but it's true. I thought I'd never get rid of that—of my dear wife, Celeste." And then John's voice had become very serious. "You know what it's been like for me these past years, Loren. Celeste trapped me—I admit that. She wanted status and money, and she got both. I got—well, now I'm getting free and I suppose I should just be grateful for the education. Loren, I don't say these things well—but I love you."

At that moment, the telephone had been a lifeline pulling Loren out of the quicksand of loneliness. She clung to it until John's voice blasted her silence.

"Well! I want an answer! Will you marry me?"

Laughing and crying, she had answered, "Yes, yes, yes, yes—"

"Hold it!" John ordered. "While you're talking, I can be flying. See you tomorrow."

Tomorrow . . .

Rain at Idlewild—hard, slanting, and completely unnoticed as John bounded off the plane like a school boy. There was much to be done before the cable from Paris announced the divorce had been granted, and one of the many things concerned a change in office procedure. Loren discovered it one morning when she found her old office cleaned out, and, investigating, a new name on the door of the office next to John's.

LOREN BANION
VICE-PRESIDENT

"Only a little premature," he explained. "You might as well get used to the name."

"It's not the name—it's the title!" Loren exclaimed.

"Why not the title? You've been doing the job for years; I've only belatedly given you the status. Belatedly," he repeated, "this, too." It was then that he gave her the ring, almost shyly. "Oh, Loren, why does it take so long to learn to distinguish the real from the phoney? You are real, aren't you, Loren? You're not one of those scheming females."

"Oh, but I am," Loren insisted. "I've been deliberately getting under your nose for years."

John had laughed. Under his nose meant only one thing at the moment. He kissed her, quickly.

"That I like. That I'll buy any day. That's not what I meant. I meant that you're not one of the phonies—the honky-tonk phonies. All out front and nothing to live with. I want to grow old with you, Loren. You're the only—" He hesitated, groping for a word, "—the only pure woman I've ever known."

It was terrible how grave John's face had become. Loren drew away.

"Please—no pedestals," she protested. "It's so cold up there!"

"It's not cold here!"

He had taken her in his arms, then, and he was right. It was warm; it was a place to rest at last. But then his arms tightened, and his fingers dug into her arms until she wanted to cry out. It was the first shadow of fear to come.

"You're real," he said. "You have to be real. I couldn't stand being fooled again!"

"*I couldn't stand being fooled again!*"

Loren stared at the telephone on the table. It was silent; but John's words were ringing in her mind. She glanced at the clock. Sleep was impossible, but nothing could be unusual tonight, and within ten minutes after Loren Banion concluded her dictation, she always turned off the lamp. The darkness came—complete at first, and then a finger of moonlight from the open window probed across the carpet. Below, the silver sound of a girl's laughter was quickly muffled in sudden remembrance of the hour.

The hour. The hour was only ten minutes spent. The long hour before four . . .

The honeymoon had been in Miami and off-Miami waters. John was a fisherman—unsuccessful but incorrigible. Monday, Tuesday, Wednesday without a catch. It was no wonder Sam Mc-Gregor, an Atlanta account they had discovered vacationing at their hotel, had insisted on an hour of solace at the Flotsam and Jetsam on the beach. It was a shanty-type bar—one of the high bracket shanties—where the drinks were long and the shadows cool. Loren was too happy to see details in the Grotto-like shadows; but someone had seen clearly. Very clearly. It was an informal place for customers in shorts and bathing suits, and the only entertainment rippled from the busy fingers of a pianist in T shirt and dungarees who wheeled his diminutive instrument from booth to booth. He wasn't meant to be heard or noticed, and only rarely tipped; and Loren wasn't really aware of him at all until, above John's and Sam's ribbing laughter, a tinkling sound became a melody. She looked up. The small piano was no more than three feet away, and behind it sat a man she had never expected to see again.

"Don't sit under the apple tree with anyone else but me, . . ."

He played not too well; but he did enjoy his work. His smile seemed to indicate that he enjoyed it very much. His smile . . .

"Loren—are you all right?"

John's voice brought Loren back from the faraway place Loren's mind had gone reeling.

"You look shook up, honey. Don't tell me that you got seasick today. Honestly, Sam, this woman can take more punishment . . ."

When John's voice stopped, he couldn't have known too much then. That was impossible. But he seemed to sense that the piano player had something to do with Loren being disturbed. He pulled a bill out of his pocket and placed it on top of the piano.

"How about hoisting anchor, sailor?" he said. "I'm afraid we're not very musical in this booth."

The piano player's smile broadened and one hand closed over the bill. "Anything you say, Mr. Banion. I only thought it would be nice to salute the newlyweds."

"You know me?" John asked.

"Why, everybody knows you, Mr. Banion. Didn't you see your picture in the paper the day you flew down? Nice catch, Mr. Banion." And then, with another smile for Loren. "Nice catch, Mrs. Banion. A very nice catch."

The piano rolled on, picking up something with a calypso beat. The incident had taken only a moment, but having sensed that something was amiss, Sam had said brightly—

"Enterprising chap. They don't miss a trick down here. How about another round?"

Loren stood up. "You two—yes," she said. "No more for me. I'm going back to the hotel."

"Loren—why? What's wrong?"

John must not ask that question; he must not look that concerned. She laughed her gayest and confessed—

"I'm afraid you'll have to stop bragging about me, John. I did get seasick this afternoon, and now I'm almost hung on one drink. No—not hung enough for you to break this up. You stay on with Sam. I'm going to get some air."

Air, wind, and a long walk along the beach—nothing erased Ted Lockard. He should be dead. Men died in a war. They stopped answering letters, and they never came back. One assumed they had died. But not Ted. Ted was alive and his smooth voice, so thrilling to a girl, had an oily quality maturity could identify. There were men who lived off their charms, even as did some women.

"A nice catch, Mrs. Banion. A very nice catch."

Loren wasn't intoxicated, but she was sick. A girl had written wild, foolish letters, and Ted Lockard probably kept all of his love letters the way some men kept hunting trophies—or securities. He would try to reach her some way—she knew that. And she was vulnerable; not because of a youthful human failure, but because of John's conception of her. She had to be perfect in order to compensate his pride, for having been so deceived by Celeste.

Luck was with her. That night, a wire from Mexico City sending John south. Loren returned to New York. But it was only a reprieve.

Celeste returned from Europe just before Christmas, *sans* bullfighter and *sans* cash. There were telephone calls and wires, all ignored, and then, one day Celeste came to the office. John saw her. Loren wasn't aware of the meeting until it was over. John had asked her to go down to the docks and see Signor Manfredi's shipment through customs. The Signor's shipping department had only a vague idea of the transoceanic hazards for breakable materials. It was a task usually delegated to an employee of lesser status; but Loren thought nothing of it until she returned in time to pass Celeste in the outer office.

Celeste was icily majestic.

"Congratulations, Mrs. Banion," she said. "John looks in the pink. You always were a good manager."

Not too much—just enough. Celeste could make a prayer sound insulting.

Inside, Loren found John not at all in the pink. He was remote and grave.

"What was Celeste doing here?" she demanded.

"She came to wish us a Merry Christmas," John said bitterly.

Loren glanced down. John's checkbook was still on his desk.

"John—you gave her money!"

He didn't answer.

"Why? Hasn't she cost you enough? You don't owe her a thing!"

"Loyalty," John said.

His voice was strange.

"What?" Loren demanded.

"It's a word," John explained. "Just a word."

Then, suddenly, he turned toward her and grasped her shoulders with both hands, holding so tightly that she remembered what had happened the day he gave her the ring. For just an instant, she was actually afraid; and then he smiled sadly and let her go.

"Forget Celeste," he said. "It's a holiday season. I felt charitable."

Loren didn't. She left John abruptly and hurried back to the front office. Celeste was nowhere in sight. Katy sat at her desk, typing letters. She looked up as Loren spoke—

"Mrs. Ban—" she began, and then corrected herself. "The former Mrs. Banion—where did she go?"

"Out," Katy said.

Katy, sweet, wholesome, naive. What did she expect to learn from Katy? She strode across the reception room and entered the hall, arriving just in time to glimpse Celeste as she was being assisted into the elevator by an attentive man. They turned and faced her, and just before the doors closed Loren got a frontal view of Celeste's new adornment. Ted looked very handsome, and he smiled.

Merry Christmas, Loren. Merry Christmas and a Happy

New Year. Santa had come early. It was the beginning of a long wait, of not knowing what Ted might have told Celeste, or what Celeste might have told John, or when Ted would make his move. John said nothing. Her own tension was the only change between them. After a time, she began to think she was suffering from nothing but the ancient feminine penchant for borrowing guilt.

Then, in the middle of January, John took the night plane to Cleveland.

"You could leave in the morning and still make that meeting in time," Loren protested.

John was adamant.

"I like to fly at night. It's smoother and I sleep all the way."

"Then I'll work on the correspondence."

"You work too hard, Loren. Why don't you let Katy do that?"

"John—please. I know these people. I've been handling your correspondence with them since dear Katy was taking her first typing lessons and getting used to having teeth without braces. Don't you know that I'm jealous of my work?"

"I should know," John said. "I'm jealous, too—of you. But I don't have to worry, do I?" His fingers stroked her cheek lightly. "No, I don't have to worry—not about Loren."

Loren, who lived on a pedestal where the life expectancy was so short.

She had worked that night until almost three, showered, and gone to bed. Sleep came immediately after work. She had to fight her way out of it when the telephone rang. Groping for the instrument, she noticed the illuminated face of the clock. It was exactly four. Nobody ever called anyone at four o'clock in the morning unless something terrible had happened.

"John—?"

She waited, suddenly fully awake and afraid. There was no answer. And then it began, so brightly, so spritely—one full chorus of a piano rendition of an old war-time melody.

"Don't sit under the apple tree with anyone else but me . . ."

That was all.

The clock had always been silent. There was no reason for it to tick so loudly now. Loren stirred restlessly against the pillows. Aside from the clock, there was no other sound. Silence from the deck below. Cherry had closed up shop for the night. The moonlight brought objects on the table out of darkness. Loren's fingers found a cigarette, lighted it, and then she sat back smoking and remembering . . .

She never told John about the four o'clock call. It was Ted's signature, obviously; but what did he have in mind? For days and nights after that call she waited for his next move. Nothing happened. John returned from Cleveland to find her thinner and tense.

"Working too hard," he scolded. "Loren, I won't allow this to go on! Katy's going to take on at least a small part of your work."

She wanted to tell him about the call; but she couldn't tell a part without revealing the whole.

"*Then reveal the whole, Loren. John is a sane, adult human being. He'll laugh about it and send Ted packing.*"

"Do you remember the McGregors?" John asked suddenly. "Miami—our honeymoon?"

Loren remembered. Her mind had just been in the same vicinity.

"I met Sam in Cleveland. He's broken—literally broken. His wife has gone to Reno, and Sam's shot. I've seen that man fight his way through tight spots that would have staggered Superman; but this has got him. You women don't know what you can do to a man."

"Reno?" Loren echoed. "Why?"

John's face hardened. "The usual reason. Sam's a busy man. Little time to play Casanova. They don't have bullfighters in Atlanta; but they do have Casanovas. You would think a woman could tell the difference between love and flattery, wouldn't you? But no, it seems they all have the same weakness." And then the bitterness ebbed out of John's voice. "Except one," he added.

She told him nothing.

She continued to wait; but there was no word from Ted. Early in February, John flew to Denver on the night plane. Loren worked on correspondence until three and then retired; but she couldn't sleep. A vague uneasiness gnawed at her mind until four o'clock when the telephone rang and the uneasiness ceased to be vague.

The call was just as it had been before. No words at all—just that same gay piano serenade . . .

For the next few months, John's trips were frequent. It was the busy time of the year. On the first night of his next departure, she didn't try to sleep. At four o'clock, the telephone rang.

". . . don't sit under the apple tree with anyone else but me."

She tried having the call traced. It was useless. The caller was too clever. Clever, but purposeless. Aside from starting her nerves on a process of disintegration, the calls were inane. Ted was too practical minded to torture without a purpose. It was the kind of sadistic trick she might expect of a jealous rival.

"Celeste!"

At one minute past four, on a morning when John was flying to Omaha, Loren placed the telephone back in the cradle convinced that she'd hit upon the source of her troubles. Ted was more clever than she'd imagined. He'd gone to John Banion's ex-wife, rather than his present wife. He'd told her his story, and now Celeste was trying to break up John's marriage by torturing his wife into a breakdown. At one minute past four A.M., immediately following the fourth of the maddening calls, the scheme seemed obvious to Loren. Wear her down, weaken her, unnerve her, and then— She wasn't quite sure what Celeste meant to do then; but there was no reason to wait and see. Two could play this game!

Loren's mind became quite clear. She began to analyze. The calls came only on the first night of John's trips. Reason: had John been at home, he might have intercepted the calls. Furthermore, there was never any way of knowing how long he would be gone. The only way of avoiding him was to make the call immediately after his departure. This meant Celeste had access to John's plans.

On the following day, Loren spoke to Katy.

"Do you remember the day the former Mrs. Banion had an interview with Mr. Banion?" she asked.

Katy considered her answer only a moment.

"Yes, I do, Mrs. Banion."

"Did she come in alone?"

This time, Katy considered a bit longer.

"I don't think I remember—yes, I do. A man came with her. He waited in the reception room."

Ted, obviously.

"Have you seen him since?"

"No, Mrs. Banion."

But there were other girls in the office—young, impressionable. Ideal bait for Ted's charms.

"Katy, I want you to do something for me. Talk to the girls, casually, of course, and try to learn if any of them has a new, dreamy boyfriend."

Katy laughed.

"According to what I pick up in the lounge, most of them have a new, dreamy boyfriend every week."

"That's not what I mean! I mean one *certain* boyfriend."

She was making a mess of it. A casual inquiry was becoming an inquisition; but there was still one thing she must know.

"And Katy, on the day when the former Mrs. Banion had the interview with Mr. Banion, did you, by any chance, overhear anything that was said?"

"Overhear, Mrs. Banion?"

There was such a thing as being too naive, and Loren's patience had worn thin.

"Accidentally or otherwise," she snapped. "Oh, don't look so wounded. I had your job once, and I was ambitious and human. I listened; I spied. I know what goes on in an office. This is important to me, Katy. I'll make it worth your while if you can tell me anything—anything at all."

It was a foolish, weak, female thing to do, and Loren regretted her words as soon as they were spoken. Had Katy been shocked, it wouldn't have been so bad; but it was all Loren could do to suppress the desire to slap the hint of a smile she saw on Katy's face.

You're cracking up, Loren. You're losing control.

She held on tight, and Katy's smile faded.

"I'm sorry, Mrs. Banion. I didn't hear anything. But if I do hear anything, I'll let you know."

Loren went back to her office shaken at her own self-betrayal. Celeste was succeeding. Whatever her diabolical plan, she was succeeding. Never had she spoken to an employee as she had spoken to Katy. Never . . .

When John returned from Omaha, he found Loren confined to her bed.

"It's nothing," she insisted. "I think I had a touch of flu."

"You've had more than a touch of over-work," John said. "I warned you, Loren. Now I'm going to send you off on a vacation."

So Celeste can have a clear field. That's her game. It must be her game.

"No—!" Loren protested. "Not now! Not at a time like this!"

John's face became very grave. He sat down on the edge of the bed, still wearing his topcoat—his brief case and newspaper in his hand. These he placed on the bed beside her.

"You've heard, then," he said. "Loren, there's no reason to be upset. It isn't as if she meant anything to me—or had meant anything to me for years. In fact—" There were times when John's mouth hardened and became almost cruel. "—I'd be a liar if I pretended to be sorry."

The newspaper had fallen open on the bed. While she was still trying to understand John, Loren's glance dropped and was held by the photograph of a familiar face. Celeste. She drew the paper closer until she could read the story. Celeste had been in an auto accident upstate. Celeste was dead.

Celeste was dead. It was horrible to feel so happy; and impossible not to. The pressure was gone. Her diabolical scheme would never materialize. Within a few days, Loren was herself again.

Three weeks later, John flew to San Francisco. Loren worked late, as usual, retired, and slept soundly—until four o'clock in the morning when the telephone rang.

The serenade continued.

A siren was sobbing somewhere in the street below. The sound brought Loren through time back to the immediate. She snuffed out her cigarette in a now cluttered tray, and her eyes found the clock again. Three forty-five. The sound of the siren faded; but now she sat upright, her heart pounding. Why was she afraid? She had been methodical and efficient and decisive. That was the important thing—decisive.

"The thing to remember about business, Miss Donell, is that an executive must learn to make decisions and stand by them. You may be right, you may be wrong—but make the decision!"

That had been John Banion instructing his new secretary—eager, ambitious, and—why not face it—already in love with her boss. It had taken six years for him to recognize that love and turn to her when he finally discovered what everyone else had known about Celeste all along; and in the meantime, Loren had learned to be decisive.

Decisive. The first four o'clock call after Celeste's death removed all doubts. It was Ted; and it was her move. But where was Ted? It would have been easy enough to trace Celeste; but Ted was another matter. She didn't want to use a private investigator and leave a trail that could be traced. The solution to her problem came from an unexpected source: Katy.

"Mrs. Banion, do you recall asking about the man who was with the former Mrs. Banion when she came to the office just before Christmas?"

It was two weeks after Celeste's death. Loren didn't look up from her desk; she mustn't betray her excitement.

"What about him?" she asked casually.

"It's a peculiar coincidence; but I had to run an errand for Mr. Banion across town yesterday, and I saw the man. He was going into a small hotel—The Lancer. I think he must live there. He had a bundle under his arm that looked like laundry."

"You're very observant," Loren said dryly.

"You did ask—"

Loren looked up, smiling.

"Ancient history," she said, "but thanks anyway. You're a diligent girl."

Loren wasn't so casual later when she drove to the Lancer Hotel, parked across the street and watched the entrance until she saw Ted come out. It was a shabby hotel in a shabby neighborhood; Celeste hadn't, obviously, contributed much to Ted's economic security. This wasn't a condition Ted could long endure. She watched him walk from the hotel to a bowling alley at the end of the block, and then went into a drug store phone booth to verify his registration at the hotel. That done, she went to work.

The first thing to be done was to obtain a recording of a piano solo of Ted's theme. This, for a small fee, was easily accomplished. For a somewhat larger fee, she then obtained a small wire recorder of a type that could be carried in a handbag or a coat pocket. At home, she transferred the record onto the tape, adding a personal touch at the conclusion, "We can reach an understanding if you will meet me behind the bowling alley at 2 A.M."

She destroyed the record and put the wire recorder away until John's next business trip. On the first Thursday in March, he took the night plane to Chicago. As soon as she knew he was leaving, Loren did two things: she recorded two hours of correspondence on the dictating machine in her bedroom, and reserved two tickets at a playhouse.

Katy begged off from the theatre.

"I'd love to, Mrs. Banion, but it's the wrong night. You see, I have a friend—"

"Then hang on to him," Loren said. "A good man's hard to find. I'll ask someone else."

An out-of-town customer had nothing to do for the evening. Anyone was acceptable as long as she had a companion. She drove to the theatre in her own car. During the first intermission, she excused herself and went to a telephone booth in the lobby. She took the wire recorder from her bag, dialed Ted's hotel, and waited for his voice. As soon as he answered, she switched on the recorder and held it to the mouth-piece. When the recording was concluded, she hung up the telephone, replaced the recorder in her bag, and returned to her place in the theatre.

It was twelve-thirty, when Loren returned to her apartment the the first time. She left her car parked in the street, as she frequently did after the garage attendant had gone off duty. It was safe. Every hour on the hour, Officer Hanlon made his rounds. She wanted the car to be seen. In the lobby, she met other theatre and party-going tenants returning home, and rode up in the elevator with them. She went directly to her room and put the wire recorder away in the drawer of the work table in her bedroom, transferring the gun to her handbag in its place. Then she set up the dictating machine, opened the bedroom windows enough to make certain the words would be heard on the deck below and waited until exactly one o'clock before turning on the machine. It was time to go.

She went down in the service elevator and left the building through the alley—unseen. She didn't take the car. She walked a distance and caught a cab, took the cab to within six blocks of Ted's hotel and walked the rest of the way. At two o'clock, she was waiting in the shadows behind the bowling alley. Ted was only a few minutes late. He advanced close enough for her to see the surprised recognition in his eyes before she fired. A strike in the bowling alley covered the shots. Ted fell and didn't move again. When she was certain that he was dead, Loren walked away—not hurriedly, but at a normal pace. The streets were almost empty at this hour, but within a few blocks she found a cab, rode to within six blocks of her apartment, and walked the rest of the way. The service entrance was locked, but the front lobby was empty.

It was exactly ten minutes before three when Loren returned to her apartment . . .

. . . The sound of the siren faded away, but not the pounding of Loren's heart. It was as if she had been in a kind of sleep-walker's trance, and now she became horribly aware of the fact that she was a murderess. The horror didn't lie in the fact that

Ted was dead—she cared no more for that than John had cared about Celeste's death. It was something else. Fear—but what could go wrong? She'd been at the theatre, with an escort, when the hotel switchboard had handled Ted's call. She'd left her windows open so Cherry Morgan could hear her voice. She left her car on the street, and come up in the elevator with friends. She'd destroyed the record—the wire recorder. Loren was out of bed in an instant. She ripped open the table drawer, opened the recorder, and pulled free the wire. She wiped it clean on the skirts of her negligee. No evidence. There was no way to connect her with the body the police would find behind a bowling alley in a shabby neighborhood across town; but there must be no evidence. The wire was clean. What else? Katy had told her where to find Ted; but she didn't even know his name. John—? No matter what Celeste might have told John, he would never connect her with Ted's murder.

But the gun. She should have gotten rid of the gun. She snatched it out of the handbag and began to look about for a hiding place. The echo of the police siren was still in her ears, and reason wouldn't still it. The gun was the one damning piece of evidence. She stood with it in her hands, turning about, directionlessly—and the doorbell rang.

When Loren went to the door, it was with a gun in her hands and doom in her mind. Just in time, she remembered to stuff the weapon under a cushion of the divan, and then go on to open the door. Officer Hanlon stood in the lighted hall looking all of nine feet tall.

"Mrs. Banion," he said, "I'm sure sorry to disturb you at this hour, but there was no one on duty downstairs."

She couldn't speak a word. Not one.

"I didn't know where to leave this."

He held up a set of keys, dangling them before her eyes. It was some seconds before she recognized them.

"You left them in your car, Mrs. Banion. I noticed the window was down when I went past at one o'clock, but I didn't think I could do anything about it without some way to turn on the ignition. It started to sprinkle a few minutes ago, so I stopped to see what I could do. I found these. You're getting careless, Mrs. Banion."

Loren saw her hand reach out and take the keys; it might have been detached from her body.

"Thank you," she said. "Is that all?"

"That's all, Mrs. Banion. Sorry to get you out of bed, but I didn't know what else to do."

Loren closed the door, then leaned against it—listening until she could hear Hanlon go down in the elevator. Only the keys? She wanted to laugh, and she wanted to cry. Most of all, she wanted John. She wanted to cling to him, to bury her head on his shoulder and be safe. The weeks of terror were over, and all Hanlon had wanted was to give her the keys! John was gone, but his room was next to hers. She ran to it, turned on the light, and went to the chair behind his desk. Soft, rich leather with the feel of John in it—the contour of his back, the worn places where he'd gripped the arm rests. And then Loren's eyes fell on the desk. For a moment, she was afraid John had gone off without his ticket. The airline envelope was there. She looked inside. The ticket was gone. *I'm becoming a neurotic woman who worries about everything*, she thought. And then she noticed what was written on the envelope in the time of departure line: 8:00 A.M.

The sixth was Friday. 8:00 A.M. was in the morning. This morning—not Thursday night.

It had to be a mistake. The airline office was open all night. She dialed quickly.

"John Banion? . . . What flight did you say? No, there was no John Banion on the nine o'clock flight to Chicago . . . The eight o'clock this morning? . . . Yes. We have a reservation for John Banion . . . Who is this calling? . . . Oh, Mrs. Banion. Your husband flies with us frequently. He always takes the daytime flights. Always."

Loren put the telephone back on John's desk, and stood listening to the words of a story. It had begun with John's fingers digging into her arms.

"*I couldn't stand being fooled again!*" he'd said.

And then, on the day Celeste had come to see him—

"*Loyalty,*" John said. "*It's a word. Just a word.*"

"Oh, no, John," Loren whispered.

"*I like to fly at night,*" John said. "*It's smoother and I—*"

"John, no—"

But it had to be John. He'd seen her face that day in Miami when Ted played an old melody. He'd gotten some story from Celeste—enough of a story to induce him to buy her silence, and immediately afterwards the calls had begun. And where was John when he didn't take the night flights he was supposed to take? With a cold certainty, Loren knew. Men lived by patterns. He had turned to his secretary once, and now—hadn't Katy been the one who had told her where to find Ted? Katy, who couldn't go to the theatre because she was expecting a friend? Katy, that not so naive child who *did* listen at the boss' door . . .

And Ted Lockard was dead. Loren remembered that when the telephone in her bedroom started ringing. She turned and walked slowly and obediently into her room. She picked up the telephone and listened to the music with an expressionless face. It was four o'clock. It was time for John's serenade.

DOROTHY B. HUGHES

1904–1993

DOROTHY B. HUGHES, at the time of the publication of her debut suspense novel, *The So Blue Marble* in 1940, had worked as a journalist and published a book of poetry, *Dark Certainty*, nine years earlier. The crime genre gave Hughes her true voice, one mixing a terse, hard-bitten style with a deep understanding of her flawed protagonists, who struggle to stay true to themselves as larger criminal forces threaten to overwhelm them.

The eleven novels Hughes wrote and published from 1940 to 1947 include incomparable classic noirs like *The Fallen Sparrow* (1942), a spy thriller and keen study of post-traumatic stress in the midst of war; *The Blackbirder* (1943), featuring a heroine of the Resistance who shows her fear but never lets it define her; *Dread Journey* (1945), which uses its claustrophobic cross-country train setting to brilliant effect as it dissects the corrosive qualities of Hollywood; *Ride the Pink Horse* (1946), where a man's revenge plans and sense of doom play out against the wide-open New Mexico plains; and her greatest masterpiece *In a Lonely*

Place (1947), in which an army veteran's Los Angeles serial murder spree turns would-be female victims into heroines, and is a masterful look at the psychopathic personality.

Hughes's writing pace trickled and then stopped completely for over a decade as she found that caring for infirm family members sapped her ability to write fiction, but her final novel, *The Expendable Man* (1963), brilliantly dissected the burgeoning Civil Rights movement and lingering racial prejudice with a single narrative twist. Hughes later published a biography of Erle Stanley Gardner, creator of the Perry Mason novels, and remained a prolific reviewer of crime fiction for the likes of the *Los Angeles Times* and the *Albuquerque Tribune*, but she didn't abandon fiction altogether, publishing original short fiction as late as 1991, two years before her death.

"Everybody Needs a Mink," which first appeared in *The Saint Mystery Magazine* in 1965, at first seems a departure from the customary foreboding dread of Hughes's best novels. Meg Tashman, a socialite living in a Westchester County town, cultivates an air of frivolity on a day trip to Manhattan as she shops for luxury goods at Randolph's department store. Lurking beneath the surface, however, is pressing anxiety about living beyond one's means, and playing the part of one class while feeling like a fraud. When Meg's desire for the mink coat is unexpectedly and shockingly fulfilled, it's just the first of a series of surprises for both Meg and the reader.

EVERYBODY NEEDS A MINK

ONE WAS dusty rose brocade, tranquil as an arras in a forsaken castle. One was a waterfall of gold, shimmering from a secret jungle cache. And there was, of course, the stiletto of black, cut to here and here—the practical one, as it would go everywhere—and she had the black evening slippers from last year, like new for they went out only to the New Year's Eve and Mardi Gras dances at the club, and the annual office executive dinner at the Biltmore. With her pearls, single strand, good cultured, Christmas present two years ago from Tashi—black and pearls, always good.

She selected the gold. She'd dash down to Florida and pick up a copper tan before the Christmas party, or maybe Hawaii. Or a week in Arizona, quite chic. She could buy gold slippers and hunky gold jewelry. When you were selecting, you didn't have to think practical, you could let yourself go.

And the only fun on a shopping tour to the city for underpants and sox and polo shirts for second-grader Ron, and two jumpers and calico blouses and sox for fourth-grader Stancia, in the before-school sale at Randolph's—the only fun was in selecting. For when the Tashman ship came in, when the long-lost uncle in Australia left them his fortune, when in the some-day, never-never land future, they became rich, astronomically rich. . . .

And now for a fur, because Meggy Tashman, that soignee young socialite of Larksville-nearly-on-the-Hudson, could hardly be expected to appear in a waterfall of gold with her old black velvet double duty raincoat and evening wrap. She moved the few steps from the French Room entrance arch to the Fur Salon entrance arch. And there it was. Like a precious jewel impaled on the arms of an emerald tree. The perfect mink. A deep brown, exquisitely matched, full-length mink.

She didn't have to look further. This was it. Practical too. Something to cover the beat-up terry jump suit when she drove the children to school. Something to sling over the faded blues and Tash's old shirt on the dash from the vacuum cleaner to the supermarket. Mink was so durable. A lifetime investment. So rich, so utter, utterly rich.

"Miss." The voice came from the Louis XV chair near the mink. In the chair was a small, elderly man. Near him, smoothed into black crepe, towered one of those living store dummies who sold furs, hair and face lacquered in gold and red and lavender.

"Miss!" the voice said just a little louder. A stubby forefinger beckoned. The button eyes held in place by a network of weathered wrinkles seemed to be looking directly at Meg. The finger seemed to be beckoning to her.

She half-shifted her position in order to glance over her shoulder. There was no one behind her. She looked in at the man again. His hat bobbed; he was wearing his hat and overcoat.

"She's just the right size," he was saying to the saleslady. He gave a very small and very timid smile at Meg. "Would you mind modeling it, Miss?"

Meg advanced through the arch to the man and the mink. "Model this?" she asked, not quite believing.

"If it isn't too much trouble."

"You're the right size, Modom," the saleslady intoned through her haughty nose. Then she tried to smile, because after all Meg was a customer, too, witness the bulging, sage-green paper sacks with the legend "Randolph's" spelled out on them in paler green. It wasn't much of a smile, but you had to be careful with lacquer.

"It's no trouble at all," Meg gave the little man a real smile. "I'd love to."

She deposited on the ocher satin love seat, the paper sacks, her own coat, and her scuffed, tan leather purse. The saleslady helped her into the mink. Exactly the right size.

As it settled on her shoulders, Meg breathed, "Ohhh!" She had meant to be sophisticated about it. As if she had a mink for every day of the week; as if she only wore the old brown and white checkered wool for sales shopping at Randolph's.

"You like it?" the man wondered.

"Ohhh!" Her voice sounded like a silly teenager but she didn't care. "It's the most beautiful thing I've ever seen." She swooped the fur about her and half-turned, mannikin style. "It is simply—simply supernal."

The old man smiled. The salesperson smiled. She ought to, with the commission she'd make on this sale.

"I've got to see it," Meg exclaimed. She half-danced to the pier mirror supported by gilt plaster cupids at the rear of the salon. When she beheld herself in the coat, she stopped breathing. She erased the young joyous excitement from her flushed face and posed in elegance, simple $10,000 mink elegance. She wished Stancia could see her. She wished Tash and Ron could see her. But she didn't wish for the coat. There was a point where wishes were too far out.

The saleslady's reflection came up behind her in the mirror. Smiling all over this time. She'd made the sale. Meggy slipped out of the coat and said, woman to woman, "It is gorgeous."

The woman placed it reverently on another Louis XV chair. "You'd like your initials in it?" Her pencil pointed on her sales pad.

"But certainly," Meg said, playing the game. "M.O.T."

"Old English? Or Modern?"

"Old English, of course," Meg said, just as hoity-toity. She went back to the love seat and retrieved her good old checkered.

The woman followed her. "May I have your name, please?"

This was carrying the game too far. "What for?" Meg asked. She wasn't about to get on any special mink list; there was enough junk mail to dispose of. She'd had her moment.

"For delivery," the woman suggested. And added, not quite so sure of herself, "You'd like us to deliver it, wouldn't you?"

"Deliver what?" Meg shouldered her oversize handbag, tried to heft the sacks into a better carrying position.

"The coat."

"That mink coat?" Meg gestured with her free elbow.

"Yes."

Meg began to laugh. "I couldn't afford a coat like that in a million years."

"He bought it." The saleslady spoke plainly. "He bought it, for you."

Meg's eyes slipped to the chair where he'd been sitting, but he wasn't there anymore. She returned her gaze to the face of the woman. Speculation in it now.

"He asked me to have it delivered, to whatever address you gave."

"Are you nuts?" Meg demanded flatly.

Sliding off her rarefied perch, the woman returned just as flatly, "No, I'm not nuts." Then awe came into her mouth. "He paid cash. Eleven one thousand dollar bills. Cash!"

Meg shook her head. "It must be a gag," she said slowly.

"I'd like to be on the receiving end of a gag like that." The pencil poised again, "Your name and address?"

Meg gave her name and address.

She went down the escalator, outside, down the subway steps, train to Times Square, shuttle to Grand Central. There was time for a coke and to buy the children each a sack of gold-covered coins. She didn't think about the mad, mad episode at all. It kept galloping through her head like a steeplechase, but she didn't think about it.

She caught the fourish, well ahead of the commuter crowds; time to get home, gather the children from neighbor Betts (look after hers next week); get dinner, pack the children to bed, wait for Tash to come home from his upstate appointment.

It was a gag, of course. One of those TV things. Instead of the coat would be delivered a toupeed, not as young as he thought he was man, who'd burble, "So sorry, Mrs. Tashman, but you made a mistake. However, we are giving you absolutely free this frying pan and one dozen eggs." She'd throw the eggs right in his toothy teeth. She decided she wouldn't tell Tash about it. Not that she'd accepted or expected the coat, but being the butt of a practical joke was too humiliating. Anyway, by now the little old man's keeper would have caught up with him and his play money.

The coat arrived on Monday. In the green van from Randolph's with a driver who couldn't care less, just sign here, Mrs. Tashman, and here's your receipt. Not like when you sent sheets or underwear; they were dumped on the doorstep.

It was the same mink. The absolute same mink. Only the initials M.O.T. were now embroidered in the satin lining. She didn't put it on. It was a firecracker ready to explode. She stroked it and looked at it and then stashed it at the deep, dark rear of her closet.

She didn't mention it until the family was at dinner. Then she said, "The funniest thing happened to me when I was shopping in the city last week."

"Like what?" Tash asked, dutiful husband, his mouth full of meat pie.

She told the story. Just as it happened. Ron couldn't have cared less. A coat was a dull coat at six and three-fourths years, something you had to wear in winter. Stancia's face shone with acceptance of all the magic in all the fairy tales. Tash queried, "You mean he gave you a mink coat, just like that?" He was a modern, intelligent young husband. Not one of those old-fashioned, suspicious, my-wife's-got-a-secret-lover guys. "The broccoli, please, Stancy."

"What'll I do?" Meg wanted to know.

"Wear it," Tash stated practically. "Everybody needs a mink. Eat your salad, Ron."

The telephone rang. It was Betts, could Meg take her children Thursday instead of Friday? Meg could. She went upstairs, unstashed the coat, put it on. She returned to the dining room.

Ron noticed first. "Is that it?" Uninterested.

Stancia and Tash popped to attention.

"It wasn't pretend?" Stancia asked.

Tash echoed his daughter. "You mean it really happened?"

"It did," Meg assured them.

They all thought up reasons. Ron settled on Superman.

"But this was an old man."

"Disguised." Ron was shrewd.

Stancia dreamed. "You reminded him of his dear daughter who died young and who never had a mink coat."

"Must have been a crook—getting rid of some dough he couldn't be caught with. Counterfeit." But Tash himself nixed that idea. "No. The store would have checked." He tried again. "Income tax write-off. You know, a gift."

Stancia was carried away. "He had only a week to live. Leukemia." Nine-year-olds knew about everything. "He was all alone. He wanted to make one beautiful gesture before joining his loved ones."

"Zrrp!" cried Ron. "Into the secret room. Put on wrinkles. Overcoat and hat. Zrrp to Randolph's."

But Meg and Tash worried it seriously. For at least a month. Tash had to have answers to problems.

Then the picture was in the paper. An old-time gangster, off to prison on income tax evasion. At first she thought it was her man. The same pulled-down hat, the same type overcoat. It wasn't of course. Her man had a sweet, secret smile not a tight-lipped glare.

But she told Tash, "It could be." And when he looked so hopeful, "It really could be." And, finally, her fingers crossed for what must be a lie, "It really is." She relaxed in his relieved sigh. Tonight he would enjoy TV. She warned, "Don't tell the children!"

"Don't tell anybody," he stressed.

The temperature dropped sharply that weekend.

Tash said, "You might as well get the good of it while you have it. Just in case Uncle Jabez decides to turn it into a pumpkin."

She wore the coat to the school dinner, explained to friends, "A gift from my uncle."

"The rich one," Tash abetted. "Lives in Australia."

She wore it to the PTA and the supermarket and the parties and the executive dinner and everywhere. Always with joy and tenderness. And a little feather of sadness.

Because she could never say, "Thank you," to the little old man. Because he could never know what it meant to her. Unless. Unless he remembered her face at that first moment when he chose her to wear mink.

JOYCE HARRINGTON

1932–2011

By the time JOYCE HARRINGTON published the very first short story she ever wrote in 1972, she had already led several lives. Born in Jersey City, New Jersey, and raised in Southern California, Harrington pursued work as an actress, training at the Pasadena Playhouse alongside Harry Dean Stanton and Robert Duvall. Upon her 1961 marriage to photojournalist Philip Harrington, she raised two children and worked for a time with the American Society of Magazine Photographers. But when *LOOK* magazine, which supplied the bulk of the Harrington family's income, closed in 1972, she turned her attention to writing. That first short story, "The Purple Shroud," was not only published in *Ellery Queen's Mystery Magazine*, it won the Edgar Award for Best Short Story the following year.

From then on, Harrington proved to be one of *EQMM's* most prolific contributors throughout the 1970s and 1980s, with her work also appearing in *Alfred Hitchcock's Mystery Magazine* on a regular basis. Harrington also wrote three novels: *No One Knows My Name* (1981), *Family Reunion* (1982), and *Dreemz of the*

Night (1987). In parallel she worked in the advertising industry and was named vice president and director of public relations for Foote, Cone & Belding in 1986. When her health began to decline in the late 1990s, Harrington retired from writing, spending the last decade of her life as a devoted reader.

Retirement, along with greater fame as a short story writer, may be why Harrington's fiction work hasn't received the attention it deserves. She was primarily concerned with human behavior and the motives for sliding into nefarious deeds, with twists that disturbed in their quiet intensity. It's no wonder "The Purple Shroud" fared so well upon publication: its depiction of a toxic marriage and how a subjugated woman finds her way out still resonates today.

THE PURPLE SHROUD

MRS. MOON threw the shuttle back and forth and pumped the treadles of the big four-harness loom as if her life depended on it. When they asked what she was weaving so furiously, she would laugh silently and say it was a shroud.

"No, really, what is it?"

"My house needs new draperies." Mrs. Moon would smile and the shuttle would fly and the beater would thump the newly woven threads tightly into place. The muffled, steady sounds of her craft could be heard from early morning until very late at night, until the sounds became an accepted and expected background noise and were only noticed in their absence.

Then they would say, "I wonder what Mrs. Moon is doing now."

That summer, as soon as they had arrived at the art colony and even before they had unpacked, Mrs. Moon requested that the largest loom in the weaving studio be installed in their cabin. Her request had been granted because she was a serious weaver, and because her husband, George, was one of the best painting instructors they'd ever had. He could coax the amateurs into stretching their imaginations and trying new ideas and techniques, and he would bully the scholarship students until, in a fury, they would sometimes produce works of surprising originality.

George Moon was, himself, only a competent painter. His work had never caught on, although he had a small loyal following in Detroit and occasionally sold a painting. His only concessions to the need for making a living and for buying paints and brushes was to teach some ten hours a week throughout the winter and to take this summer job at the art colony, which was also their vacation. Mrs. Moon taught craft therapy at a home for the aged.

After the loom had been set up in their cabin Mrs. Moon waited. Sometimes she went swimming in the lake, sometimes she drove into town and poked about in the antique shops, and sometimes she just sat in the wicker chair and looked at the loom.

They said, "What are you waiting for, Mrs. Moon? When are you going to begin?"

One day Mrs. Moon drove into town and came back with two boxes full of brightly colored yarns. Classes had been going on for about two weeks, and George was deeply engaged with his students. One of the things the students loved about George was the extra time he gave them. He was always ready to sit for hours on the porch of the big house, just outside the communal dining room, or under a tree, and talk about painting or about life as a painter or tell stories about painters he had known.

George looked like a painter. He was tall and thin, and with approaching middle age he was beginning to stoop a little. He had black snaky hair which he had always worn on the long side, and which was beginning to turn gray. His eyes were very dark, so dark you couldn't see the pupils, and they regarded every-thing and everyone with a probing intensity that evoked un-easiness in some and caused young girls to fall in love with him.

Every year George Moon selected one young lady disciple to be his summer consort.

Mrs. Moon knew all about these summer alliances. Every year, when they returned to Detroit, George would confess to her with great humility and swear never to repeat his transgression.

"Never again, Arlene," he would say. "I promise you, never again."

Mrs. Moon would smile her forgiveness.

Mrs. Moon hummed as she sorted through the skeins of purple and deep scarlet, goldenrod yellow and rich royal blue. She hummed as she wound the glowing hanks into fat balls, and she thought about George and the look that had passed between him and the girl from Minneapolis at dinner the night before. George had not returned to their cabin until almost two in the morning. The girl from Minneapolis was short and plump, with a round face and a halo of fuzzy red-gold hair. She reminded Mrs. Moon of a Teddy bear; she reminded Mrs. Moon of herself twenty years before.

When Mrs. Moon was ready to begin, she carried the pur-ple yarn to the weaving studio.

"I have to make a very long warp," she said. "I'll need to use the warping reel."

She hummed as she measured out the seven feet and a little over, then sent the reel spinning.

"Is it wool?" asked the weaving instructor.

"No, it's orlon," said Mrs. Moon. "It won't shrink, you know."

Mrs. Moon loved the creak of the reel, and she loved feeling the warp threads grow fatter under her hands until at last each planned thread was in place and she could tie the bundle and braid up the end. When she held the plaited warp in her hands she imagined it to be the shorn tresses of some enormously powerful earth goddess whose potency was now transferred to her own person.

That evening after dinner, Mrs. Moon began to thread the loom. George had taken the rowboat and the girl from Minneapolis to the other end of the lake where there was a deserted cottage. Mrs. Moon knew he kept a sleeping bag there, and a cache of wine and peanuts. Mrs. Moon hummed as she carefully threaded the eye of each heddle with a single purple thread, and thought of black widow spiders and rattlesnakes coiled in the corners of the dark cottage.

She worked contentedly until midnight and then went to bed. She was asleep and smiling when George stumbled in two hours later and fell into bed with his clothes on.

Mrs. Moon wove steadily through the summer days. She did not attend the weekly critique sessions for she had nothing to show and was not interested in the problems others were having with their work. She ignored the Saturday night parties where George and the girl from Minneapolis and the others danced and drank beer and slipped off to the beach or the boathouse. Sometimes, when she tired of the long hours at the loom, she would go for solitary walks in the woods and always brought back curious trophies of her rambling. The small cabin, already crowded with the loom and the iron double bedstead, began to fill up with giant toadstools, interesting bits of wood, arrangements of reeds and wild wheat.

One day she brought back two large black stones on which

she painted faces. The eyes of the faces were closed and the mouths were faintly curved in archaic smiles. She placed one stone on each side of the fireplace.

George hated the stones. "Those damn stonefaces are watching me," he said. "Get them out of here."

"How can they be watching you? Their eyes are closed."

Mrs. Moon left the stones beside the fireplace and George soon forgot to hate them. She called them Apollo I and Apollo II.

The weaving grew and Mrs. Moon thought it the best thing she had ever done. Scattered about the purple ground were signs and symbols which she saw against the deep blackness of her closed eyelids when she thought of passion and revenge, of love and wasted years and the child she had never had. She thought the barbaric colors spoke of these matters, and she was pleased.

"I hope you'll finish it before the final critique," the weaving teacher said when she came to the cabin to see it. "It's very good."

Word spread through the camp and many of the students came to the cabin to see the marvelous weaving. Mrs. Moon was proud to show it to them and received their compliments with quiet grace.

"It's too fine to hang at a window," said one practical Sunday-painting matron. "The sun will fade the colors."

"I'd love to wear it," said the life model.

"You!" said a bearded student of lithography. "It's a robe for a pagan king!"

"Perhaps you're right," said Mrs. Moon, and smiled her happiness on all of them.

———

The season was drawing to a close when in the third week of August, Mrs. Moon threw the shuttle for the last time. She slumped on the backless bench and rested her limp hands on the breast beam of the loom. Tomorrow she would cut the warp.

That night, while George was showing color slides of his paintings in the main gallery, the girl from Minneapolis came alone to the Moons' cabin. Mrs. Moon was lying on the bed watching a spider spin a web in the rafters. A fire was blazing in the fireplace, between Apollo I and Apollo II, for the late summer night was chill.

"You must let him go," said the golden-haired Teddy bear. "He loves me."

"Yes, dear," said Mrs. Moon.

"You don't seem to understand. I'm talking about George." The girl sat on the bed. "I think I'm pregnant."

"That's nice," said Mrs. Moon. "Children are a blessing, Watch the spider."

"We have a real relationship going. I don't care about being married—that's too feudal. But you must free George to come and be a father image to the child."

"You'll get over it," said Mrs. Moon, smiling a trifle sadly at the girl.

"Oh, you don't even want to know what's happening!" cried the girl. "No wonder George is bored with you."

"Some spiders eat their mates after fertilization," Mrs. Moon remarked. "Female spiders."

The girl flounced angrily from the cabin, as far as one could be said to flounce in blue jeans and sweatshirt.

George performed his end-of-summer separation ritual simply and brutally the following afternoon. He disappeared after lunch. No one knew where he had gone. The girl from Minneapolis roamed the camp, trying not to let anyone know she was searching for him. Finally she rowed herself down to the other end of the lake, to find that George had dumped her transistor radio, her books of poetry, and her box of incense on the damp sand, and had put a padlock on the door of the cottage.

She threw her belongings into the boat and rowed back to the camp, tears of rage streaming down her cheeks. She beached the boat, and with head lowered and shoulders hunched she stormed the Moons' cabin. She found Mrs. Moon tying off the severed warp threads.

"Tell George," she shouted, "tell George I'm going back to Minneapolis. He knows where to find me!"

"Here, dear," said Mrs. Moon, "hold the end and walk backwards while I unwind it."

The girl did as she was told, caught by the vibrant colors and Mrs. Moon's concentration. In a few minutes the full length of cloth rested in the girl's arms.

"Put it on the bed and spread it out," said Mrs. Moon. "Let's take a good look at it."

"I'm really leaving," whispered the girl. "Tell him I don't care if I never see him again."

"I'll tell him." The wide strip of purple flowed garishly down the middle of the bed between them. "Do you think he'll like it?" asked Mrs. Moon. "He's going to have it around for a long time."

"The colors are very beautiful, very savage." The girl looked closely at Mrs. Moon. "I wouldn't have thought you would choose such colors."

"I never did before."

"I'm leaving now."

"Goodbye," said Mrs. Moon.

George did not reappear until long after the girl had loaded up her battered bug of a car and driven off. Mrs. Moon knew he had been watching and waiting from the hill behind the camp. He came into the cabin whistling softly and began to take his clothes off.

"God, I'm tired," he said.

"It's almost dinner time."

"Too tired to eat," he yawned. "What's that on the bed?"

"My weaving is finished. Do you like it?"

"It's good. Take it off the bed. I'll look at it tomorrow."

Mrs. Moon carefully folded the cloth and laid it on the weaving bench. She looked at George's thin naked body before he got into bed, and smiled.

"I'm going to dinner now," she said.

"Okay. Don't wake me up when you get back. I could sleep for a week."

"I won't wake you up," said Mrs. Moon.

Mrs. Moon ate dinner at a table by herself. Most of the students had already left. A few people, the Moons among them, usually stayed on after the end of classes to rest and enjoy the isolation. Mrs. Moon spoke to no one.

After dinner she sat on the pier and watched the sunset. She watched the turtles in the shallow water and thought she saw a blue heron on the other side of the lake. When the sky was black and the stars were too many to count, Mrs. Moon went to the toolshed and got a wheelbarrow. She rolled this to the door of her cabin and went inside.

The cabin was dark and she could hear George's steady heavy

breathing. She lit two candles and placed them on the mantelshelf. She spread her beautiful weaving on her side of the bed, gently so as not to disturb the sleeper. Then she quietly moved the weaving bench to George's side of the bed, near his head.

She sat on the bench for a time, memorizing the lines of his face by the wavering candlelight. She touched him softly on the forehead with the pads of her fingertips and gently caressed his eyes, his hard cheeks, his raspy chin. His breathing became uneven and she withdrew her hands, sitting motionless until his sleep rhythm was restored.

Then Mrs. Moon took off her shoes. She walked carefully to the fireplace, taking long quiet steps. She placed her shoes neatly side by side on the hearth and picked up the larger stone, Apollo I. The face of the kouros, the ancient god, smiled up at her and she returned that faint implacable smile. She carried the stone back to the bench beside the bed, and set it down.

Then she climbed onto the bench, and when she stood, she found she could almost touch the spider's web in the rafters. The spider crouched in the heart of its web, and Mrs. Moon wondered if spiders ever slept.

Mrs. Moon picked up Apollo I, and with both arms raised, took careful aim. Her shadow, cast by candlelight, had the appearance of a priestess offering sacrifice. The stone was heavy and her arms grew weak. Her hands let go. The stone dropped.

George's eyes flapped open and he saw Mrs. Moon smiling tenderly down on him. His lips drew back to scream, but his mouth could only form a soundless hole.

"Sleep, George," she whispered, and his eyelids clamped over his unbelieving eyes.

Mrs. Moon jumped off the bench. With gentle fingers she

probed beneath his snaky locks until she found a satisfying soft-
ness. There was no blood and for this Mrs. Moon was grateful.
It would have been a shame to spoil the beauty of her patterns
with superfluous colors and untidy stains. Her mothlike fingers
on his wrist warned her of a faint uneven fluttering.

She padded back to the fireplace and weighed in her hands
the smaller, lighter Apollo II. This time she felt there was no
need for added height. With three quick butter-churning mo-
tions she enlarged the softened area in George's skull and stilled
the annoying flutter in his wrist.

Then she rolled him over, as a hospital nurse will roll an im-
mobile patient during bedmaking routine, until he rested on his
back on one-half of the purple fabric. She placed his arms across
his naked chest and straightened his spindly legs. She kissed
his closed eyelids, gently stroked his shaggy brows, and said,
"Rest now, dear George."

She folded the free half of the royal cloth over him, covering
him from head to foot with a little left over at each end. From
her sewing box she took a wide-eyed needle and threaded it with
some difficulty in the flickering light. Then kneeling beside the
bed, Mrs. Moon began stitching across the top. She stitched
small careful stitches that would hold for eternity.

Soon the top was closed and she began stitching down the
long side. The job was wearisome, but Mrs. Moon was patient
and she hummed a sweet, monotonous tune as stitch followed
stitch past George's ear, his shoulder, his bent elbow. It was not
until she reached his ankles that she allowed herself to stand and
stretch her aching knees and flex her cramped fingers.

Retrieving the twin Apollos from where they lay abandoned
on George's pillow, she tucked them reverently into the bottom

of the cloth sarcophagus and knelt once more to her task. Her needle flew faster as the remaining gap between the two edges of cloth grew smaller, until the last stitch was securely knotted and George was sealed into his funerary garment. But the hardest part of her night's work was yet to come.

She knew she could not carry George even the short distance to the door of the cabin and the wheelbarrow outside. And the wheelbarrow was too wide to bring inside. She couldn't bear the thought of dragging him across the floor and soiling or tearing the fabric she had so lovingly woven. Finally she rolled him onto the weaving bench and despite the fact that it only supported him from armpits to groin, she managed to maneuver it to the door. From there it was possible to shift the burden to the waiting wheelbarrow.

Mrs. Moon was now breathing heavily from her exertions, and paused for a moment to survey the night and the prospect before her. There were no lights anywhere in the camp except for the feeble glow of her own guttering candles. As she went to blow them out she glanced at her watch and was mildly surprised to see that it was ten minutes past three. The hours had flown while she had been absorbed in her needlework.

She perceived now the furtive night noises of the forest creatures which had hitherto been blocked from her senses by the total concentration she had bestowed on her work. She thought of weasels and foxes prowling, of owls going about their predatory night activities, and considered herself in congenial company. Then taking up the handles of the wheelbarrow, she trundled down the well-defined path to the boathouse.

The wheelbarrow made more noise than she had anticipated and she hoped she was far enough from any occupied cabin for its rumbling to go unnoticed. The moonless night sheltered her from any wakeful watcher, and a dozen summers of waiting had taught her the nature and substance of every square foot of the camp's area. She could walk it blindfolded.

When she reached the boathouse she found that some hurried careless soul had left a boat on the beach in defiance of the camp's rules. It was a simple matter of leverage to shift her burden from barrow to boat and in minutes Mrs. Moon was heaving inexpertly at the oars. At first the boat seemed inclined to travel only in wide arcs and head back to shore, but with patient determination Mrs. Moon established a rowing rhythm that would take her and her passenger to the deepest part of the lake.

She hummed a sea chanty which aided her rowing and pleased her sense of the appropriate. Then pinpointing her position by the silhouette of the tall solitary pine that grew on the opposite shore, Mrs. Moon carefully raised the oars and rested them in the boat.

As Mrs. Moon crept forward in the boat, feeling her way in the darkness, the boat began to rock gently. It was a pleasant, soothing motion and Mrs. Moon thought of cradles and soft enveloping comforters. She continued creeping slowly forward, swaying with the motion of the boat, until she reached the side of her swaddled passenger. There she sat and stroked the cloth and wished that she could see the fine colors just one last time.

She felt the shape beneath the cloth, solid but thin and now rather pitiful. She took the head in her arms and held it against her breast, rocking and humming a long-forgotten lullaby.

The doubled weight at the forward end of the small boat caused the prow to dip. Water began to slosh into the boat—in small wavelets at first as the boat rocked from side to side, then in a steady trickle as the boat rode lower and lower in the water. Mrs. Moon rocked and hummed; the water rose over her bare feet and lapped against her ankles. The sky began to turn purple and she could just make out the distant shape of the boathouse and the hill behind the camp. She was very tired and very cold.

Gently she placed George's head in the water. The boat tilted crazily and she scrambled backward to equalize the weight. She picked up the other end of the long purple chrysalis, the end containing the stone Apollos, and heaved it overboard. George in his shroud, with head and feet trailing in the lake, now lay along the side of the boat weighting it down.

Water was now pouring in. Mrs. Moon held to the other side of the boat with placid hands and thought of the dense comfort of the muddy lake bottom and George beside her forever. She saw that her feet were frantically pushing against the burden of her life, running away from that companionable grave.

With a regretful sigh she let herself slide down the short incline of the seat and came to rest beside George. The boat lurched deeper into the lake. Water surrounded George and climbed into Mrs. Moon's lap. Mrs. Moon closed her eyes and hummed, "Nearer My God to Thee." She did not see George drift away from the side of the boat, carried off by the moving arms of water. She felt a wild bouncing, a shuddering and splashing, and was sure the boat had overturned. With relief she gave herself up to chaos and did not try to hold her breath.

Expecting a suffocating weight of water in her lungs, Mrs. Moon was disappointed to find she could open her eyes, that air still entered and left her gasping mouth. She lay in a pool of water in the bottom of the boat and saw a bird circle high above the lake, peering down at her. The boat was bobbing gently on the water, and when Mrs. Moon sat up she saw that a few yards away, through the fresh blue morning, George was bobbing gently too. The purple shroud had filled with air and floated on the water like a small submarine come up for air and a look at the new day.

As she watched, shivering and wet, the submarine shape drifted away and dwindled as the lake took slow possession. At last, with a grateful sigh, green water replacing the last bubble of air, it sank just as the bright arc of the sun rose over the hill in time to give Mrs. Moon a final glimpse of glorious purple and gold. She shook herself like a tired old gray dog and called out, "Goodbye, George." Her cry echoed back and forth across the morning and startled forth a chorus of bird shrieks. Pandemonium and farewell. She picked up the oars.

Back on the beach, the boat carefully restored to its place, Mrs. Moon dipped her blistered hands into the lake. She scented bacon on the early air and instantly felt the pangs of an enormous hunger. Mitch, the cook, would be having his early breakfast and perhaps would share it with her. She hurried to the cabin to change out of her wet clothes, and was amazed, as she stepped over the doorsill, at the stark emptiness which greeted her.

Shafts of daylight fell on the rumpled bed, but there was nothing for her there. She was not tired now, did not need to sleep. The fireplace contained cold ashes, and the hearth looked bare and unfriendly. The loom gaped at her like a toothless mouth, its usefulness at an end. In a heap on the floor lay George's clothes where he had dropped them the night before. Out of habit she picked them up, and as she hung them on a hook in the small closet she felt a rustle in the shirt pocket. It was a scrap of paper torn off a drawing pad; there was part of a pencil sketch on one side, on the other an address and telephone number.

Mrs. Moon hated to leave anything unfinished, despising untidiness in herself and others. She quickly changed into her town clothes and hung her discarded wet things in the tiny bathroom to dry. She found an apple and munched it as she made up her face and combed her still damp hair. The apple took the edge off her hunger, and she decided not to take the time to beg breakfast from the cook.

She carefully made the bed and tidied the small room, sweeping a few scattered ashes back into the fireplace. She checked her summer straw pocketbook for driver's license, car keys, money, and finding everything satisfactory, she paused for a moment in the center of the room. All was quiet, neat, and orderly. The spider still hung inert in the center of its web and one small fly was buzzing helplessly on its perimeter. Mrs. Moon smiled.

There was no time to weave now—indeed, there was no need. She could not really expect to find a conveniently deserted lake in a big city. No. She would have to think of something else.

Mrs. Moon stood in the doorway of the cabin in the early sunlight, a small frown wrinkling the placid surface of her round pink face. She scuffled slowly around to the back of the cabin and into the shadow of the sycamores beyond, her feet kicking up the spongy layers of years of fallen leaves, her eyes watching carefully for the right idea to show itself. Two grayish-white stones appeared side by side, half covered with leaf mold. Anonymous, faceless, about the size of canteloupes, they would do unless something better presented itself.

Unceremoniously she dug them out of their bed, brushed

away the loose dirt, and leaf fragments, and carried them back to the car.

Mrs. Moon's watch had stopped sometime during the night, but as she got into the car she glanced at the now fully risen sun and guessed the time to be about six thirty or seven o'clock. She placed the two stones snugly on the passenger seat and covered them with her soft pale-blue cardigan. She started the engine, and then reached over and groped in the glove compartment. She never liked to drive anywhere without knowing beforehand the exact roads to take to get to her destination. The road map was there, neatly folded beneath the flashlight and the box of tissues.

Mrs. Moon unfolded the map and spread it out over the steering wheel. As the engine warmed up, Mrs. Moon hummed along with it. Her pudgy pink hand absently patted the tidy blue bundle beside her as she planned the most direct route to the girl in Minneapolis.

ELISABETH SANXAY HOLDING

1889–1955

The famously prickly Raymond Chandler said of ELISABETH SANXAY HOLDING: "For my money she's the top suspense writer of them all. She doesn't pour it on and make you feel irritated. Her characters are wonderful; and she has a sort of inner calm which I find very attractive." Holding was born in New York but spent much of her life traveling the world after marrying George Holding, a British diplomat, in 1913. The time she spent in the Caribbean, especially Bermuda, would inform several of Holding's nineteen suspense novels (she published six romantic novels in the early 1920s, switching gears when the 1929 stock market crash provided an economic incentive), including *The Strange Crime in Bermuda* (1937). But the hallmark of Holding's work was subtle, psychologically nuanced portraits of women making sense of troubled marriages, conflicted relationships with children, or intrigue thrown up by the larger world.

Holding is best known for *The Blank Wall* (1947), in which a woman covers up a crime she believes to have been committed by her daughter, and which was made into the 1949 movie *The*

Reckless Moment and remade in 2001 as *The Deep End*, with Tilda
Swinton. Other notable novels included *The Unfinished Crime*
(1935), *The Old Battle Ax* (1943), *The Innocent Mrs. Duff* (1946), and
Widow's Mite (1953), published after her husband's retirement
and their move back to New York City.

"The Stranger in the Car," first published in *The American*
magazine in July 1949, is a sly depiction of women protecting
their own familial turf. The twist is that the narrator is male, a
middle-aged husband and father content in an outwardly placid
existence that's thrown for a loop when his daughter is mixed
up in the murder of a spurned suitor. Holding brilliantly de-
scribes the disconnect between the idea of the male provider and
the seemingly passive, cared-for women who really hold all the
power, and who operate according to their needs and wants,
even in the face of a terrible crime.

THE STRANGER IN THE CAR

CARROL CHARLEROY leaned back in his chair and closed his eyes; a big, stout, handsome man, olive-skinned, with a black mustache; a flamboyant look about him, in spite of his correct and conservative clothes. Miss Ewing was playing the piano for him, and he tried to relax, to enjoy this music, but a peculiar restlessness filled him. He frowned, opened his eyes, and took out his cigar case.

He and his wife Helen never sat here in the drawing-room unless they had guests; then the room would be pleasantly lighted, there would be people moving about, the sound of voices. Now the only light came from the gold-shaded lamp beside the piano at the other end of the long room, and, in spite of Miss Ewing's music, he was aware, as never before, of the sounds from the New York street outside, the rush of wind, a car streaking past, the frantic piping of a doorman's whistle, a man's voice, hoarse and furious. This made him feel vulnerable, not comfortably shut away from the world in his own home.

"I don't like this sending Helen off to the hospital," he thought. "The flu is a treacherous disease, I grant you that. But Helen and I, and the children, and the servants, too, have all had it, at one time or the other, right here in the house, and we did very well. Can't say I care much for Dr. Marcher. Too quizzical . . .

"I've had enough of this music, too," he thought. "Very nice of her, but I wish to heaven she'd stop. I'd like to read. I wish she'd go away."

He thought she was coming to the end of a piece, but she went on and on; he lit his cigar and drew on it, and then, at last, she turned round on the piano bench to face him, a tallish woman of an age he had never tried to guess, bony and limber in her brown dress, her short, pale-brown hair curling up like dry petals from her weather-beaten face with a turned-up nose, a wide mouth, merry blue eyes.

"Very nice," Charleroy said. "Very—" He sought for a word. "Very soothing," he said.

"It *tried* to be nice!" said Miss Ewing. "It *wanted* to soothe you, Mr. Charleroy."

"Ha!" he said, with a benevolent laugh.

Miss Ewing had been in and out of the house for a good ten years; she had given music lessons to all three children. Two or three times before this she had come, in an emergency, to look after the household. Charleroy had a great esteem for her, but he found it embarrassing, almost paralyzing to be left alone with her. He was glad to see her close the piano and rise, but it would be worse, he thought, if she should sit down and try to entertain him.

"If you don't mind," she said, "if you're sure you'll be all right, Mr. Charleroy, I think I'll nip upstairs and write some letters. I've been naughty about my correspondence!"

"Certainly!" he said, with eagerness, and heaved himself out of his chair, to give her a polite bow.

He remained standing, listening to her light, quick steps running up the stairs. When he heard a door close overhead he went into the dining-room and got a bottle of whisky out of the cellarette. He brought this, with a glass and a carafe of water, into the room where he and Helen were accustomed to sit. The second parlor, this had been called in his boyhood; it was a narrow little room between the drawing-room and the queer little glassed-in room that overlooked the back yard. It had no windows, and the sounds from the street did not reach him here; he had thought he would like that, but he found it too quiet. He poured himself a drink, and took up the book he was reading.

He expected to be very comfortable, but he was not; the silence of the house disturbed him. Nobody upstairs but Miss Ewing, he thought. The room Jim and Young Carrol had shared was dark and empty; Jim in Japan, Young Carrol married and living in Philadelphia; dark and empty the room the girls had shared. Margaret had married, a month ago, and Julia had gone out dancing tonight.

"I'll stay home and keep you company, Daddy," she had said; but he had opposed that, with secret alarm. "No, no," he had said; "go along and enjoy yourself, Julia."

He had not wanted anyone to keep him company. When Helen was here he would read, she would read, or perhaps write letters; sometimes a whole evening would pass with scarcely a word, and it was very agreeable. No reason why it should not be agreeable now, to sit here and read and drink his nightcap.

The telephone rang. He dropped his book on the floor. "It's

the hospital," he said to himself, and went out to the telephone in the hall.

"Charleroy speaking," he said, with immense calm.

"Oh, Uncle Carrol?" said a little high voice. "It's Sylvie. How is Aunt Helen?"

"Well enough," he answered curtly. Half past ten was no hour to make such an inquiry.

"Uncle Carrol . . . Is Julia home?"

"What?" he said, seriously annoyed now. "I understood she'd gone out with you and Ivan."

"Oh, yes! But the party split up, and I just wondered . . . Please give my love to Aunt Helen when you see her. Good night, Uncle Carrol!"

He sat by the telephone, frowning. "*What* was the girl wondering about," he thought. "Why did she expect Julia to be home this early? Party split up, eh?"

"Well, why not?" he thought. "Julia knows what she's doing. Very levelheaded girl. Never any need to worry about Julia. I'll read for a while, and then I'll go to bed and go to sleep."

But his book did not interest him, and after a few moments he poured himself another drink. Helen wouldn't like that, he thought, and sighed. He sipped the drink, leaning back in his chair; he picked up the book again and read a page; he yawned, and closed his eyes. "Too early for bed," he thought. "But I might take a little nap . . ."

He waked with a start.

"What's that?" he asked, aloud.

He was not sure whether he had dreamed it or whether he really had heard someone fall on the stairs. It had to be looked into, though, and he got up and went out into the dimly lit hall.

Halfway up the stairs he saw his daughter Julia, on her knees, her pale satin dress trailing down behind her, her forehead rest-ing on an upper step.

He went to her and touched her arm. "Julia?" he said, in a low voice.

She raised her head and smiled, vaguely.

He tried to help her, but she was stepping all over her long skirt. "Pick up your dress!" he said. "There!"

With his arm around her, he got her up the stairs and along the hall to her own room. He opened the door and switched on the light, and she was leaning against the wall, still with that dazed smile. There was a red mark on the bridge of her nose.

"Julia," he said, "what's the matter with you?"

"I'm—all right, Daddy," she said mildly.

"Julia—are you able to get yourself to bed?" he asked.

"I'll help her, Mr. Charleroy," said Miss Ewing.

She stood there, wearing a tweed coat over her nightdress, curl-ers in her hair; the one person, he thought, whom he could have wanted here now. For she had known Julia as a little girl; she would understand that this situation could not be what it ap-peared to be.

"Yes," he said, and stepped back, closing the door.

He stood outside it, appalled. "She's been drinking," he thought. "Julia's been drinking. Julia fell down!"

"Now, look here!" he told himself. "It could happen to any-one. Anyone could take one too many, without realizing."

Anyone else, but not Julia, that girl of inflexible pride and composure, tall, handsome, superbly sure of herself. He glanced at his watch; nearly three o'clock.

"This won't do," he thought. "I've got to get my sleep, got to keep fit, look after my business. You'd think they'd realize that."

He went to his own room then, undressed, and got into bed.

He was, by habit, a heavy sleeper, but he waked at once the next morning at the sound of a light tap at the door.

"Eight o'clock, sir," said the housemaid.

He got up at once and put on his slippers and his purple brocade dressing gown; stopping before the mirror, he sighed, to see his portliness; he twisted his mustache a little, and went out into the hall.

There he paused, deeply apprehensive and troubled. "*I* don't know how to talk to Julia," he thought. "That's her mother's business. But just now Helen can't be worried. She's not to know."

He decided that he would confine himself to that, in a tone of cold disapproval. He would simply tell Julia that her mother must be protected from any knowledge of last night's disgraceful scene.

"Disgraceful scene," he repeated to himself, as he knocked on Julia's door.

There was no answer, and in the dim hall, in the silent and somehow lifeless house, that was bad. He knocked again; then he turned the knob and opened the door a little.

"Julia?" he said sternly.

"Oh . . . ! Father!" she said, sitting up in bed.

"Good heavens!" he said.

"What's the matter, Father?"

"You have a black eye," he said.

She raised her hand to the swollen and discolored eye that gave her handsome young face a look of forlorn debauchery; she reached for the dressing gown on the chair beside her and slipped her arms into it; she got up and went barefoot to the mirror over the chest of drawers.

"Heavens!" she said. "I didn't know . . ."

"How did this happen, Julia?" he asked.

"Well, I tripped on the stairs, didn't I?"

"Where had you been?"

"I went with Sylvie and Ivan to the Brocade Room at the St. Pol."

"Sylvie telephoned," he said. "Before eleven, that was. She asked me if you were home. She said the party had split up."

Julia turned toward him, tall and straight in her dark flannel robe; and, in spite of the black eye, she was impressive. "I went out for a walk," she said,

"Alone?"

"No. With a man."

"What man?"

"A friend of theirs," she said. "I don't remember his name."

"Then you went back to Sylvie and Ivan?"

"No," she said, without hesitation. "I don't know where I went."

"What do you mean?" he cried.

"I mean I just don't remember," she said. "We got into a taxi, and I think I fell asleep. Then I don't remember anything until I was going down in an elevator with him somewhere."

"Where?"

"I don't know. Then we got into another taxi, and he brought me home."

"What time did you leave Sylvie and Ivan?" he asked.

"I don't know. But if she telephoned before eleven. I must have been gone then."

"And you got home at three," he thought.

"You must try to remember more," he said.

"I can't," she said. "Only that I began to feel sick and—queer, and when Sylvia and Ivan got up to dance, I asked this man to take me out in the fresh air for a while. I must have had too much to drink. I don't know how *that* happened. It never happened to me before. It was an accident."

"It's never an accident," said Charleroy.

"It was, this time." said Julia. "I'm not like that. You know it."

He did know it. Let her stand there in front of him, with a black eye, and tell him that she had been drinking too much. He still knew she was not like that.

"We'll have to keep this from your mother," he said.

"Yes. I'll say I hit my head against a taxi door, or something."

"No," said Charleroy. "She mustn't see you like this."

"Good lord!" said Julia. "It's no disgrace to have a black eye!"

He did not answer that; only looked at her. She looked straight back at him.

"I'm sorry I worried you, Father," she said. "But I *don't* feel disgraced. I don't feel ashamed. The whole thing was an accident."

It was her magnificent innocence that disarmed him. He could not ask her anything more about that man, about those missing hours; he would not, by a single word, shake her confidence in life, and in herself. If she was not worried, not frightened, so much the better.

He looked away from her and frowned, deciding what was to be done. He was an excellent man of business, accustomed to making decisions, to accepting responsibility, and he was, above everything, a notable improviser. "No," he said. "You'd better go away for a week or so."

"Be sent away—in disgrace?"

"Nonsense!" he said curtly. "The chief thing to be considered is your mother's health. She mustn't see you like this. And nobody else must, either. You certainly can't go out anywhere—any parties, that sort of thing."

"How long will it last?"

"I don't know. We'll get a doctor to look at it. But in the meantime the best thing will be for you to go out to Meadowsweet."

"I shouldn't mind that so much," said Julia.

"And I'll send Miss Ewing with you."

"But why?"

"Because I don't want you to go alone, and she's a very fine woman."

"You and Mother always have had such a thing about Ewing—"

"Miss Ewing," he said.

The door of Julia's bathroom opened and Miss Ewing came out. She still wore the tweed coat over her nightdress, the curlers in her hair, but she had an air of dignity. "I'm sorry," she said, "but I was *trapped*. You see, I sat up here with Julia last night—"

"Oh, I didn't know that!" said Julia.

"No, dear, of course you didn't. But I thought it was *wiser*. And I think—but I don't want to be a busybody. Does anyone want to hear what I think?"

"If you please," said Charleroy, with the great courtesy he always had for Miss Ewing.

"I think Mr. Charleroy's idea is excellent," she said. "Because,

Jewel, my dear, if you go to see your mother and tell her you hit your head on a taxi door, she'll ask a very great many questions, and—" She laughed a little. "I'm sure mothers have a sixth sense," she said. "She'd *know* something was wrong."

"Nothing is wrong," said Julia.

"*I* think," said Miss Ewing, "that if you tell Mrs. Charleroy that I've had a little tiny breakdown—fatigue, you know—and that dear Jewel has carried me off to Meadowsweet, to look after me for a few days . . ."

"Excellent!" said Charleroy. "You can call up your mother as soon as you get there, Julia."

"And now," said Miss Ewing, "I'll creep downstairs and get some breakfast for you, Jewel. And then I'll just dart up to my hotel, to pick up a few things I'll need in the country."

"I'll take you there, Miss Ewing," said Charleroy.

"*Thank* you, Mr. Charleroy!" she said.

He turned back to his daughter. He wanted to say something to her, but he did not know what it was; he could find no words. They looked steadily at each other for a moment, and then he went out of the room.

After breakfast together in the dining-room, Charleroy and Miss Ewing left the house together. He went first, descending the steps to the street with his rolling gait, his overcoat open, his soft hat at a debonair angle. The taxi was waiting, his taxi.

"Good morning, Mr. Charleroy!"

"Morning, Leon. Uptown, this morning. Park Vista Hotel."

"That's a change," said Leon. "That's certainly a change."

Charleroy helped Miss Ewing into the cab, and settled back in a corner. Leon was a bore, Helen said. Very well; he, himself, was often greatly bored by Leon. But Leon belonged to him; he had for Leon the feudal loyalty that was in his nature. An old clerk, an old servant, a tradesman who had served him faithfully could be sure of his bounty.

"Now, about cutting these taxes," Leon said. "I wouldn't know. I simply would not know. How's about it, Mr. Charleroy?"

Charleroy did not answer; this was his method when he did not wish to talk. Stopping for a light, Leon turned to look back at him, a dark, emaciated young man with hollow cheeks, a mouth like a Brownie's, from ear to ear. He smiled, and Charleroy looked at him in gloomy silence.

Charleroy was thinking, "I've got to find out where Julia was, who that man was. The fellow may be going around, talking. . . . I could find out from Sylvie—but she might suspect something. I'm sure she'd suspect something if I called her up, asked her questions. Never called her up in my life. No. Julia will have to ask her for the fellow's name. . . . But I don't like that, either. All this petty intrigue . . ."

"Helen could handle this," he thought. But Helen was not to be disturbed. She was not to know about Julia, not to see Julia with a black eye. "I'm *worried*," he told himself angrily. But he would not say to himself that it was something more than worry.

He had been to the Park Vista Hotel before; two or three times in the past to bring the children home from their music lessons; once to bring Miss Ewing home to a Thanksgiving dinner. The lounge looked familiar to him, rumpled chintz covers on the chairs, everything shabby and not very clean, but, he thought, cheerful.

He had never before been above the main floor, and he had

expected to wait in this lounge for Miss Ewing. But she pushed him gently into an old grillwork elevator; they ascended to the fourth floor and got out into a corridor with green walls and a green carpet, and a peculiar airless smell.

Miss Ewing went before him and opened a door with a key. "Here's my little domain, Mr. Charleroy!" she said.

It was a big room with a high ceiling, green paint peeling off the walls, a mantelpiece upon which stood two tall, red-glass vases filled with somber leaves and, at one end, a brown curtain drawn across an alcove.

"Excuse me just a moment!" said Miss Ewing, and disappeared behind the curtain.

It occurred to Charleroy that possibly Miss Ewing's life was not quite so cozy as he had thought. He knew that she was not at all well-to-do; he and Helen were always recommending her to people as an excellent music teacher and, above all, as a fine woman. They had tried to help her in other ways, too: a check at Christmas time, a handsome payment for the three or four times she had come to look after the children and the house. But he had thought of her, all these years, as living in this hotel in a cheerful and comfortable fashion. "Not like this," he thought. "This is sordid," he thought.

Miss Ewing came out from behind the curtain now in a dark-brown dress with a little white collar; her pale-brown hair curled up wildly from her weather-beaten face. From a table she took up a tooled leather box and proffered it to him. There were four cork-tipped cigarettes in it, and he took one, out of politeness.

"I'll have one, too!" she said, and he lit it for her.

"How is Mrs. Charleroy?" she asked.

"Oh, doing very well, the doctor says. Very well."

"If there's *anything* I can do for her—" said Miss Ewing. "But I'm sure she knows how glad I'd be."

"She does," said Charleroy, drawing on the cigarette, which was dry as hay. It must have been in the box a very long time. "I appreciate your going out to Meadowsweet with Julia, Miss Ewing."

"I'm *glad* to go, Mr. Charleroy. I think it's a *very* serious situation. It happens so often."

"Don't understand you," said Charleroy.

"They forget," said Miss Ewing. "They forget names. They forget where they've been."

"*Who* forgets?"

"Those poor girls who've been given goof balls."

"Goof balls? Never heard of goof balls," said Charleroy briefly. "What are they?"

"Barbiturates. Like sleeping pills, only stronger," said Miss Ewing ominously.

"Nonsense. Julia would never think of taking—"

"I know that, Mr. Charleroy. I know that. But they could have been *slipped* to her!"

"But Ivan and Sylvie were there, plenty of people around, waiters, and so on."

"Waiters are *often* in cahoots with those men," said Miss Ewing.

"*What* men?" asked Charleroy, unable to conceal his irritation. "No. It's simply a question of taking one drink too many. You were there last night—"

"My Jewel wouldn't do that," said Miss Ewing. "She was only eight years old when she first came to me, and I made a study of her. Mr. Charleroy, you don't know how much of this drugging is going on."

"Yes, yes!" said Charleroy. "But in Julia's case—"

"Mr. Charleroy, I personally know of *two* girls—American girls in Europe—who were drugged. One of them, a beautiful girl, was missing for two days, and to this moment she can't remember one single thing about where she'd been or what happened. Then later this man appeared and began to blackmail her."

"Yes, yes," said Charleroy, and glanced at his watch. "I'm afraid we'd better be going, Miss Ewing."

"Mr. Charleroy," she said, with a passionate earnestness, "you can count on me to the *last ditch*."

"I'm sure of it, Miss Ewing," he said. "I appreciate it."

And that was true. "If the poor old girl wants to make up a sort of movie story out of the thing," he thought, "let her. Makes her happy, and it doesn't hurt anyone else."

"You'd better take some money," he said, and got some bills out of his wallet. "Might need something. I'll mail you a check tonight."

"Thank you," said Miss Ewing. "You can trust me to look after our Jewel."

Leon was waiting for them outside the hotel.

"Tell you what," said Charleroy. "When we get to the house, Miss Ewing will wait in the cab until my daughter comes out. Then I want you to drive them out to Meadowsweet. You can call me up later, let me know what I owe you."

"I'll do that, Mr. Charleroy," said Leon.

Charleroy felt somewhat better about things. He had two faithful retainers on the job now, two people to respect, cherish, and shelter Julia. He used his latchkey to enter the house on

Eleventh Street, and he hoped he would not meet the house-maid. He mounted the stairs as lightly as he could and knocked at Julia's door.

"Me," he said in a muffled voice, and Julia opened the door at once.

When he saw her, all the pain, the dread, the shocked astonishment of last night came back to him. She was dressed with her usual expensive correctness, in a tailored gray suit, a pale-blue blouse; she stood tall, straight as an arrow, her dark hair neat, close to her head. But the black eye made her look forlorn, battered; she was not the cherished young creature he wished to believe her, entirely beyond the reach of ugly misfortune. She had been hurt, and she was vulnerable.

"Better wear your dark glasses," he said.

Without a word she went to the chest of drawers and got out a pair of sunglasses with white rims; she put on a gray felt hat, and beneath it her face looked thin, even gaunt.

"As soon as you get out to Meadowsweet," he said, "call Dr. Pugh and get him to take a look at your eye."

"Yes, I will, Father," she said. "Father, I'm sorry."

His throat contracted; he gave a short cough. "Well . . ." he said. "You must be more careful in the future." . . .

He entered the office like a sultan, generous, but dangerous. A man of moods, his secretary called him to her friends.

"Get me Meadowsweet, will you?" he asked her. "I want to speak to Mrs. Brady."

He sat down before his enormous, gleaming desk in blank silence.

"I'm sorry, Mr. Charleroy," said Miss Peters, "but Meadow-sweet doesn't answer."

"Oh, thanks," he said. "It doesn't matter."

But it did matter. Throughout the cold months the Bradys were caretakers at Meadowsweet; in the summer Mrs. Brady became a cook-housekeeper and her husband a gardener; they were fine people. He had wanted to tell Mrs. Brady that Miss Julia was on her way out; make her comfortable; look after her. But, he told himself, it was quite reasonable to expect that, at this hour of the morning, Mrs. Brady had gone into the village to market and that her husband would be out, looking after the chickens, or something of the sort. "They'll be there when Julia arrives," he thought, "and she's got Miss Ewing. She'll be all right."

He now turned his attention to the mail Miss Peters had sorted for him, but there was nothing in it that interested him enough to relieve his black oppression. Unfortunately, he suddenly remembered Miss Ewing's talk about "goof balls." "Nonsense!" he told himself angrily. He had never paid too much attention to Miss Ewing's anecdotes, most of them to do with her adventures in Europe just after the first World War, and certainly he was not going to begin now to take them seriously.

But, later in the day, in the middle of a talk with a new and not too important advertiser, he suddenly remembered the tale of the American girl, tall and beautiful, who had disappeared for two days, and never knew where she had been.

"First thing is to get Julia away," he thought. "So that Helen won't be asking to see her. Then the next thing is to get hold of this fellow, find out all about him. He's a friend of Sylvie's and Ivan's; they'll be able to tell me all I want to know. Then I'll look him up, have a talk with him, size him up. No. I'm not worried."

But he could not deny the sense of urgency, of irritable haste that filled him. He rang up the Wall Street office where Ivan worked, and he was angry to learn that Ivan was out. He tried again in the afternoon, and got the same answer. "Very well; this evening, then," he thought. . . .

At five o'clock Leon drove him uptown to the hospital, and he went into Helen's room. There was a nurse there, a big, clumsy woman, and she did not go away.

"I'm *much* better, Carrol," Helen said.

He noticed that she had put on lipstick, and that worried him. Women did those things, he thought, to make themselves look better than they were.

"Helen—?" he said.

She held out her hand to him, a thin hand, but beautifully kept; colorless nail polish.

"Carrol," she said, with a drowsy smile. "I'll be home in a few days. Don't worry about anything, dear. I'll be back."

He held her hand tight. "Yes," he said. "Yes. Everything's all right, Helen. Take it easy, Helen."

Their hands clasped tight, these two who had together known love and birth and death, war that had struck twice, the anguish of seeing their sons leave, the scarcely lesser anguish of seeing their older daughter, Margaret, so gentle and bemused, marry an Englishman and go off to make her life in exile.

Then the cross, awkward nurse moved forward, and Charleroy withdrew his hand. "I'll see you tomorrow, Helen," he said. . . .

Instead of using his latchkey, he rang the bell, because he wanted someone to speak to him when he entered that silent house.

"Uncle Carrol!" said a resonant voice.

It was Ivan Barlow, husband of his niece Sylvie, a dark, handsome blue-jowled young fellow, very serious.

"I was down at the trust company all day," he explained. "When I got back to the office they told me you'd called. I tried to call you back, but you'd just left. So I thought I'd better stop by on my way home."

"Yes, yes," said Charleroy. He had meant to make his inquiries casual, very casual; he did not want it to be this way. "Nothing of any importance," he said.

"I wanted to see you, anyway," said Ivan in his serious fashion. "Sylvie and I talked it over, and we both felt that we were more or less to blame."

"For what?"

"Well, we could see that she wasn't herself."

"What are you talking about?" Charleroy demanded, so roughly that Ivan dropped his eyes for a moment. Then he looked up, with a clear and candid gaze.

"Sylvie and I were very much upset," he said, "when Julia disappeared with that fellow."

"*What* fellow?"

"I wish to heaven I could remember," said Ivan, distressed. "I'm pretty sure his name is Winter, but I can't remember who the devil he is, or where I met him. And Sylvie says she never saw him before. I noticed him standing in the doorway, and he seemed to recognize me, so I beckoned to him to come over to our table. To tell you the truth, I wanted a chance to talk to Sylvie about Julia, about what we'd better do—"

"Yes, yes! Go on."

———

"Sylvie and I got up to dance. We were talking, and we didn't notice them go out. We sat down again and waited, and after a while I went to look in the bar and the lobby. After half an hour more Sylvie went to call you up to see if Julia'd come home."

"She came in a little later," said Charleroy. "Winter, you say the fellow's name is?"

"I'm pretty sure of *that*, but I can't remember where—"

"Doesn't matter," said Charleroy. "Doesn't matter."

"Sylvie and I were worried," the earnest Ivan said again. "I called up Julia this morning, and the maid said she'd gone away."

"She took Miss Ewing away for a little rest," said Charleroy. "Nothing to worry about." He took a step forward, obliging Ivan to retire backward a little down the hall. "Very good of you to stop in," he said. "Give my love to Sylvie. And don't worry about Julia. Not now, or any other time. Julia's all right."

He advanced another step, and Ivan, slightly disconcerted, again retreated and reached behind him for the doorknob.

"Aunt Helen?" he began.

"Doing very well!" said Charleroy heartily. "Good night, m'boy!"

"Good night, Uncle Carrol," said Ivan, and opened the door.

The wind streamed in, cold against Charleroy's face; then the door closed. And, standing there in the hall of the silent house, he had a moment of desperation. If Ivan and Sylvie don't know who the fellow is, he thought, then what?

It was his conviction that there was always something to be done in any emergency. He thought for a moment; then he went to the telephone directory and looked up the Winters. There were plenty of them, and nothing in their addresses, first names, or occupations gave him any clue, or any inspiration. He thought again; then he dialed the St. Pol.

"I want to speak to a Mr. Winter who's staying in the hotel," he said.

There was no Mr. Winter in the hotel.

"See if he checked out yesterday, will you?"

No Mr. Winters had checked out yesterday, or the day before.

"Thank you," said Charleroy.

He sat with his head bent, his eyes fixed upon his glossy shoes. He began to remember Miss Ewing's stories, which he had, in the beginning, dismissed as pure romancing. Now, however, they were vivid to him; he could imagine variations. This fellow Winter might easily trace Julia. He might follow her out to Meadowsweet. He might try to blackmail her. He might be there now!

Anger began to rise in him. "I'll get to the bottom of this!" he cried to himself.

He decided to call up Leon.

"There's a business matter that's just come up," said Charleroy. "Paper, for my daughter to sign. I'll have to run out to Meadowsweet with it."

"Okay, Mr. Charleroy. Will I come early tomorrow?"

"I'll have to go tonight," said Charleroy.

"Tonight?" said Leon, and was silent for a moment, perhaps rearranging his own unimaginable life. "Okay. Mr. Charleroy."

"In an hour and a half," said Charleroy.

He ate his dinner without interest; he told Nora the tale about the paper to be signed, he made sure that she had the Meadowsweet telephone number. Then, for some reason which he did not trouble to examine, it seemed to him incorrect to leave without taking a bag. He brought a suitcase out of his closet; in it he put pajamas, clean shirt and socks, a razor, and a toothbrush, and carried it downstairs.

In his overcoat and hat, he stood in the open doorway, and it was strange to be going like this, nobody saying good-by to him, nobody expecting him anywhere. There was a wild wind blowing and the street was empty; now and then a car went by, but there was no one on foot. The taxi, when it came, looked fantastic, tinselly, with a red light, a green light, yellow lights.

He went down the steps, holding his hat.

"It's a mean night," Leon said.

"Very," said Charleroy.

"Still," said Leon, "we can make good time, a night like this. We can get out there by eleven, if we get the breaks."

Charleroy lit a cigar and leaned back. He felt like talking to Leon tonight, and he did talk, about politics, about taxes, about Russia, as they drove through the city and out onto a highway.

He dozed a little, and when he waked, the country was familiar, the gentle sweep of the dark hills, the empty fields, the bare trees rocking stiffly against the pallid sky. "Nearly there," he thought, and fear stirred in him again. Suppose he found Julia ill?

Now they were turning into the lane, and in a moment he would see the lights of the house. If there were any lights. But the Bradys always went to bed very early, and very likely Julia and Miss Ewing had done so, too. "Perhaps I should have telephoned," he thought. "But no; it's better this way. I'll see for myself..."

There was a crash that flung Charleroy down on his knees; his head banged against the wall. He thought that he was sliding down a long chute, horribly fast . . .

"Mr. Charleroy! Mr. Charleroy! Are you all right?"

"Yes," said Charleroy. "What happened?"

"I dunno," said Leon, with a sob. "I ran smack into this car here that's parked without no lights."

"Are you hurt, Leon?"

"I—wouldn't know. There's—all blood—on my face."

Charleroy recognized the note of hysteria. No matter how he felt, he had to take charge. "Have you a flashlight?" he asked. "Let's have it."

There was no answer. He got up from his knees, with a grunt, and put on his hat, which had fallen off; he opened the door of the cab and got out. The headlights of the taxi were out and he could not see Leon.

"Where are you?" he asked.

"Here," said Leon, and a flashlight shone in his eyes. He took it, and turned it on Leon, and there was a smear of blood on his cheek.

"Anyone that parks without lights ought to be hung," said Leon.

"Let's see what damage we did," said Charleroy, and turned the flashlight on the other car.

"Good heavens!" he cried. "There's someone in it!"

There was someone in the driver's seat, leaning back behind the wheel, his arms at his side, his hair glistening.

Charleroy walked forward and opened the door of the other car, to touch the driver's hand. "I think he's dead," he said, in great wonder.

"We couldn't of killed him!" Leon cried. "I wasn't going fast—"

"He's—cold," Charleroy said. "He must have been dead before we came."

"Dead!" said Leon. "And just sitting there like that?"

"We'll have to notify the police," said Charleroy. "Will your cab run, Leon?"

Leon got into the taxi and backed away. "Yeah," he said. "Yeah, she runs. But my lights are busted. I wouldn't dare drive without no lights."

"I'll hold the flashlight," said Charleroy. "There's a filling station a little way ahead, where we can telephone."

He sat in the taxi, resting the flashlight steady on the open window, so that it threw a narrow beam of light on the road before them. Leon drove slowly, past the car where the dead man sat. "Poor devil's right outside my own place," Charleroy thought.

He would not have admitted it, but he was happy. He liked this riding cautiously along the dark road, holding the flashlight; he liked the idea of notifying the police, of being the one who had discovered the body. "I reached into the car," he would say. "Felt the poor devil's hand. He must have been dead for some time. Heart attack, I suppose." . . .

He did say all this, over the telephone, in the filling station.

"Well," he was told, "you return to the scene of the accident, and we'll be along."

They left Leon's taxi at the filling station, for an overhaul, and hired another one, Leon sitting in the back as a passenger. When they reached the lane, two cars were already there, their headlights illuminating the road in both directions. As they stopped, a motorcycle policeman came up to them.

"Your name Mr. Charley?"

"Charleroy."

"You the one reported this here accident?"

"Yes."

"You'll have to come along to the station and give a full report," said the cop in a tone which greatly annoyed Charleroy.

"Certainly!" he said. "I'll be glad to see someone in authority."

"You will," said the cop, and they set off, the motorcycle cop riding beside the taxi.

They turned into a deserted village street, where two green lights burned before a neat red-brick building, and here they stopped. They got out, and followed the motorcycle cop into a bare room fitted with benches, where another policeman sat at a high desk like a pulpit; they went through this room and along a short hall, to an open door.

"Here they are, sir," said the motorcycle cop, and left them.

A man sitting at a desk rose, a very tall young man in uniform, with big ears and melancholy dark eyes. "Mr. Charley?" he asked politely.

"Charleroy."

"Mr. Charleroy. I'm Lieutenant Levy, in charge here. And you—?"

"Leon Perez, sir."

"Sit down," said Levy. "And smoke, if you like."

Charleroy lit a cigar. "Light up, Leon," he said.

"I haven't got no more cigarettes, sir."

"Here!" said Charleroy. "Have a cigar."

"Thank you, sir," said Leon, his face growing bright.

"Now—" said Levy. "Who's the owner of the car you were driving?"

"Me, sir," said Leon.

"I'd like to see your license," said Levy, and Leon sprang up and handed it to him. "A taxi?" Levy said, surprised. "You're quite a long way from New York."

"I've been using Perez's taxi for three or four years," said Charleroy. "I can vouch for it that he's an excellent driver. Great confidence in him. I had to come out to my place, Meadow-sweet, and I naturally thought of Perez."

"I see. Is your family here, Mr. Charleroy?"

Charleroy did not like this, but he could not avoid answering. "My daughter's out here," he said stiffly.

"I see," said Levy. "Is your daughter alone here, Mr. Charleroy?"

"No!" said Charleroy sternly. His daughter was never alone. "The Bradys are there, a couple, caretakers, so on. And she has Miss Ewing with her."

"Miss Ewing is a friend?"

"Yes. Friend of the family. Very fine woman."

"I see. If you have a place here, Mr. Charleroy, I suppose you know a good many of the local people?"

"Well—" said Charleroy. He could not, at the moment, think of any local people known to him. His wife, or Mrs. Brady, were the ones who dealt with the tradespeople; when he came for week ends, he walked into the house and everything was there, even the New York newspaper he preferred.

"Do you know anyone by the name of Leonard Winter, Mr. Charleroy?"

"*Winter?* Leonard *Winter?*" said Charleroy. Then he felt that his tone and his look of vast bewilderment were overdone. "Why, no," he said thoughtfully. "No. Not that I can remember."

"He's the man you found in the car, Mr. Charleroy."

"He was, eh? Poor devil! Heart attack, I suppose?"

"No, sir, it wasn't," said Levy.

Charleroy frowned, and stirred uneasily. There was something wrong here, something he did not understand.

"I don't know what you're getting at," he said. "But here are the facts. The car was parked there, without any lights, and we ran into it, head on. But we were going slowly, around the curve. I don't believe we could have caused him any serious injury. What's more, when I felt the poor devil's hand, it was cold." He paused. "Nobody would sit there in a parked car without lights unless he was very ill. Or unconscious," he said.

"Winter was shot through the heart," said Levy.

There was a moment's silence.

"Indeed?" said Charleroy coldly. He wished to believe that he was annoyed. But what he felt was a vague and cold dread.

The bare and brightly lit room was quiet.

"Suicide?" said Charleroy.

"We haven't found any weapon in the vicinity," said Levy.

"You haven't had time to look properly."

"We've had time enough to search all the likely places, Mr. Charleroy."

"Very well," said Charleroy. "Then the thing was a murder. A holdup."

"That's possible," said Levy.

"Very well," said Charleroy, again. "Perez and I can't help you there. We simply ran into the fellow's car. We didn't hear any shots, didn't see any suspicious characters, anything of that sort. We've given you all the information we can."

"I see," said Levy, in his polite and patient way. "Is your daughter expecting you, Mr. Charleroy?"

"No," said Charleroy curtly.

"Do you think that anyone in the house is likely to be up now, sir?"

Charleroy glanced at his watch. "It's nearly midnight," he said. "No. I certainly don't think anyone's likely to be up now."

"Then I won't detain you any longer, Mr. Charleroy," said Levy, rising. "I'll be around in the morning."

This unexpected dismissal was, somehow, more annoying than the questions. Charleroy waited a moment; then he rose, and Leon with him. "Very unfortunate affair," he said.

"Very," said Levy.

The taxi took them back to Meadowsweet. Charleroy mounted the steps and rang the doorbell.

A window opened upstairs, and Miss Ewing's voice called, sharply, "Who's there?"

"It's me, Miss Ewing. Charleroy."

"Oh!" she cried. "Oh, dear! Oh, I'll be right down!"

"Where are the Bradys?" he thought. They had a room on the ground floor, and the doorbell rang in it. "What's the matter with them?" He stood waiting, with the wind blowing his overcoat against his legs, and his irritability grew and grew.

A light sprang up in the hall, warmly yellow behind the fanlight; he heard the chain rattle back, and Miss Ewing opened the door.

"Oh, Mr. Charleroy!" she said. "Is she worse?"

"Who?" he asked, trying not to look at Miss Ewing.

"Mrs. Charleroy. Oh, I'm so worried."

"No, no," he said, frowning. "She's better. I happened to have a little time to spare and I thought I'd run down and see Julia."

"She's asleep now, Mr. Charleroy."

"Yes," he said. "Come in, Leon, and close the door."

There they all stood, in the wide hall with the polished floor, and the graceful stairway rising from it, so empty, so still.

"I want to put Leon up overnight," he said. "What's happened to the Bradys?"

"They went to Danbury to see their daughter's new baby," said Miss Ewing. "They'll be back in the morning."

"They had no right to go away!" said Charleroy. "They shouldn't leave you and Julia alone in the house!"

"Julia's safe with me, Mr. Charleroy," said Miss Ewing quietly.

He had to look at her then. "Sure of that," he said.

She was wearing green-and-white flowered pajamas and over them that tweed coat; her hair was again in curlers. "Julia'll have to buy the woman a wrapper, negligee, whatever you call them," he thought. "Little present. She shouldn't go around like this."

"Thing is, what rooms are ready?" he asked.

"Well, we'll see," said Miss Ewing gaily.

"The Bradys shouldn't have gone away," he said. "They're supposed to keep the place going, ready at any time."

"But they do, Mr. Charleroy! Everything was in apple-pie order when we got here. But their daughter's just had a baby, you know, so we let them go, just for one night. Nobody imagined *you'd* be coming."

"No, of course not," he said, trying to be reasonable.

But he was unreasonably disappointed not to find the Bradys here, the house alive.

"Julia— ?" he asked.

"She went to bed early," said Miss Ewing. "We stopped at Dr. Pugh's office, you know, and he said to use an ice bag for her poor little eye. She said it made her *much* more comfy."

"What else did he say?"

"What else? Why, nothing, Mr. Charleroy. Now I'll pop upstairs and see what rooms are all ready."

He went upstairs with her, and he mounted with an unusually heavy tread; when he reached the upper hall he spoke more loudly than usual. He wanted Julia to wake. "This is the room I use," he said, opening a door and turning on the switch. Everything was in order.

"Now, about Leon," said Miss Ewing. "If you'll just glance at the other rooms and see—I'll get things ready for you here, Mr. Charleroy."

"Everything's all right here, thanks."

"Just give me five seconds here!" she cried. "And you'll be surprised."

"Thank you, no!" he said, and stood holding the door until she went past him into the hall.

There were six bedrooms, each with twin beds, so that guests could be put up at any time. That, he thought, was the way you wanted a house to be, always ready, so that you could come into it whenever you pleased, bring along anyone you pleased. Julia was in the room she had always occupied; Miss Ewing had taken the room next to hers. Charleroy opened a door at the end of the hall, and the room there seemed quite in order. He went to the head of the stairs and called down to Leon.

"Here you are!" he called. "Here you are, *señor!*"

And Julia must surely hear this, directly outside her door. "This way!" he said to Leon. "Here you are!"

"Which bed will I sleep in, Mr. Charleroy?" Leon asked.

"Both of 'em!" said Charleroy, with a laugh.

But the little joke fell flat; Leon did not laugh; he looked more forlorn than ever, standing in the neat, brightly lit room.

Charleroy caught sight of Miss Ewing then, going along the hall. "Good night!" he said hastily to Leon, and went after her; he stopped her as she was about to enter his room. "Don't need anything at all, thank you," he said. "I can look after myself. Old campaigner, y'know."

"Well, if you're *sure*, Mr. Charleroy—?"

She gave him a merry smile and went away, and he closed his door. Rain came rattling against the front windows; he opened a side window, to get rid of the faint, musty smell in the room, and stood looking out over the wide, flat lawn. "It's a wonder Julia didn't hear me," he thought. "It's a great wonder."

He lit a cigar and walked about the room, the floor creaking under his portly tread. He had never before seen this room without Helen's things in it; there was nothing at all now on the chest of drawers, nothing on the dressing table. "If Helen was here," he thought, "she'd have some ideas."

"I want a look at Julia," he thought. "She can sleep all day tomorrow, if she likes, but I want to see her now." He opened his door, and the hall was in darkness, which was wrong. He pressed the switch in the wall, and a little overhead bulb came on, shedding a feeble light. He knocked at Julia's door, gently.

He waited, then he knocked a little louder. Miss Ewing's door opened.

"Sleeping the sleep of the just, Mr. Charleroy," she whispered.

"She's all right, I suppose?" he asked, not at all in a whisper.

"Oh, perfectly!" said Miss Ewing. "We cooked ourselves a nice little supper—Mr. Charleroy! I never *thought*! Would you like some of my famous scrambled eggs?"

"No, thank you," he said, and went back into his room.

"I'll give the woman half an hour to get to sleep," he thought, "and then I'll try again. She's a fine woman, very fine woman, but I wish she'd go to sleep and let me alone. I want to see Julia. . . . Maybe she was awake," he thought, "and didn't want to come out. No! She wouldn't do that. At the very least, she'd put her head out of the door and say hello."

He looked at his watch, and sat down in a basket chair. "Winter," he thought. "Sitting there in his car dead. Poor devil! But it's not the worst way to go. Quick, anyhow." . . .

"Well, I might as well be comfortable," he thought, with a sigh. "There ought to be an old dressing gown here in the closet; it was always left here." He rose and opened the closet door, and he was pleased to see the familiar object, a rather shabby robe of gray with a silver thread, a cord with tarnished silver tassels.

There was something on the floor of the neat and almost empty closet. He stooped and picked it up—a man's thin topcoat, and under it lay a man's hat. "Brady's," he thought, and closed the door with a bang. "He shouldn't leave his things here. Ought to know better."

He put on the dressing gown and started to sit down in the basket chair again. But something bothered him. You couldn't imagine Tim Brady throwing his things around like that.

He went back to the closet and picked up the topcoat again. There was something in the breast pocket, and he took it out. It was a wallet with a cellophane-faced compartment for a driving license. In it was a driving license made out for Leonard Winter.

He replaced the wallet in the jacket pocket and looked around the room; then he opened his suitcase and put the coat and hat into it.

"I'll finish this cigar," he told himself, "and then I'll go to bed and to sleep." And he knew that he would be able to sleep. He had done all the thinking he intended to do, if some horrible shrouded thing stirred in the back of his mind, he did not intend to examine it. Not now. . . .

The moment he waked he looked at his watch; it was after eight. The wind had died down; the rain fell steadily; the room was very cold. "I want to see Julia," he thought. "As soon as possible." He could make no plans, no arrangements, in a way he had to put off thinking, until he had seen her.

He went into the icy bathroom and washed; he dressed in haste, but with all his usual care. He was standing before the mirror brushing his mustache when the doorbell rang; as he stepped out into the hall it rang again. Miss Ewing was just coming out of her room, dressed in a tweed skirt and a green sweater.

"I'll go!" she cried, and went running down the stairs.

He heard her unlock the door; he heard her say "Yes?" in bright inquiry.

"I'm Lieutenant Levy, madam, from the Horton County Police. Sorry to disturb you so early, but I'd like to ask a few questions. May I see Miss Charleroy?"

"I'm afraid she's still asleep," said Miss Ewing. "She hasn't been feeling very well. Wouldn't I do? I'm staying here with her. Ewing, my name is, Katrinka Ewing."

"Thank you, Miss Ewing. I daresay you'll be able to help us. But I'd like to see Miss Charleroy later."

Charleroy went along the hall and knocked at Julia's door.

"I want to see you, Julia. At once," he said.

"I'll be down in a few moments, Daddy."

"No, now. Put on a wrapper and open the door."

"All right!" she said angrily, and turned the key.

She was wearing a blue shirt and a dark skirt; her dark hair was smooth and neat. Yet she looked wretched, woebegone, dreadful, to him, with her discolored eye, the sullen thrust of her underlip.

"There's a man here from the police," he said. "He wants to see you."

"All right," she said.

There had been no greeting between them, no pretense of their being glad to see each other.

"There's no use going into details just now," Charleroy went on, "but a man was found last night, just outside the drive here. He'd been shot. Killed."

"Really?" said Julia indifferently.

"Julia—" Charleroy began, in the very low tone he had used from the first.

"Mr. Charleroy?" said a voice behind him, and, turning, he

saw Lieutenant Levy halfway up the stairs, polite, smiling, but very alert. "Miss Ewing tells me your daughter isn't feeling very well. If she'd prefer, I can come upstairs and talk to her."

"I'll come down," said Julia clearly.

There was nothing for Charleroy to do but stand aside and let her go; he followed her down the stairs and into the sitting-room, where Miss Ewing stood before the empty fireplace. In the past, this room had seemed to him particularly colorful, with the chintz curtains, the flowered wallpaper, the bits of shining brass here and there. But on this rainy morning it was bleak and deadly cold.

"Sit down, Miss Charleroy," said Levy. "Have you heard anything about what happened yesterday, just outside here?"

"Yes. My father just told me."

"This man's name was apparently Winter, Leonard Winter. Were you acquainted with him, Miss Charleroy?"

"No," said Julia.

"Her manner," thought Charleroy, "couldn't be worse, sullen and brusque; she must be making the worst possible impression on this policeman: Better," he thought, "if Levy would speak sharply to her." His patience was somehow sinister.

"You see," Levy said, with an air of explaining everything, "the first thing we want to do is identify the body. The car has a Buffalo license and it's registered in the name of Leonard Winter, who was recently living in a hotel in Buffalo. We got in touch with the Buffalo police and they say he left there some days ago. We could get someone from Buffalo to come down and identify, but that takes time. If we could get any information locally—"

Julia said nothing.

"You see," Levy went on, "we think he must have stopped in somewhere in this neighborhood. No coat or hat, and it was a cold day."

Still Julia said nothing.

"There aren't many houses just around here," Levy went on. "And there's very little traffic, this time of the year. But, just the same, in the course of time we'll find someone who saw him, before he got where we found him."

In the course of time—Charleroy repeated it to himself. It was an ominous phrase. There would be someone—a boy on a bicycle, a busy doctor driving by, a trouble shooter up a pole—someone, surely, must have seen this man.

"You see," Levy said, "he wasn't killed in the car."

"Mercy!" cried Miss Ewing, with eager interest. "How can you possibly know *that*?"

"For one thing," Levy answered, "there was no blood in the car, and no sign of any having been cleaned up. And, for another thing, the Medical Officer says that, sitting the way we found him, the man couldn't have been shot through the heart. The bullet came from below him."

In the course of time—Charleroy said it to himself. There was a car coming up the drive now, and suppose it were to bring the boy, the doctor, the trouble shooter, the inevitable witness?

The car stopped, but there was no sound of footsteps on the veranda; the doorbell did not ring. Somebody standing outside, cautiously peering in at a window?

Then the back door closed, there were footsteps in the kitchen.

"The Bradys!" he said, with a sigh of relief.

"I'd like to see them," said Levy, and went out of the room. He was back in a moment, followed by the Bradys, still in traveling costume, and after them came Leon, very neat, his black hair sleek.

"Good morning!" Charleroy said to the Bradys, and they answered together, "Good morning, sir!"

"A fine couple," Charleroy thought; "fine people."

Tim Brady was a man of fifty-five or so, tall and gangling, with a long, rueful upper lip and a low forehead habitually wrinkled in a puzzled frown. Loretta, his wife, was a little thing, quick and lively, white-haired, still pretty. They had been at Meadowsweet for some twelve years now; they had their own bedroom, sitting-room, and bath; it was their home for the rest of their days.

"Sit down, Mrs. Brady," said Levy. "Have you heard anything about what happened here yesterday?"

"Yes, sir," answered Mrs. Brady. "The taxi driver that we took from the station told us." She brought something out of her pocket. "We told the taxi driver to let us out at the entrance to the drive; that way we'd look around and maybe pick up something, and sure enough didn't I find these in the bushes there!" She was holding out a pair of white-rimmed sunglasses, and she was proud and pleased.

"There you are, Leon!" said Charleroy. "That's where you must have dropped them."

"Yes, Mr. Charleroy," said Leon. "They're always falling out of my pocket."

It was as quick as that, as easy as that, to cross the bridge from a passive resistance to the law to an active conspiracy.

"Always losing them," said Leon, and held out his hand for the glasses.

But Levy appeared not to notice this; he put them into his own pocket.

"Well, I won't bother you any more now," said Levy. He stood up, looking at the little herd he had rounded up there. "If you come across anything that seems to have any connection with the case, you'll let me know?"

"Yes, sir," said Mrs. Brady, alone.

"Any prowlers, for instance," said Levy. "You see, Winter wasn't killed in his car."

"Ah! And where was the poor man killed, then, sir?" asked Mrs. Brady.

"We don't know—yet," said Levy. "Well, thank you all."

Charleroy went to open the door for him; when it was closed, he stood beside it. "I've got to go in to New York today," he thought. "There are things in the office—appointment with Carlsen at three— And I've got to see Helen; there's no getting out of that. And I've got to be normal. She's a very observant woman."

He opened the door and stepped out on the veranda. But the cold, fine rain drove into his face and he retreated into the house. Leon was just about to mount the stairs.

"Leon!" said Charleroy.

"I ought to thank him," he thought; "ought to say a word of appreciation." Leon had been asked to lie, and he had lied, readily; he must understand why this had been asked of him; he must understand the whole situation, more or less. Yet in his thin, dark face there was no hint of knowingness; he stood waiting, attentive and obliging, nothing more. "No," Charleroy thought. "Let it go."

"When will your taxi be ready?" he asked.

"Tomorrow," Leon answered, and explained what was amiss with it.

"Then you might as well stay here overnight," said Charleroy.

"I'll do that, Mr. Charleroy," said Leon.

Charleroy went on to the kitchen, where he found the Bradys sitting at the table, drinking coffee.

"Don't get up! Don't get up!" he said. "Station wagon in order, Tim? . . . Good! If you'll bring it around, I'd like to make the nine-forty."

He left the kitchen, closing the door behind him; in the little hall he paused for a moment. "No!" he said to himself. "I won't want to talk to Julia now. Not now."

As he started up the stairs he was saying to himself, over and over, "The less I know, the better." But he checked that. "No reason to think there is anything to 'know,' " he thought. "The only thing is, to act for the best, as things come up."

He finished packing his bag and carried it downstairs. Mrs. Brady had breakfast ready for him in the dining-room, and he sat down there alone. "Julia's got Miss Ewing to look after her," he thought. "Couldn't find anyone better, more devoted. The Bradys are here; Leon's here." He tried to take comfort from the thought of all these devoted people about her, but in his mind he saw her as forlorn, wretched, stubbornly hostile. "She's not herself," he thought.

There was no one he knew on the train, and he was glad of that; he sat in the smoker, looking out of the window at the flat country in the rain, and he made his plans.

The first thing was, to get rid of Winter's clothes. "Two angles to that," he thought. "I want to put them where they won't be found, but I don't want to destroy them. I might want to bring them out, later on. After Levy's caught the killer."

He concentrated his thoughts upon the clothes in his bag, and in a few minutes a good solution came to him, as he had expected it would. "I'll take them to the club," he thought, "leave them in my locker. No one's going to look there."

With this settled in his mind he began to think of Helen. Not of Julia. He knew already what he wanted to do about Julia; the great difficulty was, how to present it to Helen. "She must not be worried," he thought. "She's ill. She must be spared."

At the Grand Central he got a taxi and drove to the Pendleton Club; he went directly to the locker-room, which he had seldom visited before; he wrapped Winter's coat and hat in his old bath-robe, brought along for the purpose, and locked up the bundle. Nobody here would ever dream of opening his locker, and, he thought, it was improbable, almost impossible, that a Horton County policeman would enter a place like this.

Then he got into another taxi and drove off to the hospital.

He knocked on Helen's door, and she called, "Come in!" He entered, and he was not pleased to find her sitting in a chair, a blanket over her knees.

"You're up?" he said. "It's too soon."

"No," she said. "I didn't have any temperature last night, or this morning."

But she was pale, her clear features were a little sharpened; it seemed to him that she looked remote and a little strange. He went to her side, and as he bent to kiss her she put one arm around his neck; she drew his face against hers and held him fast for a moment, with that queer little fierceness which underlay her great composure. He had, in the past, seen her speak sternly to one of the children, and then suddenly catch the little culprit in her arms. "Don't do that again!" she would say.

He stood for a moment with his heavy head bent; then she released him and he stood upright. He began to ask her questions: What medicine were they giving her? How was she eating? How was she sleeping?

"I'm much better, Carrol," she answered, with impatience. "I wish I'd never let Dr. Marcher rush me off here. I wish I'd stayed home."

"You're better off here."

"No," she said briefly, and was silent for a moment. "Are you going back to Meadowsweet tonight, Carrol?"

He brought up a chair and sat down beside her. "Yes," he said. "And there's another thing, Helen. I may have to go to Chicago on Monday."

He was watching her covertly, and he saw no change, no look of surprise in her face. "I thought of taking Julia along," he said.

"That's a nice idea," she said. "Perhaps she could look up Anne Barrow there."

So it was done, and with surprising ease. He had dreaded telling her of this trip; he had expected questions, objections. But she did not seem to think the plan at all odd, or even particularly interesting. He left her a few moments later, relieved, seeing the road clear before him.

"I'll have to go to Chicago on Monday," he told Masterman, his partner, when he got to the office. "Family business."

That, too, was surprisingly easy. He talked to Masterman

about matters that would, or might, come up during his absence; he told his secretary to get plane reservations and hotel rooms for himself and his daughter. On his way out to lunch he stopped in a telephone booth in the lobby and called up a fellow club member.

"Macarren?" he said. "This is Charleroy. You're from Chicago; can you give me the name of a doctor there, a first-class man?"

"Certainly!" Macarren answered, with severity. "I'll give you the name of the best all-around man there. If he can't help you, I don't think anybody could."

Charleroy wrote down the name and address in his little blue, leather-covered book, and went on to his lunch. "I'll see this doctor alone, first," he thought. "I'll get some information about drugs; how long the effects can last, and so on. Julia doesn't remember anything about that Wednesday evening. There may be—other blackouts. It's possible, I suppose, that she'll never remember . . .

"That would be the best. If I'm satisfied with this doctor," he thought, "I'll leave her there for a while. Get her a suite in some comfortable little hotel, send Miss Ewing out to keep her company. What will I tell Helen about that? I don't know," he thought. "I'll think of something. But I'm going to get Julia away."

For a little change, he told himself, still denying, still refusing to look at the shadow that waited in the background of his mind. . . .

He was determined upon this course, impatient to embark upon it. "But we'll have to wait until Monday," he thought. "That police fellow isn't likely to object, but we don't want to seem hurried. Just two days," he thought. He would spend those two days at Meadowsweet, and he hoped, he believed, that he could keep her shut away and safe.

"I don't imagine Levy will be back," he told himself. "There's nothing to connect anyone in the house with Winter. And he seems a decent sort of fellow, Levy does. Not the type who'd want to bother respectable people."

He got out of the train at the little station that was so deserted and bleak in the March twilight. In another three months, he thought, it would be summer, alive, cheerful. Margaret and her new husband would come to visit; the house would be full again, Helen there; friends of Julia's would be there. And Julia, herself, would be recovered, calm, proud, confident.

As the taxi turned into the drive, he noticed, with surprise and uneasiness, that another car, a taxi, had turned in after him. Who could this be? he wondered. No visitor could be welcome now. His cab stopped before the house and Charleroy paid the driver and got out, just as the door of the other cab opened and that passenger descended. He was a slim, even a thin, young man, in a dark overcoat and a soft, black hat pulled down too low over his forehead. Looks queer, Charleroy thought.

"Yes?" he asked, standing at the foot of the steps.

"I came to see Miss Charleroy," said the stranger. "Miss Julia."

"I'm her father," said Charleroy, and the young man took off his hat. He had neat blond hair, a sharp and rather long nose, a look of fatigued cheerfulness about his gray eyes and his thin, wide mouth.

"My name's Winter, sir, Leonard Winter. I heard from Irene

Bascom that I'd be likely to find Miss Julia out here, so I came along."

"Leonard Winter," Charleroy was repeating to himself, in blank astonishment. "Leonard Winter, eh? But Leonard Winter is dead."

He glanced again at the newcomer; there he stood, still hat in hand, in the chill wind, patient, amiable, but, Charleroy thought, with something unbearably flippant about him. "An impostor," Charleroy thought. "I'd like to order him off the place. Tell him to get out. But better not. If he actually is the fellow Julia was out with, he'll need handling."

"Is my daughter expecting you?" he asked, with an effort.

"No, sir; I just took a chance."

"You came all the way out from New York?"

"Well, yes, sir."

"In business there?" He had to know all he could about this fellow.

"Oh, yes, sir," said Leonard Winter. "I give dancing lessons."

"Good heavens!" thought Charleroy. Then he said, "I don't know whether my daughter's seeing anyone or not. I'll find out."

He mounted the steps and rang the bell; when Mrs. Brady opened the door he stepped in, closing the door behind him. "I don't want that fellow in the house," he thought. "Miss Julia?" he asked.

"Up in her room, sir," said Mrs. Brady, and he went up the stairs and knocked at her door.

"Come in!" she answered indifferently.

In a dark sweater and skirt, she was sitting at her desk, under a rose-shaded lamp.

"Oh, Father," she said. "Hello!"

"There's someone here to see you, Julia."

"Who is it, Father?"

"No use beating about the bush," he thought. "She's got to know this, sooner or later."

"He says his name is Leonard Winter," he replied.

She rose, looking at him in dismay. "But, Father! The other one—? The one in the car—?"

"I don't know. I don't know anything about it. Simply, this fellow says his name is Leonard Winter. He says he's come out here to see you. But if you don't want to see him, I'll send him away."

"I don't want to see him," she said.

Charleroy went down the stairs again and out of the house. Leonard Winter was still standing in the drive, which was empty now, the two cabs gone; he had his hands in his pockets and he was looking up at the upper story of the house. "I don't like this fellow; I don't trust him," Charleroy thought.

"Sorry!" he said, and the young man turned. "My daughter's not seeing anyone just now."

"Oh. . . . May I leave a note, sir?"

"If you like," said Charleroy reluctantly.

The young man came forward; he took an envelope out of his pocket and a fountain pen; he began to write, holding the paper flat against the wall of the house. He doubled it over, and handed it up to Charleroy, who stood at the head of the steps.

"Sorry to bother you, sir," he said, smiling. It was a gay smile, but the long creases in his lean cheeks, the lines at the corners of his eyes gave him a battered look.

"Walking back to the station?" Charleroy asked.

"Well, no, sir. I've got a room here, at Glazener's Hotel," Winter answered. "Thank you, sir."

He turned away then, and Charleroy watched him all the way down the drive, with profound uneasiness and mounting anger. "That fellow's going to try again to see Julia," he thought. "That's why he's staying here. Very well, we'll cope with him."

He wanted to go up to Julia again, but in the hall he met Miss Ewing, coming through the swing door that led from the kitchen. She was wearing a smock over her dress and a towel pinned over her hair.

"Cooking!" she cried. "I've got a really-truly Italian dinner for you, Mr. Charleroy! I went to the village myself and got the things."

"Very nice," said Charleroy.

He felt sorry for her, seeing how pleased she looked; for the first time he noticed dimples in her weather-beaten cheeks. "Lonely," he thought. "She'd like a home of her own, poor woman. And she's not likely to get one."

Then he heard a step on the stairs, and turned, to see Julia coming down. Her eye was still discolored and half closed; she moved more slowly than was usual with her; she was pale; ill, he thought.

"Julia!" cried Miss Ewing. "You naughty girl! Go back!"

"I think I'll come down to dinner."

"No!" cried Miss Ewing. "You can't! Get right back to bed, darling, and I'll send you the nicest little tray you ever saw."

"I'd rather come down," said Julia.

"Julia, no!" said Miss Ewing, her voice unsteady. "You *said* you'd let me look after you. You *know* how good I am about looking after people. You'll just undo *all* the good I've done."

"The house is nice and warm," said Charleroy in protest. "If Julia gets to bed right after dinner, I don't see what harm—"

"No!" said Miss Ewing, in a high, trembling voice. "If I'm here to look after Julia, the *least* she can do—" A sob stopped her, and Charleroy looked hastily away.

"All right!" said Julia, and turned back, up the stairs.

Charleroy followed her halfway. "Julia," he said, very low, "the fellow's left a note for you."

"I don't want it, Father."

"Julia," he said, "that won't do. Here! Take it!"

She looked down at him, over her shoulder; then she reached her hand behind her and he put the envelope into it.

"If you find anything in it that—bothers you," he said, "anything you'd like to discuss—I'll come up later."

She went on up the stairs then, her shoulders rigid, and Charleroy went back to the hall. "She says she doesn't know Winter, but she must know something *about* him, or she wouldn't have wanted to refuse the note. She's nervous, very nervous. She shouldn't be up there by herself. She ought to be down here, with me."

He sighed at the thought of a dinner alone with Miss Ewing, and went into the dining-room to mix himself a drink; he was still there, standing by the sideboard, when she reappeared, in a lightning change of costume, a long dress of dark-red satin, with long, tight-fitting sleeves and a small white fur collar, very crooked. She lit the candles on the table and sat down, in Helen's place, smiling anxiously. Mrs. Brady brought in two plates of soup, thin and watery, with bits of sausage and cabbage floating in it.

"I made it!" said Miss Ewing. "*Minestrone.*"

"Very nice," said Charleroy.

"But it's not hot!" cried Miss Ewing, as she tasted it. "I'll tell Mrs. Brady—"

"No, no! Don't bother! I like it this way," said Charleroy. For he had noticed a look on Mrs. Brady's face, he had felt an indefinable chill in the atmosphere, and he wanted no domestic trouble. He obliged himself to swallow all of the unpalatable soup; he praised the chicken and the salad that followed; he responded as best he could to Miss Ewing's sprightly conversation; he had a cup of coffee with her and a cigarette in the sitting-room before he went up to Julia.

He found her reading in bed, with a tray on the table beside her.

"Did you eat a good dinner?" he asked.

"No," she answered. "I hate garlic. Father . . ."

"Yes, Julia?"

"Father, he's the one. He's the man."

Charleroy was silent for a moment. "The man—who brought you home Wednesday night?"

"Yes," she said. "Look!"

He rose and took the note from her.

"Dear Mlle. J. C.,

I've tried a couple of times to see you, but no luck. Didn't want to telephone. Don't worry about Wednesday night. I was your lucky escort. In case you want to talk it over, I'm at Glazener's Hotel here, and entirely at your disposal.

"Leonard Winter"

"Yes . . . I see," said Charleroy.

Julia lit a cigarette and leaned back on the pillows. "I suppose," she said slowly, "that it could be blackmail?"

That had been Charleroy's first thought, but he was sorry it had occurred to Julia. "I'll deal with him," he said. "Don't worry."

"I want to see him for myself," said Julia. "I—in a way, I've *got* to see him. I'll call him up now and tell him to come over."

"Tell him to come tomorrow morning."

"I'd rather see him tonight."

"No. Tomorrow morning," said Charleroy. "I have reasons."

His only reason was that he wanted time to think, to examine the situation suddenly so changed for him. He could admit to himself now that he had believed Winter was the man who had been with Julia Wednesday night. But if he had not been . . . ?

"Suppose I've been wrong all along?" he thought. "Suppose those clothes of his were old things he'd left here, maybe months ago? He may have got a new driving license. I don't remember the date on the one I saw. Maybe nothing happened. Not here. He was shot outside, on the road. Blackmail, murder, drugs, all a nightmare. Let it be nothing."

"I'm going to Chicago Monday, Julia," he said, "and I'm going to take you along."

"I couldn't go, Father."

"Certainly you can," he said. "Nice little change for you."

"I can't possibly," she said. "*You* ought to understand."

He leaned forward to look at her, and regretted it. In spite of her half-closed and stained eye, her glance was steady and somber, infinitely disturbing. With both hands on the arms of the chair, he hoisted himself to his feet.

"We'll discuss it tomorrow," he said. . . .

———

Charleroy was not accustomed to lying awake. But tonight he could not sleep. He could not plan a clear course of action. He could not state his problem; he did not know with what, with whom he had to deal. "*You* ought to understand," Julia had said. Understand what? What did she think he knew? He flounced, angrily and wretchedly, in bed. He wanted to do something, to take some steps. But, in a horrible fog, he dared not move, for fear of hurting the ones he was determined to protect. He thought of the clear, quiet, untarnished Helen. Scandal, blackmail, murder. . . .

When he opened his eyes, there was a pale light in the room, and he thought that perhaps it was snowing. He rose and looked out of the window. But it was only a gray day; his watch showed half past eight. "That Winter fellow will be coming," he thought. "I want to be ready."

He took a bath and shaved and dressed, and then he felt like Carrol Charleroy again. He went downstairs, portly and hand- some, and in the hall below he met Julia. She was wearing a blue dress, and her hair was tied back with a bit of blue ribbon. The black eye was little improved, but there was a change in her that gave him heart. She did not look sullen now, but resolute; she had something of her old air of assurance.

"I telephoned to that Leonard Winter man last night," she said. "He's coming this morning, at ten."

"I'll deal with him," said Charleroy.

"I want to see him myself," said Julia. "And if he's got any ideas about blackmail, all right. I'll just tell him to talk—as much as he wants, to anyone he wants. Let him spread the tale all over New York. I don't care."

"That's the way I like to hear her talk," thought Charleroy.

246 ELISABETH SANXAY HOLDING

"But it wouldn't do. Not with the other affair in the background."

"You've got to think of your mother," he said.

"Mother's the most sensible person I know," Julia said. "I'm just beginning to realize what a wonderful break it's been for all of us to have such a sensible mother. When you come to think of it, she's practically never wrong."

"No," said Charleroy judiciously. "And how about me?" he thought. He would very much have liked a word of praise from Julia, but it was not in his nature to hint for it. "Wonderful woman," he said. "But any scandal about you would upset her very much."

"I don't know . . ." said Julia. "Let's have breakfast, Father."

"Where's Miss Ewing?"

"Still asleep. And I hope she stays asleep for hours."

They sat at the table together, with Mrs. Brady waiting on them; the dining-room was warm, pleasantly redolent of coffee and bacon; the wall sconces were turned on, making the glass and silver twinkle. And for a moment Charleroy could tell himself that perhaps nothing had happened, that this was no more or less than a cozy, happy breakfast of father and daughter, safe under their own roof.

They heard a car coming up the drive; they heard the doorbell ring.

"Mr. Winter's here," said Mrs. Brady.

"Bring him in!" said Charleroy. "Sit down again, Julia. We'll give him a cup of coffee."

But Julia remained standing, and, looking at her, Charleroy felt a sharp stab of pain. He could imagine what it must be to her, to face this man, this stranger with whom she had passed those lost hours; he felt an anger against Winter that turned him pale.

"'Morning, sir!" said Winter joyously.

He looked almost handsome in his well-cut dark suit; but why so gay?

"Miss Charleroy?" he said, and held out his hand.

"Good morning," said Julia, making no move to take his outstretched hand.

"A fellow I know borrowed my car, the day before yesterday," he said. "He left me a note, to say he was driving out here to see you. And he and the car have both disappeared. I wondered if you'd have any idea where he went, after he left here?"

"Sit down!" said Charleroy, so loudly, so imperiously that Mrs. Brady was startled, and dropped a spoon on a plate, with a little clatter.

The swing door into the kitchen was open and Brady was in there. He and his wife heard what Winter said. They would, they must, surmise who the missing friend was. Had Winter meant them to hear?

Winter was holding Julia's chair, and when she was seated, he sat down across the table from her.

"Oh, thanks!" he said, looking pleased by the cup of coffee Mrs. Brady set before him.

"Nice little village here," he observed.

Everything he said had for Charleroy an undertone of ugly and dangerous meaning; his debonair cheerfulness was ominous.

"How long do you intend to stay out here?" he asked.

"Well, I don't know, sir. My plans are flexible."

"What about your dancing lessons?" Charleroy asked, with scorn.

"Oh, they'll keep," said young Winter. "Might I have another cup of coffee, please?"

"I think your friend was killed," Julia said suddenly.

"What?" asked Winter. "I beg your pardon? What did you say?"

She had grown very pale, but her voice was steady, and her glance, fixed on his face. "The police found a man in a car, just outside our grounds," she said. "The car was registered in your name."

"Lord!" said Winter. "A smash-up?"

"No," she said. "He was shot. You'd better go to the police at once. They think it was you who was killed."

She rose; they stood facing each other. "She's superb!" thought Charleroy. "She knows Winter's bound to find out the whole thing—and she's simply telling him to go to the police—and to hell with him."

"You'd better go, right away," she said, and turned and went out of the room, straight and easy. And, for all this great dread and fear, Charleroy felt an immense pride in her.

"You'd better go," he repeated to Winter.

"Yes, sir," said Winter. "Any way you say. But first I'd like to speak to you about Wednesday night. To you, or to Miss Charleroy."

"This is it," thought Charleroy. "This is blackmail."

"All right," he said.

"On Wednesday night I was wandering around in the St. Pol, and I saw Ivan Barlow at a table with two girls."

"Where did you first meet Ivan?"

"In North Africa, sir, in an officer's mess. He was there—"

"Very well. Get on with it."

"Well, Ivan gave me a sign to join them, and I did. He and his wife got up to dance and I sat at the table with your daughter. She said she wasn't feeling so well, and she asked me to take her out for a little walk in the fresh air. We got our coats and we left, but after half a block she couldn't navigate. She fell and hit her head on the pavement, which accounts for her black eye. I didn't think she'd want to go back to Sylvie and Ivan, so I got a taxi. I thought I'd take her home. But she passed out before I could get the address, and I hadn't caught her name when we were introduced. I took her to my apartment. Couldn't think of anything else to do."

"Go on," said Charleroy.

"There's an automatic elevator in the house. I'm pretty sure no one else saw her, either coming in or going out. Except Hinds."

"Who's Hinds?"

"He's the fellow I share—was sharing an apartment with. The one who came out here."

"Go on."

"He came in, soon after we got there. Let himself in with his key. She was on the couch in the sitting-room, out cold. I told him it was a cousin of mine who'd never had a drink before. But when I went out of the room for a moment he opened her evening bag, and he must have found something in it that gave him her name. Anyway, when I came back, he showed me a pill he'd found in her bag."

"*What* pill?"

"Hinds knew what it was, right off. I've forgotten the name, but it was some sort of drug. A goof ball."

"No," said Charleroy.

"Well, that's what Hinds said it was, sir. Plenty of people take them, when they can't sleep."

"My daughter doesn't."

"Maybe it belonged to someone else," said Winter politely. "Anyhow, I was sorry he'd found it. I'd only known Hinds a couple of weeks, but I'd got a pretty good idea of what he was like. I didn't think he knew who she was, though, so I didn't worry too much. Well, when she came to, I took her home. The next day I had to go to Boston, and when I got back this morning I found a note from Hinds. He said he'd called up your house in New York, and the maid told him your daughter had come out here. He said he was borrowing my car, to drive out and see her. And that—well, that had me worried."

"Why?"

Winter was silent for a moment. "Well, personally, sir," he said, "I'd rather speak ill of the dead than the living. Makes less trouble, don't you think?"

"Get on with it," said Charleroy.

"Well, I was afraid he might try to—worry your daughter. About the pill and the rest of it."

"Blackmail?" Charleroy asked evenly.

"Something along that line, sir. Hinds was broke. And plenty tough."

"You believe that this friend you lived with was a criminal?"

"We weren't what you'd call friends, sir. We'd never set eyes on each other until about three weeks ago. Hinds advertised that he had an apartment to share, and I went to look at it. I liked it, clean, plenty of light and air, a room to myself, and it didn't cost too much. We were both out a lot of the time, only now and then, when we happened to be home together, he'd get talking. He told me some things about himself that I didn't much like, but, after all . . . Well, you know what it's like these days, sir, to find a decent place to live."

"Yes," said Charleroy. "You'd better see the police now. They're anxious to identify the body."

He could stand no more then, and he went out of the room.

He went out on the veranda and paced up and down, with rain blowing cold in his face.

Long ago, when he had been a proud and rather pompous little boy, he had heard in Sunday school about Abraham and Isaac; he could still remember the picture he had seen, of a thin and resigned young Isaac lying on the sacrificial stone while his bearded father stood over him with a knife. "All right!" he thought. "I'll admit that we owe a duty to society, civilization, law, and so on. But personally, I'll put my own people first. The people who trust me. I'll do anything for them."

He felt cold now, chilled to the bone; he opened the door and re-entered the house. The sound of Winter's voice made him scowl; he went to the door of the sitting-room, and from there he could see the young man standing with one arm along the mantelpiece, talking to Miss Ewing, who sat on the sofa beside Julia.

"I thought you'd gone, Winter," he said.

"Miss Ewing asked me to wait, sir," said Winter uncomfortably.

"She *made* him wait," Julia said.

"To market, to market, to buy a fat pig!" Miss Ewing chanted gaily. "Brady's driving me in to the village in a few moments, and I've offered Mr. Winter a lift."

"I'll go, too," said Julia.

"I don't want you!" said Miss Ewing, with a little pout. "I'm going to get surprises. I'm going to cook a real French dinner tonight."

"I've got things to get in the village," said Julia.

"No!" said Miss Ewing, with a little stamp of her foot. "You *can't* spoil all my little surprises!"

"Julia doesn't want to leave her alone with Winter," thought Charleroy. "Afraid she'll talk too much, make some slip. Although I can't see how it can matter now. He'll go to the police; he's obliged to. And then . . ."

He glanced at Winter's tired, amiable face, and he could not read it. "He's a dark horse," Charleroy thought, angry and alarmed. "By heaven, it would be a relief if he'd come out in the open and ask for money to hold his tongue! I could deal with him then. But when he hangs around, grinning—I don't know whether he's a fool or a knave."

There was a car coming up the drive. "It's Levy," Charleroy thought. "I knew it would have to be this way. This is the payoff. This is it."

He went to the door himself; he opened it before the bell was rung.

"Helen!" he cried.

She stood there, pretty in her gray fur jacket and a small hat to match, calm, impeccable, finely finished.

"*Helen!*"

"Let me in, Carrol! It's chilly."

He stepped back, and she entered the hall.

"Mother!" cried Julia, in just the tone her father had used, shocked, indignant.

"I thought I'd surprise you," said Helen. "Dr. Marcher got me a nice car—heated—and a good driver. I told the doctor I couldn't stay another minute in his hospital."

"You shouldn't—" Charleroy began.

"Don't worry!" called Miss Ewing, halfway up the stairs. "We'll get you right to bed, Mrs. Charleroy."

"No, thanks," said Helen.

"Now, do what Nurse Ewing says! I really am good at looking after sick people."

"I'm not sick, thanks, Miss Ewing. I'll just step into the kitchen and speak to Mrs. Brady about lunch."

"No! I'll do that, Mrs. Charleroy! I was just going down to the village to get things."

"Maybe Mrs. Brady has things in the house," said Helen, and went off along the hall.

"Delirious," said Miss Ewing, in a low voice.

"Nonsense!" said Charleroy, frowning.

He had not recovered from his shock. "Nothing," he thought, "could be worse than for Helen to come here now, just when the situation is building up to some unimaginable climax. Winter here in the house . . ."

They all waited in the hall until Helen returned to them, followed by Brady carrying a suitcase.

"Mrs. Brady says she'll get us a nice little lunch by half past twelve," she said.

"But I asked Leonard to lunch!" said Miss Ewing. "I promised him a French casserole!"

"Leonard?"

"He's a man I met," said Julia.

"I'll just go up and leave my things," said Helen.

"Let me be sure everything is comfy!" said Miss Ewing, and went scampering up the stairs.

Helen went after her, then Brady with the bag, and Charleroy and his daughter stood side by side, looking after them.

"She never said a thing about my eye," said Julia.

"No," said Charleroy. It was queer that Helen had said nothing about that, but everything in the situation was queer and dreadful. "Possibly we'd better—" he began, and stopped as Brady came down and went past them to the kitchen.

"No!" came Miss Ewing's voice from above. "I won't do it, Mrs. Charleroy!"

Helen's voice was inaudible.

"No!" cried Miss Ewing again. "Don't ask me, Mrs. Charleroy!"

"That's going too far!" said Charleroy. "She can't be allowed to upset your mother like that."

He started up the stairs, so fast that he was a little out of breath when he reached the top. The two women were in his bedroom, Helen sitting in the basket chair, Miss Ewing standing near the open door.

"You have no right to ask me!" she said. "It's—cruel!"

"What's all this?" Charleroy demanded, and Miss Ewing turned to him.

"Mr. Charleroy," she said, "your wife is trying to drive me away. She's trying to get rid of me."

"I've found a very nice position for Miss Ewing," said Helen. She was leaning back in the basket chair, her hands on the arms, her ankles crossed; a characteristic attitude, relaxed but formal. "I spoke to Olive on the telephone, and there's a very nice position for Miss Ewing, teaching music in a private school."

"In Seattle!" said Miss Ewing. "I won't go to Seattle!"

"It's a charming city," said Helen. "Leon can drive you in to New York after lunch, and you can get a plane tomorrow. . . . Carrol, if you'll write a check for Miss Ewing—"

"I don't want a check! I won't go to Seattle."

"Mother!" said Julia's voice behind Charleroy. "Miss Ewing's done a lot for us."

"Oh, I'm sure she has," said Helen pleasantly. "And I'm sure she'll like this new position."

"Mother, if she doesn't want to go to Seattle—"

"You see, her friends are here," said Charleroy, surprised and shocked, as he was sure Julia was, by Helen's attack.

"I think it would be better for all of us if Miss Ewing leaves this afternoon," said Helen.

"After all I've done," cried Miss Ewing, "you're driving me away!"

Tears were raining down her face; she put her hands to her temples, pushing up the petallike, dry hair into two grotesque and pitiable horns.

"Helen," said Charleroy, "Miss Ewing's done—"

"Mother," said Julia, "you don't realize all Miss Ewing's done."

"I'm sure we all appreciate what Miss Ewing's done," said Helen, with a rather alarming social smile. "But I think she ought to leave, this afternoon."

"No!" said Miss Ewing, in something like a scream. "I won't! You *don't* know what I've done for you and yours!"

"Perhaps not. But I'd like to know," Helen said, in her clear, rather flat voice. "What *is* it that Miss Ewing has done for Julia?"

"Mother," said Julia, "let's drop it."

"I won't drop it!" cried Miss Ewing. "I've killed a man—"

From the pocket of her smock she brought a small automatic. "With this!" she said. "I had it in Italy—to protect myself."

"Give it to me," said Charleroy, as casually as he could, and without hesitation she gave him the gun and he dropped it into his pocket.

"I killed him," she said. "To save your child." She looked up at Charleroy, her blue eyes swimming, "Now!" she said. "Now you see!"

With a thin hand, she pushed him out of the way and ran out of the room.

"Julia," said Charleroy, "is there any truth in this?"

"Yes," Julia answered. "It's true." She went over to the bed and sat down. "Have you got a cigarette, Daddy? Thanks."

She drew on the cigarette for a moment.

"It's—here's how it was," she said. "When we got here Thursday, Miss Ewing kept at me to go upstairs and lie down and she'd make me some tea. I went, just to keep her quiet. I heard a car drive up to the door, but it didn't interest me; I thought it was a tradesman, or the Bradys coming back. I was lying down, reading, when I heard them. Heard her, rather. She was almost screaming. 'No! No! you can't see her! I won't let you go up!'

"That worried me, and I got up and opened my door. She was standing halfway up the stairs, with her arms stretched out, and he—that man—was standing a few steps below her. He looked horrible. He looked—foxy and—horrible."

"Take it easy, Julia."

"I will, Father. He started to come up, and then he saw me, and he smiled. He said, 'I'm here to take orders for more goof balls, Miss Charleroy.' He pushed Miss Ewing aside and came up the stairs past her. I was going to ask him what he was talking about, when—the shot came. I didn't know what it was. He was still looking up at me—as if he was astonished. And then he fell backward—down the stairs—with a crash. And then I saw Miss Ewing, with the gun in her hand."

"Take it easy, Julia."

"Yes, I will. By the way he was lying, by the way he looked, I felt pretty sure he was dead. I wanted to get a doctor, but Miss Ewing kept saying, no, get the police. After a while I realized what she was saying. She was saying, get the police and they'll bring a doctor, and I'll tell them I shot that man because he was attacking you."

"Attacking you?" said Helen.

"But, you see, he *wasn't*! I couldn't tell the police that. I thought—maybe he had a wife. Anyhow, I couldn't tell a horrible lie like that about him—when he was dead. But Miss Ewing was so sure she'd saved me. She said the police would let her go at once when they heard why she'd shot him. I had to fight with her, to keep her away from the telephone. In the end, I gave her some of Father's whisky and she sort of pulled herself together."

"Then what did you do, dear?" Helen asked.

"I drove his car under the window and we got him out and into the car. I drove him to the lane. It was beginning to get dark then. I took off my sunglasses and hung them on a bush. Then, later, I couldn't find them."

She dropped her cigarette on the floor, and Charleroy picked it up and stubbed it out in an ash tray.

"We fixed up the hall," she said, "and we found his coat and his hat on a chair. But she took them away. She said she put them in the closet of Father's room, but I looked the next morning, and I couldn't find them."

"It doesn't matter," said Charleroy.

Helen rose and crossed the room; she sat down on the bed beside Julia. "My dear," she said. "My baby."

"Mother! You see I *couldn't* let her go to the police. Not when she did it—for me."

"I see, my dear," Helen said.

There was a sound of footsteps in the hall, and in a moment Mrs. Brady came to the door. "Lunch is served, ma'am," she said.

"We'll be down in a few moments," said Helen.

They were silent, listening to Mrs. Brady's brisk footsteps descending the stairs.

"Julia," said Charleroy, "where did you get that pill?"

"What pill?" she asked, looking up at him.

"That—drug," he said reluctantly. "That—goof ball."

"What drug, Father?"

"That pill you had in your evening bag."

"Oh, that? That wasn't a 'drug,' Daddy. It was just some medicine to break up a cold I thought I was starting."

"You'd taken some of this stuff?"

"Why, yes. I took a couple when I was in the Brocade Room."

"Where did you get them, Julia?"

"Miss Ewing gave them to me. Daddy, d'you think they were something else? Not a medicine for colds?"

"Never mind, my dear," he said, laying his hand on her shoulder. "When did she give them to you?"

"That night, before dinner. She gave me three of them. She said a doctor had prescribed them for her and they always helped. She told me to take one or two right after dinner and then lie down for a while. You see, I wasn't expecting then to go out. Only, when Sylvie telephoned, I'd thought I'd better go. Dancing does you a lot of good, sometimes."

"Yes."

"I put the pills into my bag, and I took one in the powder-room when I first got there. Then I began to feel worse and worse, and I took another. Father, do you think that's what made me pass out?"

"That's what I think."

"But why, why should Miss Ewing do a thing like that?"

"I imagine she didn't realize," he said.

There was another silence.

"Now, wash your face in cold water, pet," said Helen, "and we'll have lunch."

"Mother, I couldn't!"

"You can," said Helen. "For the sake of all of us, you can. Go on, Julia."

Her daughter responded to the challenge; she rose and went off to the bathroom, closing the door behind her.

"Carrol," said Helen, "what can we do about that wretched woman?"

"I don't know yet," he said. "I don't know. I'll have to talk to her."

"Carrol, let's help her to get away. Anywhere she wants."

"I don't know," he said. "I'll talk to her, later. I'll see."

"But let's not waste time, Carrol. Let's get her safely away *now*, while there's time."

"Later," he said.

He was steady on his feet, but he felt as if he were reeling. He felt as if he were deaf and blind and must be left alone in this blank world until he could recover.

When Julia rejoined them they started for the dining-room and lunch, and found that they had forgotten Leonard Winter, waiting with amiable patience in the sitting-room.

"Mother, this is Leonard Winter," said Julia curtly.

Helen smiled at him and held out her hand. She was, Charleroy thought, unnecessarily friendly to the fellow.

"We'll wait a few moments for Miss Ewing," she said. "Mrs. Brady, will you go upstairs, please, and tell her we're waiting?"

"Good heavens!" thought Charleroy. "Does she really expect that wretched woman to come down to lunch, to sit at the table, chat? It's ghastly!" Turning his head, he could look into the hall, where Hinds had died. Julia, witness of the killing, sat beside her father, pale and silent, but in no way distraught. Upstairs, alone, was the woman who had killed Hinds. Ghastly, to be sitting here, talking, smiling, waiting for lunch.

Helen was talking to young Winter, and he responded to her warmly; he seemed somehow different. "But Helen does that," Charleroy thought. "She brings people out, does something to them."

"Well, no," Winter was saying. "I was graduated from an engineering school the week before I enlisted, and there are a couple of jobs, pretty good jobs, I could get now. But I was more than three years in the Navy Air Force, and I made up my mind that if"—he checked himself—"when I got back, I wouldn't take a job; I wouldn't settle down until I'd spent my last penny."

"Are you doing that?" Helen asked.

"Nearly there now," he answered.

"So he was one of those boys," Charleroy thought. "Battered and tired by that inhuman stress and effort. Not a playboy, not a whippersnapper. Not a blackmailer. Maybe he had come, honestly, to reassure Julia, in his own way, about that evening. And maybe Julia and I didn't receive him very well. We haven't got Helen's diplomacy. She brings people out."

"Miss Ewing isn't in her room, ma'am," said Mrs. Brady.

"She must have gone out," said Helen. "Well, we won't wait any longer."

"I think I'll take a look," said Charleroy.

"I'll go," said Helen.

"No. Don't climb the stairs again!" he said.

But she was quicker than he; she was coming out of their bedroom when he reached the upper hall.

"Carrol, let's have lunch, please!" she said. "She must have gone away, and it's the best thing that could happen."

He went down to lunch; he sat at the table, but he could eat nothing. They went into the sitting-room after the meal, and he sat, silent and intolerably oppressed, trying to think, to clear from his mind the intolerable dread that clouded it.

"I think I'll lie down for a while," Helen said.

"Good idea," he said. "Excellent!"

But she came down again, almost at once. "Carrol," she said, from the hall; and when he went to her there she handed him an envelope addressed to him. "It was under the chest of drawers," she said. "It must have blown down."

With all the windows closed against the raw day? He tore open the envelope and glanced at the note inside; he moved nearer to the door, to get more light through the glass. He looked and looked, at the little sheet of paper.

"Carrol?"

"Nothing," he said. "You'd better go up and lie down, Helen. Take it easy."

He waited until she was gone; then he went out of the house by the side door, hatless, coatless, in the sharp wind.

The light was on in the station wagon; it looked like a fine, royal coach in the dark garage. Miss Ewing was stretched out on the seat, her eyes closed, her lips parted, a little empty bottle beside her. Charleroy lifted her in his arms, surprised to find her light as a bird; he carried her back to the house, but she was dead when the doctor came.

"I've called up Levy," Charleroy said. "He's got to know. The whole thing's got to be cleared up."

"Yes," Helen said. "I think I will go to bed now. I'll have my supper on a tray, if you don't mind." She sat leaning back in the chair, smiling, serene; but she looked exhausted.

"You shouldn't have come," he said. "Marcher shouldn't have allowed it."

"I was worried," she said.

"Why?"

"From the very beginning, when you told me Julia had come out here to take care of Miss Ewing, I knew it was—queer. I was sure Julia would have stayed in New York, where she could see me in the hospital every day, unless there was something serious. I telephoned out here to Mrs. Brady, and then I was sure. She told me about Julia's eye; she told me that Miss Ewing was perfectly well."

"Why didn't you speak to *me* about this?" Charleroy asked.

"I knew you'd put me off, somehow," she said, and looked up at him. "You're very clever, Carrol."

"No," he said. "No."

"The more I heard from Mrs. Brady," she went on, "the more worried I was. Of course, it was plain, from the start, that it was something Miss Ewing had done."

"How was it plain?"

"When Mrs. Brady told me that the poor woman was actually bullying Julia, I knew that she must have some hold over you both. And there was only one sort of hold she could have."

"I don't quite see—"

"If Julia, herself, had done something dangerous, or wrong, she'd never have tried to placate anyone, to keep it quiet. But she's so much like you. You're both so quixotic. There's nothing you wouldn't do, both of you, to help anyone you imagined had a claim on you. You're—" She paused a moment, and he saw her lips tremble a little.

"Helen," he said, "you must take it easy."

She frowned, with tears caught in her sandy lashes.

"You don't belong in this era," she said. "You're feudal, you and Julia. Like a medieval baron and his daughter. Your vassals have to come and fight for you, if you need them; they have to grow crops for you. But, in return, you'll protect them—against anything."

"That's rather farfetched Helen."

"Leon," she said, "the Bradys. So many others. You're— romantic, Carrol."

He began to walk up and down the room. "I'm sorry," he said. "I can't tell you how sorry I am that you've got into this."

"If you'd only told me," she said, "from the beginning." She put a handkerchief to her eyes, perfunctorily, as if annoyed, "We've been married so long . . . surely there could be *frankness*."

He stopped beside her and laid his hand on her shoulder. "That note?" he said mildly.

She was silent for a moment, and very still. "I could have given it to you before lunch," she said. "But I thought she'd gone away. I thought the note would tell you where she'd gone. I knew you'd feel obliged to rush after her, and it seemed to me much better to let her get away. If I'd had any idea what she really had in mind—"

"It's better this way, my dear. Better for her."

"I know. There wasn't anything ahead of her but disgrace and misery. I know that."

"But there's one thing you don't know," he thought, "and you never will know it." Levy would want to see that note, but he had torn it up and burned the scraps. He remembered it, though, and always would. The woman had written:

"If I've got to be driven away from you, I don't want to go on living. I've got a little bottle of something that I've kept for years, in case things got too bad. Things always have been bad, for me. I never got my chance as a concert pianist, because all the people around me were so jealous and spiteful. But when I met you, so many years ago, it was all right. I felt I could do so *much* for you and your children. I saw that your wife never really cared for you or understood you, but I do think that, through the years, I have been able to make up to you for that, at least a little. When she was sent to the hospital I thought that perhaps my great hour had come. I thought that I could look after you, and cook for, and play my music for you.

"But she has come back, and she means to drive me away. I'm going over to the garage with my little bottle. It's quick stuff, but I'm going to wait there for an hour. If you can think of any way that I can live, and see you, even now and then, come and tell me before it's too late. If you don't come, it's the end for Katrinka Ewing." . . .

"It's unbelievable," he said. "The poor woman must have been out of her mind."

"I don't think so," said Helen.

"Must have been. The whole thing—giving Julia those pills. No possible sane reason for that."

"The reason is perfectly simple," said Helen. "She didn't know Julia would be going out, and she gave her the pills so that she'd go to sleep right after dinner."

"But why?"

"So that she could be alone with you," said Helen. "Play the piano for you."

"What?"

"And I'll tell you why she shot that man," Helen went on. "She didn't think he was trying to attack Julia. She did it so that *you* wouldn't find out she'd given Julia those pills. She knew you'd never forgive that. She knew she'd never be able to see you again."

"Me?"

"I've known, for a long time, how she felt about you, Carrol. But it didn't seem to me at all—dangerous."

"Good—heavens!" said Charleroy.

"She did it all for you," said Helen. "She must have been frantic when that man came and started talking about the pills.

She felt that she had to keep him quiet, before you found out anything."

"Helen," he said slowly, "I can't believe this."

She reached for his hand and laid it against her cheek for a moment; then she let it go and leaned back again, smiling a little. "I can," she said.

CHARLOTTE ARMSTRONG

1905–1969

During the 1950s and 1960s, **CHARLOTTE ARMSTRONG** was among the most prominent American writers working in the suspense realm. She wrote twenty-nine novels under her real name and an occasional pseudonym, Jo Valentine, winning the Edgar Award for Best Novel in 1957 for *A Dram of Poison*. Armstrong was nominated two other times for the same award in 1967 for the novels *The Gift Shop* and *Lemon in the Basket*, while three of her many short stories—"And Already Lost," (1957), "The Case for Miss Peacock" (1965), and "The Splintered Monday" (1966)—also garnered Edgar nominations.

Armstrong, born in Vulcan, Michigan, and at one time employed by the *New York Times* in its advertising department, spent much of her later life in Glendale, California, with her husband, Jack Lewi, and their three children. From there she had a good vantage point of Hollywood, which was naturally receptive to her type of suspense, concerned as it was with ordinary people, especially young women, getting mixed up in matters far beyond their control. *Don't Bother to Knock*, the 1952 film about a disturbed young woman entrusted to babysit young children at a hotel, marked Marilyn Monroe's move into dramatic roles and was based on Armstrong's novel *Mischief* (1951). The filmmaker Claude Chabrol also relied on Armstrong's work as a source for several films, including *La Rupture* (1970) and *Merci pour le chocolat* (2000).

I chose "The Splintered Monday" for the collection not just because of its award-nominated history, but because it shows Armstrong in fine form late in her career. The death of Alice Brady, which appears to be an accident, is the catalyst for long-simmering fissures to open up within her family. Armstrong's smooth, sophisticated writing turns what could have been a prosaic page-turner into something far more thrilling.

THE SPLINTERED MONDAY

MRS. SARAH Brady awakened in the guest room of her nephew Jeff's house, and for a moment or two was simply glad for the clean page of a new day. Then she found her bookmark between the past and the future. Oh, yes. Her sister, Alice, had died on Monday, been buried on Wednesday. (Poor Alice.) This was Saturday. Mrs. Brady's daughter, Del, was coming, late today, to drive her mother back home tomorrow.

Now that she knew where she was, Mrs. Brady cast a brief prayer into time and space, then put her lean old feet to the floor.

The house was very still. For days now it had seemed muffled, everyone moving slowly in a quiet gloom, sweetened by mutually considerate behavior. Mrs. Brady had a feeling that her own departure would signal a lift of some kind in the atmosphere. And she did not particularly like the idea.

She trotted into the guest bathroom to wash herself, examining expertly the state of her health. Mrs. Brady had an uncertain heart, but she had lived with it a long time, and she knew how to manage. Still, she tried to get along with as few drugs as she successfully could, so she opened the medicine cabinet, peered at her bottle of pills, but did not touch it.

No, on the whole, she thought, it would be better to get through the morning without a pill—at least, to see how it would go. She dressed herself briskly and set forth into the hall.

It was going to be a lovely summer day, weather-wise.

The door of the enormous front bedroom stood wide and her sister's bed, neatly made, shouted that poor Alice was gone. Mrs. Brady sampled the little recurring shock. It was not exactly lessening, but it was changing character. Yes, it was going over from feeling to thinking. She could perceive with her mind the hole in the fabric, the loss of a presence, the absence of a force.

But Mrs. Brady found herself frowning slightly as she proceeded downstairs and back through the house to the breakfast room. This was her last day here. And her last chance? Had she *cause* to feel offended? Or to feel whatever this uneasiness of hers could be called?

Henny, the cook-housekeeper and general factotum, came at once with her orange juice. She was a big, rawboned, middle-aged woman with a golden cross dangling at her throat. Henny still had that sad and wary look in her big eyes. She had been much subdued, too much subdued, since Alice's death.

She had taken to being very solicitous, treating Mrs. Brady as if *she* were an invalid. Yet Mrs. Brady and Henny had been good friends for many years. They had set up between them a kind of boisterous relationship, with a running gag that Mrs. Brady was a great nuisance to have around, and Henny, whenever Mrs. Brady visited, wished only to see the last of her.

Perhaps that gag was no longer in good taste—not today, not yet. But the continued coddling rather annoyed Mrs. Brady, who had never asked for it in the beginning and didn't particularly like it now.

When Henny brought her eggs, Mrs. Brady said, "It's surely hard to get used to Alice not being up there, in that room—she was there for so long. When did she last get out and go anywhere?"

"I don't remember, Miz Sarah." Henny obviously wanted to escape.

"Tell me, you last saw her right after she'd had her lunch on Monday?"

"Yes, Ma'am," said Henny, looking miserable.

"And so did I," said Mrs. Brady. "Karen didn't think we should tell her we were going downtown. I didn't even speak to her."

"No. No. You don't want to feel bad about that. Look, you spent the whole morning with her." Henny seemed to be cooing and she was not a cooing woman. "You couldn't know. Miz Del will be here for dinner, I guess. Right?"

"That's right. Henny?"

"Your eggs are getting cold, Miz Sarah."

"Henny," repeated Mrs. Brady sternly, "is there something I haven't been told?"

Henny was startled. Her eyes rolled, and her hand clutched at the cross. "I don't know what you mean. I just don't want to talk about it. I don't think you should talk about it, either."

"Why on earth shouldn't I talk about it?"

"I mean . . . Well, you've got to go on," mumbled Henny, "and what's the good of talking about it? Poor thing. I mean, she's probably better off."

Then Henny put her head down and seemed to butt through the swinging door into the kitchen.

Mrs. Brady began to eat her eggs, reflecting on the contradiction of the golden cross and the horror of death—if that was what Henny was trying to be rid of, by calling death "better off."

Well, Mrs. Brady herself was not so crazy about the idea of dying, but she accepted the fact that one inevitably would. It was presumptuous, in her opinion, to say that poor Alice might be better off. Maybe so. But maybe not.

Maybe Henny felt guilty because, during that seemingly normal afternoon, Henny herself had gone up to the third floor to "lie down," as usual, and had not made even a token resistance to the coming of the angel of death, by being alert to his imminence. Nobody had expected Alice to die—not on Monday.

Shock? Maybe I *am* still shocked, she thought. But it didn't click, as the truth should.

Bobby Conley came shuffling in.

"Good morning," said his great-aunt. "No school today?"

"Nope," said Bobby, getting into his chair in a young way that was far more difficult a physical feat than simply sitting down. "But I better hit the books some." Bobby was twenty, and away at college during the winters. He was taking some summer courses, locally.

"Del is coming to fetch me," said Mrs. Brady.

Bobby grunted that he knew. Henny came in with his juice and a mound of toast. Mrs. Brady poured his coffee.

"How do you feel about your parents flying off to Germany and France?" she asked him.

"That's okay," said Bobby. "I'll be living on campus, anyhow."

"And Suzanne back in boarding school. You'll be able to keep an eye on her."

Bobby gave her one blank look, as if to say, How antique to think that anybody should keep an eye on anybody. "Oh, sure," he said tolerantly.

His sister, Suzanne, bounced in, looking like something out of science fiction, with her hair wound on huge rollers all over her small head. "I don't want anything to eat, Henny. I'm reducing."

Mrs. Brady cocked an eye at the bare waistline, exposed between two pieces of cloth, that seemed to her to be tiny enough to snap in a strong breeze. But she said nothing. She was not in firm touch with these young people. They had seemed fond of her, in earlier days, but even Susie, at fifteen, had grown away. They went their own ways. And, of course, they should. Mrs. Brady thought they'd had a better break than their father.

Sarah Brady had always felt a kind of responsibility for her nephew, Jeffrey, because she could see, better than anyone else, how he had been burdened all his life. Poor Alice had believed that to be born a beautiful female was all the Lord had ever required of her, and that to have been widowed in her early thirties was surely a preposterous error of some kind. It couldn't happen to her! Poor Alice, with no personal resources, but plenty of money, had taken to the one hobby that appealed to her: she had gone in for ill health.

Sarah understood as much as there was to understand. Alice had been the golden-haired pet, the pampered darling, whereas she, Sarah, three years younger, had been the "clever" one. And the lucky one, thought Sarah now. It may be better to be born lucky than good-looking. She smiled to herself and sighed.

Alice's one child, Jeffrey, had been at his mother's mercy all his life.

But poor Alice, dead or alive, didn't seem to bother Jeffrey's children.

"You were at the beach, Susie, all day Monday," said Mrs. Brady musingly. "But Bobby, you came home for lunch and you were in your room, studying, right across the hall from your grandmother."

They both looked at her like owls.

"I didn't bother her," said Bobby, chewing.

It was Henny who had found Alice, and had called the doctor, after Henny's customary "lie down."

"And she didn't bother you, eh?" Mrs. Brady said.

Suzanne looked at her with round eyes. "If you just didn't tell her you were going anywhere."

And Mrs. Brady thought, *Touché?* Or was the girl thinking of her father?

But Susie was thinking of herself. "I never told her when I was going to the beach. She'd just have a big fit about sharks." One brown shoulder shrugged. "Or chaperones."

Bobby said, "She didn't even know I was going to summer school to pull up my grades. She'd have had a big fit about that too."

"No, it wasn't easy to tell her anything," admitted Mrs. Brady with a thoughtful air. "It never was. *I* don't operate that way. *I'll* have a big fit if I think the world is kept a secret from me."

They were eyeing her. With skepticism? Amusement? Pity? Or with a touch of wonder? Ah, thought Mrs. Brady, they are not as indifferent to death as they pretend.

"So she didn't cry out? Didn't ring her bell? You didn't hear a thing?"

"Nope," said Bobby. "Not a croak out of her." Then he turned his face to her, quickly. "I didn't mean to put it . . . I'm sorry." And for one brief moment Mrs. Brady saw an awed and shaken boy, who had never before been across the hall from where someone had died.

But now Karen came in and said, "Good morning, all." She had come in quietly. Her hand touched the young girl's shoulder. Suzanne sat perfectly still under it. Then Karen touched her stepson's hair lightly. Bobby did not flinch.

Mrs. Brady was thinking, They won't give themselves away.

Henny came to serve the mistress of the house with her normal air of devotion. This was Karen's house now. She was a pretty woman, in her thirties, small, compact, well-groomed, gracious in manner. She had been a nurse, hired to take care of poor Alice during one especially trying bout, almost six years ago. Karen and her patient had taken to each other. And when the patient's widowed son had married the nurse, whatever else it may have been, it had seemed a useful and practical arrangement.

Karen's control and gentle good manners, perhaps enhanced by her nurse's training, had been a saving and a soothing influence, all around. She was the one person, Mrs. Brady reflected, who had always given poor Alice her needed dollop of sympathy, who had never, so far as Mrs. Brady knew, been driven to protest, to say, in one way or another, Oh, for pity's sake, cheer up!

When the young people left, Mrs. Brady took another cup of coffee which she didn't want and wasn't supposed to have. She said to Karen, "You know, I've been feeling something—I don't know exactly what. But I hate to go away tomorrow without getting *at* whatever it is. Why do I feel as if I were getting special treatment—the kind that Alice always got?"

"Why, Aunt Sarah," said Karen, smiling, "Of course, you are getting special treatment. We are all so fond of you. Don't you think we realize you have lost your only sister? Oh, it is too bad that this had to happen during your visit. Poor Alice always so looked forward to seeing you."

She did? thought Mrs. Brady. She found that her feet were shuffling, her toes curling. Normally, she appreciated Karen's soothing ways, but not today, somehow.

"I hope you aren't feeling unhappy because you and I went off on a lark on Monday," said Karen gently. "Don't feel that way. Please? There was just no reason to think we shouldn't have gone. There were people in the house. We mustn't be tempted to feel guilty, must we?"

Mrs. Brady examined this. No, she thought, but then, to my best knowledge, I have not been tempted to feel guilty.

"You'll be home, back in your own place," Karen was saying, "with all the things you find to do and I know you'll just go on, because you always have." Karen had butter in her mouth. "Now, tell me, is there something Del likes to eat, especially, that I could order for dinner?"

"Nothing special," said Mrs. Brady, rather shortly. "She eats what she's given." She felt, suddenly, that she would be very glad to see her own child. "So do I," she added, "usually."

"Dear Aunt Sarah," said Karen fondly, "as if you've ever been a bit of trouble. But you know, Jeffrey is the one who has been hit the hardest. Don't you think we must try—just to go on? And let time heal? He's going to accept that European assignment. I encouraged him to. Don't you think that's wise? To get away from this house will be so good for him—new scenes and new experiences to help him forget."

"Oh, yes. *I* think it's wise for him to accept that offer," said Sarah Brady. "I thought so before, and told him so, as you know."

"He thinks so much of your judgment," said Karen, "and so

do I. It is only the shock—I think we must just plunge into our plans. Let's see. You'll be busy packing today, I suppose?"

"Yes." Mrs. Brady thought to herself, and *that* will take *all* of twenty minutes. She couldn't figure out why she felt so cross.

Karen excused herself, to make her marketing lists, and Mrs. Brady went upstairs, moving through the big pleasantly furnished house with a strong sense of its eclipse. This house was going to be closed. Jeffrey and Karen would be off, abroad, the children away at schools. What will Henny do? she wondered. But Henny was a household jewel who could write her own ticket, having become as valuable as a rare antique.

Mrs. Brady went back to thinking of Monday. She couldn't help it.

Just after lunch, on Monday, Karen had invited her to ride along downtown, while Alice rested. Mrs. Brady, who loved to prowl the streets when she was feeling spry enough, had accepted gladly.

She had gone to get her things, discovered with pleasure a legitimate errand of her own, and then had passed her sister's bedroom door. Karen, in the doorway with a tray in her hands, had made a "shushing" mouth. Alice was not to be told that they were going out. Mrs. Brady had supposed at the time—and still supposed—that to tell Alice would have meant at least five minutes of listening to Alice bemoan the fact that she couldn't go too, or the fact that she was being abandoned.

So Sarah had merely glanced in, seen her sister's head—still golden, courtesy of dye—and the prow of her sister's nice straight nose (which had always made her own nose seem even more knobby than it needed to seem), taken the sense of her sister's lair, perfumed, and cluttered with the thousand things that Alice had for her bodily comfort, and heard her sister say,

"I wish to rest now," in her piteous, imperious manner. I must be allowed to do exactly as I wish at all times, said Alice's manner, because I am so ill.

Mrs. Brady remembered Karen's saying that Henny needn't bother, Karen would take the tray down; remembered Henny's dive for the stairs-going-up; remembered seeing Bobby, flat on his stomach on the bed, a book on the floor, and his head hanging over it; remembered how the car had pussyfooted out of the driveway, and Karen's sad mischievous smile, when they were finally running free, on their way through the small city to its center.

Mrs. Brady had happily considered what she could, in all conscience, shop for. (She lived very frugally in a tiny apartment, not far from her daughter Del's house.) Karen had discussed a new bedspread for Suzanne and socks for Bobby, and her dentist appointment.

"You won't mind waiting for me, Aunt Sarah?"

"I think I'd rather poke around by myself and take the bus back," Mrs. Brady had said.

"But it's three blocks to walk, from the bus to the house."

"I don't mind. Besides, I have a little errand to do."

"Can't I do it for you?"

"No. No. It's all right, you see, when the three blocks end in a soft chair."

"Well . . . if you insist."

So Mrs. Brady had enjoyed herself in the department store, inspecting bedspreads, and had advised about socks, and then, deposited on the sidewalk near Karen's dentist's building, she had gone her own way. Not far. Not for long. She had that little errand, which gave her a bit of a purpose, and she had accomplished it, and then window-shopped her way to the bus stop, and a bus had come before she was *too* tired . . .

When she had come back into this house, Dr. Clarke was already there, and Henny was weeping. Bobby was in the living room, numb and dumb and dry-eyed. Jeffrey had been notified. And Alice was dead.

Almost as soon as Mrs. Brady had reached her own bathroom, and taken one of her pills against the shock and strain, she'd heard Karen running up the stairs. But Karen did not need her, and then she had heard Jeffrey's voice below. So she had hurried down to stand by, been delegated to watch for Suzanne and break the news gently—as Monday had splintered out of the shape of an ordinary Monday.

Remembering, Mrs. Brady shook her head. But there was no shaking the nagging notion out of it. She couldn't help imagining that there *was* something she hadn't been told.

So she marched into her bathroom and took a pill to fortify herself. She intended to fare forth. She intended to see her nephew alone. She really had not—not since, not yet.

It was almost eleven when Mrs. Brady finally made it, by bus, to Jeffrey's office, identified herself to his receptionist, and could not help but feel gratified when Jeffrey came blasting out of his inner recess.

"Aunt Sarah, what the dickens are you doing here?" He was a tall man, a bit thick in the middle these days; his hair was graying; his long face had acquired a permanent look of slight anxiety. He was a quiet man, who ran well in light harness, grateful for peace whenever he got it.

"I won't have another chance to see you alone, Jeff."

"Will you come in?" The anxiety on his face deepened. "Or

better still, let's go down to the drug store and have a coffee break."

"All right." She wouldn't risk another coffee. No matter. So he took her down in the elevator and they sat in a leatherette booth. The place was familiar. Mrs. Brady had lived in this town, herself, ten years ago. The druggist knew her. The young girl who tended the snack counter was friendly. Mrs. Brady felt personally comfortable. She ordered a piece of Danish pastry.

But now to business. Studying her nephew's face, she said, "Jeff, it's true. Poor Alice didn't *like* it. We both knew that she wouldn't. I'm sorry that your last talk with her, on Monday morning, had to be even as unpleasant as it was. But I can only say to you that *I* still think you were right to decide to go to Europe, and right to tell her that you *had* decided to go."

"Why, sure, Aunt Sarah," he said, not looking up. "I know that. And don't *you* worry about it for a minute."

"Alice would have been perfectly safe, with all the arrangements you made, and no more miserable than usual. As far as we could *know*."

"I agree. Please, Aunt Sarah, don't think for a moment that anyone is blaming *you*—for your advice or for anything else in the world."

"Oh, Jeff." His Aunt felt impatient with him. "Of course, you're not blaming me. I don't understand why there has to be any thought of blame. *I* happen to know that the Lord is running this world and hasn't yet appointed me to do it. Or you, either." She was sputtering, as of old.

He was smiling at her. "I'm all right, Aunt Sarah," he said affectionately. "It takes a little time, that's all."

"I'm leaving tomorrow."

"I'm glad—" he began, and quickly stopped.

Oh, yes, he was glad she was going. It only confirmed what Mrs. Brady had been feeling. Well? Perhaps, she must concede that she *could* be a bit of a nuisance, too. After all, Jeff was a grown man. He didn't need his Auntie to stiffen him. Or shouldn't. Time would pass, time would heal. Heal what? The truth was, a burden had been lifted from Jeff and his household. All that eternal pussyfooting would be over. Fresh winds would blow.

But they were not blowing—not yet. Was the household guilty of being just a little *too* glad? And *too* soon?

No. She still sensed that she, Sarah Brady, was being treated too gently, in some way. She couldn't pinpoint one single piece of clear evidence—but she knew in her bones that she was being "handled."

So? Had Sarah Brady come to such a pass? She didn't relish it. Why, Alice was the one who always had to be handled. All her life. In fact, that was how Alice managed the rest of the world. If it did not behave just as she wished, she simply insisted that it *seem* to—at least within her range. And had always won, because it was easier to do it that way—Alice having such a very small and narrow range.

But not I, thought Sarah. No, not I!

"I *thought* you were glad I was leaving," she said flatly.

"Not for my sake," said Jeff, too quickly. "But I want you to be busy and forget. Live your own life, Aunt Sarah." He was smiling, but she didn't like either the look or the sound of him. "You have always told me that I ought to live mine."

Forget? thought Sarah, bristling within. Even poor Alice deserved better than to be forgotten as fast as possible. Furthermore, it *isn't* possible. Alice was what she was, and she will remain a part of our lives as long as we live.

"Oh, I say a good many things," she admitted. "For better or for worse, I have always been one to trot out what's on my mind. Well, then, right now, I keep having this nagging feeling that there is something that I *ought* to say. Or do. Or know."

"All you have to do is be yourself," said Jeff, somewhat fatuously. He patted her hand. "It'll be nice to see Del. She doesn't mind three hundred miles in one day, and the same again tomorrow."

"That sort of thing doesn't bother Del," said Mrs. Brady lightly, seeing clearly that her nephew was getting rid of her.

She refused Jeff's offer to send her home in a cab, insisting that she enjoyed the bus ride. On one of her good days, the truth was, she certainly did. But she wasn't feeling as well now as she might.

When Jeff kissed her brow goodbye and said, pseudo-gaily, "Don't you worry about a thing," Mrs. Brady was contrarily convinced that there was something she *ought* to worry about.

She stood on the sidewalk and listened to one word turn into another in her mind. "Handled"? No, she was being "spared." Well! She, Sarah Brady, was not going to stand for being "spared"! Not yet and not ever—not if she could help it.

Mrs. Brady walked back into the drug store to look in the phone book, but there were several Dr. Clarkes. She had no clue. Then the druggist hailed her. "Anything else I can do for you, today, Mrs. Brady?"

"Please, Mr. Fredericks, do you happen to know which Dr. Clarke took care of my sister?"

"Surely. Dr. Josephus Clarke. You want his phone number?"

"I want his address," she said thoughtfully.

"He's in the same building where your Dr. Crane used to be."

"Oh, is he? Thank you." Now Mrs. Brady had her bearings.

Then the druggist said, "I was sure sorry to hear about your sister. A long illness, I guess." Was he, too, delicately implying cause for rejoicing?

Mrs. Brady came into the doctor's waiting room, feeling like a dirty spy. The girl who took her name seemed totally confused to hear that she wasn't a patient. Mrs. Brady had to wait out the doctor's appointments for almost two hours.

So she sat and turned the leaves of old magazines, and watched the people come and go, and pondered how to ask a question, when it was the question that she wanted to find out. Or whether there was one.

At last she was given her five minutes. "I am Mrs. Conley's sister, Sarah Brady."

"We met," the doctor said, "in sad and unfortunate circumstances. What can I do for you. Mrs. Brady?" He was benign.

"I don't know. You could tell me, please, *why* my sister died on Monday."

"Why? I . . . don't quite understand."

"I mean, should we have suspected?"

"Oh, no. Certainly not," said the doctor. "I see. I see. You have been feeling that you should have been at her side? That's a very common feeling, Mrs. Brady, but it really isn't rational. I'm sure you know what I mean." He was tolerant, gentle.

"You took care of her, as they say, for a long time?" She was groping.

The doctor said, with a sad smile, "I did all I could, Mrs. Brady."

"Of course you did," she burst out. "I'm not here to hint that you didn't. But what did my sister die of? Maybe that's how I should have put it."

"How shall I tell you?" He seemed to be countering. He was watching her, quite warily. "In a lay term? Heart failure? . . . I don't quite understand what troubles you, Mrs. Brady. But if you like, I can assure you that there is no need for you to be troubled—no need at all. We must accept these things."

"Dr. Clarke, I am *not* like my sister."

He made no direct response to this. "It is very easy to imagine things, in grief," he went on. "But when you have a bit of a heart problem, as you do, it is wise to learn serenity."

"I have a very good doctor," she snapped, "who has taught me to deal with my heart."

"I'm sure you have."

"Perhaps you know him? Dr. Crane?"

"By reputation. A very good man," he purred. "You are looking well."

Mrs. Brady shook her feathers. She was making a fine mess out of this interview. But the doctor was not. He was "handling" her expertly. In fact, he was getting rid of her. Expertly. Like Jeff.

Mrs. Brady found the old familiar bus stop. She supposed she must have put his back up, as the expression goes. I, said Sarah Brady to herself, am a terrible detective.

Well, it wasn't her *way*, to go snooping around corners and behind people's backs. It just never *had* been her way and she didn't really know how to do it. She, too, was what she was—a vinegary old soul—and her whole past wasn't going to let her be anything else. In the meantime, she hadn't found out a single blessed thing.

Wait. She had. Dr. Clarke had been told that *she*, Sarah, had a heart problem. Now, why was he told that?

Ah, now she was *sure* that she was being "spared" and "handled" and it was beginning to make her good and mad.

She almost trotted the three blocks to the house, brisk with anger, and had steam left over to pack her things with great dispatch. Then Del roared into the driveway. And when Del came, in her long-legged still puppylike way, there was a lift in the atmosphere. Something about Del. She was a young mother now, with a house of her own to run. But Del refused to be anything but cheerful. *She* didn't have to be tactful. It was impossible to be offended by her—Del was as open as the day.

"Sorry I couldn't make it to Aunt Alice's funeral," she said, "but Georgie was down with chicken pox. Sally isn't due to get them till Tuesday. So here I am. Hi, kids!"

Bobby and Suzanne regarded Del with a kind of suspicious delight. Dinner was almost easy.

Afterward, Del began to yawn. She said she went to bed with the sun these days. Why fight it? Her kids were up and roistering every dawn.

But Mrs. Brady didn't want Del to leave her side until she had said what she was going to say. She would still tear some veils. There was that anger still in her, still energizing her.

She said, rather abruptly, to the assembly in the living room, "I won't have another chance. So I want to ask you, right here and now, what's going on in this house? I've been poking around all day, trying to find out what's been hanging over my head. But I'm no detective. So now I am *asking*. Why are you keeping secrets from me? What have I ever done to make you insult me by keeping the truth away from me?"

"Why, Mama!" said Del, with nothing but surprise.

Jeff looked at Mrs. Brady with a reddening face. The others seemed to hold their breath. "I am sorry," Jeff said stiffly, "if you feel we've been insulting you, Aunt Sarah. That's the last thing any of us would want to do."

"Oh, Aunt Sarah," said Karen with gentle woe, "how can it be an insult to try not to keep talking about unhappy things?"

"I don't want to talk about unhappy things *because* they are unhappy," said Sarah. "I know how Alice trained you all—to keep unhappy things outside her door. But I don't like things kept outside *my* door—*any* things. And, as far as I know, I don't deserve to be treated this way."

Jeff was looking stricken and his wife put her hand on his knee. "Oh, Aunt Sarah, dear," she said softly, "you mustn't, you really mustn't. I'm so sorry that you feel as you do. I wish you didn't. Del?" She looked to Del for help.

But Del said, "I don't know what Mom's talking about."

"Neither do I," said Suzanne abruptly, from the heap she was on a floor cushion.

Mrs. Brady kept sternly to her course. "I want to know why you are all handling me with kid gloves. In fact, I think I want to know exactly what happened here on Monday."

"Children," said Karen, "she's had a shock. She's—"

But Bobby sat up in his chair and used his spine. "I know what she means," the boy said.

Mrs. Brady nodded to her unexpected ally. Karen's hands

were moving in a protective flutter, but now Jeffrey said, "The fact is, we can't be quite sure what did happen. If we chose not to tell you of a certain possibility, that was because it is very distressing to think about, and it certainly need not be true."

"There," said Karen. "Now, surely, that is no insult. When is it an insult to be kind? Del, dear, would you like something to eat or drink, before bed?"

Del said cheerfully, "You won't brush her off that easily."

And Jeffrey said painfully, "No, I guess not."

Karen said, "Oh, Jeff, this is *too* bad. Oh, please, all of you. Let it go. It's all over. There is nothing anybody can do or even really *know*."

But Bobby said, "I guess you'd better tell us, Dad."

And Suzanne said, with a burst of anger, "Don't you think we can take it?"

And Mrs. Brady was nodding and sparkling her approval. These kids will do, she thought.

So Jeffrey lifted his head and spoke in a blurting way. "All right. There is a possibility that my mother took her own life."

"Doesn't the doctor know that?" asked Del, breaking the silent moment of shock with an air of intelligent interest.

Karen said, "No, No. That is, he suspects that she may have had too much of her medicine. By accident. Or just in ignorance. He doesn't know, you see, that she happened to be feeling rather upset and hurt that day."

Bobby was on his feet. "Oh, come on, Dad! You know darned well Grandmother never would have cared *that* much. So you told her you were taking off to Europe—so what? Listen, *she* knew she'd have a ball, bossing a crew of nurses and telling everybody how you ran out on her. Well, it's the truth!" He looked around, belligerently.

Suzanne said, "She was spoiled rotten—we all know that. But nothing was going to get *her* down."

Karen said, "Oh, my dears. Oh, I don't think this is very kind. You are making your father feel very bad. None of us want him feeling any worse. Please?"

Del said, "I don't see what you're all so upset about."

And Karen said, "There now. That is *very* sensible. Isn't it?"

"It certainly is," snapped Mrs. Brady. "You haven't said a word so far that was worth keeping secret. You think she might have, in one of her moods, taken too much medicine on purpose? But the doctor thinks not? I can't see anything in *that* worth lying to me about."

"But we can't *know*," said Karen, "and why should *you* be worried?"

Mrs. Brady answered in ringing tones. "Why not? I'm alive."

Her nephew looked at her and said, "I beg your pardon, Aunt Sarah. We should have told you. I think you knew that your heart medicine is the same as hers? And you knew that her pills were very much weaker than yours—almost placebos, in fact? Karen spoke to you of that, didn't she? The day you unpacked."

"Yes."

"Well, my mother evidently crossed over to your room on Monday, took your bottle of pills, got back into bed, and then swallowed enough to be too many for her. She took them herself—no doubt of that. So it just seemed—after the doctor had gone—"

Jeff began to flounder. "When we found—we didn't want

to—we felt—" He put his hands over his eyes. "For Bobby's sake, who didn't notice that she crossed the hall, and for your sake, Aunt Sarah, who *did* encourage me to tell my mother I was going away—well, we saw no reason, since we can't be *sure* of the truth, why you should be tortured by this doubt."

"By which *you* are being tortured?" said Mrs. Brady. Then she closed her mouth and set herself to manage her treacherous heart.

"It is perfectly possible—in fact, it is probable," Jeff said, straining to believe, "that she forgot. Or never realized that your pills were so much stronger. It may have been just that her own supply was low—"

Del said alertly, "Mama?"

Sarah Brady had shrunken in the chair. She was hunched there like a little old monkey, and the agitation of her heart was now visible to all.

Her daughter came to her and said again, "Mama?"

"Get my handbag—pills," Mrs. Brady mumbled through numb lips.

Karen said, "Oh, Aunt Sarah!" She clapped her hands and called, "Henny! Bring a glass of water—quickly." She stood by Mrs. Brady and her nurse's fingers felt for the pulse. Sarah kept breathing as slowly and as deeply as she could.

Bobby said, "Listen, everybody! If I'd seen her, which I didn't, I wouldn't have known to *do* anything. It's a lot of malarkey! Keeping stuff from *me*."

Suzanne said, "Listen, if Grandmother had *wanted* to kill herself she'd have done it. What's the difference how? But I'll never believe she *did* do it."

Henny was there and Del ran up with the handbag. Del

grabbed the glass of water, pushing Karen away. Mrs. Brady swallowed a pill, then some water, and sighed.

In a few moments she said, "How do you know she took *my* pills?"

"Oh, Miz Sarah," wailed Henny, "why did you have to find out about that? It was me who saw your bottle under her bed—after the doctor went."

"And who," said Mrs. Brady, lifting her voice a little, but not looking up, "put it back in my room?"

"Me," said Henny. "Miz Karen, she recognized it. And she said—and Mr. Conley, he felt so terrible—so they both said, Well, the *least* said the better. *I* didn't want you to feel bad, either." Henny was ready to weep. "Listen, you got to pray Miz Alice didn't sin, not that way."

Mrs. Brady shook her head. "Jeff, did you see this bottle, *my* bottle, on Monday?"

"Yes, I saw it." Her nephew bent forward, alarmed for her. "Now, don't worry, Aunt Sarah—forget it. We shouldn't have told you."

Mrs. Brady could feel her blood beginning to flow less turbulently.

"I can't," she said. "I can't forget it. My bottle was downtown when Alice died—I *know* it was!"

"Why, no," said Jeff. "I'm sorry, Aunt Sarah, it couldn't have been—it was under Alice's bed."

"I *was* surprised," said Mrs. Brady in a stronger voice, "to see so many of my pills gone at noon. But I carry Dr. Crane's prescription with me all the time, so after Karen left me and went to the dentist, I dropped into Mr. Fredericks' drug store."

In the silence that followed, she looked only at Karen.

"Oh, but then *she* must have—" said Karen. "Poor Alice must have—"

Mrs. Brady sighed again. No. Definitely not. Alice, dead, had put no bottle under her deathbed.

She said, without anger, "I guess you wouldn't have talked them quite so desperately into 'sparing' me if you hadn't finally noticed Mr. Fredericks' name and *Monday's date* on this label? Oh, Karen, I told you I had an errand to do on Monday!"

No one spoke.

"When did Henny find it where you put it?" Mrs. Brady pressed on. "After I'd brought it back from Fredericks' drug store, of course. But by that time Alice was already dead of what you'd given her. At noon, was it, before we went downtown, when *you* took away her tray?"

"No," said Jeff. "No. *No!*"

"If there is another secret around," said Aunt Sarah sadly, "please trot it out."

In a moment Karen said sullenly. "She's buried. Now we can go to Europe. We can all live, for a change." The skin of her face was suddenly mottled, and her eyes had clouded over. "She was going to raise such a fuss. Jeff wouldn't have stood up to it—he'd have given in, the way he always did. She wasn't any good, even to herself. You all know that. *I* had to take it, all day, every day. You can call it mercy."

But no one was calling it mercy. The two children had drawn close to their father. Henny went to stand behind them. Jeffrey Conley stared at his second wife with wide and terrified eyes.

"You can do what you want," whined Karen viciously, "but you had all better stop and think. What good will it do to let the truth out now?"

The room was still, without an answer.

Mrs. Brady took another sip of water, although her heart felt steadier now as she sensed the old familiar comfort that always sustained her.

"The quality of truth," she said, "is that it's really there. Poor Alice taught me that."

It was Del who said, "I'll call the police—it has to be done. I'll do it."

Poor Karen.

DOROTHY SALISBURY DAVIS

1916–

DOROTHY SALISBURY DAVIS is the lone author in the collection who is still alive, and at ninety-six years old, Davis's spirit remains unimpeded—she described herself as "gregarious and socially vibrant" in a May 2012 interview. Born and raised in Illinois, Davis worked as a research librarian in the advertising world and as an editor for Chicago-based magazine *The Merchandiser* before finding her calling in fiction. Though she published two short sets of series novels, one featuring the housekeeper Mrs. Norris and police detective Jasper Tully, along with another starring a different sleuth, Julie Hayes, Davis's stand-alone novels, including *The Judas Cat* (1949), *The Pale Betrayer* (1965), and, most recently, *In the Still of the Night* (2001), feature her very best work.

Sara Paretsky, one of the pioneers of female private-eye fiction and a fellow Illinois author, hailed Davis for her hallmark "awareness of how easy it is for ordinary people to do nasty or wicked deeds . . . She lived among bootleggers, immigrants, sharecroppers, and itinerant workers in her early years, and there's a richness to her understanding of the human condition that is missing from most contemporary crime fiction."

That deep well of understanding and empathy suffuses Davis's short fiction as well, much of it collected in *Tales of a Stormy Night*, published a year before she was awarded the Mystery Writers of America's Grand Master designation in 1985. Instead of being concerned with black-and-white notions of good and evil, Davis's characters are flawed, doing their best to transcend their failings even when, more often than not, they cannot do so. They act with sincere motives and deep feelings, even when events conspire to turn out very badly or dampen success with a terrible but necessary sting in the tail.

"Lost Generation" may seem an unorthodox choice for the anthology, at least at first blush, since it's told from and features the perspective of men, a perspective Davis renders with unfailing and subtle insight. It disturbs in the way that only quiet, stomach-clenching horror can, as it roots out a mother's darkest nightmare and makes it feel utterly real. Upon first publication in *Ellery Queen's Mystery Magazine* in September 1971, editor Fred Dannay flat-out told readers, "this is not a pleasant story, we warn you. . . . you'll find no 'sheer entertainment,' no 'escape fiction' . . . But if you want to look into the hearts of men—rather, into the heart of a man—into the confusions and contradictions of today's prejudices, then we urge you not to skip the next six pages." Today, I urge readers as strongly as Dannay did more than forty years ago.

LOST GENERATION

THE SCHOOL board had sustained the teacher. The vote was four to three, but the majority made it clear they were not voting for the man. They voted the way they had because otherwise the state would have stepped in and settled the appeal, ruling against the town . . .

Tom and Andy, coming from the west of town, waited for the others at the War Memorial. The October frost had silvered the cannon, and the moonlight was so clear you could read the words FOR GOD AND COUNTRY on the monument. The slack in the flagpole cord allowed the metal clips to clank against the pole. That and the wind made the only sounds.

Then Andy said, "His wife's all right. She came up to Mary after it was over and said she wished he'd teach like other teachers and leave politics alone."

"Politics," Tom said. "Is that what she calls it?"

"She's okay just the same. I don't want anything happening to her—or to their kid."

"Nothing's going to happen to them," Tom said.

"The kid's a funny little guy. He don't say much, but then he don't miss much either," Andy said.

Tom said nothing. He knocked one foot against the other.

"It's funny, ain't it, how one man—you know?" Andy said.

"One rotten apple in the barrel," Tom said. "Damn, it's getting cold. I put anti-freeze in half the cars in town today, but not my own. In his even."

"The kid—he's just a kid, you know," Andy said.

Tom wiped the moisture from beneath his nose. "I told you nothing's going to happen to him."

"I know, I know, but sometimes things go wrong."

The others came, Frankie and Murph, walking along the railroad tracks that weren't used any more except by the children taking a short cut on their way to and from school. You could smell the creosote in the smoke from the chimneys of the houses alongside the tracks. One by one the railroad ties were coming loose and disappearing.

The four men climbed the road in back of what had once been the Schroeders' chicken coops. The Schroeders had sold their chickens and moved down the hill when the new people took over, house by house, that part of town. One of the men remarked you could still smell the chicken droppings.

"That ain't what you smell," Tom said. "That coop's been integrated."

Frankie gave a bark of laughter that ricocheted along the empty street.

"Watch it, will you?" Tom said.

"What's the matter? They ain't coming out this time of night."

"They can look out windows, can't they? It's full moon."

"I'd like to see it. I'd like to see just one head pop out a window." Frankie whistled the sound of speed and patted the pocket of his jacket.

"I should've picked the men I wanted," Tom said, meaning only Andy to hear. "This drawing lots is for the birds."

"You could've said so on the range." The town's ten police-men met for target practice once a week. They had met that af-ternoon. After practice they had talked about the school-board meeting they expected to attend that night. They joked about it, only Andy among them having ever attended such a meeting before.

"I'd still've picked you, Andy," Tom said.

"Thanks."

Frankie said, "I heard what you said, Tom. I'm going to re-member it too."

Andy said, "You might know he'd live in this part of town. It all adds up, don't it?"

No one answered him. No one spoke until at the top of the street Murph said, "There's a light on in the hallway. What does that mean?"

"It means we're lucky. We can see him coming to the door."

Tom gave the signal and they broke formation, each man moving into the shadow of a tree, except Tom who went up to the house.

The child was looking out the window. It was what his father made him do when he'd wake up from having a bad dream. The trouble was, he sometimes dreamed awake and couldn't go back to sleep because there were a lot of people in his room, all whispering. What kind of people, his father wanted to know. Men or women? Old people or young? And was there anyone he knew?

Funny-looking people. They didn't have any faces. Only eyes—which of course was why they whispered.

His father told him: Next time you tell them if they don't go away you'll call your dad. Or better still, look out the window for a while and think of all the things you did outdoors today. Then see if the funny people aren't gone when you look around the room again.

So at night he often did get up. The window was near his bed and the people never tried to stop him. Looking out, he would think about the places he could hide and how easy it would be to climb out from the bottom of his bed. He had a dugout under the mock-orange bushes, and under the old cellar doors propped together like a pup tent in the back of the garage; down the street were the sewer pipes they hadn't used yet, and what used to be the pumphouse next to Mrs. Malcolm's well, which was the best hiding place of all; the big boys sometimes played there.

Tom passed so close that the boy could have reached out and touched him.

The doorbell rang once, twice, three times.

The man, awakened from his sleep, came pulling on his bathrobe. He flung open the door at the same time he switched on the porch light.

A fusillade of shots rang out. The man seemed frozen like a picture of himself, his hand stretched out and so much light around him. Then he crumpled up and fell.

Twenty minutes later Andy was sitting on his bed at home when the ambulance siren sounded somewhere up the hill. His wife put out her hand to see if he was there. "Andy?"

"Yes?"

She went back to sleep until the town alarm sounded, four long blasts for a police emergency.

Andy dressed again and once more took his revolver from the bureau drawer.

"What time is it?" His wife turned over at the clicking sound as he refilled the chamber of the gun.

"Almost half-past three."

"It isn't right, a man your age."

"Someone has to go." In the hall he phoned the police station for instructions.

This time Andy drove, as did the other deputies. Cars clogged the street where lights were on in all the houses, and people stood outdoors, their coats over their nightclothes, and watched the ambulance drive off. They told one another of the shots they took for granted to have been the backfires of a car.

Doc Harrington drove up. Black bag in hand, he went into the house. Andy followed on his heels. Both men stepped carefully around the bloodstains in the front hall.

The woman was hysterical. "They took our little boy. They killed his father and they took our little boy." She kept crying out for someone to help her; anyone. The Chief of Police and Tom, who was in the room with them, tried to calm her down. She couldn't say who "they" were.

When Doc appeared and commanded that someone get a neighbor woman in to help him, Tom started to leave. Andy caught his arm.

"I don't know what she's talking about," Tom said. "She says the boy's been kidnapped. More like a neighbor's got him, but I'm going to organize a search. If we don't find him it'll be the State Police, and after that the F.B.I."

"The kid's not here?"

"Maybe you can find him. I've been from basement to roof."

Room by room Andy searched the house. The child's bed

had not been slept in much that night. You couldn't really tell, the things a youngster took in bed with him. The window was open just a little and it was hard to raise it higher. The back door to the house was open and Andy would have said the kid had gone that way because on the back steps was a woolen monkey, its ears still frosty damp with spittle.

Andy got a flashlight from the car and joined the other deputies, Tom, Murph, and Frankie among them. They went from house to house to ask if anyone had seen the child. No one had and the mother's cry of kidnapping had gone the rounds.

They searched till dawn. By then the State Police were in the town; the Chief cordoned off the house and set a guard. The house was quite empty. Doc Harrington had given the woman an injection and driven her himself the eight miles to the hospital.

The men, chilled to the bone, were having coffee at the station house when old Mrs. Malcolm, on her way to early Mass, stopped by to say she'd heard a noise that sounded like a kitten's mew at the bottom of her well. The well had long been dry and she'd had it boarded up after the Russo dog had fallen in and died there. But the kids kept coming back. They pried loose the boards and played at flushing "Charlie" from his underground hideout.

Tom and Andy were already in the Malcolm yard when the fire truck arrived. With their own hands they tore away the boards that weren't already loose at the well's mouth. The shaft was dark, but there were steps at least halfway down the shoring. It was decided, however, to put a ladder down.

Tom, again making himself the boss, said *he* was going down. The others linked themselves together, a human chain, to keep the ladder from striking bottom. The depth was about thirty feet. Andy was the signalman. He reported every step Tom took, and he cried out the moment Tom's flashlight discovered the child on the rocks heaped at the bottom of the dry well.

"He's sleeping," Tom shouted up. "He's sleeping like a little baby."

"He can't be, falling that far down. Be careful how you lift him," Andy said.

Tom steadied the ladder among the rocks, draped the limp child over his shoulder, and started up. The firemen went back to the truck for their emergency equipment. Andy kept up a singsong cautioning: a kid was just a little thing, it got hurt real easy. Tom was too large a man for such a job, and he ought to have more patience.

"Will you shut your damned mouth up there?" Tom shouted. "I'm coming up the best I can."

He'd got past halfway when the boy recovered consciousness. At first he squirmed and cried. The men crowded in to watch. Andy begged them not to block the light.

"Just keep coming easy," Andy crooned, and to the child, "There's nothing you should be a-scared of, little fella. You're going to come out fine."

Then—it was at the moment Tom's face moved into the light—the child began to scream and beat at him with fists and feet, and a rhythm of words came out of him, over and over again, until no one who wasn't deaf could mistake what he was saying: "My dad, my dad, you shot my dad!"

Tom tried to get a better hold of him, or so he claimed when he got up, but the child fought out of his grasp. Tom caught him by the leg; then the ladder jolted—a rock displaced below. The child slipped away and plummeted silently out of sight. That was what was so strange, the way he fell, not making any cry at all.

Tom lumbered down again. He brought the child up and laid him on the ground. Everyone could see that he was dead, the skull crushed in on top.

Andy searched the wrists anyway and then the chest where the pajamas had been ripped, but he found no heartbeat, and the mouth was full of blood. He looked up at Tom who stood, dirty and sullen, watching him.

"I didn't want to let go of him. I swear it, Andy."

Andy's eyes never left his face. "You killed him. You killed this baby boy."

"I didn't, Andy."

"I saw it with my own eyes." Andy drew his gun.

"For God's sake, man. Murph, Frankie, you saw what happened!"

They too had drawn their guns. The Chief of Police and the State Troopers were coming up the hill, a minute or two away. The two firemen coming with the resuscitator were unarmed.

Tom backed off a step, but when he saw Andy release the safety catch he turned and ran. That's when they brought him down, making sure he was immediately dead.

MARGARET MILLAR

1915–1994

MARGARET MILLAR is best known as the wife of Kenneth Millar, better known to the reading public under his pseudonym Ross Macdonald. But remembering her that way ignores her excellent literary suspense career—and the fact that with *The Invisible Worm* (1941), she published several years before her husband did. A native of Kitchener, Ontario, Millar immigrated to California with her husband and spent the bulk of her time in Santa Barbara, which proved a fitting, sunny locale for a number of her books that explored the psychological underpinnings of crime and, in particular, crimes affecting domestic situations and the inner lives of women.

Millar's 1955 novel *Beast in View*, in which an invalid woman is increasingly harassed by terrifying phone calls, won the Edgar Award for Best Novel from the Mystery Writers of America, and she was nominated for the same award two years later for *Stranger in My Grave*, a disquieting account of a young woman oppressed by marriage and a domineering mother who finds emotional freedom after a dream of her own death. *The Fiend*

(1964) is an empathetic account of a pedophile, a risky subject few other than Millar could pull off with any success, while *Banshee* (1983) is one of Millar's most emotional works, dealing with the disappearance of a young girl named Princess. All told Millar published twenty-five novels, the bulk of them crime fiction; a memoir; and a posthumous short story collection, *The Couple Next Door* (2004). She was named Grand Master by the Mystery Writers of America in 1983.

It was from Millar's posthumous story collection that I discovered "The People Across the Canyon," first published in *Ellery Queen's Mystery Magazine* in 1962. In it she takes familiar feelings of insecurity and curiosity and mixes them with something more sinister when a family moves across the way from the Bortons, who instantly rue the loss of privacy and then grow more suspicious of their new neighbors as time wears on. But nothing compares to the twists in store when their daughter, Cathy, takes a shine to the new family, giving Millar a chance to comment, brilliantly, on the dark side of aspirational desire and wish fulfillment.

THE PEOPLE ACROSS THE CANYON

THE FIRST time the Bortons realized that someone had moved into the new house across the canyon was one night in May when they saw the rectangular light of a television set shining in the picture window. Marion Borton knew it had to happen eventually, but that didn't make it any easier to accept the idea of neighbors in a part of the country she and Paul had come to consider exclusively their own.

They had discovered the site, had bought six acres, and built the house over the objections of the bank, which didn't like to lend money on unimproved property, and of their friends, who thought the Bortons were foolish to move so far out of town. Now other people were discovering the spot, and here and there through the eucalyptus trees and the live oaks, Marion could see half-finished houses.

But it was the house directly across the canyon that bothered her most; she had been dreading this moment ever since the site had been bulldozed the previous summer.

"There goes our privacy." Marion went over and snapped off the television set, a sign to Paul that she had something on her mind which she wanted to transfer to his. The transference, intended to halve the problem, often merely doubled it.

"Well, let's have it," Paul said, trying to conceal his annoyance.

"Have what?"

"Stop kidding around. You don't usually cut off Perry Mason in the middle of a sentence."

"All I said was, there goes our privacy."

"We have plenty left," Paul said.

"You know how sounds carry across the canyon."

"I don't hear any sounds."

"You will. They probably have ten or twelve children and a howling dog and a sports car."

"A couple of children wouldn't be so bad—at least Cathy would have someone to play with."

Cathy was eight, in bed now, and ostensibly asleep, with the night light on and her bedroom door open just a crack.

"She has plenty of playmates at school," Marion said, pulling the drapes across the window so that she wouldn't have to look at the exasperating rectangle of light across the canyon. "Her teacher tells me Cathy gets along with everyone and never causes any trouble. You talk as if she's deprived or something."

"It would be nice if she had more interests, more children of her own age around."

"A lot of things would be nice *if.* I've done my best."

Paul knew it was true. He'd heard her issue dozens of weekend invitations to Cathy's schoolmates. Few of them came to anything. The mothers offered various excuses: poison oak, snakes, mosquitoes in the creek at the bottom of the canyon, the distance of the house from town in case something happened and a doctor was needed in a hurry . . . these excuses, sincere and valid as they were, embittered Marion. *"For heaven's sake, you'd think we lived on the moon or in the middle of a jungle."*

"I guess a couple of children would be all right," Marion said. "But please, no sports car."

"I'm afraid that's out of our hands."

"Actually, they might even be quite *nice* people."

"Why not? Most people are."

Both Marion and Paul had the comfortable feeling that something had been settled, though neither was quite sure what. Paul went over and turned the television set back on. As he had suspected, it was the doorman who'd killed the nightclub owner with a baseball bat, not the blonde dancer or her young husband or the jealous singer.

It was the following Monday that Cathy started to run away.

Marion, ironing in the kitchen and watching a quiz program on the portable set Paul had given her for Christmas, heard the school bus groan to a stop at the top of the driveway. She waited for the front door to open and Cathy to announce in her high thin voice, "I'm home, Mommy."

The door didn't open.

From the kitchen window Marion saw the yellow bus round the sharp curve of the hill like a circus cage full of wild captive children screaming for release.

Marion waited until the end of the program, trying to convince herself that another bus had been added to the route and would come along shortly, or that Cathy had decided to stop off at a friend's house and would telephone any minute. But no other bus appeared, and the telephone remained silent.

Marion changed into her hiking boots and started off down

the canyon, avoiding the scratchy clumps of chapparal and the creepers of poison oak that looked like loganberry vines.

She found Cathy sitting in the middle of the little bridge that Paul had made across the creek out of two fallen eucalyptus trees. Cathy's short plump legs hung over the logs until they almost touched the water. She was absolutely motionless, her face hidden by a straw curtain of hair. Then a single frog croaked a warning of Marion's presence and Cathy responded to the sound as if she was more intimate with nature than adults were, and more alert to its subtle communications of danger.

She stood up quickly, brushing off the back of her dress and drawing aside the curtain of hair to reveal eyes as blue as the periwinkles that hugged the banks of the creek.

"Cathy."

"I was only counting waterbugs while I was waiting. Forty-one."

"Waiting for what?"

"The ten or twelve children, and the dog."

"What ten or twelve chil—" Marion stopped. "I see. You were listening the other night when we thought you were asleep."

"I wasn't listening," Cathy said righteously. "My ears were hearing."

Marion restrained a smile. "Then I wish you'd tell those ears of yours to hear properly. I didn't say the new neighbors had ten or twelve children, I said they *might* have. Actually, it's very unlikely. Not many families are that big these days."

"Do you have to be old to have a big family?"

"Well, you certainly can't be very young."

"I bet people with big families have station wagons so they have room for all the children."

"The lucky ones do."

Cathy stared down at the thin flow of water carrying fat little minnows down to the sea. Finally she said, "They're too young, and their car is too small."

In spite of her aversion to having new neighbors, Marion felt a quickening of interest. "Have you seen them?"

But the little girl seemed deaf, lost in a water world of minnows and dragonflies and tadpoles.

"I asked you a question, Cathy. Did you see the people who just moved in?"

"Yes."

"When?"

"Before you came. Their name is Smith."

"How do you know that?"

"I went up to the house to look at things and they said, Hello, little girl, what's your name? And I said, Cathy, what's yours? And they said Smith. Then they drove off in the little car."

"You're not supposed to go poking around other people's houses," Marion said brusquely. "And while we're at it, you're not supposed to go anywhere after school without first telling me where you're going and when you'll be back. You know that perfectly well. Now why didn't you come in and report to me after you got off the school bus?"

"I didn't want to."

"That's not a satisfactory answer."

Satisfactory or not, it was the only answer Cathy had. She looked at her mother in silence, then she turned and darted back up the hill to her own house.

After a time Marion followed her, exasperated and a little

confused. She hated to punish the child, but she knew she couldn't ignore the matter entirely—it was much too serious. While she gave Cathy her graham crackers and orange juice, she told her, reasonably and kindly, that she would have to stay in her room the following day after school by way of learning a lesson.

That night, after Cathy had been tucked in bed, Marion related the incident to Paul. He seemed to take a less serious view of it than Marion, a fact of which the listening child became well aware.

"I'm glad she's getting acquainted with the new people," Paul said. "It shows a certain degree of poise I didn't think she had. She's always been so shy."

"You're surely not condoning her running off without telling me?"

"She didn't run far. All kids do things like that once in a while."

"We don't want to spoil her."

"Cathy's always been so obedient I think she has *us* spoiled. Who knows, she might even teach us a thing or two about going out and making new friends." He realized, from past experience, that this was a very touchy subject. Marion had her house, her garden, her television sets; she didn't seem to want any more of the world than these, and she resented any implication that they were not enough. To ward off an argument he added, "You've done a good job with Cathy. Stop worrying . . . Smith, their name is?"

"Yes."

"Actually, I think it's an excellent sign that Cathy's getting acquainted."

At three the next afternoon the yellow circus cage arrived, released one captive, and rumbled on its way.

"I'm home, Mommy."

"Good girl."

Marion felt guilty at the sight of her: the child had been cooped up in school all day, the weather was so warm and lovely, and besides, Paul hadn't thought the incident of the previous afternoon too important.

"I know what," Marion suggested, "let's you and I go down to the creek and count waterbugs."

The offer was a sacrifice for Marion because her favorite quiz program was on and she liked to answer the questions along with the contestants. "How about that?"

Cathy knew all about the quiz program; she'd seen it a hundred times, had watched the moving mouths claim her mother's eyes and ears and mind. "I counted the waterbugs yesterday."

"Well, minnows, then."

"You'll scare them away."

"Oh, will I?" Marion laughed self-consciously, rather relieved that Cathy had refused her offer and was clearly and definitely a little guilty about the relief. "Don't you scare them?"

"No. They think I'm another minnow because they're used to me."

"Maybe they could get used to me, too."

"I don't think so."

When Cathy went off down the canyon by herself, Marion realized, in a vaguely disturbing way, that the child had politely but firmly rejected her mother's company. It wasn't until dinnertime that she found out the reason why.

"The Smiths," Cathy said, "have an Austin-Healey."

Cathy, like most girls, had never shown any interest in cars, and her glib use of the name moved her parents to laughter.

The laughter encouraged Cathy to elaborate. "An Austin-Healey makes a lot of noise—like Daddy's lawn mower."

"I don't think the company would appreciate a commercial from you, young lady," Paul said. "Are the Smiths all moved in?"

"Oh, yes. I helped them."

"Is that a fact? And how did you help them?"

"I sang two songs. And then we danced and danced."

Paul looked half pleased, half puzzled. It wasn't like Cathy to perform willingly in front of people. During the last Christmas concert at the school she'd left the stage in tears and hidden in the cloak room . . . Well, maybe her shyness was only a phase and she was finally getting over it.

"They must be very nice people," he said, "to take time out from getting settled in a new house to play games with a little girl."

Cathy shook her head. "It wasn't games. It was real dancing—like on *Ed Sullivan*."

"As good as that, eh?" Paul said, smiling. "Tell me about it."

"Mrs. Smith is a nightclub dancer."

Paul's smile faded, and a pulse began to beat in his left temple like a small misplaced heart. "Oh? You're sure about that, Cathy?"

"Yes."

"And what does Mr. Smith do?"

"He's a baseball player."

"You mean that's what he does for a living?" Marion asked. "He doesn't work in an office like Daddy?"

"No, he just plays baseball. He always wears a baseball cap."

THE PEOPLE ACROSS THE CANYON · 313

"I see. What position does he play on the team?" Paul's voice was low.

Cathy looked blank.

"Everybody on a ball team has a special thing to do. What does Mr. Smith do?"

"He's a batter."

"A batter, eh? Well, that's nice. Did he tell you this?"

"Yes."

"Cathy," Paul said, "I know you wouldn't deliberately lie to me, but sometimes you get your facts a little mixed up."

He went on in this vein for some time but Cathy's story remained unshaken: Mrs. Smith was a nightclub dancer, Mr. Smith a professional baseball player, they loved children, and they never watched television.

"That, at least, must be a lie," Marion said to Paul later when she saw the rectangular light of the television set shining in the Smiths' picture window. "As for the rest of it, there isn't a nightclub within fifty miles, or a professional ball club within two hundred."

"She probably misunderstood. It's quite possible that at one time Mrs. Smith was a dancer of sorts and that he played a little baseball."

Cathy, in bed and teetering dizzily on the brink of sleep, wondered if she should tell her parents about the Smiths' child—the one who didn't go to school.

She didn't tell them; Marion found out for herself the next morning after Paul and Cathy had gone. When she pulled back the drapes in the living room and opened the windows, she heard the sharp slam of a screen door from across the canyon and saw a small child come out on the patio of the new house.

At that distance she couldn't tell whether it was a boy or a girl. Whichever it was, the child was quiet and well behaved; only the occasional slam of the door shook the warm, windless day.

The presence of the child, and the fact that Cathy hadn't mentioned it, gnawed at Marion's mind all day. She questioned Cathy about it as soon as she came home.

"You didn't tell me the Smiths have a child."

"No."

"Why not?"

"I don't know why not."

"Is it a boy or a girl?"

"Girl."

"How old?"

Cathy thought it over carefully, frowning up at the ceiling. "About ten."

"Doesn't she go to school?"

"No."

"Why not?"

"She doesn't want to."

"That's not a very good reason."

"It's her reason," Cathy said flatly. "Can I go out to play now?"

"I'm not sure you should. You look a little feverish. Come here and let me feel your forehead."

Cathy's forehead was cool and moist, but her cheeks and the bridge of her nose were very pink, almost as if she'd been sunburned.

"You'd better stay inside," Marion said, "and watch some cartoons."

"I don't like cartoons."

"You used to."

"I like real people."

She means the Smiths, of course, Marion thought as her mouth tightened. "People who dance and play baseball all the time?"

If the sarcasm had any effect on Cathy she didn't show it. After waiting until Marion had become engrossed in her quiz program, Cathy lined up all her dolls in her room and gave a concert for them, to thunderous applause.

"Where are your old Navy binoculars?" Marion asked Paul when she was getting ready for bed.

"Oh, somewhere in the sea chest, I imagine. Why?"

"I want them."

"Not thinking of spying on the neighbors, are you?"

"I'm thinking of just that," Marion said grimly.

The next morning, as soon as she saw the Smith child come out on the patio, Marion went downstairs to the storage room to search through the sea chest. She located the binoculars and was in the act of dusting them off when the telephone started to ring in the living room. She hurried upstairs and said breathlessly, "Hello?"

"Mrs. Borton?"

"Yes."

"This is Miss Park speaking, Cathy's teacher."

Marion had met Miss Park several times at P.T.A. meetings and report-card conferences. She was a large, ruddy-faced and unfailingly cheerful young woman—the kind, as Paul said, you wouldn't want to live with but who'd be nice to have around in an emergency. "How are you, Miss Park?"

"Oh, fine, thank you, Mrs. Borton. I meant to call you yesterday but things were a bit out of hand around here, and I knew there was no great hurry to check on Cathy; she's such a well-behaved little girl."

Even Miss Park's loud, jovial voice couldn't cover up the ominous sound of the word *check*. "I don't think I quite understand. Why should you check on Cathy?"

"Purely routine. The school doctor and the health department like to keep records of how many cases of measles or flu or chicken pox are going the rounds. Right now it looks like the season for mumps. Is Cathy all right?"

"She seemed a little feverish yesterday afternoon when she got home from school, but she acted perfectly normal when she left this morning."

Miss Park's silence was so protracted that Marion became painfully conscious of things she wouldn't otherwise have noticed—the weight of the binoculars in her lap, the thud of her own heartbeat in her ears. Across the canyon the Smith child was playing quietly and alone on the patio. *There is definitely something the matter with that girl*, Marion thought. *Perhaps I'd better not let Cathy go over there anymore, she's so imitative.* "Miss Park, are you still on the line? Hello? Hello—"

"I'm here," Miss Park's voice seemed fainter than usual, and less positive. "What time did Cathy leave the house this morning?"

"Eight, as usual."

"Did she take the school bus?"

"Of course. She always does."

"Did you see her get on?"

"I kissed her goodbye at the front door," Marion said. "What's this all about, Miss Park?"

THE PEOPLE ACROSS THE CANYON • 317

"Cathy hasn't been at school for two days, Mrs. Borton."

"Why, that's absurd, impossible! You must be mistaken." But even as she was speaking the words, Marion was raising the binoculars to her eyes: the little girl on the Smiths' patio had a straw curtain of hair and eyes as blue as the periwinkles along the creek banks.

"Mrs. Borton, I'm not likely to be mistaken about which of my children are in class or not."

"No. No, you're—you're not mistaken, Miss Park. I can see Cathy from here—she's over at the neighbor's house."

"Good. That's a load off my mind."

"Off yours, yes," Marion said. "Not mine."

"Now we mustn't become excited, Mrs. Borton. Don't make too much of this incident before we've had a chance to confer. Suppose you come and talk to me during my lunch hour and bring Cathy along. We'll all have a friendly chat."

But it soon became apparent, even to the optimistic Miss Park, that Cathy didn't intend to take part in any friendly chat. She stood by the window in the classroom, blank-eyed, mute, unresponsive to the simplest questions, refusing to be drawn into any conversation even about her favorite topic, the Smiths. Miss Park finally decided to send Cathy out to play in the schoolyard while she talked to Marion alone.

"Obviously," Miss Park said, enunciating the word very distinctly because it was one of her favorites, "obviously, Cathy's got a crush on this young couple and has concocted a fantasy about belonging to them."

"It's not so obvious what my husband and I are going to do about it."

"Live through it, the same as other parents. Crushes like this are common at Cathy's age. Sometimes the object is a person, a whole family, even a horse. And, of course, to Cathy a nightclub dancer and a baseball player must seem very glamorous indeed. Tell me, Mrs. Borton, does she watch television a great deal?"

Marion stiffened. "No more than any other child."

Oh dear, Miss Park thought sadly, *they all do it; the most confirmed addicts are always the most defensive.* "I just wondered," she said. "Cathy likes to sing to herself and I've never heard such a repertoire of television commercials."

"She picks things up very fast."

"Yes. Yes, she does indeed." Miss Park studied her hands, which were always a little pale from chalk dust and were even paler now because she was angry—at the child for deceiving her, at Mrs. Borton for brushing aside the television issue, at herself for not preventing, or at least anticipating, the current situation, and perhaps most of all at the Smiths who ought to have known better than to allow a child to hang around their house when she should obviously be in school.

"Don't put too much pressure on Cathy about this," she said finally, "until I talk the matter over with the school psychologist. By the way, have you met the Smiths, Mrs. Borton?"

"Not yet," Marion said grimly. "But believe me, I intend to."

"Yes, I think it would be a good idea for you to talk to them and make it clear that they're not to encourage Cathy in this fantasy."

The meeting came sooner than Marion expected.

She waited at the school until classes were dismissed, then she took Cathy into town to do some shopping. She had parked the car and she and Cathy were standing hand in hand at a corner waiting for a traffic light to change; Marion was worried and impatient, Cathy still silent, unresisting, inert, as she had been ever since Marion had called her home from the Smiths' patio.

Suddenly, Marion felt the child's hand tighten in a spasm of excitement. Cathy's face had turned so pink it looked ready to explode and with her free hand she was waving violently at two people in a small cream-colored sports car—a very pretty young woman with blonde hair in the driver's seat, and beside her a young man wearing a wide friendly grin and a baseball cap. They both waved back at Cathy just before the lights changed and then the car roared through the intersection.

"The Smiths!" Cathy shouted, jumping up and down in a frenzy. "That was the Smiths."

"Sssh, not so loud. People will—"

"But it was the *Smiths*!"

"Hurry up before the light changes."

The child didn't hear. She stood as if rooted to the curb, staring after the cream-colored car.

With a little grunt of impatience Marion picked her up, carried her across the road, and let her down quite roughly on the other side. "There. If you're going to act like a baby, I'll carry you like a baby."

"I saw the Smiths!"

"All right. What are you so excited about? It's not very unusual to meet someone in town whom you know."

"It's unusual to meet *them*."

"Why?"

"Because it is." The color was fading from Cathy's cheeks, but her eyes still looked bedazzled, quite as if they'd seen a miracle.

"I'm sure they're very unique people," Marion said coldly. "Nevertheless, they must stop for groceries like everyone else."

Cathy's answer was a slight shake of her head and a whisper heard only by herself: "No, they don't, never."

When Paul came home from work, Cathy was sent to play in the front yard while Marion explained matters to him. He listened with increasing irritation—not so much at Cathy's actions but at the manner in which Marion and Miss Park had handled things. There was too much talking, he said, and too little acting.

"The way you women beat around the bush instead of tackling the situation directly, meeting it head-on—fantasy life. Fantasy life my foot! Now, we're going over to the Smiths' right this minute to talk to them and that will be that. End of fantasy. Period."

"We'd better wait until after dinner. Cathy missed her lunch."

Throughout the meal Cathy was pale and quiet. She ate nothing and spoke only when asked a direct question; but inside herself the conversation was very lively, the dinner a banquet with dancing, and afterward a wild, windy ride in the roofless car . . .

Although the footpath through the canyon provided a shorter route to the Smiths' house, the Bortons decided to go more formally, by car, and to take Cathy with them. Cathy, told to comb her hair and wash her face, protested: "I don't want to go over there."

"Why not?" Paul said. "You were so anxious to spend time with them that you played hooky for two days. Why don't you want to see them now?"

"Because they're not there."

"How do you know?"

"Mrs. Smith told me this morning that they wouldn't be home tonight because she's putting on a show."

"Indeed?" Paul said grim-faced. "Just where does she put on these shows of hers?"

"And Mr. Smith has to play baseball. And after that they're going to see a friend in the hospital who has leukemia."

"Leukemia, eh?" He didn't have to ask how Cathy had found out about such a thing; he'd watched a semidocumentary dealing with it a couple of nights ago. Cathy was supposed to have been sleeping.

"I wonder," he said to Marion when Cathy went to comb her hair, "just how many 'facts' about the Smiths have been borrowed from television."

"Well, I know for myself that they drive a sports car, and Mr. Smith was wearing a baseball cap. And they're both young and good-looking. Young and good-looking enough," she added wryly, "to make me feel—well, a little jealous."

"Jealous?"

"Cathy would rather belong to them than to us. It makes me wonder if it's something the Smiths have or something the Bortons don't have."

"Ask her."

"I can't very well—"

"Then I will, dammit," Paul said. And he did.

Cathy merely looked at him innocently. "I don't know. I don't know what you mean."

"Then listen again. Why did you pretend that you were the Smiths' little girl?"

"They asked me to be. They asked me to go with them."

"They actually said, Cathy, will you be our little girl?"

"Yes."

"Well, by heaven, I'll put an end to this nonsense," Paul said, and strode out to the car.

It was twilight when they reached the Smiths' house by way of the narrow, hilly road. The moon, just appearing above the horizon, was on the wane, a chunk bitten out of its side by some giant jaw. A warm dry wind, blowing down the mountain from the desert beyond, carried the sweet scent of pittosporum.

The Smiths' house was dark, and both the front door and the garage were locked. Out of defiance or desperation, Paul pressed the door chime anyway, several times. All three of them could hear it ringing inside, and it seemed to Marion to echo very curiously—as if the carpets and drapes were too thin to muffle the sound vibrations. She would have liked to peer in through the windows and see for herself, but the Venetian blinds were closed.

"What's their furniture like?" she asked Cathy.

"Like everybody's."

"I mean, is it new? Does Mrs. Smith tell you not to put your feet on it?"

"No, she never tells me that," Cathy said truthfully. "I want to go home now. I'm tired."

It was while she was putting Cathy to bed that Marion heard Paul call to her from the living room in an urgent voice, "Marion, come here a minute."

She found him standing motionless in the middle of the room, staring across the canyon at the Smiths' place. The rectangular light of the Smiths' television set was shining in the picture window of the room that opened onto the patio at the back of the Smiths' house.

"Either they've come home within the past few minutes," he said, "or they were there all the time. My guess is that they were home when we went over, but they didn't want to see us, so they just doused the lights and pretended to be out. Well, it won't work! Come on, we're going back."

"I can't leave Cathy alone. She's already got her pajamas on."

"Put a bathrobe on her and bring her along. This has gone beyond the point of observing such niceties as correct attire."

"Don't you think we should wait until tomorrow?"

"Hurry up and stop arguing with me."

Cathy, protesting that she was tired and that the Smiths weren't home anyway, was bundled into a bathrobe and carried to the car.

"They're home all right," Paul said. "And by heaven they'd better answer the door this time or I'll break it down."

"That's an absurd way to talk in front of a child," Marion said coldly. "She has enough ideas without hearing—"

"Absurd is it? Wait and see."

Cathy, listening from the backseat, smiled sleepily. She knew how to get in without breaking anything: ever since the house had been built, the real estate man who'd been trying to sell it always hid the key on a nail underneath the window box.

The second trip seemed a nightmarish imitation of the first: the same moon hung in the sky but it looked smaller now, and paler. The scent of pittosporum was funereally sweet, and the hollow sound of the chimes from inside the house was like the echo in an empty tomb.

"They must be crazy to think they can get away with a trick

like this twice in one night!" Paul shouted. "Come on, we're going around to the back."

Marion looked a little frightened. "I don't like trespassing on someone else's property."

"They trespassed on our property first."

He glanced down at Cathy. Her eyes were half closed and her face was pearly in the moonlight. He pressed her hand to reassure her that everything was going to be all right and that his anger wasn't directed at her, but she drew away from him and started down the path that led to the back of the house.

Paul clicked on his flashlight and followed her, moving slowly along the unfamiliar terrain. By the time he turned the corner of the house and reached the patio, Cathy was out of sight.

"Cathy," he called. "Where are you? Come back here!"

Marion was looking at him accusingly. "You upset her with that silly threat about breaking down the door. She's probably on her way home through the canyon."

"I'd better go after her."

"She's less likely to get hurt than you are. She knows every inch of the way. Besides, you came here to break down the doors. All right, start breaking."

But there was no need to break down anything. The back door opened as soon as Paul rapped on it with his knuckles, and he almost fell into the room.

It was empty except for a small girl wearing a blue bathrobe that matched her eyes.

Paul said, "Cathy. Cathy, what are you doing here?"

Marion stood with her hand pressed to her mouth to stifle the scream that was rising in her throat. There were no Smiths.

The people in the sports car whom Cathy had waved at were just strangers responding to the friendly greeting of a child—had Cathy seen them before, on a previous trip to town? The television set was no more than a contraption rigged up by Cathy herself—an orange crate and an old mirror that caught and reflected the rays of the moon.

In front of it Cathy was standing, facing her own image. "Hello, Mrs. Smith. Here I am, all ready to go."

"Cathy," Marion said in a voice that sounded torn by claws, "what do you see in that mirror?"

"It's not a mirror. It's a television set."

"What—what program are you watching?"

"It's not a program, silly. It's real. It's the Smiths. I'm going away with them to dance and play baseball."

"There are no Smiths," Paul bellowed. "Will you get that through your head? *There are no Smiths!*"

"Yes, there are. I see them."

Marion knelt on the floor beside the child. "Listen to me, Cathy. This is a mirror—only a mirror. It came from Daddy's old bureau and I had it put away in the storage room. That's where you found it, isn't it? And you brought it here and decided to pretend it was a television set, isn't that right? But it's really just a mirror, and the people in it are us—you and Mommy and Daddy."

But even as she looked at her own reflection, Marion saw it beginning to change. She was growing younger, prettier; her hair was becoming lighter and her cotton suit was changing into a dancing dress. And beside her in the mirror, Paul was turning into a stranger, a laughing-eyed young man wearing a baseball cap.

"I'm ready to go now, Mr. Smith," Cathy said, and suddenly all three of them, the Smiths and their little girl, began walking away in the mirror. In a few moments they were no bigger than matchsticks—and then the three of them disappeared, and there was only the moonlight in the glass.

"Cathy," Marion cried. "Come back, Cathy! Please come back!"

Propped up against the door like a dummy, Paul imagined he could hear above his wife's cries the mocking muted roar of a sports car.

MIRIAM ALLEN DEFORD

1888–1975

MIRIAM ALLEN DEFORD was a prolific writer in the mystery, science fiction and fantasy, and true crime fields. She was first published at the age of twelve, and by fourteen was making her mark in the early feminist movement as a campaigner and disseminator of birth control information to underprivileged women, first in her native Philadelphia and later, in Boston, New York, and the San Francisco area. DeFord, along with her first husband, Maynard Shipley, were active against the rising tides of antievolution fights in the 1920s. She also worked for Charles Fort, the famed researcher into paranormal phenomena, and for a time for the magazine *Humanist*. She was one of the first female insurance claims adjusters, and was actively involved in civil rights organizations, including the ACLU.

Her science fiction and fantasy stories, with themes of alienation and changing sexual roles, were largely published in the *Magazine of Fantasy and Science Fiction* when Anthony Boucher—also the mystery critic for the *New York Times* and a well-published writer in his own right—was editor, and later collected in *Xenogenesis* (1969) and *Elsewhere, Elsewhen, Elsehow* (1971). DeFord's mystery short stories, many of which appeared in *Ellery Queen's Mystery Magazine*, were collected in *The Theme Is Murder* (1967). She also won an Edgar Award for Best Fact Crime for *The Overbury Affair* (1960), about the murder of Thomas Overbury during the seventeenth-century reign of King James I in England, and garnered further acclaim for *The Real Bonnie and Clyde* (1968), a corrective account of the notorious outlaw couple published a year after the commercially successful film was released. DeFord was also an active editor of anthologies, how-to manuals, and practical guides for writers. She died in San Francisco's Ambassador Hotel, where she made her home, in 1975.

"Mortmain," first published in *Ellery Queen's Mystery Magazine* in 1944, further mines deFord's recurring interest in the alienated self through the prism of a nurse caring for elderly patients in a hospital ward. The work is tough and frustrating, the rewards few, the indignities mounting. So it's only natural that tension would build to a boiling point, with the nurse seeking personal redemption in the only manner she appears to have left.

MORTMAIN

"I'LL BE back on Thursday, Miss Hendricks, and I'll drop in here in the afternoon. It's only three days, and I don't anticipate any change. You know what to do. If anything happens, you can call Dr. Roberts; he knows all about the case. I wouldn't go away, with Marsden like this, but—well, it's my only daughter, you know, and she'll never be married again—at least, I hope not!—and she'd be heartbroken if her old dad weren't there to give her away."

Dr. Staples turned to his patient.

"Good-bye, old man; I'm leaving you in Miss Hendricks' charge till Thursday. You won't be sorry to have three days free of me, eh?"

Dr. Staples put on his gloves and picked up his hat from the table by the bed. The sick man nodded feebly, essaying a slight courteous smile. The nurse nodded too, her eyes downcast. She was afraid to look at the doctor—afraid to let him see the incredulous joy in her face.

"So long, then." He was gone, shutting the door quietly after him.

What unbelievable luck! Cora Hendricks felt herself trembling with excitement. How she had schemed and planned—and it had never occurred to her that anything would keep Staples from his daily visits to his patient. Now she had three whole days and nights.

Today. It was only three o'clock. She could do it today. His four o'clock medicine. By five she would be finished here; by six she could be on a train. By Thursday she could be where Staples would never find her. No—that was foolish. She mustn't disappear. She would phone Dr. Roberts, and he would come. Perhaps he would summon Staples back, perhaps he would take the whole responsibility. Either way, it would make no difference to her. Afterwards, she could go, and then—then her new life would begin.

She sat silently by Marsden's bed, on the other side of the table, and let her eyes, that she had not dared to let the doctor see, rove around the big room. Back of the framed photograph of Marsden's dead wife was a sliding panel that hid a safe. She knew the combination; Marsden had given it to her when he wanted her to bring him the insurance papers for the doctor to look at. Marsden knew he was going to die soon.

At night, when he was asleep, she had opened the safe again. It was full of money. She had not counted it all, but without the bonds—they would be dangerous—there was nearly ten thousand dollars in currency. Her hands shook at the memory.

She could have taken it then, and gone away, but three things had restrained her. First, there was a lingering scruple of professional ethics, at deserting a patient in the middle of the night. Then, he might waken suddenly and understand, and she knew that in a drawer of the bedside table was a loaded revolver.

He was probably too weak to use it, but once in a while he gathered sudden accesses of strength. And finally, it would be quite obvious where and how the money had gone. Marsden would tell the doctor in the morning, and they would have hold of her in short order.

But she must get it. She must. There were urgent reasons. There was her own realization that time was slipping past her, that professional calls were growing fewer, that there was nothing saved. And there was Terry.

Terry had been her patient once, long ago, before she knew anything about him. He was just a rich man taken ill in a hotel. That was when she was young and full of ideals and rigorous virtues. Probably, if she had never met Terry, the money would have lain in that safe forever for all of her. But after they had fallen in love she had found out—gradually. Terry was a professional bank-robber: that was the bald truth of it. He was also handsome, cultured, fascinating, and she was mad about him. Slowly his influence conquered all the ideals and most of the virtues. If she had been scrupulous and honest since, it was from expediency, not from principle. And then Terry had been caught. But he had not been armed—Terry was too wise ever to carry a gun—and he had received a light sentence—ten years. He was a model prisoner; with good behavior, his term would be over now in three more months. They were going to be married when he got out. He must never run such risks again; she must have money for him—plenty of money. They must be able to go away somewhere, change his name, live new lives. It was with Terry, in whispers across a high-ridged table in the visitors' room, that she had planned this thing.

Marsden would never need that money. There wasn't anyone

for him to leave it to: his wife was dead, he was childless and without brothers or sisters. He had told her himself that his will left everything to various charities. Everything about him was eccentric. Living alone in an apartment, eating in restaurants, hiring no servant—that was eccentric too, not miserly. He paid Cora Hendricks well, and he paid the woman well who came in once a week to clean. It was eccentric to refuse to go to a hospital when his illness became acute; Staples was an old friend and humored him. It was eccentric to keep his valuables in a safe built into the wall instead of in a safe-deposit box in a bank. It was surely eccentric to keep a loaded revolver in a table-drawer when he was too weak to lift it and had no occasion to use it anyway.

At first she had suspected he was contemplating suicide as a quick way out of incurable disease, but he had disabused her mind of that.

"I like to feel that I am still in touch with the active world I shall not rejoin," he had said a little shamefacedly, in his precise voice. "When I was well I spent all my summers in Maine, in the town where I was born. Up there in Squanscutt I'm somebody important; here in New York I'm just a fairly prosperous man with nothing to do.

"Do you know, Miss Hendricks"—his voice slumped to a conspiratorial whisper like a small boy's—"when I'm at home, in the summer, I'm a deputy sheriff! I have all the accoutrements—I keep it here by me, to look at and remember, because I shall never wear the things again. In fact, I never did need them, but there was always a chance of—oh, let's say adventure—a rumrunner, perhaps, before repeal, or an escaping bandit. Nothing exciting ever happened to me in my life," he added wistfully. "This junk here represents my dream that something might have happened."

He opened the drawer confidentially—it was one of his good days—and let her look at everything. There was the badge, with "Deputy" on it in blue enamel; the revolver in its holster; the pair of handcuffs; even, crushed and folded, the hat, looking more like a western bad man's than a Maine deputy sheriff's. Cora, with a transient twinge of pity, realized that in Squanscutt they must laugh at him and indulge him and love him—probably he had been the town's benefactor in more ways than one. He was no millionaire, but the bonds must run to a hundred thousand in value, and he had a good-sized checking account in two banks. The cash in the safe was all that mattered to her—just spending money to him, but imperative, vital, to Cora Hendricks.

She could reach across him right now, open the drawer—it had no lock — and shoot him as he lay there with his eyes closed and his breath coming in irregular gasps. She would do nothing so ridiculous, of course. Marsden was going to die naturally—perhaps from the excitement of seeing his old friend and physician leave him for three days. That was what she would suggest to Dr. Roberts when she called him.

She had the stuff ready: Terry had told her where and how to get it. It could be poured into the four o'clock medicine, and he would never know the difference. Neither would anyone else—who would order an autopsy on a man who had been dying for weeks? In ten minutes now he would be dead.

Then she went over the plan mentally, while she sat watching the sick man's troubled breathing. First she must wash out the glass thoroughly. Next she must dispose of the little vial which had been constantly in her apron pocket for a week while she awaited her chance. She could take it away with her, and throw it somewhere when she was on the train. She would get the money out, close the safe again—it was unlikely that anyone, even Staples, knew just how much currency Marsden had there, or if he had any at all. Fingerprints wouldn't matter—Staples had seen her open the safe at Marsden's order.

Ten thousand dollars made a big bundle. But there was room in her suitcase. When Roberts was through with her she would pack and return to her rented room. She would give her name in at the registry at once. She might even go out on another case if one presented itself. Nothing suspicious; no running away. When Marsden was buried, when Terry was about to be released, she would go to the place where they had agreed to meet, and take the money with her.

Would the clock ever move to four? She felt her nerves fraying with impatience to have it over with. She got up softly and walked to the window. It was open a little. Cora gazed meditatively at the building opposite. No one could possibly interfere. Even if some fool stood there with a spy-glass, what would he see? A uniformed nurse giving her patient his medicine. She smiled, and returned to the chair on the left side of the bed.

Four o'clock. She stood up briskly. Marsden opened his eyes and turned his head inquiringly to her.

"Your medicine," she said soothingly. She caught her breath; she must not betray her agitation.

"Which one?" he asked feebly. He lost track of time easily.

"The digitalis mixture."

"Oh, yes."

He watched her while she poured a little water in the glass

and then with the dropper measured the eight drops into it. The medicines were not on the bedside table—that was sacred to his personal belongings, his glasses and a book or two, and the touching little bunch of flowers the cleaning woman had brought him that very morning.

She turned away from him to stir the mixture. In that instant the little vial came from her pocket and was emptied into the glass and returned to its hiding-place. The liquid was colorless and odorless.

She marveled at her steadiness as she brought the glass to him, propped him on his high pillow so that he could drink. He took the glass in his veined hand and laid it beside him on the table.

"Sit down, Miss Hendricks," he said gently.

Cora dropped into the chair by the bed. Could he possibly have seen that her legs were trembling?

Marsden half-smiled, and stared at the half-full glass. In the same mild tone he spoke again.

"Will it hurt?"

For a second she could not answer: the shock drove the blood from her heart. Then she summoned her voice.

"Why, Mr. Marsden, you've had it three times a day, right along. You know it doesn't hurt."

His mind must be beginning to wander; he couldn't last much longer in any event. Perhaps if she had let him alone he would have died without her help. But she couldn't take that chance; he might outlast the time when Terry was due to meet her, or die when Staples was there.

"I don't mean the digitalis," said Marsden evenly. "I mean the other stuff you put into it. From the bottle in your pocket."

She stared at him, speechless, paralyzed.

"It's for the money in the safe, isn't it? I've been watching ever since you saw it. I could have given it all to you, and saved you from having to do this. But you see, I'm tired of all this nonsense. Staples wouldn't finish me off, I know that. But you will. Thank you, my dear. I'm glad I had enough in the safe to tempt you."

She sat stunned, unable to look at him.

"Only, it doesn't seem fair to other people, later on. Money doesn't last forever, you know, and you might be tempted again to —"

He summoned all his strength for the last effort. His movements were quick and sure. He even managed to get the glass on the table again before he fell back on the pillow.

On Thursday afternoon, Dr. Staples, smiling as he remembered his daughter's radiant face, rang the bell softly so as not to disturb Marsden. He waited. He rang again. Then, with a frown, he searched his pockets for the extra key which his friend had given him in the early days before a nurse had been needed. He frowned again, indignantly. He had never employed Miss Hendricks before — his regular nurse was ill — but the registry had recommended her highly. Surely she had not deserted a patient in the condition Marsden had reached.

At the door he stood stock-still, feeling his face grow white.

The room was full of flies. Marsden lay obliquely across the bed; brown patches had formed on his stringy neck, his mouth and eyes were open. On the bedside table, beside some wilted flowers, was a glass, with a little liquid still in the bottom. Dead flies lay in it and around it. The table-drawer was open.

On the other side of the bed, slumped by an overturned chair, crouched Miss Hendricks. Her hair was disheveled, her uniform torn. There was dried blood on her right arm, and a long green bruise over a puffy swelling.

Dr. Staples walked quickly to the bed, pulled back the tumbled covers.

Miss Hendricks opened blank eyes. The doctor's flesh crawled, as she began to giggle.

Her right wrist was handcuffed to the left wrist of the corpse.

CELIA FREMLIN

1914–2009

CELIA FREMLIN was born in Kingsbury, Middlesex, and studied classics at Somerville College of the University of Oxford. After her mother died in 1931, she looked after her father and worked a number of domestic service jobs, which was a way, Fremlin once said, to "observe the peculiarities of the class structure of our society." That experience informed her first book, *The Seven Chars of Chelsea* (1940), while *War Factory* (1943), cowritten with Tom Harrisson, grew out of Fremlin's wartime work with the British government's Mass Observation unit polling people about how they felt about their daily lives, the war, and government.

Fremlin married in 1942 and had three children, and in the midst of raising her family found the seeds for her first published novel, *The Hours Before Dawn* (1958), which won the Edgar Award for Best Novel in 1960. Fremlin's debut is a disquieting look at a young mother with two small children and a baby, clearly in the throes of postpartum depression, who's neglected and treated cavalierly by her distant husband, friends, and family, until the arrival of a lodger leads to strange events that have the heroine doubting her sanity.

After such an auspicious start, Fremlin wrote fifteen other domestically oriented suspense novels over the course of her career, including *Uncle Paul* (1959), *The Jealous One* (1964), *The Parasite Person* (1982), and *King of the World* (1994). She also published dozens of short stories that were eventually collected in *Don't Go to Sleep in the Dark* (1970), *By Horror Haunted* (1974), and *A Lovely Day to Die* (1984), the last in which I found "A Case of Maximum Need."

Originally published in 1977 by *Ellery Queen's Mystery Magazine*, it introduces eighty-seven-year-old Emmeline Fosdyke making a most unusual request of those who work at the Sheltered House of the Elderly, where she's recently moved: "No, no telephone, thank you, it's too dangerous." Naturally, the workers are puzzled. What happens if Emmeline injures herself, or worse? But as Fremlin details with chilling effect, Emmeline isn't just trying to protect herself but other people, who are in even more danger from the consequences of conversation.

A CASE OF MAXIMUM NEED

"NO, NO telephone, thank you. It's too dangerous," said Miss Emmeline Fosdyke decisively; and the young welfare worker, only recently qualified, and working for the first time in this Sheltered Housing Unit for the Elderly, blinked up from the form she was filling in.

"*No telephone?* But, Miss Fosdyke, in your—I mean, with your—well, your arthritis, and not being able to get about and everything . . . You're on our House-Bound list, you know that, don't you? As a House-Bound Pensioner, you're entitled—well, I mean, it's a *necessity*, isn't it, a telephone? It's your link with the outside world!"

This last sentence, a verbatim quote from her just-completed Geriatric Course, made Valerie Coombe feel a little more confident. She went on, "You *must* have a telephone, Miss Fosdyke! It's your *right*! And if it's the cost you're worrying about, then do please set your mind at rest. Our Department—anyone over sixty-five and in need—"

"I'm not in need," asserted Miss Fosdyke woodenly. "Not of a telephone, anyway."

There had been nothing in the Geriatric Course to prepare

Valerie for this. She glanced round the pin-new Sheltered Housing flatlet for inspiration, but she saw none. Its bland, purpose-built contours were as empty of ideas as was the incomplete form in front of her. "Telephone Allowance. In Cases of Maximum Need . . ."

It was a case of maximum need, all right. Valerie took another quick look at the papers in her file.

Fosdyke, Emmeline J. Retired dressmaker, unmarried. No relatives. One hundred percent disability: arthritis, diabetes, cardiovascular degeneration, motor-neurone dysfunction.

The case notes made it all so clear. Valerie glanced up from the precise, streamlined data and was once again confronted with a person—an actual, quirky, incomprehensible person, a creature whose eyes, sunk in helpless folds of withered skin, yet glittered with some impenetrable secret defiance.

Why couldn't old sick people just *be* old and sick, the poor girl wondered despairingly. Why did they have to be so many other things as well, things for which there was no space allotted on the form, and which just didn't fit in *anywhere*?

"But suppose you were *ill*, Miss Fosdyke?" Valerie hazarded, her eyes fixed on all that list of incapacitating disabilities "Suppose—?"

"Well, *of course* I'm ill!" snapped back Miss Fosdyke. "I've been ill for years, and I'll get iller. Old people do. Why do I have to have a telephone as well?"

Valerie's brain raked desperately through the course notes of only a few months ago. Dangers to Watch Out For in Geriatric Practice. Isolation. Mental Confusion. Hypothermia. Lying dead for days until the milkman happens to notice the half-dozen unclaimed bottles . . .

An *easy* job, they'd told her back in the office—an easy job for Valerie's first solo assignment. Simply going from door to door in the Sheltered Housing block, and arranging for a free telephone for those who qualified, either by age or disability or both. She'd pictured to herself the gratitude in the watery old eyes as she broke the good news, imagined the mumbling but effusive expressions of gratitude.

Why couldn't Miss Fosdyke be like that? Eighty-seven and helpless—why the hell couldn't she?

"Miss Fosdyke, you *must* have a telephone!" Valerie repeated, a note of desperation creeping into her voice as she launched into these unknown waters beyond the cosy boundaries of the Geriatric Course. "Surely you can see that you must? I mean, in your situation—suppose you needed a doctor?"

"Nobody of my age needs a doctor," Miss Fosdyke retorted crisply. "Look at my case notes there, you can see for yourself the things I've got. Incurable, all of them. There's not a doctor in the world who can cure a single one of them, so why should I have to be bothered with a doctor who can't?"

Obstinate. Difficult. Blind to their own interests. Naturally, the course had dealt with these attributes of the aging process, but in such bland, non-judgmental terms that when you finally came upon the real thing, it was only just recognizable.

But recognizable, nevertheless. Be friendly but firm, and don't become involved in argument. Smilingly, Valerie put Miss Fosdyke down for a free telephone, and left the flat, all optimism and bright words.

"Hope you'll soon be feeling better, Miss Fosdyke," she called cheerfully as she made her way out, and then on her long lithe young legs she almost ran down the corridor in order not to hear the old thing's riposte: "Better? Don't be silly, dear, I'll be feeling worse. I'll go on feeling worse until I'm dead. Everyone does at my age. Don't they teach you *anything* but lies at that training place of yours?"

"*What* a morning!" Valerie confided, half laughing and half sighing with relief, to her lunch companions in the staff canteen. "There was this poor old thing, you see, getting on for ninety, who was supposed to be applying for a free telephone, and do you know what she said . . . ?"

And while the others leaned forward, all agog for a funny story to brighten the day's work, Valerie set herself to making the anecdote as amusing as she knew how, recalling Miss Fosdyke's exact words, in all their incongruous absurdity: "No, no telephone, thank you. It's too dangerous."

Too dangerous! What *could* the old thing mean? Ribald suggestions about breathy male voices late at night ricocheted round the table; anecdotes of personal experiences almost took the conversation away from Miss Fosdyke and her bizarre attitude, and it was only with difficulty that Valerie brought it back.

At *eighty-seven*!—she should be so lucky!—this was the general reaction of the others. Of course, the girls admitted, one did read occasionally of old women being assaulted as well as robbed—look at that great-grandmother found stripped and murdered behind her own sweet-shop counter only a few months ago. And then a few years back there had been that old girl in an Islington basement defending her honor with a carving knife. Still, you couldn't say it was common.

"At *eighty-seven*!" they kept repeating, wonderingly, giggling a little at the absurdity of it. Consciously and gloriously exposed to all the dangers of being young and beautiful, they could well afford to smile pityingly, to shrug, and to forget.

It was nearly three months after the telephone had been installed that Miss Fosdyke first heard the heavy masculine breathing. It was late on a Sunday night—around midnight, as is usual with this type of anonymous caller—and it so happened that Miss Fosdyke was not in bed yet; she was dozing uneasily in her big chair, too tired after her hard day to face the slow and exhausting business of undressing and preparing for bed.

For it *had* been a hard day, as Sundays so often were for the inhabitants of the Sheltered Housing block. Sunday was the day when relatives of all ages, bearing flowers and pot plants in proportion to their guilt, came billowing in through the swing doors to spend an afternoon of stunned boredom with their dear ones; or, alternatively, to escort the said dear ones, on their crutches and in their wheel chairs, to spend a few hours in the tiny, miserable outside world.

Just *how* tiny and miserable it was, Emmeline Fosdyke knew very well, because once every six weeks her old friend Gladys would come with her husband (arthritic himself, these days) to take Emmeline to tea in their tall, dark, bickering home—hoisting her over their awkward front doorstep, sitting her down in front of a plate of stale scones and a cup of stewed tea, and expecting her to be envious. Envious not of their happiness, for they had none, but simply of their marriage. Surely any marriage, however horrible, merits the envy of a spinster of 87?

Especially when, as in this case, the marriage is based on the long-ago capture by one dear old friend of the other dear old friend's fiancé—a soldier boy of the First World War he'd been then, very dashing and handsome in his khaki battle dress, though you'd never have guessed it now. Emmeline remembered as if it was yesterday that blue-and-gold October afternoon, the last afternoon of his leave, when she had lost him

"He says you're frigid!" Gladys had whispered gleefully, brushing the golden leaves from her skirt, all lit up with having performed a forbidden act and destroyed a friend's happiness all in one crowded afternoon. "He says . . ."

Details had followed—surprisingly intimate for that day and age, but unforgettable. Only later, emboldened partly by old age and partly by a changing climate of opinion, had Emmeline found herself wondering how responsive Gladys herself had proved to be over the subsequent 55 years. Naturally Emmeline had never asked, nor would Gladys ever have answered. But maybe Gladys' tight bitter mouth and the gray defeated features of the once carefree soldier boy were answer enough.

The visit on this particular Sunday had been more than usually exhausting. To start with, there had been seedcake for tea instead of the usual scones, and the seeds had got in behind Emmeline's dentures, causing her excruciating embarrassment and discomfort; and on top of this, Gladys' budgerigar, who had been saying "Percy wants a grape!" at intervals of a minute and a half for the last eleven years, had died the previous Wednesday, and this left a gap in the conversation which was hard to fill.

And so, what with the seedcake and the car journey and the boredom and the actual physical effort of putting up with it all, Emmeline Fosdyke arrived back at the Sheltered Housing unit in a state of complete exhaustion. She couldn't be bothered even to make herself a cup of tea, or turn on the television; she didn't feel up to anything more than sitting in her armchair and waiting for bedtime.

She hadn't meant to fall asleep. She'd learned long ago that when you are old, sleep has to be budgeted just as carefully as money: if you use up too much of it during the day, there'll be none left for the night. So she'd intended just to sit there, awake but thinking of nothing in particular, until the hands of her watch pointed to a quarter to ten and it would be time to start preparing for bed.

But it is hard to think of nothing in particular after 87 years. Out of all those jumbled decades heaped up behind, *something* will worm itself to the surface; and thus it was that as Emmeline's head sank farther and farther toward her chest, and her eyelids began to close, a formless, half-forgotten anxiety began nibbling and needling at the fringes of her brain—something from long, long ago, over and done with really, and yet still with the power to goad.

Must hurry, must hurry, must get out of here—this was the burden that nagged at her last wisps of consciousness. Urgency pounded behind her closed eyes—a sense of trains to catch, of doors to bolt, of decisions to make. And now there seemed to be voices approaching—shouts—cars drawing up—luggage only half packed.

Slumped in her deep chair, Emmeline Fosdyke's sleeping limbs twitched ever so slightly to the ancient crisis; the slow blood pumped into her flaccid muscles a tiny extra supply of oxygen to carry the muscles through the dream chase along streets long since bulldozed; her breath came infinitesimally quicker, her old lungs expanded to some miniscule degree at the need for running, running, running through a long-dead winter dawn . . .

It was the telephone that woke her. Stunned by the suddenness of it, and by its stupefying clamor erupting into her dreams, Emmeline sat for a few moments in a state of total bewilderment. Who? Where? And then, gradually, it all came back to her.

It was all right. It was here. It was now. She, Emmeline Fosdyke, eighty-seven years old, sitting comfortably in her own chair in her own room on a peaceful Sunday evening. She was home. She was safe—safe back from that awful outing to Gladys' house, and with a full six weeks before she need think about going there again. There was nothing to worry about. Nothing at all. Nothing, certainly, to set her heart beating in this uncomfortable way, thundering in her eardrums, pulsing behind her eyes.

Except, of course, the telephone, which was still ringing. Ringing, ringing as if it would never stop. Who could possibly be telephoning her on a Sunday evening as late as—oh, dear, what *was* the time? With eyes still blurred by sleep, Emmeline peered at her watch and saw, with a little sense of shock, that it was past midnight.

Midnight! She must have been dozing here for hours! That meant that even with a sleeping pill, she'd never—

And still the telephone kept on ringing; and now, her mind slowly coming into focus, it dawned on Miss Fosdyke that she would have to answer it.

"Hello?" she half whispered, her old voice husky and tremulous with sleep. Then from force of habit she said, "This is Emmeline Fosdyke, 497-6402. Who . . . ?"

There was no answer. Only the slow measured sound of someone breathing—breathing loudly, and with deliberate intention; the sounds pounded against her ear like the slow reverberation of the sea. In, out. In, out.

For several seconds Miss Fosdyke simply sat there, speech-less, the hand that clutched the instrument growing slowly damp with sweat, and her mind reeling with indecision. During her long decades of solitary bed-sitter life, she'd had calls of this nature quite a number of times, and she knew very well there was no infallible method for dealing with them. If you simply hung up without a word, then they were liable to ring again later in the night; if on the other hand, you *did* speak, then they were as likely as not to launch forth immediately into a long ram-bling monologue of obscene suggestions. It was a nerve-racking situation for an old woman all on her own in an empty flat and late at night

Miss Fosdyke decided to take the bull by the horns.

"Listen," she said, trying to speak quietly and control the quivering of her voice. "Listen, I don't know who you are or why you're calling me, but I think I ought to tell you that I'm—"

That I'm what? Eighty-seven years old? All on my own? Crippled with arthritis? About to call the police?

That would be a laugh! Anyone who has been an elderly spinster for as long as Emmeline Fosdyke knows well enough what to expect from officialdom if she complains of molestation. No, no policemen, thank you. Not any more. Not ever again.

But no matter. Her decisive little speech seemed to have done the trick this time. With a tiny click the receiver at the other end was replaced softly, and Emmeline leaned back with a sigh of relief, even with a certain sense of pride in what she had accomplished. Funny how these sort of calls always came when you were least prepared for them—late at night, like this one, or even in the small hours, rousing you from your deepest sleep.

Like that awful time five years ago—or was it six?—when she'd been living all alone in that dark dismal flat off the Holloway Road. Even now she still trembled when she thought about that night, and how it might have ended. And then there was that other time, only a few years earlier, when she'd just moved into that bed-sitter in Wandsworth. There, too, the telephone had only recently been installed, just as it had been here . . .

Well, I *told* her, didn't I? That prissy, know-it-all little chit of a welfare worker—no one can say that I didn't warn her! I *told* her that a telephone was dangerous, but of course she had to know better, she with her potty little three-year Training Course which she thinks qualifies her to be right about everything for evermore!

Training Course indeed!—as if life itself wasn't a training course much tougher and more exacting than anything the Welfare could think up, if it sat on its bloody committees yakketty-yakking for a thousand years!

Nearly one o'clock now. Emmeline still had not dared to undress, or to make any of her usual preparations for the night. Even though it was more than half an hour since she'd hung up on her mysterious caller, she still could not relax. Of course, it was more than possible that nothing further would happen, that the wretched fellow had given up, turned his attentions elsewhere. Still, you couldn't be sure. It was best to be prepared.

And so, her light switched off as an extra precaution, and a blanket wrapped round her against the encroaching chill of the deepening night, Emmeline sat wide-awake in the velvety darkness, waiting.

It was very quiet here in this great block of flats at this unaccustomed hour. Not a footstep, not a cough, not so much as the creaking of a door. Even the caretaker must be asleep by now, down in his boiler room in the depths of the building.

Emmeline had never been awake and listening at such an hour before. Her mind went back to earlier night calls when the sounds outside had grown sharper, louder. Did she hear them again?

Emmeline was trembling now, from head to foot. She'd never get out of it this time, never! Ten years ago—even five— she'd at least have been mobile, able to slip through a doorway, to get away from the house, and if necessary stay away for days, or even for weeks.

Not now, though. This time she would be helpless, a sitting duck. And as this thought went through her mind, she became aware, through the humming of her hearing aid, of a new sound, a sound quite distinct and unmistakable, the sharp click of the latch as her door handle was being quietly turned.

Softly, expertly, making no noise at all, Emmeline Fosdyke reached into the darkness for the long sharp carving knife that always lay in readiness.

It was a shame, really, having had to do this to them, after having been so nice to them on the phone, after having given them her name and everything, and encouraging them to think that her tense husky whisper was the voice of a young girl. It was a real shame; but then, what else could she have done?

In the deep darkness, the unknown male lips coarse and urgent against her own, she would have her brief moment of glory, a strange miraculous moment when it really seemed that the anonymous, ill-smelling mackintosh of some stranger was indeed a khaki battle dress of long ago, that the blind clutchings in the darkness were the tender caresses of her first love. For those few wild incredible seconds, in the meaningless grip of some greasy, grunting stranger, she would be young again, and loved again, under the poignant blueness of a war-time summer sky.

During those mad brief moments she could allow hard masculine fingers to fumble with her cardigan in the darkness, and with the buttons of her blouse, scrabbling their way nearer and nearer . . . a shame it was, a crying shame, that at exactly that moment, just before the eager questing fingers had discovered the sagging, empty loops of skin and had recoiled in horror—that was the moment when she'd had to stab the poor nameless fellow, if possible in the heart.

Had to: It was self-defense. Even the law had agreed about that, on the rare occasions when the law had caught up with her.

She'd *had* to do it—*had* to stab them all, swiftly and surely, before they'd had a chance to discover how old she was.

"No, no telephone, thank you. It's too dangerous"—for them.

SUGGESTIONS FOR FURTHER READING

THIS BIBLIOGRAPHY includes all sources used in the writing of this book's introductory essay or the individual biographical notes. It also includes certain biographies, books, articles and Web sites related to the topic of domestic suspense, and other commentaries on particular authors and themes.

Abbott, Megan. *A Hell of a Woman*. Texas: Busted Flush Press, 2007.

Connolly, John, and Declan Burke. *Books to Die For: The World's Greatest Mystery Writers on the World's Greatest Mystery Novels*. New York: Atria/Emily Bestler Books, 2012.

Cypert, Rick. *The Virtue of Suspense: The Life and Works of Charlotte Armstrong*. Susquehanna University Press, 2008.

DeAndrea, William L. *Encyclopedia Mysteriosa. A Comprehensive Guide to the Art of Detection in Print, Film, Radio, and Television*. New York: Macmillan, 1994.

Foxwell, Elizabeth. *Clues: A Journal of Detection*, various issues. MacFarland.

George, Elizabeth. *A Moment on the Edge: 100 Years of Crime Stories by Women*. New York: HarperCollins, 2004.

Marks, Jeffrey. *Atomic Renaissance: Women Mystery Writers in the 1940s and 1950s*. Delphi Books, 2003.

Nolan, Tom. "Ross Macdonald and Margaret Millar: Partners in Crime." *Mystery Readers International* 17(3), 2001.

Paretsky, Sara. *A Woman's Eye*. New York: Delacorte Press, 1991.

Schenkar, Joan. *The Talented Miss Highsmith*. New York: St. Martin's Press, 2009.

Steinbrunner, Chris, and Otto Penzler. *Encyclopedia of Mystery and Detection*. New York: McGraw-Hill, 1976.

Swartley, Ariel. "Fever Pitch." *Los Angeles Magazine*, May 2004.

Swartley, Ariel. "Guns and Roses: The Women of Noir." *LA Weekly*, 1999.

Winn, Dilys. *Murder Ink: The Mystery Reader's Companion*. New York: Workman, 1977.

Web Sites

The Bunburyist: elizabethfoxwell.blogspot.com

Ellery Queen's Mystery Magazine Author Index, 1941–1972: rimes12.tripod.com/eqmm.html

The Fiction Mags Index: www.philsp.com/homeville/ fmi/ostart.htm#TOC

Golden Age of Detection Wiki: gadetection.pbworks.com/w/ page/7930628/FrontPage

Recovering Nedra: www.recoveringnedra.blogspot.com

CREDITS